Readers love
the Hockey Ever After series
by Ashlyn Kane and Morgan James

## *Winging It*

"This book was filled with wonderful characters in addition to a lot of information about what goes on off the ice, injuries, trades and a look at what the players go through."

—Paranormal Romance Guild

"From the terrific world building, the endearing characters and the solid plot and timelines, this book was simply so much more than I could have hoped for."

—The Novel Approach

## *Scoring Position*

"This is a book that anyone who loves hockey should definitely read."
—Paranormal Romance Guild

"The pace was even faster, the characters even more lovable and the chemistry even hotter, and I loved meeting some of my favorite characters from the first book again. This book truly warmed my heart!"

—Annie's Reading Tips

By Ashlyn Kane

American Love Songs
*With Claudia Mayrant & CJ Burke:* Babe in the Woodshop
A Good Vintage
Hang a Shining Star
The Inside Edge
The Rock Star's Guide to Getting Your Man

DREAMSPUN BEYOND
Hex and Candy

DREAMSPUN DESIRES
His Leading Man
Fake Dating the Prince

*With Morgan James*
Hair of the Dog
Hard Feelings
Return to Sender
String Theory

HOCKEY EVER AFTER
Winging It
The Winging It Holiday Special
Scoring Position
Unrivaled

Published by DREAMSPINNER PRESS
www.dreamspinnerpress.com

By Morgan James

Purls of Wisdom

DREAMSPUN DESIRES
Love Conventions

*With Ashlyn Kane*
Hair of the Dog
Hard Feelings
Return to Sender
String Theory

HOCKEY EVER AFTER
Winging It
The Winging It Holiday Special
Scoring Position
Unrivaled

Published by DREAMSPINNER PRESS
www.dreamspinnerpress.com

# UNRIVALED

## ASHLYN KANE
## MORGAN JAMES

Published by

DREAMSPINNER PRESS

5032 Capital Circle SW, Suite 2, PMB# 279, Tallahassee, FL 32305-7886  USA
www.dreamspinnerpress.com

Unrivaled
© 2023 Ashlyn Kane and Morgan James

Cover Art
© 2023 L.C. Chase
http://www.lcchase.com
Cover content is for illustrative purposes only and any person depicted on the cover is a model.

Mass Market Paperback ISBN: 978-1-64108-547-2
Trade Paperback ISBN: 978-1-64108-521-2
Digital ISBN: 978-1-64108-520-5
Trade Paperback published February 2023
v. 1.0

Printed in the United States of America
∞
This paper meets the requirements of
ANSI/NISO Z39.48-1992 (Permanence of Paper).

# Ashlyn's Acknowledgments

THIS BOOK is the direct result of interference and meddling from Aurora Crane. Thank you. I'm so glad we're friends.

I also owe thanks to a huge team of cheerleaders and alpha readers: Laura, Sibel, Amanda, Curry, JEB, Rufus, and more. Thank you for loving my gremlins (almost) as much as I do.

# Pregame

"WOW, TRY to look less like you're having fun."

Grady Armstrong self-consciously pulled his hand away from his cuff link and realized he was scowling. "I can't help it. You know I hate these things."

His sister, Jessica, rolled her eyes, unsympathetic. "Yeah, it's so terrible being paid millions of dollars with the catch that you're expected to put on a tux once a year and go to a fancy party."

Grady flinched. Jess had three Olympic hockey medals and she'd made more in one season as an NHL scout than she had in her entire professional hockey career. "It's not like they're gonna *give* me the Lady Byng."

Sure, he was nominated. He'd been nominated three times now, not that he cared about individual trophies. If he couldn't have the Cup, nothing else mattered. But they kept nominating him for the Lady Byng— hockey's sportsmanlike conduct award—so he had to come, basically.

"Maybe if you didn't keep letting Mad Max goad you into a fistfight at the end of the season, they would."

Grady flushed. "I don't let him *goad me*—"

Jess snorted.

Fine, he did. It wasn't his fault Max Lockhart had such a punchable face and insisted on putting it in front of Grady's fist.

He'd played in the NHL for over a decade. He prided himself on his clean play, or he'd never have been nominated for so many useless Lady Byngs. Chirps didn't get to him. He had thick skin and he was proud of it.

Max Lockhart got under it like a twelve-gauge needle, which was why Grady didn't *have* any Lady Byngs.

Besides, he started it when he broke Grady's arm. Even if general consensus said it was an accident.

Grady sighed.

Ever the big sister, Jess patted him on the back in faux sympathy. "It's fine. The Art Ross would get jealous if you had to put it next to another trophy anyway."

Even if he'd won that this year instead of last, Grady wouldn't get to *keep* the award for being the season's top scorer. It lived in the Hockey Hall of Fame. But he guessed that wasn't the point. "Thanks for the perspective," he said dryly.

A server stopped by their table with a tray of champagne, and Grady took two glasses with a nod of appreciation.

She raised her flute to him. "What are siblings for?"

They touched glasses.

"Other than an excuse not to bring a real date to the NHL Awards, obviously."

Grady downed the glass in one go out of pure spite. They'd had *that* conversation one too many times. "Jess—"

"It's not like you'd be the only one!" She gestured over his shoulder to a table three rows over, where a couple of the Orcas were making sappy heart eyes at each other. Kirschbaum was getting the Hart—league MVP. His boyfriend wasn't nominated for anything.

That wasn't the problem.

"It's not the attention." Grady was out, but he was a low-key kind of guy. He didn't go around in a rainbow-flag cape at Pride like some players he could mention—not because he wasn't proud, but because he only cared about parades if there was a Stanley Cup involved.

Jess rolled her eyes. "Yeah, duh. You've always had that." No trace of bitterness, even though she was objectively the better player of the two of them. "Who has time to date with hockey?" she mimicked in a fake baritone that sounded nothing like Grady. His voice wasn't that deep. "Literally everyone else, bro. But you don't have to date to get laid. Like, I wasn't out there living a life of celibacy."

As if he needed the reminder. "Thanks for that."

She grinned. "Welcome." Another server came around—hors d'oeuvres this time—and she snagged a couple plates. "Anyway. The point is you could have someone if you put the effort in. Your personality leaves a lot to be desired, but you're rich and you have a nice face. Plenty of guys would hit that."

Grady dragged one of the plates of crostini over in front of him. "Stop. I'm blushing."

Jess didn't have time for a rejoinder, because the microphone made a godawful screech as the commissioner stepped up to the podium.

Fantastic. Time for the show to begin.

BY THE time the awards were over, Grady had loosened up a little, mostly because of the champagne. Jess left him to mingle, and he spent some time circulating, talking to the guys who'd passed through his team over the years, guys he knew from the American national team, and his usual competition for the Lady Byng. He didn't enjoy it—he knew he came across as awkward and as aloof as he felt—but it would be worse to keep to himself, and when no actual games were on the line, Grady could be a gracious loser.

"Congrats," he said to Caelan Murphy, this year's winner.

Murphy accepted Grady's handshake with a laugh. "Yeah, thanks. Glad I'm not in your division. I'd never get to take the thing home either."

At least Grady wasn't the only one who found Lockhart so aggravating. "I should have better self-control."

Murphy snorted and shook his head. "If you say so." Then his wife caught his arm and he smiled. "Sorry, looks like duty calls. Have a good one, eh?"

Grady acknowledged him with a tilt of his head and started to plan his escape. Now that the awards had been handed out and he'd been seen making nice, he could sneak away. He'd use the restroom and then track down Jess to let her know he was leaving.

It seemed like a solid plan until he was washing his hands at the Luxor bathroom sink and Max Lockhart came out of the stall behind him like a demon emerging from the bowels of hell.

Fuck.

"Armstrong," Lockhart said cheerfully. Whatever his many other sins, apparently he wasn't one of those guys who used the washroom without cleaning his hands afterward. He wristed the tap on and slathered himself in soap. "My condolences on your Lady Byng loss."

Grady had never spoken to Lockhart off the ice and couldn't decide if he was being an asshole or being sincere. Maybe he was a sincere asshole. "You could always decide not to provoke me next year."

Lockhart met his eyes in the mirror and cracked a shit-eating grin that still had all its original teeth, despite his punchable face. "You could always decide not to rise to the bait."

Grady never felt like he could, was the problem. Something about the guy gave him itchy mitts. "Guess we're at an impasse." He made for the door before the tension in his shoulders could coil any tighter. You weren't allowed to punch people in real life either.

This time Lockhart laughed at him outright. "Yeah, all right, bud. Hey, who's the rocket you brought tonight? Thought you were queer."

Fuck's sake, could this guy leave nothing on the ice? Grady gritted his teeth. "That's my sister."

Now he was cackling. "Oh shit, my bad." He turned the sink off with his forearm and turned toward Grady. "Don't worry, though." He flicked his wet fingers at Grady, splashing tiny droplets on his face. "You're prettier."

There he went, right under the skin again. Was Grady supposed to be flattered or simply knocked off-kilter? Maybe he was supposed to be offended. *Pretty* wasn't always a compliment when you were talking to a dude. "Prettier than you," he agreed.

Lockhart grabbed a couple paper towels and dried his hands. "Too bad." With a wink, he dropped them in the trash. "If I were up to your standards, we could probably have some fun together."

And then, before Grady could process his own horror, Lockhart was gone.

What. The *fuck*.

# Warm-ups

**NHL Announces Return of World Cup of Hockey**
**By Kevin McIntyre**

With the off season well underway, you might be asking yourself—wait a second. Isn't the World Cup in May? Didn't we just do that?

And you're right. The International Ice Hockey Federation World Cup is in the spring, when playoffs are going on in the NHL.

The World Cup of Hockey is a different animal—distinguishable by its logo, which resembles a certain type of hygiene product. Depending on your philosophy and the year, it's either a fun way to launch the season, a paltry offering to appease NHL players who are salty they can't go to the Olympics, or a money grab. It's probably the inconsistent schedule that lends credence to that last theory. There have been four World Cups of Hockey, played anywhere from 3 to 15 years apart.

Unlike Olympic and IIHF hockey, the World Cup of Hockey is played by NHL rules on NHL-size ice. This year's teams include Canada, the US, Russia, Czechia, Finland, Sweden, Europe (comprised of players from European nations not otherwise represented), and North America (Canadian and American players 23 and under).

The tournament will once again take place in Toronto. Preliminary games begin on September 10 when Czechia faces off against Russia.

GRADY TRAINED hard all summer.

That wasn't unusual. Grady trained hard every summer. Throwing himself into the hockey season was one way he distracted himself from the anniversary of his parents' death at the end of August. Besides, you didn't keep your spot on the top line of a professional hockey team without putting in the work. He liked to push himself, challenge himself to do better than he had in previous years.

This year was the first time he resented it.

He used to love getting back to work. Each season was like a freshly resurfaced sheet of ice, waiting for his mark. But that was the problem too—at the end of each season, the Zamboni went by again and any impression Grady might have made was erased. Without that big win, or even just a handful more wins than losses.

He tried not to think of it that way. He couldn't *afford* to think of it that way. But it had been years since the team did more than limp pathetically into the playoffs for a first-round exit. Usually they didn't even get that far.

Grady was a gifted hockey player. When Philadelphia drafted him, they were supposed to turn a corner. But they kept driving straight toward the cliff's edge, and they'd taken his career with them.

He liked to push himself, but he didn't have the drive to push a whole team.

He was thirty years old and he was tired of bearing the brunt of the expectations of a perennially disappointed fan base. If they couldn't turn things around by November, he'd told his agent to request a trade.

They might not give him one, but his contract expired at the end of the season, and he wouldn't extend his stay in Philly. If they didn't trade him, they'd lose him for nothing.

The request would probably make him a pariah. Fans hated players they saw as disloyal, but what was Grady supposed to do? They were tired of losing, and half the time they blamed him. There was only so much he could do on the ice.

So he trained hard all summer, but he wasn't eager for training camp. A few years ago, management had tried to make him captain, but he'd declined, and now everyone looked at him like he had one foot out the door. Like he thought he was too good for them.

Okay, not *everyone*.

A familiar hand clasped his shoulder. "At least pretend you're optimistic."

"I'm too old to have to fake it." But he pasted on a smile for Cooper, who'd taken the C instead. Grady wasn't a people person. He'd learned his lesson back in juniors. For him, being captain would've been a nightmare. Coop's mix of cockiness and approachability made him perfect at the job.

"Your acting skills aren't up to it anyway."

No shit.

Grady half turned toward Coop on the bench. If they were having this talk, the least he could do was face it head-on… more or less.

"So. This is the year, eh?"

Grady let out a long, slow breath. "Looks like it."

Coop nodded. "We better make it count, then." He rolled his shoulders and then tapped his stick against Grady's leg. "Come on. Fresh ice awaits."

If Grady was going to set himself up to be trade bait, he needed to be in top form. He stood. "Let's do it."

**Player Profile—Max Lockhart**
**By Natasha Chu**

As part of our series leading up to the World Cup of Hockey, we'll be profiling players to watch from every team. Today it's left-winger Max Lockhart's turn.

If your team plays in the Eastern Conference, you already know him by reputation. Lockhart plays a major part in the powerhouse New Jersey Monsters lineup. To put it bluntly: he's a pest.

No, that's not fair. Lockhart is a gifted goal scorer in his own right and has been a contender for all the NHL's major scoring trophies. He's had multiple hundred-point seasons. That's part of what makes him so annoying. He makes you mad, and then he makes you pay, and he grins the whole time.

I go into our interview expecting he'll make me mad too. As a dyed-in-the-wool Shield fan, I'm no stranger to hating on Max Lockhart.

So of course the first thing he does is turn my expectations on their head.

There's a formula to how these interviews generally go. I meet players in the bar at the hotel they're staying at. I offer them a drink. The ones with the serious image—the ones who don't eat sugar during the season and drink kale smoothies three times a day—order water. The more casual guys order beer or, occasionally, Jack and Coke.

Max Lockhart—"Hey, I'm Max"—orders a frozen margarita and asks if I want to go halfsies on a plate of nachos.

He's casual in jeans and a Raptors T-shirt, his dishwater-blond "hockey hair" somewhat windblown. His blue eyes are very bright, and he smiles a lot. He's not handsome, exactly. But something about him is magnetic. It makes it hard to look away.

I already like him more than I expected to. Though I suppose that could be the margarita talking.

"You don't mind if I record this, do you?" I have to ask.

"Nah, I know how it goes." He gestures vaguely. "Besides, hard to eat nachos if you've got to take notes by hand."

He has a point. And they're very good nachos. I'd hate to miss out. I set my phone to record and reach for my list of prompt questions.

Except I never quite get to it. Before I can ask the first one, Lockhart's phone pings. He's cursing and apologizing and putting it on silent, but then he lights up a little. "Sorry, I'll put this away in a second. Just, my sister sent me a picture of my dog and it's super cute—want to see?"

I obviously want to see the dog. He's got wavy brown fur and big brown eyes and a stub of a tail. In the picture, he's holding a battered yellow doll shaped like a stick figure. His name is Gru, Lockhart—Max—tells me, but when I ask what kind of dog, he laughs.

"He's a rescue. Someone asked me that once and I was like, 'I don't know. Brown?' What, am I going to 23andMe my dog? He's maybe part Lab, part cocker spaniel... part someone's leg for all I know."

Was that a Terry Pratchett reference, I wonder. But instead I take the opportunity to ask about his family. "So you have a sister—older or younger? Any other siblings?"

"A sister and a brother. Nora's the youngest. She just graduated dentistry school in April, so that's why she's watching Gru. Nora couldn't get off work, so she volunteered to dog-sit. Then there's me, typical middle child. My older brother Logan's married now—he totally married up—and he's got two kids who fortunately take after his wife. My parents have always been super supportive, even though the three of us were hellions as kids. I've got a couple duds for aunts and uncles—no, I'm kidding. I have a big family, though. We'll be here all night if I have to make fun of all of them."

He says this with a gleam in his eyes that makes it hard to believe he harbors anything but love for these people, whatever his mouth might say.

I've thrown out my whole script at this point, but I need to get something that relates to hockey, so I ask him, "Sounds like your family, uh, shows their love in a certain way…?"

He laughs out loud. "We're all a bunch of shit-disturbers."

I reach for another chip. My margarita is almost empty. "So your role as, let's say an agitator on the ice— that's something that comes naturally to you?"

Max signals our server to bring another round. He grins again, then chomps down on a nacho. "God, yeah. We were always needling each other at home. You should've seen my brother's face when my little sister called him the first pancake—you know, the one that comes out a little funky because the pan wasn't hot enough yet. Never really expected that playground skill to come in so handy professionally, but I guess it translates."

Considering he's drawn a penalty nearly every game I've watched him in, I'd guess so too. "World Cup of Hockey games can be a little different from the regular season," I say diplomatically. What I mean is, no one's working that hard to sacrifice their body when they'll be playing for their regular team in three weeks. "How is your role with Team Canada different from the one you play with the Monsters?"

"Well, I'm hoping not to get punched in the face as much. Maybe score a couple goals. It's not every day you get to play with the country's best, so I'm looking forward to rolling with that."

Well, sure. Who wouldn't?

Max and I are talking like we've been friends for years by the time we polish off the plate and the server brings the bill. "I know I said we'd go halfsies, but I definitely ate more of the nachos," he says as he reaches for the folder.

Who is this guy? And can we get him traded to Toronto? "I'm expensing it anyway," I tell him.

He grins and lets me get it. "Oh, well in that case." It feels like we're sharing a joke.

It remains to be seen if, when the regular season starts in a few weeks, the joke's actually on me.

IF ANYONE asked what Grady thought about the NHL's World Cup of Hockey gimmick, he'd lie.

It originated when the NHL decided players couldn't go to the Olympics anymore—something they'd waffled on several times since. Instead they held the World Cup of Hockey, a glorified All-Star tournament, on top of the regular one, with a bunch of made-up teams like Team North America, with the Canadians and Americans who were under twenty-three, and Team Europe, because most of continental Europe couldn't ice a competitive team alone. But you could never say you weren't proud to wear your country's flag, even if it was a meaningless tournament based on money and offered as a shitty consolation prize.

"Wow, Grades." Jess slid his beer toward herself in their corner booth at the bar. "Tell me how you really feel."

Grady scowled slightly as he realized he'd run his mouth after all, even if Jess wasn't just *anyone*. Still, he felt like a bratty kid. "Sorry. I know I'm being ungrateful—"

She snorted. "Save it. It's nothing everyone doesn't already know, but most people have more sense than to say it out loud."

Grady made a face. "Cowards," he said hypocritically.

Jess laughed, but her amusement disappeared quickly. "Anyway, I didn't come to get you drunk or impugn Old Glory or whatever. We can get to that later." She stirred her own drink, the ice clinking gently against the sides of the glass. "I came to ask you something."

Grady wasn't even buzzed, but the words sobered him. When he was fifteen and she was twenty-five, their parents died. Jess had taken on the role of his parent ever since. She'd made every sacrifice to make sure Grady got to the NHL. "What's up?"

She traced a water droplet down the outside of her glass. "So, some of my old teammates are doing a ski trip this year."

*Some of my old teammates.* That probably meant Amanda, the ex-girlfriend Jess had never gotten over. They'd broken up just after Jess and Grady's parents died. "Sounds fun. Why are you freaking about it?"

Jess sighed, her face etched with misery. "It's over Christmas. I don't want to leave you alone. And this is definitely a 'no boys allowed' kind of event."

They were all each other had, so they always spent the holiday together. But Jess had given up so much for him—Grady could suck it up for one year. "So I'll find something else to do. I'm a grown man. You don't have to take care of me forever."

"Shut up, I do too. You're just a baby."

"Come on." She never asked for anything. After fifteen years, maybe she could finally get some closure. "What do I have to do for you to be okay with going?"

Jess rattled the ice cubes in her glass of vodka soda. "God, I don't know. Fall in love and go spend Christmas with your boyfriend's family?"

Grady snorted. "You don't ask for much." Jess had opinions about his love life—or lack of one.

But a strange light had come into her eyes—the one she got when she was about to snipe the puck off his stick and embarrass him in front of all his friends—and she speared him with a sharp look. "Actually...."

Oh God. Had he given her some kind of horrible idea? "Why am I suddenly afraid?"

"I'll make you a deal." She sipped the last of her drink. The slurp of it echoed through her straw. "I'll go on one condition—you have to try online dating."

She probably thought he'd push back on that the way he'd been doing for years. But honestly, Grady didn't even think twice about it. If this was what it took for Jess to do something for herself, it was the easiest decision he'd ever made. He held out his hand. "Deal."

"Wait, seriously?"

"No take-backs."

"I'm going to make you tell me about the dates."

He could just lie to her. He wouldn't, though, except as a last resort. She was the only family he had left. "I would expect nothing less."

Jess eyed him with suspicion, but she finally shook his hand. "Okay." But when the handshake ended, she left her palm out. "Now give me your phone so I can download the app."

Despite the fact that Jess was even worse with tech than he was, Grady didn't argue.

"That went better than I thought," Jess said a few minutes later, when a server had brought them another round. "I was worried about it. I wanted to break it to you now instead of, like, before a game that actually counted for something." She paused. "Although maybe you should be careful of those baby Germans. Didn't Europe get runner-up last time?"

"That was, like, eight years ago," Grady said, but he'd forgotten about Kirschbaum and his Hart trophy. Team Europe was absolutely capable of kicking their ass.

Jess patted his shoulder. "It's okay. I played Olympic hockey, remember? I know the only thing that matters is beating Canada."

Grady allowed himself a small smile. "You were never tempted to marry one of them?" There was a strong legacy of American and Canadian female hockey players marrying each other. More recently, a few male couples had joined them.

"Eh." Jess waggled her hand back and forth, playing along. "Never *seriously*." Then she propped her chin on her hand and said, "Have you?"

"Fuck no." He laughed at the idea. "As a breed, we are horrible, gross, overly competitive assholes. Why would I saddle myself with that?"

She crossed her arms on the table and leaned forward. "What *is* your type, then, baby brother? Since you have such strong opinions on the topic." She was eyeing his phone again, like she wanted to start filling out his dating profile right now.

The million-dollar question. "I don't know, someone nice?"

For some reason that set Jess into peals of laughter.

"What?" He hunched his shoulders. It wasn't that funny. Just because he wanted to come home from a road trip to some physical affection, someone who was easy to be around, someone he could let his guard down and relax with. What was wrong with that?

"Grades, I mean this with all the love in my heart." She reached across the table and took his hand. "But *you're* an overcompetitive asshole. What nice guy is going to sign up for you?"

Grady pulled his hand back. "Wow. Thanks for the support, sis."

"I didn't mean it like that. I get that you don't want every day to be a battle. Just… I don't know. *Nice* is all you can come up with? I'm not saying go date someone who hates your guts and kicks puppies, but that sounds…."

"What?"

"I don't know. Kind of a low bar?" she suggested. "*Boring*? Like, you don't want a doormat, Grades. You like a challenge."

"I challenge myself professionally. Every day." Couldn't he have something easy? Just one part of his life where he didn't have to be at the top of his game all the time?

Jess shrugged. "I guess. What do I know about romance anyway, right?"

Oh God, was this conversation some kind of older-sibling-projection nonsense? "Are you having a midlife crisis?"

She gasped. "How dare you!"

"That's not a no."

"I see how it is." But instead of answering the question—which was telling in and of itself—she signaled the server to bring another round.


LIKE EVERY good East Coast Canadian kid, Max grew up dreaming of playing hockey with the maple leaf on his chest.

Of course, he imagined wearing it in a tournament that mattered, but just because this one had no real stakes didn't mean he didn't want to win. He just wouldn't sacrifice his body for it.

But he *would* bring his A game for the chirps. Team USA was playing Grady Armstrong on their first line, and there were few players Max had more fun riling. His sister, Nora, had been in town for one of their regular season games against each other, and back at his house later, they got high and giggly as they watched the replay of Armstrong in the penalty box. "No, but check out the muscles bunching in his jaw when he clenches it," she'd half *tsk*ed, half giggled. "I mean, the look works for him, but he *definitely* grinds his teeth."

"Guy's strung way too tight," Max agreed sagely. Then he restarted the video so they could watch him lose his shit again.

So maybe Max had had an idle fantasy or three about how to help Armstrong unwind. Or, honestly, not—he'd probably be equally good in bed cranky.

Max would've enjoyed the World Cup of Hockey experience either way, was the point. Go team and all that. Plus events like this were prime hookup opportunities—hockey players, hockey fans, hockey capital of the country.

Unfortunately, tonight he didn't have the energy to hook up in person—not after practice and then drinks with the boys, and with practice again tomorrow. Putting an effort into his appearance at 10 p.m.? In this economy?

Pass.

This was why God invented Grindr.

Max flopped on his hotel bed and thumbed open the app.

He didn't use it often. Max's charm was more potent in person and in limited doses. He knew his strengths. But he was pretty good at taking dick pics that were sexy but still anonymous. Everybody should have a plan B.

He perused the app's offerings.

The first three guys he passed on were like beers. Young, blond, inoffensive profiles. Not memorable or particularly potent, but they'd quench your thirst. One of them had actually posted the lyrics to "867-5309" under his profile pic, which made Max suspect he was either a douchebag or lying about his age.

*Not tonight, Jenny.* He swiped on to the next guy.

The following one, Jordan, was a mixed drink. Could be watered-down and flavorless, could knock you on your ass. No way to know until you took a sip. Jordan was cute, but not what Max was looking for tonight. He just wanted to get off and go to bed.

He swiped again.

… and then there was this guy. His face and dark eyes promised the potency of a shot.

The fact that it was *Grady Armstrong*'s face meant it was a straight-up catfish.

"Seriously, dude?" Max navigated to the message icon before his brain could even engage. Who did this guy think he was kidding? They were in Toronto. If Grady Armstrong wanted to get his dick wet, all he had to do was go outside and smile at someone.

The smiling would probably hurt him, though. It was not the guy's natural expression. See: evidence of teeth grinding.

Max debated a handful of seconds before settling on the fishing emoticon. He followed up with *nice try asshole*, in case the message wasn't totally clear.

A moment later a checkmark popped up to indicate the message had been read.

Max had intended to jerk off tonight, but getting into a fight on the internet was almost as good. He settled in to wait for the reply.

*What?* came through a minute later.

Eloquent. Max snorted. *Gimme a break, bud. u think just cause the wcoh is in Toronto that people are gonna believe ur Armstrong? U took his headshot from nhl.com. 0 effort.*

Grady Armstrong would never. Guy was the biggest try-hard Max had ever met.

*What's wrong with my head shot?*

Max rolled his eyes. *aside from the fact that its obviously not u? like at least crop a pic from the team's insta or something, god damn. gimme something to suspend my disbelief on*

*Not my problem you don't believe me.*

What, he wasn't going to take a candid photo to prove it? Big shock there.

*It is tho. Bc I have too much self-respect to sext a guy whos catfishing as a dude with a hockey stick up his ass*

*That definitely sounds like a you problem.*

Max laughed. He knew this was a good idea. *Your loss, Fakey Armstrong.* To rub it in, he scrolled through the folder of his borderline-obscene photos and sent a shot of his chubbed-up dick in his favorite pair of sweat shorts. No nudity; Max wasn't an asshole. He wasn't gonna send unsolicited dick pics.

*Guess I'll have to take the L since nothing I say will convince you.*

Now he was getting it. Still… Max was having fun. He hated to have the whole thing end just like that. Besides, it was entertaining to pretend that Grady Armstrong *did* have Grindr on his phone and was somewhere in one of Toronto's hotels, getting salty about Max chirping him. Well, Grindr profile MXLmillion—because Max had the brains to avoid accusations of catfishing and also didn't want casual users identifying him by name—chirping him.

It was a good fantasy. Almost as good as the idle daydreams Max had about needling Armstrong until he finally gave in and fucked Max against a wall. The guy was tightly strung. Max wanted to know how hard he had to pluck to get him to snap. The sex would be *phenomenal*.

But in the meantime, he had to deal with Mr. Catfish.

*Tell u what*, Max said, because he had spent his entire life making sure he got the last word. *If ur really Armstrong u can prove it. Meet me in the arena basement after the Canada/young guns game. Ill be wearing the team Canada shirt.*

This time the response took longer to come through. Perhaps the guy had finally realized Max had him. *What's in it for me?* he finally said.

Seriously? Was this guy new or something? *If ur grady Armstrong?? An orgasm.*

*What's in it for you, then?*

Grady Armstrong's dick, if Max was lucky. *When I prove u are not grady Armstrong u will delete this account and stop trynna catfish horny queers.*

*See you then*, came the immediate reply. This was followed by a row of American flag emojis.

Max laughed again and sent back a middle finger. Whoever this guy was, he was committed to the bit.

Satisfied, he set his phone on the nightstand to charge and flicked out the light.

Sleep came easily.

GRADY HAD never been in love. Jess, like any overly invested older sibling, thought this was her fault and therefore her job to fix.

When Amanda broke up with her, she was a wreck. She tried not to show it in front of Grady, but there'd been no hiding it.

Grady could admit—to himself, anyway—that it had left its mark. He'd already lost his parents. He couldn't imagine being in Jess's shoes and losing his partner too. It was bad enough when he overheard one of the friends he had in juniors talking to a teammate about how everyone treated Grady like he was special "just because he's an orphan." The betrayal still stung over a decade later. So he'd never put much effort into relationships. Grady had suffered enough losses.

But Jess didn't have to know he was looking for a holiday date and not a happily ever after.

It was just as well that guy on the dating app only seemed to want him for sex, because what did Grady know about relationships?

It was that, more than anything, that convinced him to go through with the meetup. At this point, what could it hurt? Grady would show up, his "date" would be surprised it was actually him, and they'd have sex. At least he'd get some physical gratification out of it. Maybe he could even get in a few verbal jabs at the man who said he had a hockey stick shoved up his ass.

He considered no-showing—how was some random going to get into the arena's basement anyway, unless he was one of the army of staff members it took to keep the place going?—but at the end of the day, his pride wouldn't let him.

It wouldn't let him dress up for the occasion either. Sweats and a T-shirt would do. He was an athlete. It was practically his uniform.

So half an hour before the game, Grady entered the players' area of the arena, the same way he would if he were going to do a workout, but instead he took a left turn into a small lounge and put the game on the TV. He needed to know the competition.

The game ended in Canada's favor. No surprise—Grady figured them for the strongest competition at the tournament. But that meant it was time to meet his mystery date.

So. He'd go, he'd have casual anonymous semipublic sex, and then he'd go out tomorrow and play hockey for his country.

What could go wrong?

THE KIDS, Max decided after the game, were not all right.

The kids were fast, hungry, and young enough to think they were bulletproof, and they played today's preliminary matchup like it was game 7 of the Cup Final.

The kids also hadn't had defensive responsibility beaten into them yet, so Team Canada won 5–3, but it cost Max more in bruises than he wanted to admit to hold on to the puck for his two goals and an assist.

Worth it, though, obviously.

"Hey, Mad Max!"

And now his team was going to want to go out to celebrate, or play video games to bond, or both, but Max had an appointment to undress an internet stranger. Literally or metaphorically, depending on whether he showed and how hot he was.

Max looked up from pulling on his T-shirt and met Coop's eyes. "Present."

They weren't friends, which, like, Max wasn't *upset* about. He knew he was better at leaving rivalries on the ice than 98 percent of the league. But Coop and the other Philly guys always gave him a little extra side-eye because they were protective of Armstrong and somehow thought Max had broken his arm on purpose or that he was out to personally destroy the guy's carefully controlled on-ice persona. It wasn't Max's fault he was good at distracting him from doing his job. It was Armstrong's fault for being so easy to nettle.

Coop rolled his eyes. "Cute. You coming to dinner?"

Oh, wow, an official invitation.

Coop gave a sheepish smile. "Your pickpocket move saved me from looking like a pylon. Figure I owe you a drink."

Howard Barclay, Team North America's nineteen-year-old hotshot captain, had faked Coop out and intercepted a pass he never should've made, but Max had it covered. They scored on that play too.

"Nah, that was my pleasure." Max wasn't going to rub it in—if Coop was going to treat him like a human being for the next week, he'd lean into it. "Gotta keep the kids in their place, obviously."

"Obviously," Coop laughed. "But you're not coming to dinner? You got a hot date or something?"

One of Max's teammates from Jersey raised his head and glanced over. "Oh no. I know that look. It's dick o'clock."

Max blew him a kiss. "I'll catch up with you guys at the restaurant. Text me details?"

"As long as you promise *not* to text *me* any."

"Your loss." He had the feeling today's story would be a good one. He saluted the room with his phone and then shoved it in his pocket. "If

I don't text you by ten, assume I'm dead and send someone cute to look for my body."

The idea made him snicker a little as he navigated the depths of the arena. Like, imagine the cops delving into his app history and finding out he'd set up a meeting with someone claiming to be Grady Armstrong, and Armstrong having to answer questions about his Grindr use.

He'd look like a wet, grumpy cat, and he'd be about as friendly about it. Max was getting a warm, fuzzy feeling. Sure, in this hypothetical scenario he'd be dead, but he'd be dead and *still pissing off Grady Armstrong*. God was good, et cetera.

It wasn't that security was lax. It was just that Max was in the players-only area already—no extra measures required to keep people out.

If he'd thought about that a little longer, he'd have realized sooner. But he didn't have time to think about it, because when he rounded the corner to the league's best-worst-kept secret hookup spot, he came face-to-face with the grumpy wet cat himself.

Oh *shit*.

Max could feel his mouth dropping open, but he didn't have the motor control to do anything about it.

For his part, Armstrong didn't seem to have put two and two together yet. He glanced at Max and curled his lip in a sneer. "Get your own dark corner, Lockhart. I'm meeting someone."

"I mean, I could leave," Max said. "But then who's gonna give you that orgasm?"

From the looks of it, that realization hit like a six-five defenseman twelve inches from the boards. Armstrong flushed an unfortunately attractive red from the apples of his cheeks down to his collarbones, lovingly displayed in the slutty V-neck T-shirt he was wearing. Damn, he'd dressed to impress in that shirt—Max wanted to put his hands all over him. Mouth too, if Armstrong was amenable.

It would really suck if Armstrong wasn't amenable, but at least Max would have solid gold chirp material for the rest of his career.

"You're…?" Armstrong said. Even his eyes were unfairly pretty, a blue-green color a model would die for. Right now they were as big as hockey pucks.

"A man of my word," Max filled in. He stepped into the role he'd made for himself like he was stepping onto the ice. It was easy—right foot forward, then left, until he didn't *quite* have Armstrong boxed in against the wall. He was going for sexy, not threatening.

He and Armstrong were the same height, which Max always forgot on the ice, where the twenty pounds of muscle Armstrong had on him made him seem enormous. Not that Max let that stop him from checking the guy every legal chance he got. It was fun.

This was fun too, and something else besides.

Armstrong met Max's gaze, but he'd schooled his expression. Max couldn't tell what he was thinking. "You want on my dick that bad?"

"Hockey players who live in glass houses, bud." Max flicked his eyes down Armstrong's broad chest to his crotch. He was wearing sweatpants. His dick wasn't all the way hard, but he wasn't soft either. "You're telling me you never thought about it?" Yeah, right. Max would bet his lucky cuff links he had.

Armstrong wet his lips. He'd thought about it, all right. Maybe only since Max made that pass at the NHL Awards, but Max wasn't gonna get in his feelings about that. Armstrong was thinking about it now, and that was all that mattered. "Thinking about it's not the same as acting on it."

Max leaned closer—close enough that Armstrong would feel the words leave Max's mouth when he spoke, voice a low promise. "Don't you want to know what's better? Your imagination…" He took a half step forward, so his thigh wasn't *quite* between Armstrong's. The heat from his body radiated through Max's leggings. "… or my reality?"

Armstrong inhaled sharply. He was either going to break or balk.

For a second, Max was sure he'd balk. Disappointing, but he wasn't going to be an asshole about it. But then, before he could take a step back, Armstrong put his hands on Max's hips.

A challenging light came into those pretty eyes.

Energy zinged up Max's spine. He should've known. Armstrong never backed down on the ice either. It was *on*. But he was going to make Armstrong say it. Max was a good multitasker. He could get his ego and his dick stroked at the same time.

"Tick tock," Max said. "I'm into informed consent. You wanna take this for a test-drive or what?"

Armstrong's eyes slammed closed and his head thunked back against the wall. He made a noise like he was in deep physical pain.

But Max didn't have time to be disappointed, because the next second he'd been spun around and *he* was up against the wall, Armstrong crowding into his space, shoving his massive thigh against Max's hard-on.

Max opened his mouth to swear, but he didn't get a sound out before Armstrong's crashed down over his and swallowed every syllable.

*Oh fuck yes.*

Grady Armstrong wasn't fucking around. He kissed with his whole body—all two hundred pounds of it. He was mean about it too, tightening his fingers on Max's shoulders and scoring his teeth over Max's lip.

Max knew he'd be like this. He gasped under the onslaught and scrambled to shove down Armstrong's waistband. That was the unspoken rule of the hookup basement—don't linger. Get down, get it up, get off, and get out.

They'd checked off the first two, judging by the firm line of pressure against Max's hip, and they were making excellent progress on the third.

This probably wasn't going to last long enough to warrant the condom Max had optimistically shoved into the tiny pocket of his leggings.

The lube, on the other hand—

Armstrong pulled his mouth from its bruising campaign on Max's lips and bit at the hinge of his jaw when Max wrapped his hand around his dick. Just like Max figured: thick to match the rest of him, and cut—too much friction.

Max snagged the lube from his pocket and shoved his own leggings down while ripping the packet open with his teeth.

"Really?" Armstrong said with more than a hint of judgment. "You brought lube?"

Max emptied the contents into his palm and took them both in a rough grip. "You're welcome, bro."

Armstrong sucked hard on the side of Max's neck, right where he was sensitive. "Don't call me bro when your hand's on my dick."

Somehow Max got out a breathless laugh instead of a moan. "What, you need some sweet nothings?" Thank God his mouth worked on autopilot. His brain was busy thinking *fuck, fuck, that's so good* as Armstrong's cock leaked all over both of them. "Want me to call you Daddy?"

The suck became a bite that made Max's cock jerk and his knees try to buckle. "You're such a shithead."

The world narrowed down to Armstrong's hand—in Max's hair now, pulling like he knew how much Max loved it, or maybe like he didn't *care*, which might be hotter—the warm, salty scent of him, the pressure of Max's palm, and Armstrong's dick next to his. Max was riding the edge.

"A shithead who's gonna make you come," Max pointed out, light-headed. Armstrong's cock was hot and hard against his own. He had to be close.

"You first," Armstrong growled, and he tugged Max's head back hard enough to make his eyes water and bit the base of his throat.

Max couldn't argue. He was too busy coming his brains out. The pleasure coursing through his body spilled over his fingers in a hot flood. Armstrong came too, groaning softly against Max's neck, his stubble burning perfectly against Max's sensitive skin.

*Oh my God*, Max thought as he tried to catch his breath. He'd known the sex would be good, but simultaneous-orgasm good? For a quickie hand job in the arena basement?

Would they even *survive* if they fucked in a bed?

Max wanted to find out, like, yesterday. It left him wrong-footed.

"Holy fuck," he said finally. His voice sounded hoarse. Had he been screaming?

Armstrong didn't answer. He was leaning his full weight against Max, breathing heavily into the damp skin of Max's neck. Max probably looked like a chew toy. Worth it.

But this was getting a little too… cuddly. Max was generally a fan of cuddling, but Armstrong wouldn't be into it, at least not with him. He needed to remind them both of that before he got too comfortable.

Carefully, Max withdrew his hand from their cocks and then, less carefully, wiped it on Armstrong's T-shirt.

That got his attention. "What the fuck!" He jolted like Max had electrocuted him.

"Don't be such a baby. You left your mark all over me. Fair's fair." At least Armstrong could wash the shirt. Max raised his clean hand to his neck and touched the side of it. He was going to hear all about *that* at dinner.

Still worth it.

"I'm supposed to walk out of the arena like this?" His face was scarlet. His lips were swollen. He looked halfway between fucked out and ready to go another round. If Max didn't have dinner plans, he'd be tempted.

Hell, he was tempted anyway.

Max needed to get a grip on himself. "I still have a spare shirt in my stall." It was a Team Canada shirt with Max's number on it. He was pretty sure Armstrong would prefer to wear jizz. "I guess I can part with it for a good cause."

"You're all heart."

Despite himself, Max laughed. "You're so salty." Max made an effort to be cheerful. That was what people expected from him. Grady Armstrong obviously didn't give a fuck about expectations. Max respected that.

He tucked himself back into his leggings. "I can't believe you made a Grindr profile with your NHL profile picture. The hell were you thinking, bud?"

"It's Grady," Armstrong—Grady—said grumpily. "I'm not your bud."

"You could be," Max said impulsively. Off the ice, anyway. Max wasn't gonna stop chirping, checking, or getting in his face, but he was willing to add sucking, fucking, and coming *on* his face. Or vice versa. He wasn't picky. "Anyway, the Grindr profile? You didn't wanna be a little more subtle?"

Grady sighed. "My sister set me up with an online dating… thing."

*Oh my God.* Max bit his lip hard and took a deep breath to rein in the laughter. He doubted Grady would appreciate it, and it might keep him from agreeing to a round two in the future. "She downloaded and filled out the app for you, didn't she."

This time the sigh was longer and deeper. "How'd you know?"

Max cleared his throat. "Well. For one thing, Grindr's a hookup-and-sexting app."

"Fuck."

"Yeah. She got you, bud." It slipped out. Max didn't bother to correct himself.

Grady let it slide. "She probably didn't realize it was the wrong app. But that does explain a lot."

It sure did. Max pushed open the door to the locker room and waved him in. It was empty. "Yeah, if you're looking for more than a half hour of romance, you're better off looking elsewhere."

With an expression of distaste, Grady pulled off his shirt. Max didn't hurry to find him a replacement. "Grindr's never heard of foreplay, I guess." He tossed the shirt in the trash.

The shoulders on this guy. The waist-to-hip ratio. There was just so much of him, all round with muscle and… biteable.

Max didn't need to know Grady was into a lot of foreplay. Not if he wasn't going to give a hands-on demonstration, at least. He tore his eyes away and dug in his duffel for that T-shirt. "Grindr *is* foreplay."

"If you say so."

"Here." Max thrust a bundle of red-and-black cotton at him. "No more wardrobe malfunction."

Grady took the shirt and unfolded it. The expression of distaste returned. "I can't wear this. It has your number on it."

Max gave him a smile full of teeth. "My number or my DNA. Your call."

Grady glowered. "What am I going to tell people if they see me wearing this?"

Max spent a few seconds imagining it. God, it would be glorious. "I don't know, not my problem. Tell them you lost a bet."

"*You're* the one who lost the bet."

"Did I, though?" Max asked. "Doesn't feel like I lost. Feels like I got exactly what I wanted."

A muscle at the corner of Grady's jaw twitched. Nora was totally right about the tooth grinding. "Just… take your shirt off."

The sudden change in tactic had Max blinking. "Round two already? I have dinner plans, but I could be convinced—"

"The shirt you're wearing doesn't have a number on it, at least."

Max could've argued, but the thought of Grady Armstrong putting on clothing still warm with Max's body heat tickled something primal in the back of his brain. He took the shirt off and traded it.

"I can't believe this," Grady muttered.

"What? That you're wearing my shirt, or that you ravished me in the hookup basement?"

The scowl deepened. "I didn't *ravish*—"

Max cleared his throat as he caught his own reflection in the locker room mirror. Yep, Grady did a number on him, all right. He gestured to his neck. "You were saying?"

Grady smoothed his hands down the front of his—Max's—shirt. "You didn't exactly complain about it at the time."

"I'm not complaining about it now."

That earned him a twitch. Max couldn't tell if it was an irritated twitch or if he was trying not to smile.

God, this was fun.

Perhaps sensing he couldn't win, Grady changed the subject. "That one wasn't me." He pointed to a livid purple bruise running from Max's hip to shoulder. "That from the game?"

"Wow, are you studying for the detective's exam?" Max pulled his shirt on. He didn't need Grady knowing where to land a hit to make it hurt. "Yes, it's from the game."

"Who did that?" He sounded impressed.

So maybe his interest was academic. Max could relax a little. Grady wasn't a dirty player—at least not without a little effort on Max's part. He offered a wry smile. "Eric Chen, if you can believe it."

Grady's eyes went wide. "Chen? That kid weighs, like, a buck fifty!"

"Tell that to my ribs." Max grabbed his bag from the stall and slung it over his shoulder. "Either he hit a growth spurt this summer or he discovered the joys of anabolic steroids."

Grady snorted. "Thanks for the warning, I guess." The US was playing Team North America next.

"No charge."

They left the locker room, and Max realized it was time to part ways. They'd have to travel through public areas, and while he didn't care about being seen fraternizing with the enemy, Grady would.

Especially when wearing the enemy's shirt.

Max didn't want to examine the twinge of sadness he felt at that, so he said sunnily, "Okay, well, this is where you leave me. I recommend you call an Uber for the ride back to the hotel. If you jog through the lobby, maybe no one will notice your shirt."

"I hate you," Grady told him, voice flat.

Max only grinned wider. "I know."

GRADY HAD taken a hit to the head in practice.

That was the only explanation he could come up with for why he'd agreed to meet a stranger for sex in the depths of another team's arena.

It was definitely the only explanation for why he'd gone through with it after learning the stranger was Max Lockhart.

And then, of course, reality reasserted itself, Max returned to being a shithead, ruining Grady's shirt, which he had to wear *in public*, and Grady had regrets—regrets he couldn't put words to, not that he *wanted* Max to know about them. It made Grady feel like a pod person, reverting to small talk with a guy he'd always gone out of his way to avoid, but Max was… distracting.

Fuck, that was probably part of Max's plan all along—throw Grady off his game with sex, then humiliate him by sending him out into the world in a Team Canada T-shirt that smelled like Max.

After he made his graceless escape, Grady put on his sunglasses and speed-walked with his head down to the nearest shop, where he bought a Toronto Raptors shirt. He was thankful the clerk was too busy looking at her phone to pay him any attention.

He took the long route back to his hotel. He needed the exercise to clear his head.

What had he been thinking? No, this wasn't the first time Grady'd hooked up with someone from another team, but it *was* the first time he'd done it with someone he actively disliked. Maybe the reality wasn't as dramatic as sports media liked to pretend, but *archnemesis* was only an exaggeration because neither of them had superpowers.

And now Grady was spiraling because he'd handed Max a free pass to get into his head whenever he wanted. For what? A hand job in a deserted hallway? Had he lost all self-respect?

It was a *good* hand job, though. That annoyed him. Maybe he had a previously undiscovered public sex kink or something. Maybe he'd been getting off on being kind of mean to a guy he didn't like. Grady didn't get rough with his partners. He was a big guy, and it wasn't the kind of thing he'd do with someone he just met. Even when he hooked up with other players, they went pretty easy. The last thing anyone wanted was a sex injury keeping them out of the lineup. And honestly… he'd never thought about it.

It figured that Max would be into a little pain with his pleasure. Ruining Grady's life by making him realize Grady was into giving that to him was probably a bonus.

Grady needed to stop thinking about it. He had a game tomorrow. He couldn't be up all night dissecting what it meant that Max Lockhart gave him a hand job and he liked it. It meant he had a dick and enjoyed having someone else touch it for once. The end.

Focus on the game.

That reminded him. He called up highlights from the Canada-North America game and scanned through until he found Chen's hit on Max.

Oof. That was a big hit, all right. Grady smiled to himself as Max went ass over teakettle. Should've kept his head up. Rookie mistake.

He was still smiling at it when the Team USA group chat notification lit up with an invitation to meet for drinks and second dinner at the hotel bar.

Grady understood team bonding was important, especially for short tournaments like this. He'd just sucked at it ever since his first year of junior hockey, when he'd caught a teammate mocking him behind his back for being an orphan.

But he did need to eat again, and the invitation came from Dante Baltierra—Baller—who Grady had known since his parents were still alive, and who'd sat outside development camp with him after he got the news so he wouldn't be alone while he waited for Jess to show up.

Hockey players being hockey players, neither of them mentioned it again, but Grady wouldn't forget it. Nor would he forget the—well, *balls* it took to be one of the league's first out players, paving the way for Grady's much quieter and less dramatic exit from the closet of professional sports.

For one thing, Baller would never let anyone forget it. He'd appointed himself the league's queer mascot.

Grady always tried to pick up the tab when they got together as a means of saying thanks.

Unfortunately, this time when he showed up, it was him, Baller, Tom Yorkshire, and Jack Hedgewood.

He considered turning around.

Baller must've seen it in Grady's face, because he said, "Relax, Ace. Hedgie doesn't bite. Unlike his teammate."

Hedgewood played for the New Jersey Monsters with Max. Considering how much the league loved to play up the rivalry between Grady and Max, he didn't have to guess who Baller was referring to.

*Actually,* he *doesn't bite, but it turns out I do*, Grady thought, and was immediately appalled. "I'll take your word for it," he said, but he mustered a smile.

Grady didn't know Hedgewood as well as he knew the other two. He'd played with Yorkie on the national team over the years. Hedgewood was a little younger, and various injuries and schedules had kept them from being on the US team at the same time.

But Hedgewood held out his hand for a fist bump and said, "Hey, we're all competing under the same flag. Until the preseason. Then we'll crush you."

Grady laughed and bumped his knuckles. "Guess we'll see."

"First we gotta beat Finland," Yorkie pointed out as he clapped Grady on the shoulder. "Eyes on the prize, boys."

The four of them squeezed into a booth, and Grady ended up having a nice night, even if he had to rely on Hedgie for conversation because Baller and Yorkie spent the evening exchanging pictures of their kids.

Grady debated taking out his own phone. He'd been considering getting a dog, and maybe Hedgie would have a comment on the offerings at his local animal shelter. But he knew he'd never actually go through with it. He hated the idea that something he could love so much could have such a short life. Besides, considering the number of obscene pictures that had ended up on his phone since Jess installed that stupid app, showing his screen to anyone was probably a bad idea. He kept his phone in his pocket.

By the time he got back to his room, he'd regained his equilibrium. So he fucked around with Max Lockhart. That wasn't any worse an indiscretion than spearing him in the ribs last time they played each other.

The bruises were even smaller this time… if also more visible.

But he did need to deal with his phone, because it was only a matter of time before he accidentally gave someone an eyeful of someone else's junk.

So, after his bedtime routine, he shoved down the covers of the hotel bed, propped himself up on his pillows, and prepared to deal with Grindr.

Or he tried to prepare, anyway. Every time he thought he'd figured out how to delete his profile, he accidentally touched something and ended up looking at another poorly lit dick pic, or reading a horny sext from someone who couldn't spell, or—most exasperating—getting accused of catfishing.

It took him a couple minutes, but he managed to delete his profile picture. He was pretty sure he could delete the app from somewhere *else*, but would that get rid of the pictures in his phone? Shit.

Grady knew how to use his phone, but he'd never used a dating app, and after this he never wanted to again. If he wanted to see someone's dick, he'd ask.

He was about to give up when a familiar username flashed in his messages.

*MXLmillions.* He should've guessed that'd be Max's handle. It seemed obvious now.

The first message was just a shot of the side of his neck, the string of bruises Grady left with his mouth.

The second read *my team thanks u 4 giving them something 2 talk about @ dinner.*

For a few seconds, Grady stared at his own handiwork. Apparently he'd been very… focused. Looking at the picture, he could almost taste the salt of Max's skin.

Then the annoyance kicked in. *What the fuck. You better not have told them anything.* The last thing Grady needed was to have to deal with stupid chirps about this.

And maybe he wasn't exactly *proud* of the way he felt about those marks on Max's neck. He didn't regret it, he just didn't need the whole universe knowing Grady was the one who put them there.

*Ya I definitely told team Canada I slept with the enemy.* Max followed that with an eye roll emoji. *Relax. U didn't invent discretion.*

Obviously, because if he had, he'd have used it to not sleep with Max Lockhart. *Whatever*, he sent back.

Then he turned his phone off before he could get drawn into anything else. Like looking at that picture again.

Once was more than enough.

GRADY THOUGHT his own regrets were sufficient punishment, but then they dropped the game against Team North America in overtime, off an unbelievable goal from Eric Chen, who dodged around three Americans like he was playing *Chel*, passed to his rushing teammate, and picked up the rebound without stopping.

"What the fuck, Yorkie?" Grady asked. "Did you teach him that?"

"I fucking wish."

Their next game, the last of the round robin, was against Canada.

Grady had a love-hate relationship with US-Canada games. Love, because they tended to be great hockey since both teams had deep talent pools to draw from. Hate, because Canadians thought they owned the game and took every win as proof. The only thing worse than losing to Canada in an international tournament was losing to Canada in an international tournament that took place in Toronto.

Which was why Grady didn't intend to lose.

*Do not take a penalty*, he reminded himself in warm-ups. *Whatever he says to you, you cannot take a penalty.*

Grady was on his fifth warmup lap and his hundredth repetition when a stick brushed his legs at center ice.

*Fuck.*

He sprayed to a stop. He'd only look more petty if he didn't. "What do you want, shithead?"

Max leaned on his stick and batted his eyelashes. "Aw, baby, why you treat me so mean?"

Grady gave him a flat look. "How long do you have?"

Max barked with laughter. "Hey, if I tell you to suck my dick during the game, will they suspend me? Like, how does that work if it's a sincere invitation?"

Fuck's sake, Grady thought. "Try it and find out."

Then he skated away to get his head in the game.

The minute the puck dropped, Grady knew it was going to be one of those games he loved.

The teams were well matched, with more scoring power on the American side balanced out by an absolutely psychotic Canadian goaltender. Grady would've had to dislocate every joint in his body to make half those saves. The guy was part jellyfish.

Coach kept matching Grady's line with Max's, which Grady expected—the NHL higher-ups probably told him to. Grudge matches were good for viewership. Grady braced himself for Max to say something horrible, but by the end of the first period, he hadn't come up with anything newly disgusting.

With two minutes left until the buzzer, Grady's line was out trying to increase their one–nothing lead. He kept his head up going into the corner after the puck, but he could feel Max's gaze on the back of his neck. He gritted his teeth. *Don't take a penalty.*

A second later Max's shoulder slammed into his. "Hey, bud, didn't your mom warn you your face would stick like that?"

Grady gritted his teeth harder and shoved him back. "Thought you liked my face."

Max dug at the puck, but Grady had it trapped between his skates. However tenacious Max might be, Grady was stronger. He flipped a pass to Yorkie, Max cursing behind him all the while.

Good.

The ensuing rush gave Grady a chance to show off. He wasn't the flashiest guy on the ice, but he had good vision, always knew where he needed to be. Today he slipped into a gap left by two defenders in time to get his stick on Yorkie's shot and tip the puck over the goalie's pad.

2–0. Suck it, Canada.

He caught Max's eye as he was crossing behind the net on his way to the group celly. Max was red-faced and narrow-eyed.

Grady smiled wider to rub it in.

For some reason, that only made Max laugh and turn back to his team, but whatever. Grady was winning. He didn't care what was going on in Max's head.

The second period started out chippy, and Canada scored while Baller was in the box for holding. Half a dozen more plays that should've been penalties went uncalled.

Including one where Grady was against the boards with Max *again*, with Max's stick hooked around his ankle while Max kicked at the puck. "Hey, so I was thinking—"

Fuck it. *Nothing* was getting called in this game. Grady brought his elbow back and Max's breath whooshed out.

But he didn't back off. "There's a great little food cart outside my hotel. Let me treat you to a sausage—"

Grady snorted in spite of himself.

That moment of distraction was all it took. Max worked the puck off Grady's stick and took off down the ice. It was in the back of the US net two seconds later.

Fuck.

Max clipped Grady's shoulder as they skated back toward their respective benches, and winked when Grady glowered at him.

Grady couldn't let that slide. He brooded a little in the locker room when the period was over, which prompted Baller to tap his shins. "Eyes on the prize, Ace. Where's your head?"

In the arena hookup basement, also known as his own personal hell.

Grady shook himself. "Sorry. I let Lockhart get to me."

"Well, stop it." Baller flicked him between the eyes. "You need some earplugs?"

Grady batted his hand. "No. I got it."

"Attaboy."

Baller's actual pep talk was a little more dramatic, and involved standing in his stall and quoting something that might have been from *The Mighty Ducks*. Grady didn't watch a lot of movies, even about hockey. Eventually someone threw a ball of sock tape at Baller, and he interrupted himself mid monologue. "Fine, you ungrateful fucks." He threw the tape back, grinning. "Go beat Canada so I can lord it over my husband."

Gabe Martin was retired now. Would retirement make beating your international hockey rival any less sweet—or losing to them any less bitter? Grady wasn't sure. Maybe if he wasn't playing, he'd simply be happy to participate in victory sex.

In the end, it turned out it didn't matter if Baller had only been talking to himself. They peppered the Canadian goaltender with fifteen shots, but Baller was the one who poked the puck through five-hole with thirty seconds before the clock ran out. The team mobbed him behind the net as the home crowd booed.

Music to Grady's ears—almost as sweet as the scowl on Max's face. Maybe if Grady had less of a stick up his ass, he'd blow the guy a kiss.

Probably not, though.

With the victory, the US team secured a spot in the semifinal without having to play in the quarter. This was Canada's first loss, so they'd take another semifinal spot. Europe would play Finland to determine the opponent for the US team, and Canada would play the winner of the Russia-Team North America quarterfinal.

Grady was just glad he wouldn't have to face Canada or Team North America again until the final.

"We're going out!"

Hedgie rolled his eyes. "Obviously."

"Everybody hit the bikes. Meet back here in forty."

Grady stuck his earbuds in, cued up his postwin playlist, and started his cooldown.

He had five minutes left to go when his phone beeped with a notification.

*So hear me out.*

Grady snorted. Who else would it have been?

*No.*

*Come on. Its a good idea.*

Grady doubted it. *None of your ideas are good.*

*Thats not what the cum all over ur shirt says.*

Fuck. There was a difference between something *feeling* good and being a good idea. But answering with that would be admitting that it felt good, and if Grady gave Max that inch, Max would throw him in the trunk of his car and gun it for the border. Metaphorically speaking. They were already in Canada.

He still hadn't decided how to reply when Max messaged him again.

*So heres my idea. If Canada wins this tournament ill suck ur dick. Your team wins, u suck mine.*

Grady's body was still buzzing with postwin adrenaline, and the image hit him low in the gut and made his dick twitch.

He shouldn't answer. Any engagement would only encourage him. Grady really wanted that blow job, though.

*Don't you have it backwards? Why doesn't the winner get the blow job?*

*U gonna trust me w my teeth around ur dick after u beat me?*

He made a good point. Grady was also more likely to feel magnanimous after winning than gracious after losing.

*Besides*, Max continued, *a blow job is a good consolation prize.*

Grady knew he should've turned his phone off. *Fine*, he messaged.

In response he got a string of smug-looking emojis and a few clasped hands. *Knew ud see it my way. Cant wait 2 suck ur dick!*

Grady refused to spend any brain power analyzing *that* message. He turned off his phone and finished his cooldown in silence.


To say Max was disappointed in the outcome of the Canada-North America semifinal would have been like saying water was wet.

He couldn't believe they'd lost to a group of children, most of whom were still on entry-level contracts. He was thankful none of the Team North America guys were on the Monsters. Their egos were going to be out of control.

On the other hand, maybe Max's team could use some young talent. Apparently he was old and sad now.

And Canada's loss happened *after* the US lost their semifinal against Europe, which meant that not only would Max not be winning the tournament and getting Grady's dick in his mouth, he also would not be getting his dick in Grady's.

It also meant Canada got a rematch against the US for third place, which was basically the definition of *consolation prize*, but Max wasn't going to turn it down.

Unlike the last time they'd played against each other, it was *boring*. Max didn't know if everyone was tired or if, like him, they couldn't bring themselves to care enough to put everything into a match for third place. Canada won 3–2, and Max went through the handshake line without even coming up with something annoying to say to Grady. He was off his game in more ways than one.

He answered questions for the media on autopilot, and then he went back to his hotel, ordered room service, and put on the North America-Europe game. Kirschbaum was playing in full beast mode, but North America had three forwards just as good and hungry as he was, and while Europe might have more experience, North America had youth and speed on their side.

Halfway through his dinner, Max found himself rooting for North America. After all, they were basically half Canadian, so….

A thought hit him, and he blinked at the television screen. The score was tied at 1. The game could go either way. If he messaged now, he wouldn't look *too* thirsty.

Fuck it.

*If u think about it, if North America wins, both Canada and the US also win.*

Then, in case that wasn't clear, he added a pair of mouth emojis and two eggplants.

He refused to stare at his phone while he waited for an answer, so he finished his dinner and brushed his teeth, just in case.

When he returned to the game, North America was up 2–1 with thirty seconds to go in the third.

His phone beeped.

*1573.*

What did that mean? Was it some kind of code? He refused to believe there was a sex code Grady Armstrong knew about and he didn't. But then what—

*Fairmont.*

That was Max's hotel. 1573 must be the room number.

Fuck yes.

IF ANYONE asked, Grady would blame his appalling lack of judgment on a head injury.

Or, shit, was that the same excuse he'd decided to use the first time? Did he need another one? Maybe he was so crushed after losing two games in a row, the second one to Canada of all teams—

No. That lie was even more embarrassing than the truth. He'd just have to make sure no one found out.

In the minutes after he sent the first message, he glanced around at his hotel room and wondered if he should clean up. The room-service tray was still sitting on his desk, there was a pile of folded clothes on top of his suitcase, and he'd left his toiletries on the bathroom counter.

But who was he trying to impress? Max was the one who'd suggested the bet in the first place.

"I'm overthinking this," he muttered.

As if on cue, someone knocked on the door.

Grady opened it without comment. The less time Max spent standing in the hallway where someone could see him, the better.

Fortunately he didn't seem to be in the mood to linger. He swanned into the room like he owned the place, but it wasn't like he'd dressed up for the occasion. He was wearing his Team Canada shirt and track pants. Grady didn't know how to feel about that. He was *also* wearing his team-branded athletic gear, but like, did Max think Grady was so easy that he didn't have to put any effort in?

Why did Grady care? He was here to get his dick sucked.

"Nice digs," Max commented. He had a smear of toothpaste at the corner of his mouth, so he'd put in some effort. Maybe. Grady didn't know if that made him feel better.

He rolled his eyes. "It's probably exactly the same as your room."

Max's smile went sharp. "Nah. This one has you in it."

Jesus. "You actually manage to get laid with lines like that?" Not to mention the heavy sarcasm in the delivery.

The once-over Max gave him lingered on Grady's crotch. Grady felt his ears heat up. It was the anticipation that had him half-hard, nothing more. He'd been promised an orgasm. The reaction was natural. "Was kinda under the impression that you're a sure thing."

Grady must hate himself. That was the only explanation. "Like I'd turn down a blow job."

"We *do* have something in common." Max helped himself to a seat on Grady's bed. "But who says you're going first?"

Uneasy, Grady took a step back. He didn't want to be the first to get on his knees here. Not with Max, who was as much of a competitive asshole as Grady, if not more so. And there was no way in hell Max was leaving here thinking Grady was worse at blow jobs than he was. Which meant Grady wanted to go last.

"I'm the one who lost our last game," Grady said. "How did you put it? Are you really gonna trust me with my teeth around your dick right now?"

Apparently it was Max's turn to roll his eyes. "I'm definitely not going to return the favor if you bite my dick off, so I think I'm safe." He was very confident in Grady's desire to put his dick in his mouth. Unfortunately that confidence was well-founded for reasons Grady didn't want to examine. "But we can sixty-nine if you think that's more democratic."

It was a reasonable solution, and Grady hated it. "I wouldn't want you to get distracted." Even worse if Grady got distracted and gave Max ammunition to make fun of him.

Max snorted and beckoned him closer, and Grady obeyed without thinking about it. "Relax. I literally engineered this situation so I could get your dick in my mouth. I'm just giving you a hard time." He slid his fingers into the waistband of Grady's pants, and Grady sucked in a breath. "It's foreplay."

"It is not." Grady was proud of how level his voice was.

Max looked up and quirked a knowing eyebrow. "No?" He pressed his hand over Grady's erection. "Seems effective to me."

Grady didn't have a rebuttal. There was no way he could make words make sense when Max's face was that close to his cock. When the slight pressure of his palm had Grady's blood up and his dick leaking.

"Thought so," Max said, the smug set of his mouth turned up to insufferable.

The skin over Grady's spine prickled with exasperation. "Shut up."

Max batted his eyelashes. "Yeah? You gonna make me?" The backs of his fingers teased the sensitive skin of Grady's abs.

Grady knew a challenge when he heard one. He knew the tone of Max's voice too—it was the same one he used on the ice when he was goading Grady into taking a penalty. He wanted Grady to give in.

And Grady was frozen to the spot.

"You waiting for a formal card?" Max curled his fingers and dragged his nails a few inches down to the tops of Grady's hip bones. He was still smirking. "You are cordially invited to fuck my face."

Grady shoved his pants down. "I hate you." He was starting to sound like a broken record.

Max grinned. "Prove it."

Grady gripped his shaft in one hand and Max's jaw in the other and pushed his hips forward.

If Max had a gag reflex, Grady couldn't tell. His eyes were wet and his mouth was hot and his face was red, and Grady would never hear another word that passed his lips without thinking of the muffled groans and obscene sucking noises that escaped around his cock.

Of course Max was good at this too. Fuck.

"You're such a *shithead*," Grady groaned.

Max hummed in agreement and gripped the backs of Grady's thighs to pull him closer, like an asshole. An asshole who was really into sucking cock. Grady wasn't insecure about the size of his dick, but Max was acting like there wasn't enough of it.

Did he have to be like this?

Grady needed to get laid more if he was reacting like this to Max, of all people. He swept his thumb over Max's bottom lip and cursed when Max slipped his tongue over the pad of it.

Max blinked at him, then licked against the underside of Grady's dick. The firm, wet stroke made Grady throb with want.

There was no way Grady could last, and he was pissed off about it. Was he supposed to be polite and warn the guy? Normally he would. But fuck it. He didn't even *like* Max. Besides, the way he was going at Grady's cock, he wasn't going to mind.

Grady would have to watch out that Max didn't return the favor. Still, he wasn't a complete jerk—he let go of Max's face when he came and shoved the heel of his hand in his own mouth to muffle anything embarrassing.

Max narrowed his eyes when Grady came, but he didn't pull off— pointedly, Grady thought. Like he was proving something.

Grady locked his knees and sternly commanded his lungs to stop heaving. It was undignified.

Judging by the smirking mouth around his dick, Max wasn't fooled. He took his time cleaning every molecule of come off Grady's cock with his tongue, until Grady had to pull him off by the hair because he was oversensitive.

Max licked his lips and fluttered his eyelashes. Apparently if he couldn't kill Grady on the ice, he was going to give it his best shot in the bedroom.

Two could play at that game too.

"Lie back on the bed," Grady rasped. For some reason he sounded like he was the one who'd just had his face fucked.

Laughing, Max elbow-crawled backward, the front of his sweatpants tented obscenely. "How are you still this uptight after getting your dick sucked?"

Grady pulled Max's waistband down so it snugged behind his balls. He was already wet at the tip, hard enough that he was almost purple. Evidently the noises he'd made hadn't been for Grady's benefit—he really did enjoy giving head. "What can I say, you bring out the best in me."

Max was still laughing when Grady put his mouth on his cock.

The laughter choked off into a hiss. Max bucked off the mattress, as if he hadn't been expecting it. He might not have a gag reflex, but Grady did, so he slung his left arm over Max's hips to pin him down.

"Fuuuuck, sorry. I—"

Max cut off when Grady muscled his thighs farther apart to make more room between them.

*Sorry?* What, was he pretending to have manners now? Grady bit the inside of his thigh.

Max yelped and his erection jerked against his stomach.

Grady took that in—the slightly pink skin with the faint impression of his teeth, then the puddle of precome pooling on Max's stomach. He rubbed his thumb over the mark he'd made, and Max shivered and flung his arm over his eyes.

He remembered the obscene photo of his bruises Max had sent him the other day. Maybe that had been a hint, not a taunt.

He took Max down again. He kept his mouth gentle, teasing, but he pushed his thumbnail into the bite.

Under him, Max writhed. "Should've known you'd get—fuck—competitive about this—"

*You started it.*

It was easy to make him fall apart. Grady already knew everything he needed to—Max liked it when Grady was mean to him. Someone would have to Eternal Sunshine that knowledge from his mind, because it would be inconvenient when Grady had to play against him. But right now he was all ego, basking in the trembling of Max's thighs and the hitching of his breath when Grady pulled his mouth off to stroke him slowly while he sucked a bruise into the crease of Max's groin.

Max made a muffled noise that was all vowels, and his erection twitched in Grady's hand.

Grady let go and drank in the curse of protest as he scored his fingernails down the opposite thigh.

"You're an asshole," Max said.

No, he wasn't. Not *usually*. Max brought out the worst in him. "You're into it."

"Yeah," Max agreed, easy, and he wailed when Grady carefully raked his teeth up the head of his cock.

Fucking figured, with that comment about trusting Max with his teeth around Grady's dick, that he'd be the one who got off on it.

Grady brought him to the edge twice more, hypnotized by the jerking and twitching of Max's body, the heaviness of his breathing. Every time he pulled his hand and mouth away, Max swore at him, and Grady had to suppress a shiver at having that kind of power.

Then he realized he was getting hard again from making his most loathed opponent writhe in pleasure, and came to his senses. He covered the head of Max's cock with his mouth and pumped his hand over the base of the shaft, and this time when Max stiffened, Grady grazed his teeth

over the crown as he pulled off. He stroked Max through a surprisingly
silent orgasm and held his weight firm over Max's hips just because he
could. Max kept his arm over his face until his legs stopped shaking and
Grady finally let go.

After a moment's thought, he wiped his hand on Max's shirt. He
still had the one from the other day anyway.

"Wow," Max said finally as he let his arm flop back to the mattress.
"I'm impressed with your level of pettiness."

Grady rolled onto his back. "Learned from the worst. Gotta sink to
the level of the competition."

Max snorted. "I was counting on it. Why d'you think I wanted
to go first?" He was going for smug, Grady could tell, but he mostly
sounded sex-dumb. "Right to edging me 'til I cried on the second date.
You're something else."

Something in Grady's chest went feral at that, like a wild animal
showing off its kill. Which was fucked up. Grady wasn't going to *tell* anyone
about this. Max really had cried too; the sides of his face were damp.

Fuck, Grady wanted to make him cry again. What was wrong
with him?

"This isn't a date" was the only protest he could come up with. He
swung his legs over the side of the bed and went to the bathroom to wash
his hands.


MAX FELT like he'd just invented a new superweapon, but with sex.

On the one hand, woohoo, his team would be winning at orgasms
forever. On the other hand, mutually assured destruction.

Or at least the destruction of his wardrobe. He grimaced as he
pulled his T-shirt off. He probably deserved that.

It figured that even Grady's sense of humor was kind of bitchy. Max
had him pegged as a stick in the mud, but obviously he'd miscalculated.
Somewhere under the frowny grump and the laser-focused drive was an
actual personality Max wouldn't mind getting to know.

He tugged his sweats up the rest of the way, sat up against the
headboard, and tried to regain his equilibrium.

Once was luck… or coincidence, or novelty, or whatever. But now
Max's brain was leaking out his ears again and, well, he was a twenty-
eight-year-old professional athlete who liked sex and he was very

interested in having more of it with Grady. The guy didn't have to like him—hell, the sex was probably hotter because he didn't.

Getting Grady Armstrong to like him would be an incredible achievement, though. Max believed in himself. He could win this guy over. Maybe they'd never be friends, but they could be friendly acquaintances who had a lot of sex.

Max couldn't just, like, suggest they keep fucking, though. Grady would turn him down on principle. Max would have to antagonize him into it.

Fortunately Max had plenty of experience antagonizing men into doing what he wanted. Getting a guy to fuck you and slap your ass wasn't all that different from getting one to crosscheck you and punch you in the face.

He started with helping himself to a bottle of water from the mini fridge. Then he grabbed Grady's phone while he was in the bathroom. It was locked—Grady wasn't stupid—but Max had fun trying to guess his passcode anyway.

When Grady returned, the signature Grumpy Cat expression came with him. "What are you doing?" His eyes flicked to the water bottle. "You're paying for that."

"You can send me a Venmo request after I finish fixing your internet dating game. Cheapskate." Max flipped the phone around and pointed it at Grady's face, hoping that would do the trick. Yup—facial unlock. He grinned and pulled it back toward himself. "If you wanna make a love connection, you need the right app." Also probably a good deal of luck, but Max didn't want him to get lucky. Max wanted him to get frustrated, give up, and decide to fuck Max instead.

He had a plan for that.

Grady made a sour-lemon face. "Why should I trust you to do that?"

"Hey, your sister's the one who said you should get a hookup app. It's not like I'm going to sign you up for Chaste Christian Singles." The app finished installing, and Max typed in a username and password, saved them to Grady's password-manager app, and navigated over to the profile questions. "I'm already being way more helpful."

"I don't need your help."

Yeah, right. Max snorted. "Okay, bud. Have you gotten any messages that aren't dick pics or accusations of catfishing?"

He took Grady's stony silence as an answer.

"Look, this is easy. I bet I can fill out most of it for you anyway. Then all you have to do is check yes or no on the people you match with. If you hate it, you can delete the app and no harm done, right?" Max put on his best Helpful Teammate face. He needed to remind Grady that Max was a different guy off the ice. Grady, who wasn't, kept forgetting.

"Do what you want," Grady said reluctantly. "You will anyway."

Now he was getting it. Hopefully it took him longer to catch on that Max was actively sabotaging him. "Awesome." He left the personal information to fill in later and scrolled down to the fun part. He cleared his throat and made a show of getting comfortable against the headboard, legs crossed like a pretzel. The more annoying he was, the less attention Grady would pay to what he was doing. "So, Grady." He looked up and injected his voice with gravitas. "Are you looking for someone to go out with, or someone to come home to?"

Grady's cheeks went red. "That is not one of the questions."

"It is too." Max held out the screen to prove it. "See? They want to match you with someone who wants the same things you want."

He half figured Grady was going to call the whole thing off right there, but finally he said, "Come home to."

"Aww," Max said, more sincerely than he intended. Grady scowled anyway, so at least his slipup went undetected. Then he scrolled down to the notes section underneath the answer. "I'm going to add that you're an antisocial dick who travels too much and you want someone to bone when you get home."

"Helpful," Grady said, flat. "Appreciate it."

"Next question," Max went on without acknowledging him. "Which is bigger, the earth or the sun?"

Grady gave him a flat stare to match his voice.

Yeah, okay, fine. "My dick," Max said aloud as he filled in the comments section under the question.

Grady made an indignant noise.

"When do you expect to have oral sex? Second date, obviously. Next question, who calls the shots in bed?" Max didn't bother waiting for a verbal response for that either.

Apparently not being included was getting to Grady, because he asked, pissy, "Do you actually need my input for this?"

Max paused for a sip of water and considered. "Probably not." He went back to the questionnaire. "What is your attitude toward polygamous or open relationships?" He snorted. "Yeah, no, you're a possessive asshole, so—"

"Hey! What makes you say that?"

Max lifted his head. "Really?" Then he tilted it to one side and pointed. "I'm literally wearing your teeth marks on my neck and we're not even dating."

Grady exhaled loudly through his nose.

"You going to tell me I'm wrong?"

"No," he said through aforementioned teeth.

Beaming, Max moved on to the next question. "Okay, essay portion. Hit me with your ideal first date. What are you, a coffee guy? Do you like to torture men by making them go on a run with you? I'm assuming hand jobs in an arena basement is not your go-to."

Grady flopped backward on the bed.

Holy shit, had Max actually annoyed him to death? If so, talk about a plan backfiring.

"Uh. Grades?"

Grady mumbled something inaudible. Okay, good, he was still alive. Max wanted to have sex with him again someday and he wasn't into necrophilia.

"Sorry, I didn't catch that."

A long, resigned sigh. Grady made no move to sit up. "I said I hate going on dates."

Max blinked. "Okay, well, I think we pinpointed your problem."

"It's just—it's so normal to go out to eat on a date. But I do that eighty-something times a year. I don't want to eat any more restaurant food. But I don't want to cook with a stranger in my house either."

Huh. Max hadn't expected to get an answer he related to, but he also got sick of catered and restaurant food. Things tasted better in his own kitchen. "I mean, I think that's why people get coffee?" he said. "Also because if they suck, you can chug your drink and run away."

Grady lifted his head. "Speaking from experience?"

Max quirked a smile—automatic, not even on purpose. Unlike some people, he didn't mind laughing at himself. "I'm not telling you from which side."

"Ugh." Grady flopped back again. "Maybe I should become a hermit."

"Which is different from now how, exactly?" The guy's sister had set him up with a hookup app. That was telling. "Just say mini golf or something. Having something to do gives you something to talk about, you get to move around a little, and if they're terrible, you can accidentally whack them in the shins."

"You're putting a lot of thought into this," Grady said after a moment.

Yeah, thanks, Max had been trying not to notice. He was supposed to be laying the groundwork for his own sex life, not giving half-decent advice. "Don't let it go to your head. It would be a shame if your dick went into early retirement. I'm only looking out for my community."

"You're all heart."

That was the second time Grady had accused him of that. Sarcastically, but still. Max noticed. He felt weird about it, so he deflected with "And elbows." He finished the questionnaire and scrolled back up to fill in Grady's biography details with something approximating the truth. "Done. All you have to do now is set your geographical area and decide what you're looking for in a man. Other than someone who doesn't mind the occasional expedition to remove the stick from your ass, I mean."

"I take back every nice thing I ever said about you."

Max huffed. "404 error. File not found, buddy." That *all heart* thing didn't count. It might be true, but Grady didn't mean it. He closed the app, but before he put the phone down, he navigated over to the contacts and added himself. Then he sent himself a text message. Now he could live rent-free in Grady's head *and* his phone. "Well. This has been fun, but I'll leave you to your inevitable crisis." He handed the phone back. "Best of luck with dating. Hope you choke in the preseason."

Grady's expression went from annoyed to closed-off. "Yeah, go fuck yourself."

"I meant on my dick," Max said cheerfully. "But I can bring the tools for that too." He heaved himself off the bed and shoved his shoes on. He'd spent way too long in Grady's bed already. He was starting to get comfortable. "See you next week. Bring your A game."

He was halfway to the elevator before he realized his shirt was still smeared with come.

# First Period

MOST OF the time, Grady loved being right.

This was not one of those times.

"He's going to be really good," Coop said. The preseason would start tomorrow, and they were enjoying the mild September weather by sitting on his back step with his low-calorie beer.

"Yep," Grady agreed.

"In, like, another season or two," Coop finished.

"Yep."

Management had been promising a goaltender upgrade for years. They'd finally gotten one in Colton Barnes, a twenty-year-old who'd just left college. But he'd *just left college*—hadn't finished, just joined the show because he could. He was green. Grady thought he'd be a Vezina contender eventually, but by that time, Grady could be retired.

"He could surprise us," Coop offered.

"Stranger things have happened." Like Grady hooking up with Max at the World Cup.

Twice.

Barny wasn't going to surprise them.

Grady glanced at his phone for what felt like the third time in ten minutes, and Coop laughed. "Am I boring you? Or do you have something you want to share with the class?"

For a second, Grady debated whether a confession about his love life would be more painful than contemplating their team's chances this year.

Sadly, it wouldn't.

"I had a date yesterday."

Coop snorted beer up his nose. Grady glowered at him for the unnecessary drama while he cleared his nostrils. "Sorry, uh, you were saying. A date?"

At least he didn't say what he was obviously thinking, which was *God, why?*

Yeah…. Grady had been open with him about how much he hated dating, if not the actual reason why. He'd had more than his share of heartache. The more people he let get close to him, the greater the chances he'd get hurt.

He might as well answer the unspoken question. Coop would find out sooner or later. "It was Jess's idea."

"Uh-huh," Coop said, kind of faintly, like he didn't quite believe what he'd heard or had somehow missed that Jess could talk Grady into anything.

Grady grimaced. "She wants to ditch me for the holidays to spend time with her girlfriends and won't go if she thinks I'll get lonely."

"Will you?" Coop asked mildly.

"I don't spend enough time alone to be lonely." If he wasn't practicing, playing a game, working out, or eating with the team, he was probably asleep or close to it. He could definitely handle three days of R & R at Christmas.

When Grady didn't elaborate, Coop said, "Why'd you go along with it, then?"

That was harder to explain. It wasn't as simple as *I like sex*. If he wanted sex, he could find someone willing. Now that he had a little experience with Grindr, it'd be laughably easy. How hard could it be to take a decent dick pic? *Max* could do it.

Grady tried not to think about the fact that he hadn't deleted that photo.

"Jess won't go on her trip if I don't."

"Okay. So you went on a date. And?"

"Well," Grady said dryly, "no one died."

This time Coop had paused before taking another sip of his beer, so he didn't spray hops everywhere when he snorted. "What happened?"

"It started out okay. He was nice to chat with. It seemed like we might have some stuff in common. He played baseball in college, so he had some understanding of the kind of discipline and time commitment it takes to play a sport professionally. And he was cute. Nice. Decent sense of humor." Didn't send a single unsolicited dick pick. "He wanted to go out for ice cream. Apparently there's this local place he wanted to introduce me to. I thought, okay, it's still the preseason, I can have ice cream." A little extra fat and sugar wouldn't kill him.

Coop's impassive mask was slipping, which told Grady that he should've nixed the date, or done more research or something, because it seemed obvious to Coop how this could go wrong, and Grady hadn't even told him anything. "And?"

"And it wasn't even ice cream. There was palm oil in the ingredients. It tasted awful." If Grady was going to go off his meal plan, it wasn't going to be for fake ice cream that wasn't even made out of dairy. Cream was *literally* in the name. "So I had a few bites and then I threw it in the garbage."

"And?"

Damn it. "And I figured that would be the end of it, but this guy— Brian—he would *not* let it go. Like, 'Oh, did you get brain freeze, were you not as hungry as you thought, do you want to try another flavor?'" He let out a noise of frustration. "He was taking it really personally that I didn't want any more shitty ice cream. So finally I snapped that the ice cream sucked and I wasn't going to waste my sugar allowance on food with a mouth feel like motor oil."

Coop didn't bother trying to cover his laugh. "Okay. Not the most polite, but he had it coming, if he was pushing."

"Yeah." Grady sighed. "Except it turns out the place is his family business, and it's dairy-free because they're all lactose intolerant."

"Oh, buddy. I don't think he's gonna call you."

Grady didn't think so either. Clearly he could not date someone who thought palm oil was an acceptable ingredient in ice cream.

But he hadn't meant to offend the guy. It was hard not to see this as a test that he'd failed. Even if he was only looking for someone to spend the holiday with for Jess's sake and not a lifelong love connection.

"Cheer up." Coop nudged him with his foot. "There'll be other dates."

For some reason, that didn't make Grady feel better.



BECAUSE MAX was borderline codependent, he lived next door to his best friend and teammate, Jack Hedgewood, and his other best friend, Hedgie's wife, El. On game days at home, they carpooled because Max's nagging was the only way Hedgie got anywhere on time. El said she was happy to be a housewife, but she wasn't going to be his mother.

Max wasn't going to be Hedgie's mother either, but he didn't mind playing sheepdog.

"Hey, El," he said cheerfully when she opened the door. "How far behind are we running?"

"I'm just getting in the shower!" Hedgie yelled from upstairs.

El stepped back with a knowing look and gestured Max inside. She had her long dark hair up in a ponytail, and she was wearing her yoga gear. "Right on time."

With a snicker, Max followed her to the back of the house and into the sunroom that she used as a yoga studio. He didn't do a ton of warming up with her—it was too long before the game—but it was a good way to kill time while he waited for Hedgie, and it gave him an excuse to hang out with his favorite Hedgewood.

Besides, he liked yoga. It kept him limber for non-hockey activities—a fact he'd mentioned to El more than once, and now she looked at him speculatively as he started in on his hip-flexor stretches. "Big plans after the game?"

"If I'm lucky." They were playing Grady's team, the Firebirds, a big rivalry game to open the preseason. The Monsters were based in Newark, and Philly was only an hour's drive away, so the teams played each other frequently in the preseason. But Max was still waiting for Grady to text him back about hooking up after. So far Grady had left Max on read, which was rude but not unexpected.

"You ever going to tell me who gave you the souvenirs in Toronto?"

"No can do. You know the drill." El was his go-to confessor for steamy sex stories, but if he hooked up with another player, he never gave her names. It would be just his luck that Hedgie would get traded to their team one day, or one of them would end up on Max's team, and El would know a little too much about them.

Max didn't need a reputation for being indiscreet.

He hoped no one had gotten a picture of him leaving Grady's hotel room in Toronto.

"Boo." But she grinned as she settled into lotus position and straightened her back and shoulders.

Max put his right leg out in front of him and pushed his face down toward his knee, but he kept his eyes on El. "Did you get a new bra? Your tits look amazing lately."

She laughed out loud. "God, you're so lucky you can pull that off without coming across as skeezy."

"It's a gift." It probably had more to do with the solid friendship they'd built—and the fact that Max was generally more into men than women. "Seriously. You're all...." He didn't have words, so he sat up and made an hourglass with his hands.

El's gaze went to the staircase to the second floor. The shower was still running.

Did Hedgie not know about the bra or something?

She cleared her throat. Her cheeks were pink. "It's not a bra."

Okay, so, what, did she get a boob job? Max didn't think the change was dramatic enough to be the result of surgery, and anyway he'd have known about it, so—

It dawned on him right as El said, around a small, secret smile, "The titty fairy came early."

"Holy shit!" Max said. El shushed him, and he lowered his voice. "How far along are you? Does Hedgie know?"

"Like six weeks, no he doesn't, and *don't tell him*."

Hedgie was going to flip his shit. Max grinned. "This is so exciting. When are you going to tell him?" He paused. "Also, how did he not notice?" He held his hands to his chest. "Like.... El. Seriously."

"I don't know! He's a straight guy, boobs are boobs. They're inherently wonderful."

"Well, I'm judging him on your behalf." Obviously Hedgie was not paying enough attention.

Damn. They were going to be such great parents. Max couldn't wait to see it.

But it also felt bittersweet. It was all well and good for Max to tag along with them once in a while now, when it was the two of them. But they would need time to spend as a family with their new baby, without him. And if El had a difficult pregnancy, he'd have to find alternative arrangements for Gru when he was out of town with the team. Not a big deal in the grand scheme of things, but Gru and El would miss each other.

He let the thought fade. He'd still be Hedgie's best friend and El's partner in crime, and now he'd get to be their kid's Uncle Max too. They'd still have plenty of shared meals together, between Hedgie's grilling, Max's cooking, and El's baking.

Heh. Usually it was cookies and brownies and pie, but now she had a bun in the oven.

Upstairs, the bathroom door closed, and El cleared her throat. "So. No hints about tonight's plans? Really?"

If Max gave her anything, she'd figure out who he was planning to see. "No! Stop fishing or I won't give you all the dirty details."

"Ugh, fine." She shook her head. "You'll have to let me know how it stacks up to Mr. Toronto."

"Deal." Fuck, Max was probably going to slip up somehow and let on that they were the same person, and then El would figure the whole thing out.

The alarm on Max's phone went off then, prompting him into motion. He got off the floor and shouted up the stairs, "Ten-minute warning, Hedgie!"

"Fuck! Okay!"

"Dry-cleaning's in the guest bedroom closet," El said wryly.

Max smacked a kiss on her cheek. "You're the best."

He put on his suit, made sure his lucky cuff links were securely fastened, and tucked his yoga gear into the bag he kept in the back seat of his car. He was just zipping it up when his phone buzzed.

*Finally.* Part of him had expected Grady to leave him hanging indefinitely.

He opened the message.

*Can't tonight.*

That was it. No apology, no explanation.

Not that Max expected one, but he shoved down his disappointment. It didn't matter. He could find someone else to fuck. Or he could go home alone and jerk off to the memory of Grady sinking his teeth into the inside of his thigh.

He shoved the phone into his pocket without replying, but when he turned to leave the room, El was leaning on the doorframe. She had her arms crossed—the pose did even more for her boobs; Hedgie was a lucky guy—and tilted her head.

Max should probably start closing doors when he got changed in their house, but he'd been a hockey player for too long. Body shyness was a thing that happened to other people.

"You're making a face," she accused. "And you're giving off, like, weird vibes. What's up?"

*"Weird vibes?"* Max said incredulously. He had no defense for his face; it only did what he told it when he was smirking.

"If you can make deductions based on my boobs, I can do it with your vibes."

It would've been easier if he could tell her. El was a good friend and Max couldn't trust his own head, because his dick was involved and it wasn't exactly impartial. But he couldn't ask her opinion without revealing who he was conflicted about, and worst of all he'd have to admit, out loud, that he was upset Grady Armstrong didn't want to sleep with him.

Max hadn't had a complete personality transplant in the last week, so that wasn't happening. In another few days, maybe he could admit it to himself without wanting to take a header into the boards.

"Sorry," he said, off her raised eyebrow. "I think you're going to have to remain in suspense."

He really was sorry, was the worst part.

El's eyes went wide and round, and he knew she was about to question him further, but for once in his life, Hedgie appeared at exactly the right moment, bounding to the bottom of the stairs and sweeping her into a kiss.

"Sorry, sorry, I swear I'm ready now," he said when he pulled away.

El met Max's eyes. He shook his head. "Wish us luck."

CONSIDERING THE long history of bad blood between their two teams, Grady went into the match expecting a shitshow.

The match delivered in the best worst way possible. Neither team had iced their first-string goaltender—the Firebirds were trying out their college boy, and the Monsters put in their minor-league guy—and by the end of the second, the score was 5–5. Miraculously, the refs hadn't called any penalties, mostly because even a rivalry this deep didn't warrant bloody sacrifice in the preseason.

Which wasn't to say that Grady didn't have battle wounds. He'd made and taken his share of checks, and his body was pleasantly warm with it. Two of the goals were his, which meant even the resentful dicks on Grady's team were passing to him in front of the net to get him the hatty, and every guy on Max's team was up his ass.

*That* meant Grady was doing his job, so he let it slide off him and kept his head in the game. He had another first date tomorrow, this time with an architect named Chris.

After the last disaster, he'd taken Max's advice and decided on mini golf.

Speak of the devil—

"Fuck!" Grady's shoulder crunched against the boards as a familiar body rammed into his side. Served him right for letting himself think about Max for even a second.

"Aw, baby, did you miss me?" He didn't stop to bat his eyelashes, just gave Grady's ankles a tap with his stick and left with the puck before Grady could get his feet back under him.

Did Grady *miss* him? How could he? He wouldn't leave Grady the fuck alone.

Grady took off after him down the ice.

He never did finish the hat trick, and the game ended in a tie. Grady did his cooldown and put in an obligatory word with the limited media who cared about a preseason match, then showered and put his headphones in and took his spot on the team bus. There was no point flying to Newark, even in the regular season. It was an hour by bus. They never even stayed overnight.

Coop tapped his thigh when he sat down, and Grady paused his music.

"You all right?" Coop asked. "You checked out in the third."

Grady bristled with the need to defend himself, but it was true. He hadn't gone after that hat trick like he could have. "Fine."

"Mad Max was riding you pretty hard."

By this point in their friendship, Grady knew that Coop knew exactly how that sounded, and he wasn't going to rise to the bait. "Nothing I can't handle."

"Uh-huh," Coop said. "You guys beef at World Cup or what?"

Grady turned to him in disbelief. "Did we *beef*?" he repeated. "When have we *not* 'beefed'?"

Coop raised his hands. "It just seemed intense for a preseason game, that's all. Like it was personal."

"It's always personal with him," Grady muttered. Which wasn't fair *or* true. Max hadn't said anything particularly personal, apart from that whole *baby* thing. Grady wasn't and would never be his baby.

"Okay," Coop said, backing off. "Sorry if I touched a nerve."

Sighing, Grady leaned back in his seat. He knew he was being a dick, but he felt unsettled and it made him prickly. "Not your fault. It's not even about this. It's just some... stuff. I'm dealing with it."

Mercifully, Coop let him get away with it.

But his comment brought up a point. What if it *was* personal? Was Max pissed Grady wasn't meeting him for sex? How was he supposed to do that? He'd had to get on a bus less than an hour after the game.

And it wasn't like they'd made each other any promises. Even if they had, Grady would expect Max to break them, just to mess with him.

Maybe that was what Max thought Grady had done.

And okay, that didn't feel *great*. Grady's team could beat Max's without sex mind games. They hadn't done it tonight, but that didn't mean anything. Grady wasn't interested in victories obtained through anything but pure hockey skill. It felt like cheating.

He *was* interested in having sex with Max again, though. Unfortunately.

Grady was debating whether to offer a rain check as a peace offering—they had another preseason game in Philadelphia next week— when his phone buzzed.

Grady unlocked it to a message from Shithead. Max had entered his contact as MAXIMUM ORGASM followed by multiple eggplant emojis, so Grady didn't feel the slightest bit of guilt renaming it.

But he *did* feel a jolt of lust when he opened it, because Max had sent him a picture of his come-covered abs.

A second rush went through him when he realized it wasn't a picture but a video, only about three seconds long, but he could make out the heaving of Max's stomach and the splatter of the last few drops of come. His dick wasn't in the shot, but that almost made it filthier.

*Jesus.* Grady turned his phone screen off and pushed it facedown against his thigh, suddenly furiously hard. Fortunately Coop was ignoring him, probably texting his wife. Fuck.

Grady bit his lip and chanced another look at his phone when it vibrated again, keeping the screen tilted carefully away from anyone else.

*Wish u were here*, Max had sent, followed by an angel emoji.

Grady wanted to throw himself out the bus window. He really needed his date tomorrow to go well. He had to be hard up for regular sex if he was fantasizing about running his fingers through the mess on Max's belly and using it to open him up for Grady's cock.

He took a deep breath through his nose, released it slowly, and counted to three.

Fuck it.

*Rain check for next week?*

If his date went well, he could always cancel.


MAX WAS aware that sending the video was not a great look for him. He tried to tell himself he didn't actually want on Grady's dick that bad, but lying to himself wasn't one of his strengths.

Besides, it worked, so Grady either didn't notice that it reeked of desperation or didn't care.

Grady didn't sext, which was criminal, because Max knew he had an absolutely filthy mind hidden behind those intense frowny eyebrows.

But two days after Max sent the video, Grady sent something almost as interesting.

*Did you sabotage my dating profile?*

Not, like, actively. It was possible Max had exaggerated some of Grady's characteristics or the things he'd look for in a partner, and maybe he'd steered him toward a disaster or two, but he had faith in Grady's ability to fail at dating all by himself. Either way, this was going to be good. Max pulled his feet up on the couch. *Only by being funnier than u could be irl.*

For a few minutes, he was afraid Grady wasn't going to elaborate. The three little dots flashed at him for ages.

Then Grady said, *Do you actually take guys mini golfing?*

Fuck, did Grady fuck up a slam-dunk date like mini golf? Max couldn't wait to find out how. *Ya what's not to love? Nice walk, lots of bending over.* Great for setting the mood.

Another pause. Then, *And you don't, like… piss them off?*

An array of witty comebacks cycled through Max's brain. *Aww, babe, no, that's* our *special thing*, for example. But if he said something like that he ran the risk of, well, pissing Grady off, and then Grady might not tell him how he fucked up mini golf.

*How would I piss them off*, he sent.

*Apparently I'm "too competitive" and it "isn't fun."*

Max put the phone down on the table, pressed his face into a throw pillow, and howled with laughter. Fuck, he could imagine Grady's wet-cat face. Had he lost at mini golf? Did he get cranky about it? Or was his date the one who couldn't handle Grady beating him, and got progressively colder as the gap increased, while Grady struggled to figure out what he was doing wrong?

He couldn't decide which was funnier.

Gru thought it was pretty funny too—or that was what Max gathered from his dog's reaction to Max's laughter. He yipped and wagged his stub of a tail and licked Max's ear, which tickled and only made Max laugh harder. Apparently Gru didn't want to be left out. Max let go of the pillow and tickled the dog instead, and Gru flopped over on his back and writhed in ecstasy while Max provided belly rubs.

*Did u not tell him ur a professional athlete?* he asked when he had custody of his thumbs again. Like, what did the guy expect? People like Max and Grady weren't programmed to be gracious losers.

The whole thing was hilarious. Even if he now kind of wanted to throw down with Grady over mini golf.

Sadly, Grady remembered who he was talking to and stopped giving Max chirp material. But that was okay. He didn't need it. The point of setting up Grady's online dating account wasn't for Grady to whine to Max about bad dates so Max could make fun of him, it was to get him frustrated with dating so he'd sleep with Max.

They'd already arranged their next meeting, so maybe the internet dating was redundant, but it wasn't like Max could tell him to cut it out because it served its purpose. Just because he actually was that thirsty didn't mean he had to admit it.

He spent the days before the next Firebirds game in his usual preseason routine, drawing in for enough games to get his body conditioned the way he liked it. When he wasn't playing, he was eating, sleeping, working out, or doing yoga with El and suggesting silly nursery themes. So far she'd nixed Jurassic Park and Jumanji, because she had no vision. Max thought a giant T. rex would be a great addition to any baby's room.

"It would scare away the monsters under the bed," he argued.

El threw a pillow at him. Gru barked at it, wagged his tail like he'd done a great job, and then made an appeal for more belly rubs.

El fell for it. She was no more immune than Max was.

Time seemed to pass slowly, like the last drops of maple syrup clinging stubbornly to the bottom of the bottle. Max worked out, he practiced, he walked Gru, and he waited. He couldn't remember the last time he was this pumped to play a preseason game.

So it really sucked when Coach told him the morning of the game that they were going to take another look at Jenssen, one of the rookies, so there was no reason for Max to make the trip to Philly.

He could go anyway and sit in the press box, but that would look suspicious. Most guys weren't eager to travel with the team before they had to, especially during the preseason.

If he drove himself, he wouldn't have to sit in the press box, and he wouldn't have to figure out a way to get home. Grady's dick was probably worth an hour of driving each way, though there was no way to know for sure without taking it for a test ride. It was probably even worth the chirping Grady'd give him for going so far out of his way to get it.

But something held him back. Hell, maybe he was still salty and wanted a way to inflict his own disappointment on Grady. Either way, he didn't examine it, just pulled out his phone and texted, *So, bad news.*

*You're not playing tonight,* Grady guessed.

*Ur smarter than u look,* Max replied. Then, *Sorry.*

*Guess I can't complain.*

Max sighed and flopped back against the couch.

Gru looked up from the floor, one ear standing straight up, the other flopped over. He tilted his head to the side.

"Yeah, a walk's a good idea," Max agreed. "Come on."

He ended up following the game on Twitter that night, sprawled out on his couch with Gru on his legs because he believed with his entire fifty-pound being that he was a lapdog. It was the opposite of their previous game, tied at nothing until Grady buried what turned out to be the only goal of the game five minutes from the final buzzer.

Max dropped his phone in disgust and ruffled Gru's ears. "He probably would've been a beast tonight," he said mournfully.

Gru licked his fingers and wagged his tail against Max's knees.

"Not exactly the kind of action I was looking for," Max told him. "I bet you're a better cuddler, though."

Gru rolled over for belly rubs and elbowed Max in the nuts.

"Or not," Max wheezed.

BY THE third first date, Grady was convinced he had missed a class at school or something. Maybe he'd been a terrible person in a previous life and this was his cosmic payback. Maybe the price for being really fucking good at hockey was his deplorable lack of social skills.

It was October now. Time was ticking down on his deadline to make holiday plans and make sure Jess got her girls' trip. Two days after the last preseason game of the year, and Grady was sitting at a beer garden downtown, wishing he'd ordered a single pint so he could down it and leave. Instead, he had a whole flight of tiny glasses. He *could* knock back six miniature beers in a row, but that would make it obvious that he was ditching, and they were in public, so someone would make a dumb internet post about it.

Grady had been a meme once. Someone had tried to pass through his legs while he was skating through the neutral zone, and he'd stepped on the puck and face-planted. He would prefer to avoid a repeat.

His date this afternoon was Tony, twenty-five, which Grady had decided was the lower limit for "you must be at least this old to ride." Tony was beautiful, Grady would give him that. He had smooth skin and lean muscles and thick, dark eyelashes. He had *smolder*.

He wore a black sleeveless shirt that showed off the curve of his biceps and, when he moved right, a flash of nipple. It also drew plenty of attention to the big red heart-shaped tattoo on his forearm, which had the word *Mom* written in it, in scrolling font.

Grady didn't want to ask about it, exactly. He figured if someone got a heart tattoo with *Mom* in it, they'd probably been through some shit. Maybe the guy's mom had had breast cancer or something. Grady knew about that kind of trauma, and it wasn't a first-date topic. So he didn't ask.

But he must've kept looking at it, because about five minutes into their date, Tony noticed him looking and beamed. "Cool, isn't it?"

Caught off guard, Grady stammered, "Uh, yeah, it's really… interesting."

"I know, right?" Tony flexed his forearm. "I saw it in the artist's flash book and I just *had* to have it."

"O-oh?" Grady asked. "I thought maybe you were really close to your mom or…." *Or maybe we had something in common.*

"Nah." Tony flashed some expensive veneers. "I mean, my mom's great. But I thought this was such an original piece, you know?"

With some alarm, Grady realized that he had no idea if Tony was fucking with him. He could've understood if Tony had gotten it to be ironic. And if he'd liked the design, sure, it was his skin, and he could do what he wanted with it. Grady made a living out of the slow destruction of his body. He couldn't fault anyone for decorating theirs.

But there were *Looney Tunes* episodes that involved a tattoo like that, for fuck's sake. *Original?* Was he living in the Twilight Zone?

Worse, was he too young to remember those cartoons?

Grady hated dating.

Weren't there professionals he could pay to screen his dates for him? Some kind of matchmaking service?

Ugh, no, that made him look desperate.

Tony was still talking about the tattoo. "… been thinking about what I want for my next one. I think it'd be cool to get a Chinese character, you know? Something that means, like, 'strength' or something."

Grady was pretty sure he knew the answer to this question, but something compelled him to ask anyway. "Do you speak any Chinese?"

"No," Tony answered easily. "But it looks cool, right?"

Fuck it. Grady finished the first beer in his flight and picked up the second. "If you can't read it, how will you know the artist didn't write 'fuckface'?"

Tony shrugged. "I won't, I guess. But, like, no one else is going to be able to read it either."

Grady downed the second beer. Was he going to do this?

He was going to do this.

He picked up the third glass. "Pretty sure a lot of people can read Chinese." He was dimly aware that there was more than one Chinese language, but he doubted Tony could grasp the concept and he didn't remember enough details to fake confidence in the knowledge. "Like Chinese people, for example. More people speak Chinese than English."

Snorting, Tony reached for his own beer. "Yeah, okay, but not *here*."

Jesus Christ. Grady took a deep breath and then a deep sip, because if he didn't, he was going to throw the beer in Tony's dumb face. That would *definitely* be a meme.

Then he set the glass back on the pretentious wooden serving board. "Tony, I'd like to tell you it's been nice getting to know you, but you're a racist asshole and your tattoo is basic." He tilted his head toward the remaining drinks. "I'll settle the tab on my way out."

He called a cab and spent the ride back to his place stewing.

All that negative energy needed an outlet or it was going to build up inside him and give him indigestion, so he started a text to Coop. *I'm starting to think celibacy is underrated.*

He was expecting sympathy, or maybe a tiny violin, or a question about what fresh dating hell Grady had discovered, but the message that pinged back fell firmly in the category of *none of the above.*

*Am i supposed to take that personally? i think i take that personally.*

Grady blinked, then groaned. He'd selected the most recent text thread, which was Max's, not Coop's. *Take it however you want.*

Not ten seconds later, he got a reply. *Now theres an invitation !!*

Despite his sour mood, Grady snorted. It wasn't like he didn't know Max was easy for it.

*but srsly did u fuck up another date? I need the deets. Spill the tea*

Grady felt a very inconvenient need to defend himself. *This one wasn't my fault. The guy had a heart tattoo with "Mom" on it because it was "original."*

*ok ill give u that 1*

Grady rolled his eyes. *Thanks.*

*But like how r u striking out this bad all over. I dont get it. do the guys in philly just suck*

*Oh my god that's it isn't it*

*Its not u. its philly*

*Sorry bud*

Bristling on Philadelphia's behalf, Grady gritted his teeth and responded. *Don't blame this on Philly.* Then, a minute later, *And don't call me bud.*

*Tell u what tho,* Max went on, ignoring Grady's messages, *its such a shame for ur dick to go to waste. So ill make u a deal.*

There was a 100 percent chance Grady was going to regret this, but apparently he was a glutton for punishment. *What kind of deal?*

*I will go on a practice date with u & tell u how ur fucking it up.*

Grady frowned. *What do you get out of it?*

*I pick the date. U pay.* Then, a moment later, *also u have 2 tell me all about all ur other shitty dates so I can laugh at u.*

That seemed… reasonable. Semi reasonable. Worth the risk, at least. Grady didn't want Jess to miss out on her trip, but she wouldn't go if it meant he was alone at Christmas . He didn't want to die of mortification either, which was what would happen if it ever got out that he'd gone to Max Lockhart for dating advice. But if Grady could trust anyone on the planet to give him the unvarnished truth about what was wrong with him, it was Max.

Fuck.

*Deal.*


EVENTUALLY THEY settled on the Wednesday before the season opener for their "date." Max booked the facility and sent Grady a Venmo request ten seconds later.

Grady sent him one back—six bucks for the bottled water Max drank in his hotel room. Max texted him a middle-finger emoji, but they both paid, so that was all debts cleared. Frankly he was impressed Grady had gone along with it. Max hadn't exactly picked a cheap date option, and he'd been cagey about what they were doing. On top of that, while Max *had* dated some, he didn't have the smoothest track record with relationships either. Getting someone to like him and have sex with him was easy. Connecting with them on an emotional level was a skill he hadn't mastered.

Grady must really be desperate for his help.

Max wasn't above taking advantage of that. It was just that the advantage he wanted wasn't financial.

If Grady got overly competitive about mini golf, Max couldn't *wait* to see what he made of this.

Wednesday morning, Max parked in the lot at the gym and got out of the car to enjoy the crisp fall day. He was a couple minutes early, which he wasn't going to analyze. There'd been less traffic than he anticipated, that's all.

Grady pulled in exactly on time. He made it a point to park a couple spots over from Max in the deserted lot. When he got out, Max saw he'd taken Max's instructions seriously—he was wearing a T-shirt and shorts and carrying a bag with his sneakers, same as Max. Though was it really necessary to show up with his facial hair perfectly groomed, just to highlight the sharp lines of his jaw and cheekbones? Max had made it clear they were going to be sweating, but he wasn't supposed to be sweating about *Grady* yet.

Oh well. He could hardly complain about the eye candy.

Grady shut the car door and shouldered his bag. "Did you bring me out here to kill me?"

"Don't be dumb. I'd hire a professional for that." Max hit the Lock button on his remote. "Now, no more smart remarks. We're here on a *date*, remember? How can I fix your form if you don't play along?"

Grady's pained grimace would sustain Max through so many ugly losses. But to be fair, he added, "You can still back out."

Grady squared his shoulders. "No." He schooled his features too, the furrow of his brow smoothing out. "I'm game. I can do this."

Because now that Max had offered him an out, his pride demanded he not take it. Max knew how to handle him. "Cool," he said breezily and gestured toward the gym. "So, how about I tell you where you're taking me on our date."

"That sounds like a good place to start." Grady cut him a sideways look. "You know, since this is the most expensive first date I've ever been on."

"Bzzz." Max backhanded him gently in the gut. "First offense. No talking money on the first date."

"What? Come on, you set me up—"

Max raised his eyebrows. "You gonna argue with me about the criticism?"

Grady's shoulders slumped. "You're enjoying this way too much, aren't you?"

"Oh bud, we're just getting started." Pointedly, Max stopped at the door to the gym.

Grady gave him a capital-L Look, but he got the door, so at least he wasn't a complete lost cause, etiquette-wise. "What is this place?"

Max walked in and spread his arms. "This… is a gym where they train for *American Ninja Warrior*."

Grady's mouth dropped open, but before he could say anything, Brad stepped out of the office. "Max! My man."

Max greeted him with a high-five bro hug. "Thanks for coming in on your day off." The gym didn't normally open on Wednesdays.

It definitely didn't normally open for two people, which was why their reservation was so expensive. But that was fine. Grady could treat him. Max was worth it.

"For glass seats to the next game?" Brad laughed and released him. "My wife's gonna flip. I've got your paperwork all set if you want to follow me into the… office…."

Ah. He'd recognized Grady, who looked like a bug under glass.

"Uh," Brad said.

Time for Max's charm to come to the rescue. "Brad, Grady. Grady, Brad." They shook hands, bound by Max's invocation of social norms. "Don't worry, Brad's not going to tell anyone we're actually friends."

"No one would believe me," Brad said.

"We're not friends," Grady said at the same time.

"You'll get used to his sense of humor," Max promised Brad. Since he couldn't reprimand Grady for his bad date manners in front of Brad, he said, "Let's go sign some waivers."

Grady made the patented Wet Cat face, but he didn't argue.

"So the course is pretty simple right now," Brad said as he led them into the main room. "Training starts in September and ramps up from there. We just shocked the drop pool, so your clothes are probably going to discolor if you fall in. Sorry."

"Drop pool?" Grady repeated.

"Dude, are you not familiar with your country's greatest cultural export?"

"It's for when you fall off the Shrinking Steps," Brad said.

"Shrinking Steps. Are those the things that look like… demented lily pads?"

"Aww, look at him learning new things!" Max elbowed Grady in the side. "I don't suppose you want to give us a demonstration before we start?"

Brad grinned. "Thought you'd never ask. Though I have to say, your friend's going to be at a disadvantage."

Max and Grady looked at each other. Max took a little extra time on the breadth of Grady's shoulders and the thickness of his thighs.

Finally Grady cleared his throat. "How so?"

"Upper-body strength-to-weight ratio." Brad stretched his shoulders and back. He was half a head shorter than Max and a lot leaner. "You're huge. No offense." He grabbed his right foot and stretched his quad. "The course is usually easiest for smaller people."

A lot of the obstacles involved hanging from bars and swinging from platforms.

Grady said, "I think I'll be fine," practically grinding his teeth, because he could not stand to be challenged.

Max couldn't wait until he did Wet Cat for real.

"Yeah, you're probably right," Brad said, because he had better people skills than Grady. "Okay, so the first section is balance. See those padded benches? They're designed to wobble. So the first obstacle is to run across them until you reach the second platform."

He pointed to the next section of the course. "Then there's the Ring Toss. You're going to jump up and grab those rings, one in each hand. They're not attached to the pegs. So you're going to use your body weight to stretch out and snag one ring on those green hooks hanging down from the bar. Then you pull the other ring off the first hook and stretch to the next one, until you get to the platform."

That didn't sound so bad, and it was only a short drop to a well-padded floor.

"Then you're on to the Shrinking Stairs and—yeah, maybe I'll just demonstrate?" Brad said dubiously. Max followed his gaze to Grady, who looked unimpressed.

Oh yeah. Max was gonna laugh so hard when he fell in the pool.

All limbered up, Brad handed Max a stopwatch. "See if I can beat my personal best."

Max heard, *Let's see how wound up your cranky friend gets when he can't match my time.* "Okay. On your mark… get set…." The watch beeped.

And Brad was off.

He ran straight across the padded benches with nary a wiggle. When he grabbed the rings, he switched right from a jog into a sort of monkey-swinging motion. Five rings later he was on the third platform.

Then he sprinted across the Shrinking Stairs—they wobbled too, and they got taller and smaller as they crossed the pool. Brad made it look like a breeze. Next up was—

"What the fuck," Grady muttered.

Next up was the Salmon Ladder, a bar you had to hang suspended from and then sort of jump, but with your arms, until the bar caught on the next set of rungs. There were five sets. At the top, Brad grabbed a rope, which he used to swing fifteen feet to a metal bar mounted on a horizontal wooden beam.

"Still think this is gonna be easy?" Max asked as Brad bouldered along the beam.

"Fuck you."

Brad dropped to the padded platform and descended the steps to the final obstacle—the wall.

Which he proceeded to run up. He grabbed the metal bar at the top and swung his body up like it was nothing.

Max hit the button on the stopwatch. "Two minutes, eight seconds."

Brad flopped dramatically onto his back. "Two seconds too long."

"This is batshit insane," Grady said.

"Fuck yeah it is." Max grinned at him. "Fastest time tops? Or you want to make it first through without falling?"

Grady didn't even think about it. "First through."

Good idea—otherwise they might use too much energy trying to one-up each other. "Deal." Then Max grinned. "And since *you're* taking *me* out on this date, I think that means I get to go first."

He could tell Grady wanted to argue, but somehow he swallowed the impulse. "Please," he said through clenched teeth. "Be my guest."

Max had done a few stretches before he left home, but he did a few more now to make sure he still felt limber and also to make Grady sweat when his shorts rode up. He climbed the first platform and jogged in place for a few seconds to psych himself up.

*Now or never.* He launched himself onto the first bench.

He almost face-planted when the bench lurched to the side because he didn't put his foot right in the center. Only years of balancing on skates kept him upright. But he stumbled across the second and third benches to the next obstacle.

Grady's laughter reached his ears. Max shot him the finger.

All going according to plan.

"Hey! Bad etiquette," Grady scolded.

"I'm not the one who needs a lesson!" The rings sucked. Max was *heavy*, and most of his strength was in his lower body. But if it was bad for him, it would be worse for Grady, who was heavier in the ass and thighs as well as everywhere else. He missed the final hook and ended up dropping the ring in his left hand, but he swung his body and got enough momentum to fling himself onto the platform.

He flopped there for a moment on his hands and knees, milking the appearance of trying to catch his breath. "This is the part where my concerned partner checks if I'm still alive."

"Well, your mouth still works, but that's no guarantee there's no brain damage."

Rather than attempt a response, Max attempted the next obstacle. For Max, the test was a big step onto a tiny wobbly lily pad over a pool. For Grady, it was whether he could have—or fake—a normal reaction.

Max took the big step and let himself lose balance. He flailed spectacularly to no avail and hit the water sideways.

*Graceful.* He came up sputtering. Chlorine stung his eyes as he front-crawled to the ladder.

"You okay?"

Max wiped a hand down his face and blinked up at Grady. Did he look a little green, or was it a trick of the light? "Nothing hurt but my dignity," he said damply. He swung himself out of the pool, and Grady handed him a towel.

Weird. Max had expected him to fail.

"Can't hurt what you don't have."

That was better. Max dried his face and hair and then wrapped the towel around his shoulders. "Looks like you're up."

Maybe it was because he had the advantage of learning from Max's mistakes, but Grady didn't have trouble with the benches. He *did* have an issue with the rings, though, because they'd forgotten to reset the course. Max collected them and handed them up.

To his surprise, Grady didn't start on the obstacle. Instead he sat on the edge of the platform and cracked his neck.

"What are you doing?"

Grady stretched his arms. "It's first through the course without falling, right? Time doesn't count. So there's no hurry. I'll take my time to make sure I win."

For a second, Max didn't know what to say. "Are you that obsessed with winning, or do you just want my ass that bad?"

"Don't flatter yourself. It's definitely about winning." But his cheeks were pink, and not with exertion. This was a carrot-*and*-stick scenario.

Max *tsk*ed. "It's not nice to let your date think you're not attracted to them, you know," he said as Grady hooked the first ring.

"Are you"—he hooked the third ring—"actually fishing for compliments right now?"

Of course he crossed the obstacle easily. The guy was superhuman. Max could see his nipples straining against his shirt. Nice.

Grady could probably see his too, now, since his shirt was wet.

"I'm preparing you for a life beyond practice dates. Come on, tell me something you like about me."

He thought Grady might get distracted and lose his balance on the Shrinking Steps, but no such luck. He made it to the platform and then sat down again.

"Really?" Max said judgmentally.

"I'm concentrating on the question! Wouldn't want to lose my focus and fall in the water. That would be embarrassing." He said the last part smugly.

"Don't strain yourself thinking too hard."

"Okay, okay. How about, you give good head."

Max made himself smile, because he knew Grady meant it, because it was expected, and also to cover the sting of hurt. All the texts they'd exchanged in the past couple weeks and that was all he could come up with? "Good effort, also very believable delivery, but how many first dates are you going to be able to say that on?"

With a huff, Grady crossed his arms. "Look, we've established that I'm bad at this. You're supposed to be teaching me. So… teach by example."

"Oh for—" Max couldn't believe it. Grady didn't want to give him a compliment because, what, he was afraid Max would hold it over his head? How insecure could he be? "All right. Grady." He settled the towel more securely around his shoulders, like it could protect him from Grady's judgy face. "You're a good hockey player. I like how controlled you are on the ice, how tough it is to make you lose your cool. I admire that. It makes you challenging to play against, and I like challenges."

He waited a moment for that to sink in—waited while Grady's cheeks went a little redder and he dropped his gaze.

Then he added, "Also you have a really nice dick."

Grady jerked his eyes up again and narrowed them in anger. "If you—"

Max tilted his head. "Feels different, doesn't it."

Grady closed his mouth, his lips pursed. Point made. He wouldn't forget that lesson.

Max almost expected him to sit there pouting and not try the exercise again, but Grady surprised him. "I like the way you leave everything on the ice," he said quietly. "You don't take work home with you. I envy that."

Oh Lord, what had Max unleashed? He pulled the towel from his shoulders, suddenly too warm, and cleared his throat. Whatever that *feeling* was when Grady complimented him sincerely, it needed to go back in the box. "See? You're coachable."

Grady shot him an amused look. "I think you're supposed to say thank you."

"Oh, *accepting* compliments is a whole other ball game." Not Max's wheelhouse. He gestured. "Come on, next obstacle. The point of an active date is you don't have to make small talk."

"Didn't you basically just say it's my small talk that needs work?" Grady grumbled. But he got to his feet and gripped the bar for the Salmon Ladder.

Max's mouth went dry.

Grady wasn't a small guy, especially after spending a summer bulking up. His body was solid. He had to weigh 220. He exhaled and squared his shoulders before heaving himself and the bar upward.

The bar caught. Four more to go.

His body jolted with every step, but his grip held. So did Max's attention. If he *did* accidentally win today, it wasn't like Grady's ass would be a consolation prize.

"As an FYI, you should definitely do this on all your first dates." *Damn.* "It really plays to your strengths."

Grady heaved himself up the final step of the ladder. "I'll keep that… in mind." He jumped for the rope and swung.

For a minute it looked like he wouldn't make the transfer to the bouldering obstacle. He hit the wall and bounced off, as much as a six-foot-plus man could bounce. But on the second swing, he got a grip on the bar.

Now he was dangling from it, and Max could see the strain in his body. His shoulders ached in sympathy, and part of him wanted to cheer Grady on.

Another part of him knew that wasn't the best way to motivate him.

"What, you're not feeling it now, are you? Fingers cramping?"

Grady's chest heaved, but he didn't waste breath with a reply. He grabbed the first handhold and shimmied along the beam.

"There's no shame in falling, you know. It's more fun if we're both wet."

On the next handhold, Grady's grip slipped. Max was sure he'd hit the pool, but he recovered and made the third grab.

Max needed to up his game or Grady was toast. "Bet your arms are tired. Or maybe not, I mean, you've been carrying your team for long enough—you're probably used to it."

Grady let out a muffled curse, but he finished the obstacle and dropped onto the second-last platform, then rolled onto his back. "What kind of date talk is that?" he panted.

"Motivational."

Grady snorted and turned his face toward Max. "How do you figure?"

Max grinned. "What's better than proving me wrong?"

"Trick question."

"Exactly."

After that, Grady's ascent up the Warped Wall was almost anticlimactic. Max wolf-whistled while he made the victory V with his arms.

Mission accomplished.

Part one of the mission, at least.

Max scrubbed his hair again and dropped the towel in the industrial-size bin. Then he grabbed a spare set of rings and climbed onto the first platform.

"Hey!" Grady shouted across the gym. "What are you doing? I won!"

"What, so you think we're going home now?" After what he spent renting out this place? Well, what *Grady* spent. "Patience, Grasshopper."

This would be more challenging now that his shoes were wet, but Max could do it. He shook out his muscles.

Grady descended the wall and watched from the base of the first platform. "Are you a glutton for punishment or something?"

*Yes, but I'm saving that reveal for later.* "You don't think I can do it?" Max *tsk*ed. "Grady, Grady, Grady. Anything you can do, I can do better."

"If you really want to fall in the water again—"

Max ignored him and sprinted across the benches. This time he made sure to stick to the middle.

He barely paused before launching into the rings. One, two, three, four, five, and he was across. The Shrinking Steps were tricky with wet shoes, but he didn't slip until the final one, and he landed on his feet on the platform.

Then the Salmon Ladder—he hated that thing; his core felt like it was on fire and his triceps were always jelly by the end, not to mention keeping his grip on the rope afterward gave him trouble. But he knew how to use his lower body to swing from grip to grip across the bouldering obstacle.

"You were saying?" Max said from the top of the wall a few seconds later.

He could practically feel the heat coming off Grady's red face. "Did you *practice* this?"

Max smirked at him. "Maybe."

Oooh, that frown was like a thundercloud. "So you lost on purpose?"

"Bud, I don't think we're playing the same game." Max hopped down the stairs on the back side of the wall. "This happened once before, remember?"

A muscle at the corner of Grady's jaw twitched. "Would it kill you to be straightforward about anything for once in your life?"

Max beamed. "Probably not, but why risk it?"

Now there was a vein bulging in his forehead. "Why are you like this?"

"Mom says it's because I'm a middle child."

Grady made a noise like the kitchen sink disposal.

Max patted his shoulder and headed for the exit. "You want to follow me back to my place, or should I send you the address?"


GRADY PROBABLY should have turned around and gone home. He was irritated with Max. If he wanted Grady to fuck him so bad, he could've said so. He didn't have to make a stupid bet about it. And he didn't have to let Grady win—that was *annoying*. Grady wasn't a kid. He didn't need to be *handled*.

Max was just… outrageous. Grady could never get away with half the things Max said, but Max had everyone conned into thinking he was *charming*. Even Grady caught himself falling for it from time to time.

He was also irritated with himself. He'd said some dumb things that he regretted. He hated the moment of panic he'd felt when Max hit the water. Max was never in any danger. He was falling in a pool—and now Grady knew that'd been on purpose.

Which made him *more* irritated. What did Grady care what happened to Max? He didn't even like the guy.

Okay, Grady didn't have to like someone to not want them to get hurt. But he felt like Max's intentional fall was some kind of cosmic "gotcha" moment. Like it had been meant to catch Grady caring when he shouldn't.

And then Max had the nerve to get out of the pool looking like *that*. He should've looked like a drowned rat, with his dumb, too-long hair soaked and clinging to his scalp and his athletic shirt plastered to his body and his shorts leaving nothing to the imagination.

Fuck. *Fuck.* Wasn't it bad enough that he made Grady lose control on the ice and annoyed the hell out of him off of it? Did Grady have to find him sexually attractive too?

For once in his life, could Grady have a normal reaction to someone acting like a pest?

It was possible he was thinking about it a little too hard.

But apparently the answer to all of that was no—it *wasn't* bad enough, and he *did* have to find him sexually attractive, and his reaction to Max annoying him on purpose was, evidently, to get a boner he could pound nails with, so he practically tailgated Max back to his place.

By the time he pulled into the driveway, he was *really* frustrated. He'd been stuck looking at the ass end of Max's ugly lime-green Land Rover for fifteen minutes when he parked and stalked out of the car toward the front door.

Max didn't hold it for him, so they were past the pretense of their date, which was a relief. Grady didn't feel like faking social niceties.

"You want a bottle of water or something?" Max asked as he tossed his keys in a dish by the door.

Grady had chugged a Gatorade in the car. "I'm not thirsty."

"What're you doing here, then?" But he clearly didn't care about the answer, because he grabbed a fistful of Grady's shirt and pulled him into a kiss.

Max kissed the way he played hockey, fast and hard and with an edge of teeth, always daring Grady to push back harder, to take him to the boards. Grady tried to hold back on the ice, but fuck if he was doing that here. He fisted a hand in Max's damp hair and bit his lower lip. "Where's your bedroom?"

Max hissed into his mouth and then pulled away. "Upstairs. Come on."

This time Grady didn't ask about foreplay. If he'd learned anything about Max, it was that the competition *was* foreplay.

Grady couldn't say it didn't work for him.

Max's wet T-shirt hit the hardwood at the top of the stairs. He didn't even look back at it. If he wanted to wreck his floor, Grady wouldn't stop him. He pulled his own shirt off, tossed it in a corner where no one would trip on it, and followed Max into his bedroom.

Any other time, he might have looked around to see what the room said about its owner. But Grady was a little busy right now, because Max had shoved his hand down the front of Grady's shorts.

His enthusiasm was contagious, or at least that was what Grady told himself. He bit Max's lower lip again as Max thumbed the head of his cock and then slid his hands over Max's ass and squeezed.

The space between them evaporated, so Max had to move his hand. But that was okay, because now Grady could grind their cocks together while kneading Max's cheeks. Whatever Max's many other flaws, he had a great ass, and Grady looked forward to getting to know it better.

Maybe Max was thinking the same thing about Grady's dick, because he started tugging at Grady's waistband. "Off, come on, get these off."

But—"Fair's fair," Grady said, and when he stepped back to undress, Max did the same.

Then, for the first time, they were naked together.

Max had a body built for hockey—thick, well-defined thighs and strong arms, abs hidden under a layer of fat. This was a man who valued function over form—he needed the extra weight now because he'd burn through it and then some by the end of the season. It looked good on him.

Not as good as Grady would look on him, though. He shoved Max backward onto the bed, climbed up after him, and straddled his waist.

"Thought you were gonna fuck me." Max squirmed under him. He raked his nails up the inside of Grady's thigh and then wrapped his hand around Grady's dick. "Gonna be kind of tough in that position."

Grady thrust into his grip. "I thought you were gonna let me be in charge."

Max laughed and raised his eyebrows, telegraphing *I dare you*.

Well, they weren't on the ice. Grady didn't have to feel guilty about giving in. He rose onto his knees, shoved Max onto his belly, and then settled his weight on his ass. That should keep him out of trouble for the next few seconds. "Where's your lube, if you're so hard up for it?"

Max scrabbled under the pillows at the head of the bed and retrieved a strip of condoms and a half-empty bottle. At least it was a decent brand. Not as nice as the one Grady preferred, but beggars and choosers.

Except Grady wasn't going to be the beggar in this scenario.

He shifted down the bed so he was sitting on Max's thighs. Then he uncapped the lube… and stopped. "What the fuck is that?"

Max turned to look over his shoulder, his hair half falling in his face. "What—oh, that's Larry."

"*Larry*?" Grady repeated. Without meaning to, he traced his fingers over the bright red cartoon lobster tattooed on Max's left asscheek. "*You named your tramp stamp?*"

"Excuse you, it's not a tramp stamp, it's a testament to my cultural heritage." He wiggled his ass. "Is this going to be a deal-breaker for you?"

Unfortunately, it was not. Grady's brain tried to point out that he'd rejected a guy for questionable tattoos last week, but his dick overruled the objection. "Why a lobster?"

He could practically hear the eye roll. "I'm from New Brunswick. They give us those when we're born."

Smartass. Grady slapped him on the lobster—not hard enough to hurt, just to sting a little.

Max jolted and flushed bright red from his nape down his shoulders.

Grady stared. Fuck. Of *course* he'd be into that. Of course Grady would find out by accident.

Of course Grady would feel compelled to do it again.

"At least it's not crabs, I guess," Grady said, feeling insane, and when Max laughed, Grady shoved two slick fingers into his hole. His body was hot and he opened easily for it.

"Jesus, tell me that's not something you'd say on a date."

Grady scissored his fingers. If Max wasn't into foreplay, there was no point wasting time; he was as hard as Grady. "No, only with you."

"Aw, bud, you say the sweetest—"

*I dare you*, Grady heard. Well, if another spank wasn't what Max wanted, Grady was pretty sure he'd hear about it.

*Smack.* This time Grady watched the hit land, watched the ripple of round fat and muscle, watched the pink stain spread over the skin.

Max inhaled sharply and clenched around Grady's fingers.

Enough. Grady pulled his fingers out and ripped open the condom. "You good?"

"What, you can't tell?"

Grady took that for a yes and pushed inside.

It felt like his spine had liquified. Max's ass fit perfectly into the bowl of his pelvis. The heat of him was blistering. The lines of his body, stretched sinuously on his bed, hips tilted to take Grady's cock, etched themselves into Grady's lizard brain.

And the sound Max made when Grady bottomed out made Grady's nipples hard.

Of course, the next second, Max ruined it by using words. "So are you gonna fuck me now or what?" He tried to squirm backward on Grady's dick, like he could control the situation that way.

Grady grabbed Max's hips. "Quit it." Couldn't he get two seconds to keep from coming immediately? Max was the one who wanted this in the first place.

"Come on, you don't really expect me to lie here and take it—"

Oh, fuck him very much. Grady pushed him flat to the bed, still inside him, his chest to Max's back. "Maybe I do," he said, digging his chin into Max's shoulder. He didn't have any physical leverage like this, but the metaphorical kind worked for him too. "What are you going to do about it?"

Max said, "Uh."

Grady bit the side of his neck. Beneath him, Max shuddered deliciously. "That's what I thought."

Grady was out of his depth. He had no idea what had gotten into him. He had no plan for where to take this next. But Max pushed all Grady's buttons, and it was only fair to push back.

Max should have come with an instruction manual. Grady didn't even know where his buttons were. He couldn't just lie here on top of Max—

"Hey! Did you fall asleep up there?" Max tried to work his arm underneath his body. "Some of us are trying to get off—"

Grady pulled his wrist behind his back. "Some of us threw a game on purpose, and now they're going to get off when I say they do." The movement put him back up on his knees—and gave him his leverage back.

God, who *was* he? What had come over him?

"Fuck you," Max said, but his voice was breathy, with only the hint of a snarl.

Grady shifted closer and leveraged Max's hips up with his thighs so his ass was in the air, weight on his shoulders. He looked amazing. "Maybe next time." Grady thrust experimentally. Max muffled a noise in his pillow.

Okay, well, *that* button he could find, no problem. He pushed it again and the tension sapped out of Max's body.

Grady's lizard brain hissed in triumph.

The part with actual cognitive ability went *oh no*.

Then Max said, "Is that all you got?" and Grady lost his entire mind.

He switched his grip on Max's wrist to his other hand and snapped his hips forward hard enough to fill the room with the slap of skin on skin. "Is this enough for you?" Grady rasped. He barely recognized his own voice.

Blessedly, Max seemed beyond words. He huffed out tiny, wrecked-sounding moans with every thrust, like Grady was fucking them out of him, but otherwise didn't respond.

Grady wanted to take that for a yes too, but he needed to be sure. If Max wasn't going to give verbal confirmation, Grady needed to see his face.

"Max," Grady said.

Max moaned like a porn star but didn't otherwise respond.

"*Max*—" That one slipped out unbidden. The tension in Grady's body was coiling ever tighter, but he wasn't going to come before Max did. That was a point of personal pride.

But if Max didn't tell him anything—

Grady gave up trying to get his attention with his words, fisted his free hand in Max's hair, and tugged his head back.

But he never got to ask anything, because the second Max turned his blotchy red face toward him, his whole body seized.

"Oh *fuck*," Max said. His eyes squeezed closed and his mouth dropped open, and Grady could *feel* it when he came, clenching around his cock so tight Grady was helpless to do anything but bite his lip and follow him down.

He returned to himself breathing like he'd been bag skated, lying flat against Max's back. At some point he'd let go of Max's wrist and hair. It took him a moment to find the coordination to prop himself up on shaky arms and pull out of Max's body so he could collapse next to him.

"Well," Max said faintly, "I think we can rule out bad sex as a problem."

Grady couldn't make words, so he made a rude gesture instead. Of course sex wasn't a problem. Having sex with someone he actually *liked*—that was the problem.

Maybe that wasn't completely fair. Objectively, off the ice, Max wasn't terrible.

Okay, he was, but Grady had developed a tolerance for it. They weren't *friends*, but Grady could be civil to people who weren't his friends.

Which reminded him… he owed Max an apology.

Ugh.

Better get it over with now, while Max was still facedown on the mattress and not scrutinizing him. "I'm sorry I made the brain damage comment."

Predictably, that made Max turn his head and look at him. He furrowed his brow in confusion. "What?"

"When you were doing the ring thing. I shouldn't have made a joke about brain damage. We play a contact sport. We both know enough guys who have it to know that shit isn't funny."

"I didn't think twice about it. I wasn't offended." Max tucked a hand under his cheek. For once his eyes looked serious. "You're right, though—it's not funny."

Grady blew out a breath. "That's why I don't like losing control on the ice." And why he hated it when Max got under his skin. It would be so easy to hurt someone because he got angry and made a bad hit.

Max tilted his head. "It's a contact sport. No one gets here without knowing the risks."

"Yeah. Including me." Suddenly it was important that Max understood what Grady meant and why. "Including the risk that if I don't pay attention, I could put someone through what I went through as a kid." He'd never forget watching from home as a player had a heart attack on the ice, or the sinking sensation in his gut when a pileup happened and someone got a skate blade too close to the neck.

Grady'd never seen anyone die during a game, but it could happen.

Max absorbed that for a moment. For once he didn't seem inclined to poke or prod or make fun. He was listening like he was really thinking about it. "Don't take this the wrong way," he said at last. "Because I mean, you're right, and it… I get why you'd feel, um, strongly about that." Everyone knew what happened to Grady's parents. "But… you talked to someone about this stuff, right? Like… professionally."

*I'm talking to you*, Grady thought. But that wasn't what Max meant. And since he seemed sincere in his concern—rare, for him, and unnerving for Grady—Grady answered honestly. "Yeah."

"Okay, good," Max said. "In that case, I need to tell you that you *suck* at pillow talk."

Oh fuck. Grady startled into embarrassed laughter. "God, I really do." Only Max could get away with saying that after such a serious conversation and come across as funny instead of dismissive.

"Like, buddy… that's a problem." He made an exaggerated grimace and then smiled and patted Grady on the hip. "Nice job until then, though. Ten out of ten, would lose a sex bet to again."

Right. That reminded him why he was here in the first place. "Thanks, I think. How's the rest of my report card?"

Max waggled his hand. "You're not the world's most hopeless case. You really only have one problem. It's just that it's a really big problem." He shrugged. "You've got no people instincts."

Grady opened his mouth to object… then closed it. "Oh."

"Yeah. It's pretty brutal. Which is weird," he went on, rolling onto his back, "because it's not like you have trouble reading people on the ice. But, like, your dates… have been bad."

Understatement. "Believe me, I'm aware."

"I don't mean the dates themselves. I mean the guys you went out with. You had a bad time because you picked some real losers." He rolled his eyes. "I mean, a guy who thinks ice cream should have palm oil in it?"

"*Thank* you." At least someone understood.

On the other hand, that someone was Mad Max. Maybe Grady shouldn't feel too comforted.

"Speaking of people instincts, how do you feel about dogs?"

"Uh." Grady blinked. He loved dogs in general. He was just wary of loving a single dog in particular. "I like them? But I don't have time for one, so if you're suggesting I get a dog to validate my taste in guys—"

"I wasn't, but that's not a terrible idea." Max reached onto the floor for his shorts and pulled out his phone. "Electronic baby gate. Well. Puppy gate." Then he whistled. "Gru! Come here, baby." And, to Grady, as an afterthought: "You might wanna shield your junk, he's not great about landings."

There was the excited clack of nails on hardwood, then coming up the stairs. Then a midsize chocolate-colored mutt launched itself onto the mattress.

"Hi, baby. Did you miss me?" Max ruffled the dog's ears as it licked Max's chin. "You did, huh? What a good boy."

Grady cleared his throat as a stubby tail covered in curly brown fur wagged in his face. "Should I give you two a minute?"

But as soon as the words were out, Gru turned his attention to Grady. He put his nose right up to Grady's and sniffed him while Grady petted his shoulder. "Hi. I normally have more clothes on when I meet people for the first time."

Gru smacked Max in the face with his tail stub.

"I guess you don't mind."

"He's got low standards," Max confided as he swung his legs over the side of the bed. "And also he wants his dinner. Shower's through there if you want to help yourself."

"Thanks." A shower sounded pretty good.

Max had good water pressure and about a thousand mismatched towels in his linen closet, some of which should be put out of their misery. Grady picked one of the nicer ones and stood under the fancy showerhead for an indulgent five minutes. Then he wiped the water from his face and reached for the shampoo.

The only bottle on the shelf read *Men's 3-in-1 Shampoo, Conditioner, and Bodywash*. Grady couldn't even identify a brand name.

"Oh Jesus," he said out loud. "*Why?*" No wonder Max's hair looked like that.

Reluctantly, he soaped his body—no way was he using that stuff on his hair—and rinsed off.

When he'd dressed, he went downstairs and found Max feeding Gru dinner from a bag labeled *Premium Local Organic Dog Good*. Grady's head hurt. He wondered if Max bathed Gru at home. Gru had pretty nice fur. It was soft and glossy. There was no way the dog got washed with men's three-in-one bodywash. He probably got pampered at the doggy spa with something that had oatmeal and jojoba oil or something.

Grady should stop thinking so hard about this.

But he couldn't help it. "You're out of shampoo."

Max set the dog-food scoop on the counter and turned around. Grady had left beard burn on the side of his neck. "I just bought a bottle last week."

"No." Grady shook his head. He took a step forward and held out the bottle. "*This* is not shampoo. This has no business in anyone's hair." It had no business in anyone's shower, but maybe he needed to start small. "You make millions of dollars a year. Why are you putting this on your scalp? Did the straight guys on your team get to you?"

"Hey!" Max frowned. "Seriously. Do I smell bad? Is it not doing its job?"

Grady sighed. "Do you wash your dishes with toilet bowl cleaner?"

For some reason, Max glanced at the cupboard beneath the kitchen sink. "I don't *think* so…."

Augh. "Same concept." Grady plunked the bottle down on the kitchen table. He was tempted to throw it in the garbage, but that seemed rude. Besides, if it was the dog's dinner time, it was probably long past time for him to hit the road. "Anyway, I… I should go. Thanks." Wait, *what*? Why was he thanking Max for sex? It had been Max's idea. "For the, um. Help." Right. Help. With his socialization skills. Because that was why Grady was here in the first place.

Could he get more awkward?

Somehow, instead of making fun of him the way Grady deserved and expected, Max just kind of smiled. Grady's appreciation must've taken him off guard, because he blinked a few times and his mouth moved soundlessly before he finally said, "Sure. Um, good luck on your next date."

"Thanks," Grady said again.

Then, before he could say anything else ridiculous, he made a tactical retreat.

NOW THAT Max had gotten what he wanted out of Grady's online dating experience, he stopped steering him toward disaster. Max didn't want to get invested in "winning" that game when winning was starting to look less casual and more… intentional.

If Grady were less intense in bed, or less hilariously bitchy, or an uptight prick all the way through instead of just on the surface, he'd have had no problems. But Max was starting to *get* him, what made him tick, what made him laugh. He'd gotten a glimpse of the real person under the Wet Cat face, and he liked him. But he wouldn't put himself in a position where he got more out of this whatever-it-was with Grady than Grady did.

Which meant it was time to, like, give back. And what better way than walking Grady through the finer points of weeding out losers from their online profiles?

The Monsters started their season with a road trip, so Max had plenty of travel time to spend texting Grady his tips. Mostly this involved reviewing screenshots and circling red flags—guys who mentioned a "crazy ex" in the first ten minutes of texting were an automatic no; Max couldn't believe he had to spell that out—but when he wrote *lol that guy is such a beer*, he found himself explaining Drink Theory.

*There's nothing wrong w beer. Theres a beer for everyone. It quenches ur thirst. But its empty calories, bro. no substance. Beers are for sex, not long term relationships.*

The three dots on his screen flashed at him for a few seconds before Grady's reply appeared. *Mixed drinks and shots aren't empty calories?*

Damn it, he had a point, but Max wasn't going to admit it. *Caesars come w pickles*, he said instead.

*Anyway, I don't agree. If you're going to drink consistently, isn't something less intense better? Doing tequila shots all night will kill you.*

Hmm. It was possible Max needed to rethink Drink Theory to account for relationships rather than hookups. *But what a way 2 go!!!*

Grady sent him an incredibly judgmental emoji. Then he said, *What if I'm a beer drinker?*

Max snorted. *Ur not. mixed drinks 4 u. a beer will bore the fuck out of u within 10 minutes. U need some1 on ur level.*

*So I'm a mixed drink?*

Fishing for compliments? Something made Max glance at Hedgie, passed out in the plane seat next to him. He curled his body against the side of the plane anyway, which felt… stupid. It wasn't like he was doing anything suspicious. But he didn't want to explain. He liked having this part of Grady to himself.

*Ya. Alcohol content varies depending on the pour. Can last all night… or pound it back in 1 go.* He added a halo emoji in case the innuendo was too subtle.

Predictably, Grady ignored the bait. *What about you? Are you a mixed drink?*

Oh, flattery! Max smiled in spite of himself. *Nah. Shot. Packs a punch.* And Max didn't have a track record of relationships himself. He knew his strengths.

*Can't argue with that,* Grady replied.

Well, no. He had firsthand knowledge.

Max told himself he wasn't disappointed Grady agreed. *Anyway. My vote is bachelor number 3. Lmk how it goes.*

In reply, he got a thumbs-up emoji, so at least Grady was embracing some of the trappings of modern communication.

"No sexting on the plane," Hedgie mumbled beside him.

Max looked up from his phone. "I'm not sexting. Get your mind out of the gutter."

Hedgie could barely keep his eyes open, so Max didn't know how he managed to do the judgmental eyebrow. "Who're you talking to, then? Holding your phone like you're afraid I'll see it."

How could Hedgie be this observant with Max when he was half-asleep and not have noticed his wife was pregnant? "Your mom."

"Ew, dude."

"Mind your business." Max turned the screen off and tucked his phone into his pocket.

"Wow, touchy." Hedgie suddenly seemed wide-awake. "Something going on? You're, like, unusually glued to your phone lately."

Was he? "Checking on my fantasy team."

Hedgie snorted at the obvious deflection, but he let it slide. "Did you draft me again this year?"

"Yeah, but I traded you for Grady Armstrong." The Firebirds had started the season 1–2–0, but Grady had four goals and an assist.

If fantasy hockey gave Max an excuse to check up on him, that was Max's business.

"Ouch, bro."

Max jostled their arms together in an attempt to elbow his stomach. "That's what you get for being nosy."

Hedgie rolled his eyes, but he wasn't mad. "Oh, excuse me for caring." His body sagged next to Max's, and he put his head on Max's shoulder. "Can I go back to sleep now?"

Max patted the top of his head. "Yeah, you can go back to sleep now. Baby."


AS GRADY had suspected, the Firebirds continued to struggle. They only had one solid defenseman, and their forwards were weak down the middle. Grady centered their top line, and he and Coop worked well together, but no one else had any reliable chemistry.

And then there was Barny, who showed such flashes of brilliance that it frustrated Grady when he let in those wobbling shots two minutes later. If he could play consistently, at least Grady would be able to make up his mind if he was staying.

He was pretty sure he wasn't.

And he was also pretty sure most of the team knew it, which made things awkward. He felt like he was abandoning them. They probably felt the same way. Gatherings with the team carried an undercurrent of tension that made Grady's shoulders ache.

Grady would've liked to say that dating was a pleasant distraction from work. However….

"I asked for this with no onions," his date of the evening, Chad, told their server.

Grady knew he shouldn't have broken his no-dinner rule, but Chad insisted they *had* to try this new place, it was so "on trend." He'd heard their mushroom risotto was to die for.

Grady certainly felt like dying.

"I'm so sorry," said their server, her face a picture of misery, because this was the third thing Chad had sent back to the kitchen and he had absolutely made no such request. "I'll take this back."

Grady met eyes with the server and tried to convey through his expression that he was sorry for inflicting this on her. She grimaced at him behind Chad's back and sped away with the plate.

Once she was out of earshot, Grady snapped. "Why do you keep doing that?"

Chad plucked a piece of bruschetta from their antipasto plate. "What, the food thing? It's her job to keep us happy."

Grady considered swearing off men. "No it isn't. It's her job to bring you the food you asked for. Which didn't include a special request for no onions."

"Sure," Chad said with a shrug, "but if I keep her running, she'll pay more attention to us and we'll get better service."

*We'll get our food spat in and we'll deserve it.* He looked down at his own plate. The food smelled incredible. Grady had no appetite for it. "Would you excuse me for a minute?" He didn't wait for an answer.

In the hallway by the restrooms, he took out his phone. What time was it in Vancouver? Was Max's game tonight or tomorrow? He couldn't remember, but this was an emergency. For the first time, he hit the little phone icon next to Shithead.

Max picked up on the third ring. "Hhhhwha?"

So, pregame nap time. Oops. "Did you pick this guy on purpose?" Grady hissed. He and Max had gone through the options together before settling on Chad. "He's awful."

"Armstrong?" Yeah, Max had definitely been asleep. "Are you calling me while you're on a date?"

"I'm calling you to ask how I get out of it!" Leaving Tony on the patio was one thing. They were in a fancy restaurant. Grady couldn't just walk out. Could he?

"It's that bad?"

"He's sent back everything he ordered," Grady said. "He says it's because if he keeps our server busy, she'll pay more attention to us and we'll get better service."

For several seconds Max didn't reply. Had he fallen asleep again? "Max?"

"I'm here," Max said. "Sorry. The first five minutes after waking up aren't my sharpest. Where are you? Dinner?"

"Yeah. I faked a bathroom break."

Max's laugh sounded invitingly sleepy. "A classic. Okay. First you're going to find your server, explain what's happening, and pay the bill. Make sure to tip."

"I mean, obviously." Grady didn't want to be associated with Chad's shitty behavior.

"Right. Then you're going to go back to the table and say you're sorry, but something urgent came up, you took care of the bill but you have to go. Don't make up a story, don't elaborate. I'll call you in seven minutes so you can pretend it's related to your emergency and ignore any questions while you leave. Got it?"

Grady exhaled. "Got it."

He hung up.

It took almost five minutes to square things with Quinn, their server. "No hard feelings," she assured him as she handed back his credit card. "He's not the first asshole to try it."

"Doesn't mean you should have to deal with it." Grady signed the receipt and added a big tip to make up for Chad's assholery. "All right. I'm going to go make an emergency exit, I guess. Wish me luck."

"Go Firebirds!"

Then he just had to lie to Chad. Fortunately Chad had been lying his ass off all night, so Grady didn't feel guilty. He didn't even have to put on a show of being contrite. He *was* sorry—sorry he'd agreed to go on this date.

Grady put on his best apologetic "disappointing fans who want an autograph" face. "Hey, sorry to do this to you, but something urgent came up and I've gotta go. I let Quinn know to box up your order. She's going to bring it by." Paying the bill early had the bonus of getting Chad out of Quinn's hair before he could pull any more stunts.

Chad's mouth opened. Grady could tell he didn't buy the line, but he didn't want to risk questioning Grady and finding out for sure. His fragile ego probably couldn't take it. "Wait, what? Is everything okay?"

Right on cue, Grady's phone rang and he picked up. "Hey, sorry, I'm leaving the restaurant now."

"I can't believe you *hung up on me* after *waking me up from my pregame nap*," Max whined. "Talk about ungrateful."

"Uh-huh, probably about ten minutes?" Grady replied as he waved at Chad over his shoulder. He could not get out of here fast enough. "As soon as I can, I promise."

"Good sell, though. Is this Chad? I knew I should've thrown a flag on this play when I saw his name."

Grady took a step out the door and into the sweet air of freedom. "Some of my best friends are Chads."

Max laughed. "Seriously, though, you owe me one for the get-out-of-date-free call. Don't you know you're supposed to set that up beforehand? Plus waking someone up during their pregame nap is bad luck."

"Why'd you have your ringer on, then?"

"Even professional nappers make mistakes sometimes."

"Anyway, you don't need luck." Grady unlocked his car and slid behind the wheel. The car picked up the phone call and transferred him to hands-free. "You play for the best team in the league."

"Provided we all get enough *sleep*," Max agreed. "Which I'm currently not. So I think you can make it up to me."

His voice still sounded rough with sleep, but now there was a deliberate innuendo to it. Grady swallowed as he put his car in gear. "What did you have in mind?"

"Ever had phone sex?"

Jesus. "Not while I'm driving."

"How long until you make it home, do you think?" Max asked, faux innocent. "Wonder how much trouble I can get into before then."

Grady's dick twitched against his thigh. "I'm hanging up."

Max chuckled, low and sexy. "Call me back in ten."

Grady made it home in eight.

THE MONSTERS beat the Vancouver Orcas in overtime, thanks to Max's tricky mitts and a nice feed from Hedgie.

Max sent Grady a text afterward, *thx 4 the good luck sex*, followed by the water-drop emoji and the little siren that looked like the goal light.

Then he passed out in his hotel bed for nine hours, woke up, got on the bus, got on the plane, and passed out for seven *more* hours. By the time he pulled into his driveway, he had no idea what time it was, only that he wanted a dinner cooked in his own kitchen and about a thousand doggy kisses.

But before he could get to either, he half tripped over an Amazon box sitting in front of his door.

Max was pretty sure he hadn't ordered anything. Had one of his neighbors been waiting for this while he was away? He hoped not. But the package had his name on it, so he shrugged and unlocked the door. It could wait until after he and Gru had some face time.

He set the package on the console table inside and knelt down as Gru ran up, wagging his tail and barking like Max had come back from the dead.

"Missed you too, baby." Max kissed his nose. Gru kissed him back. "Thank you. Yes, I love you too. Is it time for some belly rubs?"

Gru gazed at him in adoration and flopped over.

"If only humans were this easy to please, eh?" Max made a claw with his hand and ruffled Gru's curly tummy fur.

Gru kicked his back leg reflexively, tongue lolling out toward the floor. Max snorted at him. "On second thought, I don't think that's as good of a look on us."

They played a quick game of fetch in the backyard to work off Gru's excitement, and then Max reacquainted himself with his kitchen.

He'd just finished dinner in front of the TV, Gru lying on his feet, when there was a knock, followed by the sound of the front door opening. "Max?"

Max had a dog walker for when he was out of town, but Gru stayed with El when he was away, so she had her own key. "Come in, El." He paused the movie and turned the TV off.

She did, waving the little yellow person-shaped squeaky toy. Gru didn't move from Max's feet. He was always extra clingy after a road trip, especially the first one of the year. "I brought Gru's baby—I forgot I had it when I dropped him off this morning." She paused beside the console table. "New toy?"

"No idea," Max said. "Toss it here?"

The box rattled when he caught it. It felt like a couple of items rather than only one.

"You don't know what it is?" El frowned as she sat in the armchair. "Should we be concerned it's a bomb?"

Max looked up from peeling up the tape long enough to raise an eyebrow. "A bomb? What is this, a bad spy movie?" Stupid Amazon tape. He gave up and yanked at the cardboard instead. "It's only October. I haven't had a chance to piss anyone off yet."

Finally the box opened and Max stuck his hand inside. "Survey says it's...." A bottle of something. He pulled it out and looked at the label. "Shampoo?"

El laughed. "What? Let me see that."

Shrugging, Max handed it over and dove into the box to pull out the other item.

Conditioner. *All-natural Nourishing Formula.*

"What the fuck?"

"This is nice stuff." El whistled. "Somebody must like you a lot. It's, like, fifty bucks a bottle."

Max's mouth dropped open. "*What*? Come on. They don't make shampoo that costs that much."

El looked at him with a pitying expression. "Oh, honey." She touched his hair, which was perfectly *fine*, thanks.

But then Max remembered the last time someone else touched his hair… and put the pieces together. "Oh my God. I know who this is from."

"You do? Because you should commend them on their good taste. I'm jealous." Then her tone turned suspicious. "Wait a minute. Is this from Bud?"

Bud was Max's code name for Grady, since he didn't want to tell El his real name and talking about him without one had gotten annoying. "Probably. He was here before the season started and he definitely made a comment about me using bodywash on my hair."

"Max Lockhart! You do *not*!"

"What?" She sounded as scandalized as Grady had been. "It gets the job done!"

"Oh my God." She put her hands over her face like she couldn't bear to face the reality of Max's hygiene decisions. "Tell me that after you've used this stuff for a week."

Max started to scoff—she couldn't think he'd actually bother using shampoo *and conditioner* when he was perfectly fine doing what he'd always done—but then he remembered they played in Philadelphia this week.

And *then* he started thinking about driving Grady crazy because his hair smelled like the products Grady bought him.

He wanted to know how Grady would react to that.

Damn it, he was definitely using the fancy shampoo.

"Anyway, I thought you said your thing with Bud is just sex."

"It is," Max assured her. "Very hot, very casual sex."

El seemed skeptical. "Uh-huh. And this guy is either very loaded or very judgmental?"

He swallowed a laugh. "Oh, definitely both."

"Well, remember to thank your sugar daddy properly next time you see him. And tell me about it."

That reminded him. "Speaking of telling people things…." He gestured.

She tucked her legs up into the chair with her. "I know, I know. I'll tell him soon. I just… Is it bad that I want him to notice? I mean…." She made a gesture Max interpreted as *These boobs, am I right?* "He brought home my favorite bottle of wine tonight and didn't even blink when I said I didn't want a glass."

"Are we sure he doesn't think you're a body snatcher?"

"I have no idea what he thinks." She shook her head. "Or *if* he thinks. Maybe he'd notice me if I wore hockey gear around the house. Ugh, that's the hormones talking."

"Bad?" Max asked.

El snorted softly. "While you were gone, I teared up because Gru put a hole in his baby. You know, the toy you keep three extras of on hand at all times because of how fast he goes through them."

"Gru," Max chided as he scratched under the dog's chin. "Did you make Auntie El cry?"

"It definitely wasn't his fault. Poor guy was very concerned about me. I got a lot of kisses."

"Good boy," Max crooned.

Gru's tail stump swished against the couch.

"Anyway, speaking of the hormones." El waggled her eyebrows. "Any more salacious stories for me? Do you have another appointment with Mystery Man?"

"Not officially." Max was pretty sure they were going to hook up again after the game this week, but he couldn't give El too many details. She already knew Bud was a hockey player. There were enough teams in driving distance from Newark that she wouldn't be able to narrow it down yet, but if Max's stories all started lining up with Firebirds games.... "He called me while I was in Vancouver, though."

"*Called* you. Not even sexted. I'm intrigued." El propped her head on her arms. "How's his phone sex game?"

"He's very good at breathing loudly into the phone." Grady's dirty talk was better when Max was there to physically goad him into loosening up. The phone thing was a work in progress. Max thought they should do some remedial sexting first and see if that helped. "Fortunately I'm good enough at talking for both of us."

"No doubt," El said. "And you don't mind doing all the work?"

"Not really. He makes up for it in person." Besides, Grady's ego wouldn't let him slack off like that forever.

"No evidence left behind, though," she teased, pointing at his neck.

Max sighed gustily. "Well, you can't have everything."

"How's Larry doing? No lasting damage?" He'd gone into detail about Grady's reaction to his tattoo.

"He didn't even bruise." Max wouldn't have minded a little memento of their time together. He could take a little locker room ribbing for a reminder that he'd made Grady Armstrong lose his mind in bed. "But there's always next time."

Now El sat forward, her eyes going sharp. "Oh? Always, hmm?"

Max backpedaled. "It's a figure of speech." Thank God El didn't know Bud's true identity.

She tapped her finger against her lips. "Is it? Or is it a slip of the tongue revealing a truth you're hiding from yourself? *Always*. That's downright romantic for you, Max."

Max knew, from the glint in her eyes and the tease in her voice, that she was fucking with him.

From the slight sinking sensation in his own stomach, however, Max wasn't fucking with Grady.

"I told you, it's not like that."

Completely true.

And, so far, not a problem.

In honesty, Max had written off the idea of a serious relationship. He spent half the year on the road, and when he was home, his off hours didn't leave a lot of time to spend with someone who kept a regular nine to five. He was in a weird platonic codependent relationship with his captain and his wife. He liked casual sex and he was very good at getting it.

Besides, Max was familiar with his own flaws. Part of his job description was to be as irritating as possible. Somehow that had become part of his personality. Most of the time he didn't take his work home with him, but he couldn't turn off who he was. That made it difficult to have a relationship.

The thing was, sleeping with Grady was hot. But it was also *fun*, in a slightly demented, competitive way. Max liked the challenge of finding all Grady's buttons and pushing them one after the other, and it was even better when Grady stepped up and tried to match him move for move.

But he also just liked *Grady*—prickly, funny, technologically inept grump that he was. Max could see their hookups of convenience evolving into something else. A house somewhere between Newark and

Philly, a rivalry they played up in public and laughed about in private, maybe another dog.

Grady would never go for it, though. Max should put the idea out of his head too, even if sometimes he wanted more—not necessarily from Grady but in general. His brother Logan had a family and was living his best life as a stay-at-home dad. Max had Gru, and hockey, and his teammates, and Hedgie and El….

But Hedgie and El also had each other and a baby on the way, even if Hedgie didn't know it yet.

Max had grown up in a loving, loudmouthed family. Now he was part of a loving, loudmouthed hockey team. But one day his career would be over. What would he be part of then?

He dismissed a sudden vision of himself and Grady bickering over whose turn it was to walk the dog.

"I know, I know. You're not the type. I remember." She shook her head. "Sorry. I'm gonna blame hormones for this. And for the fact that I'm going to go home now and flash my husband my tits."

Max laughed in an effort to cover how shaky his unbidden fantasy had left him. "Get it, girl."

"But first I'm going to pee again." El grinned. "I'll see myself out. Night, Max." She stood and leaned over to ruffle Gru's ears. "Night, sweet Gru."

The door clicked closed behind her, and Max picked up the remote. With El gone, it was safe to continue watching his romcom.

But before he hit Play, he picked up his phone. *R u tryin 2 say something w this?* he asked, and sent along a picture of the shampoo.

*You are a 28 year old professional athlete. Your dog's food says LOCALLY SOURCED ORGANIC on the label. Why the fuck are you washing your hair with bodywash? What's wrong with you?*

What was wrong with him was that he'd spent his formative years playing hockey, and he'd never had enough energy to do more than train, eat, shower, and sleep. Washing his hair with a different product would've taken too much effort.

But the truth made him sound soft and kind of pathetic, so he said, *Ur right. Should wash body w fancy shampoo instead. Thx bud!*

*Just put it in your shower so my hair doesn't smell like a teenage boy next time I'm over*, Grady replied.

*Next time*, Max thought.

The fantasy replayed. In this version, he and Grady kept up their argument pro forma while walking the dog together, hand in hand.

It was probably the romcom talking, but he could deal with next time.


THE MONSTERS played in Philly the third week of October. Uncharacteristically, Grady looked forward to it. Sure, he could almost guarantee Max would do something to piss him off on the ice. But it was hard to be mad about it knowing Max would make it up to him with an orgasm later.

*Not staying in philly :( down side of being so close*, Max texted the day before the game. *Your arena has a designated dtf zone right?*

Grady had googled DTF two days into his internet dating adventure. *I'll come up with something.* A players' lounge or a trainer's room would do.

Maybe he really had lost his mind, but when he and Jess were both in Pittsburgh last week for work, she commented on how much more relaxed he seemed. "Did you make a decision about the trade?" Then she narrowed her eyes. "Did you meet someone?"

"No." If Grady hemmed and hawed, she'd smell blood in the water. In under a minute, she'd suss out that dating was terrible but he was getting laid semiregularly, and then she'd ask pointed follow-up questions that would quickly reveal the truth. "I'm trying a new tactic. It's called not giving a fuck."

Jess's laughter startled the people at the next table. "That's new?"

Grady mock glowered at her.

"Hey, I thought you were trying not giving a fuck."

He dropped the act and replaced it with a smile. "Old habits."

"Uh-huh," Jess said, but she didn't pursue the topic. "Speaking of not giving a fuck, how's the team?"

That was a different kettle of fish. "Hit-and-miss. Some of them are convinced I think I'm too good for them, and nothing I say or do will change that." If the coaching staff played them fewer minutes or in positions that played to their strengths, or if front office traded them or they retired, the Firebirds might have a fighting chance and Grady wouldn't feel like he'd anchored himself to a sinking ship.

Grady didn't blame them for not retiring, so he didn't think it was fair they blamed him for wanting to leave.

"Sucks, bro." Jess stabbed a roasted potato. "You wanna split dessert?"

In any case, Grady liked sex, and sex with Max was fun and easy. Therefore, he was looking forward to the game.

"You're in a good mood," Zipper commented when Grady joined the group for two-touch warm-ups. Zipper was fast, but he'd earned his nickname from the string of stitches he got for a high stick a few years ago, which had left a zipper-like scar along the corner of his jaw, bisecting a shaggy blond beard. "It's weird."

Coop hooted with laughter. "Grades, your *face* right now."

"Aw, leave him alone." Mack caught the ball on the top of one of his size-fourteen feet and then headed it across the circle to Grady. "You'll embarrass him and he'll turn into a dick and start avoiding us again."

Grady let the ball hit his chest and roll down to his knee, bounced it up, and then kicked it to Coop. "Thanks for the support, assholes."

He wasn't really upset, though. Chirping felt warmer and more natural than the stilted avoidance that had become the norm.

They finished the warmup, and Grady took his phone to his usual quiet spot.

This habit probably didn't endear him to his teammates either. You could only get away with sitting alone in a dark room before a game if you were a goalie. It made Grady look like an antisocial snob, but he played better when he had a few minutes to decompress before joining the chaos in the locker room.

Normally he spent five minutes scrolling through a curated section of Instagram—mostly cute animals—or meal prep TikToks. But tonight when he opened Instagram, he got a suggested post from the Monsters' account.

@NJMonsters: Mad Max lettuce on point

Instead of including one shot of Max in his pregame outfit, they'd done a whole faux fashion spread—Max laughing as he got off the bus, Max doing very dumb finger guns at the photographer, Max winking as he signed an autograph for a fan on the way into the arena. His hair did look good, damn it, wavy blond dishwater locks shining in the autumn sun. It looked soft. Grady wanted to touch it.

No, he wanted to *pull* it.

Then he made the mistake of glancing at the comment section.

*His hair looks so good asdf;lkajd;sflkja;dsf,* read the first.

*My mans discovered shampoo! Happy for him!* said the second.

How dare other people notice how good Max's hair looked. And if they *did* notice, they should be giving Grady the credit, not Max. *And* it was more likely the *conditioner* that was making the real difference here—

Grady realized this was not helping his pregame chill session and turned off his phone.

When the puck dropped, Grady was as in the zone as he ever got against the Monsters. He played center while Max played wing, so they usually didn't cover each other during five-on-five.

But when teams had the kind of heated history theirs did, penalties happened, which resulted in—

"Hey, bud, miss me?" Max shouldered into Grady as Grady cleared the puck into the offensive zone. "I missed you. That's why I coaxed Coop into that little slash—"

Because of course Max had drawn the penalty, standing in the paint in front of the Firebirds' net and hacking at the puck until Coop had enough.

Grady didn't reply. He was busy covering Max's center, who was trying to carry the puck into the Firebirds' defensive zone.

Grady stick-checked him, stepped over Max's attempted trip, and followed the puck toward the Monsters' net. The goalie blocked his shot, but Zipper got a piece of the rebound before the goalie froze the puck and the ref blew the whistle.

Max made an exaggerated sad face at Grady. "I thought we had something special, bud."

With great effort, Grady managed not to bite through his mouth guard.

Zipper nudged Max farther away from Grady, as though Grady needed a string-bean winger to fight his battles. But Zipper was full of piss and vinegar—not unlike Max had been when his rivalry with Grady started.

Maybe they shouldn't *both* start shit with the same guy. Especially not when Coop was already in the box and would still be there for another minute and a half.

"Hey." Grady used his stick to separate them before Zipper could earn an additional penalty. "He's not worth it. Chill out."

Max turned up the act. "Baby, how could you?"

*Not worth it.* He took a deep breath through his nose and skated to the faceoff circle.

"Don't walk away from me when I'm talking to you!" Max yelled at his back.

Grady won the faceoff, but Max intercepted Zipper's pass back to him, and they had to haul ass to defend in their own end.

By the time they killed the penalty, Grady was fuming and exhausted. It didn't help that Max shoved the puck under Barny's pads and into the net fifteen seconds after the penalty expired.

Coop pushed him. Max pushed back. The game deteriorated from there.

Six penalties and forty-three minutes later, the final buzzer sounded. The Firebirds won 3–2, on the strength of a three-assist night from Grady.

Naturally Max one-upped him by getting both of the Monsters' goals and by goading Grady into taking a cross-checking penalty when Zipper was already in the box. The Monsters' second goal had come on the resulting five-on-three advantage. Max blew him a kiss when he skated by the penalty box, and Grady could still hear the smug lilt in his voice as he said, "C'mon, Armstrong, we both know you want to hit me harder than that."

Maybe Grady did, but he didn't have to be proud of it, and Max didn't have to bring it up *during a game.* That felt dirty and unfair.

He did his postgame routine on autopilot. Fortunately his brain reached for "no comment" by default when reporters asked what Max had said to get a reaction.

Grady hated that it happened often enough that it had become an automatic process, though. He'd thought he was making progress keeping Max from getting to him. Mostly he was annoyed with himself because he expected Max to use their sex life against him on the ice and it had worked anyway. He shouldn't be upset.

But he was. If that made him weak or emotional or whatever, fine.

When he finally got out of his team duties, he had twenty-five minutes to meet Max before the Monsters' bus left.

He could skip it. Max would probably get the message. But if Grady was going to go home pissed off, he wasn't going to be the kind of pissed off that had held his tongue all night. He was going to be the kind of pissed off that had given Max a piece of his mind.

He pushed open the door to the least-used trainers' room—the Firebirds' arena was old, and this one had a faulty lock—and went inside.

"Finally." Max sat on the padded table, swinging his feet. He was still wearing his cooldown gear; he'd hung his suit beside the door. Probably smart, but Grady didn't feel like giving him credit. "I was starting to think you were gonna stand me up."

"Thought about it," Grady said shortly.

Max blinked and his eyes went wide. Then he raised his brows. "Do we have a problem?"

*What "we"?* "*I* have a problem. You have a decision to make. Are we gonna fuck around, or are you going to run your mouth about it when we're working?"

Max flushed. Grady could see him fluffing himself up like a rooster trying to look bigger and tougher than he was. "Hey, if you can't take it—"

"I can take it. But I won't." Grady never should've let things get this far. "What happens between us off the ice stays off the ice, or it doesn't happen. Sex with you's not good enough to fuck up hockey for."

He expected Max to try to argue, to get angry or defensive or simply leave. Instead he looked at Grady for a long moment and visibly backed down. His expression seemed almost quizzical, like he didn't understand why Grady was upset or he didn't believe it. But eventually his forehead creased in a frown and he nodded. "All right. I crossed a line. I'm sorry. It won't happen again."

Given their history, Grady shouldn't believe him. He did, though. Which made it awkward to be standing there in the training room with Max, who he wasn't friends with and wasn't angry with anymore. Being annoyed with Max had never stopped Grady from wanting to fuck him, but actual anger did.

God, how did *not* having sex make this more awkward?

Grady cleared his throat. "Good. Well. Now that's settled…."

Max shook his head. "No, wait, I need clarification. Is it just sex that's off-limits? Or, like, anything personal that I know about you because we're having sex? Do I get to chirp you for losing *American Ninja Warrior*?"

"I was the one who finished first by the rules we established. Besides, you *cheated*," Grady said before he could stop himself.

"I came prepared," Max countered. "The question stands. I need to know where the line is so I don't cross it."

Part of Grady wanted to tell him that if Max couldn't put the effort into figuring it out himself, Grady wasn't going to do it for him. But that seemed like a bad faith stance. Max was trying.

Grady didn't care if Max chirped him about losing *American Ninja Warrior*. Sure, someone might realize they'd gone to a gym together if they looked into that, but the risk was small compared to the actual fucking around they were doing. He wouldn't care if Max talked smack about Grady's shitty dates either. Even Grady thought he deserved any mockery he got. So what else was off-limits? "No sex stuff," he reiterated. "No personal stuff either, like about my family."

"I wouldn't," Max said. "Jesus. What the fuck?"

"I don't just mean my parents. There's my sister too. If we keep sleeping together, you might learn things." Jess called him all the time, and either sex made Grady say things he wouldn't or postorgasmic Max was too easy to talk to. Either way, Grady would spill something private sooner or later.

Max nodded. "Okay. That's fair." He offered a wry half-smile. "Sorry for killing the mood."

Grady snorted in spite of himself. Time to offer... not a whole olive branch, but maybe a dirty martini. "I mean, trainers' rooms don't exactly set the mood either."

"Poor ambience didn't stop us in the basement in Toronto."

Unfortunately, that was true. Before Grady could admit it, Max changed the subject. "But look... let me make it up to you. Late dinner on me?"

"Your bus is going to leave in, like, ten minutes."

Max shrugged. "So I'll take an Uber home."

All the way back to Newark?

But Grady *was* hungry, now that Max mentioned it. "All right," Grady said. "You need a restaurant recommendation?"

"Nah." Max grinned at him. "Let me get dressed. You good to drive?"


MAX HAD always known his mouth would get him in trouble one day. It was kind of what it did.

But if someone had told him he'd be biting his tongue because he went too far chirping Grady Armstrong and Grady threatened to stop having sex with him, he'd have laughed in their face. And that wasn't even the whole truth. He was mad at himself because Grady had been *angry* with him, not annoyed.

Max made his living getting other players to react emotionally instead of with their brains. But even though it was his job, he didn't actually want to make Grady angry. At least, he didn't want Grady to be angry with *him*.

It made him wonder where that anger came from. Max didn't think he said anything egregious. But Grady's anger was sincere, and whatever he felt was strong enough that he was ready to sacrifice filthy hot sex.

Max mulled it over while Grady followed the GPS to the restaurant Max had suggested, which was twenty minutes outside Philly. The thought he kept coming back to unsettled him.

Grady felt used. Not only for sex, but so Max could get an edge in the game.

Which… when they started fucking had kind of been Max's plan, or at least something he considered. He expected Grady to do the same. Only now those expectations were upside-down, because Grady got mad at him and Max felt shitty, and what did that mean?

Well, for starters, it meant he hadn't gotten laid tonight.

"This the place?"

Suddenly Max realized the car had stopped, and he looked out the window. "Yeah. Best late-night diner in two states."

"I drove ten miles for a *diner*?"

"You know a lot of restaurants where the kitchen's open after eleven on a weekday?" Max countered. "Besides, you haven't seen their milkshakes."

Grady's stomach growled so loud Max could hear it. "Milkshakes?"

"Eleven flavors."

He looked torn. "That's not on my nutrition plan."

Max eyed him up and down. "I think you can get away with it this once." Then he smiled. "And did I mention the burgers?"

"Okay, all right, stop tormenting me. Let's eat."

The diner existed in a kind of weird space. Because it was late, people minded their business. No one batted an eye at two huge guys in suits sitting down across from each other, or at the loud clack and scrape of Max's lucky cuff links against the Formica table. Probably anyone who glanced at them would assume they were in organized crime, which was either hilarious or horrifying. He wondered what they'd make of the jeweled sea monster on his left cuff.

Max didn't recognize their server—her name tag said Marcie—and she didn't seem to recognize them either. "What can I getcha, hon?"

"Hi, Marcie. I'll have the strawberry cheesecake shake and the house special burger, fries on the side, hold the gravy, please."

"Sure thing." She scrawled something on her pad. "And you?"

They'd barely had time to open the menu. Grady raised panicked eyes to Max. Yeah, the milkshake menu alone was overwhelming. Max would give him that.

"He'll have the same, gravy on the side, vanilla milkshake." Somehow Max managed to keep a straight face for that last part, even when Grady wrinkled his nose. "Trust me." He handed his menu to Marcie.

She put her pen away. "Got it. Coming right up."

When she was out of earshot, Grady said, "Vanilla?"

"Hey, you're the one who froze. Besides, vanilla is a classic." If he didn't like it, Max would trade him.

"Gravy on the side?"

"Some of my fellow Canadians profane their fries with gravy. I can look the other way for you, even though you're American and don't have a cultural excuse."

Grady snorted. "Big of you, but I'm not a fan."

"I knew I liked you for a reason."

This time Grady didn't smile, but he was thawing. Not all the way. Maybe, like, milkshake consistency. "You're laying it on kinda thick tonight."

"Bud, you know better than to give me an opening like that." He did deserve an explanation, though. "I wasn't trying to be an asshole before, but that's different from trying not to be an asshole. Which is what I'm doing now."

The smile was lurking just under the surface. Max knew it. Grady cleared his throat. "Interesting distinction."

Max propped his chin on his hand. "I have hidden depths."

Marcie swung by with the milkshakes—served in giant soda fountain glasses with a cherry on top of each. Max reached for his, giddy with anticipation. "Thank you."

Grady pulled his drink toward himself. "Seriously, though, how are you getting away with this?"

Max wrapped his lips around the straw and held eye contact while he sucked down the first few delicious mouthfuls. Then he pulled back and licked ice cream from the corner of his mouth. "I've lost five pounds since the beginning of the season." Max had a ridiculous metabolism, but that was too fast. "Nutritionist basically said eat some calorie bombs and worry about it later."

"Well, this should qualify." Grady took his first sip of milkshake, and his eyes widened. Then he took another sip, and another. "Okay, wow. Ten miles is nothing for this."

"Right?" Max beamed.

Grady smiled back, and Max felt a rush of triumph—success at last. "Although I admit I thought you were going to tie a knot in the cherry stem."

"Maraschino cherries are gross."

Grady picked up his spoon and scooped Max's cherry off the top of his milkshake. "More for me."

He popped the whole thing in his mouth. Fortunately for Max's sanity, he didn't do the cherry-stem trick either, just pulled it out and set it aside. "Strawberry cheesecake, huh? Pretty good."

Max took a big sip of his own to wet his dry mouth. "Yeah."

Their meals arrived in short order. If the milkshake impressed Grady, Max was pretty sure the burger had him ready to forgive and forget. He only made one guilty face before he wolfed down the plate full of food.

Max felt smug, which was a much more comfortable emotion than guilt.

Somehow they ended up talking about kids' movies, because Grady had never seen *Despicable Me* and didn't get why Max's dog was named Gru. "You know, it's the one with the Minions? Little yellow guys, obsessed with bananas?"

When no little light bulb came on in Grady's eyes, Max reached for his phone. "Here, I'll show you." He didn't want to explain his attachment to a movie about a self-proclaimed villain with a marshmallow center who ended up adopting a bunch of adorable children and falling in love with the woman who started off his enemy. Safer to stick to the slapstick comedy of the Minions.

"Seems like it's just your speed," Grady quipped, like he was supposed to, and Max relaxed.

"Whatever, dude. The Minions are comedy gold."

By the time they'd finished their plates, Max had his footing back and the suspicion had faded from Grady's posture. Something inside him loosened. Max really hadn't been trying to be a dick. It was good to know he hadn't ruined this.

But he discovered he had fucked up in an unexpected new way when he called up the rideshare service on his phone. "Shit."

Grady raised his eyebrows. "Problem?"

Max put his phone away. "I forgot what you forgot earlier—it's late on a weeknight. Nobody around to drive me home. I'll have to ride with you back to Philly and get a car from there or call a cab." Which would take forever.

Grady checked the time and made a face. "I'm not handing you over to some random in the middle of the night."

How valiant of him. Lucky for that milkshake, or Max might start feeling warm and fuzzy. "Afraid I'll get mugged?"

"Hey, don't laugh. There was that guy in Toronto who got carjacked last year."

"Won't be a problem for me since there's no car."

Grady bit his lip and shook his head. "Look, it's late and I don't want your mysterious disappearance coming back to haunt me. But I'm also tired, and I don't want to drive all the way to Jersey *and back* in one night, so…."

Oh God, was he offering to drive Max home in exchange for a bed for the night? That would be perfect. Except tonight was supposed to be about Max fixing his fuckup, not making Grady go out of his way for him. "You don't have to do that."

Grady gave an abortive, self-conscious shrug. "It's no big deal. Wouldn't want to leave Gru without a father."

"He would probably turn to a life of crime," Max agreed. "I mean, if you're sure, I'd appreciate it."

"I don't have to be anywhere until two tomorrow—flying out for the Eastern Canada trip." He looked like he couldn't believe he was offering, but he didn't sound like he wanted to take it back. "It's just an extra twenty minutes' driving tonight. No big deal. And you'll probably annoy me enough that I don't fall asleep at the wheel."

Max laughed, because otherwise he'd start thinking about how Grady had said *it's no big deal* twice, like repeating it could make Max believe it. It *was* a big deal. So far they'd only hooked up, and only when they were both getting something out of it. This was Grady going out of his way for Max the same day Max casually used sex with him against him in a game.

It was better for Max's sanity if he didn't think about that.

"All right," he said. "Thanks."


GRADY DIDN'T know what possessed him to offer to drive Max home. He just did it, and they got there, and Max said, "Hey, so… want a thank-you handy?"

… Okay, so maybe he *did* know.

Grady was too tired and full of forbidden foods to enjoy anything more vigorous. He ended up on his back in Max's bed with Max braced above him, Max's hands on their cocks and one of Grady's in Max's hair. He could smell the shampoo he'd bought, and the strands were soft and smooth around his fingers.

In the morning he woke up blinking at Max's bedroom ceiling, still sticky. When he turned his head, he saw Max passed out on his face, Larry the Lobster on full display. Grady had left a halo of fingertip-shaped bruises around it.

Oops.

He helped himself to Max's shower to wash away their indiscretions. By the time he emerged, Max was downstairs making breakfast.

Gru greeted Grady at the bottom of the stairs, prancing in a circle and wagging his tail. Grady devoted a few minutes to stroking his soft fur and then joined Max in the kitchen and washed his hands.

Max looked up from an enormous skillet of scrambled eggs. "Hungry?"

So Grady was getting fed now too? Max must really feel shitty about yesterday's game. "Yeah, thanks. You want help?"

"Sure. Can you do the smoothies? They're basically premade, only have to stick 'em in the blender. Bottom drawer of the freezer."

Grady's kitchen skills were up to a lot more than smoothies, but in the two seconds Grady had spent looking over Max's shoulder, he hadn't found anything to fault, so he figured the eggs were taken care of. The blender was already on the counter, and the toaster held six slices of whole-grain bread, ready to be toasted.

Grady pushed the bread down and peeked over Max's shoulder again when the smoothies were blended. "You put sour cream in the eggs?" he asked in surprise when he saw the container on the counter.

Max snorted. "What am I, a heathen? Obviously."

"Well, you also obviously use store-bought eggs, so I thought it was a fair question." Grady snooped around for the butter dish. Or was Max a margarine guy?

"By the toaster," Max said, and Grady found the dish right as the toast popped. "Also, what the hell, where else would I get eggs? I'm not keeping my own chickens. Hedgie and El live next door. They'd kill me." He added a glop of sour cream to the eggs. "Or are you some kind of egg thief? Is it the buying part you object to? Do you drive around the wilds of Pennsylvania slinking into chicken coops?"

Grady rolled his eyes. "I buy eggs from the *farm*, idiot."

"God, of course you do, you insufferable organic-food hipster." Max laughed. Grady didn't take it personally. If Max wanted to eat inferior eggs, that was on him. "Can you get the plates? These are done. Cupboard beside the sink."

Max had practice at ten, so they sniped lazily at each other as they ate and Max fed Gru his egg-covered bread crusts.

"You're spoiling him," Grady commented.

"Buddy, that ship sailed a while back."

With breakfast and coffee taken care of, Grady's blood sugar went up and a hint of surreality slipped in. He couldn't actually be sitting in Max Lockhart's kitchen, eating food he made. Casually noting that they had the same taste in expensive cookware. Rubbing the belly fur of his very cute dog.

Had he slipped into another dimension?

He was about to pinch himself to check when a godawful noise set his teeth on edge. "Oh Jesus, what the fuck?"

"Dishwasher." Max patted the countertop above the offending appliance, which wailed like an injured pterodactyl. "We've been through a lot together."

"Like a car accident?" Grady had to raise his voice to be heard. Now that he was looking at it, the dishwasher did look kind of dinged up. "Did you go to the draft together?" It was probably old enough.

"All right, so most of what we've been through is the dishwasher running twice to get the dishes clean."

The offending machine hit a new decibel level.

Good Christ. "It sounds like that and it doesn't even *work*?"

Max shrugged sheepishly. "I mostly set it to run and then leave for practice."

Grady looked at the dog. "Your dad's been tormenting you."

"Hey!"

But Grady ignored him and took out his cell phone.

"What are you doing?"

Grady looked up from the screen. "Your dishwasher sounds like a dying vibrator, Max. It's sad. And it doesn't even work. Where's your wallet?"

Max pulled it out of his pocket and handed it over.

Grady took out his credit card and put it on the table.

"First of all, I have no idea what a dying vibrator sounds like. I'm a responsible adult and my toys are always charged—"

"It sounds like your dishwasher," Grady interrupted. He navigated to the dishwasher reviews section of the Consumer Reports website. "Which doesn't work and also might explode at any moment, Mr. Responsible Adult." He screenshotted the three top-rated models and opened a browser window to find the nearest appliance store that did installation.

"Second of all…." Max sat down at the table again. "Are you researching dishwashers for me?"

"No." Grady scrolled down the site and started entering Max's credit card information.

"No?"

"I am researching dishwashers for me, because if I ever have to hear this noise again, I'm going to kill someone, and they don't have hockey in jail." He looked up from his phone. "What's your game schedule? I need to give them a delivery window."

Max got up again and pulled a schedule off the fridge. Grady glanced at it and then finished the transaction and handed Max his credit card back. "Congratulations. Your new appliance will arrive next Tuesday."

"I'll make sure to send out an announcement," Max said faintly. He was looking at his wallet like it might bite him.

"I expect to be named godparent." Grady glanced at the time and grimaced. He still had to pack for the trip. "I gotta get going. Thanks for breakfast."

Max waved it off without looking at him. "Thanks for the ride."

Right. Grady cleared his throat. "Well… see you later."

# Second Period

SOMEHOW MAX got through practice without skating into the boards, missing too many passes, or maiming anyone with a high stick.

He got home without incident too, which was great because El would kill him if he caused any injury to the daddy of her unborn child.

But Max's good fortune ended there.

How had he let this happen? This thing with Grady had gotten out of hand. Max had signed up for hot mutual orgasms as a much-needed pressure release valve on the stress of a hockey season. He wasn't prepared for Grady Armstrong sitting at his kitchen table, researching which dishwasher to get and then taking care of the chore in minutes, like Max hadn't been putting it off for months. Like it was nothing.

Like Max hadn't gone and fallen completely in love with him, after sliding into it by reluctant degrees over the past month and a half.

"Hello? Max?" Hedgie poked his shoulder, and Max jolted back to the present—his car, in his driveway, with his best friend. "Are we gonna talk about it?"

"Talk about what?"

Hedgie turned to face him. "You didn't take the bus home last night, which means you hooked up in Philly. There was a car in your driveway this morning with Pennsylvania plates. Oh, and there's a handprint-shaped bruise on your ass. Or did you miss all the chirping in the locker room earlier?"

*Fuuuuuuck.* Max slumped in the driver's seat and put a hand over his face. The panic he'd sublimated all morning surfaced with a vengeance. "I did something really dumb."

Hedgie exhaled audibly. "Physical dumb or emotional dumb?"

When Max laughed, it came out tinged with hysteria. "Oh, definitely both, but we had safe sex if that's what you're asking."

"Fuck." There was a thump and the SUV jolted as Hedgie's head went back against the seat rest. "Tell me you're not hooking up with one of the Firebirds' girlfriends."

Max had never been a homewrecker, but he couldn't find the energy to be offended at the question. "Not a WAG, no."

The interior of the SUV filled with a gradual, oppressive silence.

Then the penny dropped and Hedgie said, "Jesus fuck, Max."

"I didn't mean to!" He should've seen this coming, but he had *tried* to keep a lid on things. Everything would have been fine if Grady had kept treating Max like a very irritating itch he had to scratch. Max wouldn't have gotten in his feelings about that.

Probably.

"*Grady Armstrong*, though?" Hedgie paused. "I'm assuming it's Armstrong. Unless it's another Firebird who's not out or whatever."

At this point Max might as well own up. "It's Grady."

"*First-name basis*," Hedgie wailed.

"This isn't helping."

Finally Hedgie unclenched. "Yeah, okay, sorry. It's been an interesting few days for surprise revelations, between you and El."

"Oh thank fuck she finally told you." At least Max could stop worrying he'd spill the beans.

"We're gonna come back to why you knew before I did, but let's focus on the crisis at hand."

"It's because your wife's tits got bigger and I noticed."

Now Hedgie was the one with his hand over his eyes. "You're the worst gay best friend ever."

"I'm bi," Max said. "And my eyes work fine."

"Max. Focus." His tone went sober. Max slouched further. "You and Grady Armstrong. Is it serious?"

"Define 'serious.'" Max wasn't having this conversation in the car. "Can we go in? Gru's probably losing his mind."

Unfortunately Hedgie didn't let it go once they were in Max's kitchen, with Gru thumping his tail on the floor as Hedgie rubbed his chest. "So," he prompted. "You and Armstrong. You were about to tell me how that happened."

Max sighed and opened the dishwasher. "I thought he was catfishing on Grindr. We made a bet. Imagine my surprise when I showed up and it was actually him." Ugh. There was still a ring of coffee in his favorite mug. He took it to the sink.

Hedgie's judgmental gaze bored into his back. "And he just... went along with it."

Max scrubbed out the mug. "I promised an orgasm."

"Of course you did." Hedgie paused. "You really need to get a new dishwasher."

*Not anymore*, Max thought. His shoulders sagged. "Yeah," he said. Once he explained about his appliance-related insanity, there was no going back. Hedgie would read between all the lines and judge him, because Max did something stupid and he should know better.

But at least he'd have someone to whine to. Max sighed. "You wanna call El over so I only have to go through this once? Because it's funny you should mention the dishwasher...."

THE ROAD trip started fine.

The Firebirds downed the Ts 4–2 in regulation, and the team risked going out to the bars even though they were in Toronto, where someone always had something to say about it. Grady stuck with Coop and Zipper in a booth in the back corner and tried not to feel hunted every time one of the other guys glanced his way.

"We're celebrating," Coop reminded him. "Stop looking over there."

Grimacing, Grady reached for his beer. "Easy for you to say. You're not the one whose Gatorade they want to piss in."

"Okay, that was weirdly specific. Something we need to go to management with?"

It wouldn't make anything better. "No." They hadn't done anything. He just had residual paranoia from his teenage years. He never should've told Jess what he overheard his teammate say. Furious, she'd told the coach, and the other player had gotten traded. Unfortunately the other guy was well-liked, so Grady got branded a traitor and a tattletale. It wasn't the greatest year of his life. "It's nothing new, anyway. I'm used to it."

"You're pissed at them when they let in more goals than you score, they're pissed at you when you don't score more goals than they let in. But we won, so relax." Zipper was a pacifist when he was drunk.

Coop took the opportunity to change the subject. "Speaking of scoring. How's that internet dating thing going?"

Zipper hooted. "Seriously, bro?"

With a poisonous look at Coop, Grady admitted, "It's a moral support thing for Jess, okay?" That was at least sort of true, or true enough that Zipper wouldn't care about the difference. "The ladies from her team are doing a Christmas ski trip this year and Amanda is going. I want her to get some closure. But she won't go if she thinks I'm spending the holiday alone."

Amanda had been Jess's goalie.

"I always thought they'd end up together," Zipper commented. "Teenage fantasy destroyed."

"Dude." Grady shuddered. "Gross."

Zipper made a face. "Yeah, my bad. Sorry. Anyway." He propped his chin on his hand, and for a second, he reminded Grady of Max. "Internet dating. You were about to tell us how it's going."

"It's brutal," Grady said, which led to a breakdown of the dates and much laughter on Zipper's part.

By the end of the story, he felt lighter, distracted from team drama— until Coop swigged back the last of his bottle of beer and shook his head. "I was so sure you were finally getting laid."

A small, very annoying part of Grady—the tattletale left over from childhood—sulked when Grady didn't cop that he was. "Your comment on my attitude is noted. Also, fuck you."

When Zipper had finished laughing, he leaned back in the booth, loose-limbed and smiley. "We're gonna miss you around here, bro."

Nights like tonight, Grady could admit he'd miss them too.

Their game in Ottawa the following night was another story.

This time Barny was starting, and he was shaky. Fletch and Taylor didn't help; Taylor'd clearly drunk too much the night before, and he hung Barny out to dry a couple times. Only luck saved the Firebirds from going up in smoke—the Tartans hit the crossbar three times, and two shots missed by chance.

In contrast, Grady'd gotten to bed at a decent time, after just enough beer to put the situation with Max out of his mind. He felt rested. He and Coop and Zipper clicked.

They were tied at 2 going into the third period. Grady had both goals, so despite the fact that they were getting outshot two to one and their defense was as effective as wet tissue paper, spirits were high.

Coach clapped his hands as they prepared to go back to the ice. "All right, boys, let's tighten up in our own end and help Aces here finish it off, eh?"

Half the team might not like Grady very much right now, but a potential hat trick fired them up all the same. They hit the ice for the third period with energy and confidence.

That lasted for a minute and a half. Then the Birds got caught flat-footed on a line change. On the bench, Grady barely contained a grimace as the game suddenly went from five-on-five to five-on-two.

And the two were Fletch and Taylor, who were tired from their shift and supposed to be coming off.

"Fuck's sake," Grady groaned as the puck hit the back of the net, a snipe from the top of the circle. A cheer went up in the arena.

Coop gave him a bracing smile. "Looks like you're on tap for the equalizer."

But twenty-seven seconds later, before Grady even got on the ice, the Tartans scored again, a dirty goal from inside the paint.

The Firebirds' energy and positivity evaporated. Barny visibly tried to shake off the second goal, but he was rattled, too reactive.

It was a bloodbath.

The Tartans must've smelled fear, because they put another six shots on goal in the next two minutes. One of them went in, leaving the Birds trailing 5–2. At the play stoppage, Grady glanced over to the bench and saw Coach conferring with their backup goalie and their goaltending coach, but they didn't pull Barny out.

Tough on the team, and tough on the kid, but it was the right call. Barny'd either get used to playing after he made a mistake or he'd wash out. The only way to get used to it was to do it.

It didn't make Grady feel better when he finally caught that pass from Zipper with two minutes left and finished the hat trick. It was a beautiful pass—tape to tape, with Coop acting as a screen until suddenly he wasn't and Grady had a clear shot. Half-clapper, top shelf, where Mama keeps the peanut butter.

But it was a meaningless goal, because the Tartans put two more in the net, one after the other.

The buzzer went seconds after Grady put the fourth goal past the goalie's pads. Final score Tartans 7, Grady 4.

It was a team game. But wasting a four-goal night on a loss sickened him. Disgusted, he snapped his stick over his thigh and got slapped with an unsportsmanlike fine and a game suspension, even though it was after the buzzer.

He didn't care. He tossed his stick in the trash on his way to the locker room and didn't talk to anyone through the process of cooldown, showering, and dressing. Even Coop gave him a wide berth.

On the bus, Grady shoved his earbuds in and pressed his shoulder against the window.

Then he stared down at his phone, willing it to buzz. Max always texted him after games, usually to chirp him. At some point it had stopped being annoying and become part of how Grady unwound. Maybe Max was losing his touch.

Maybe Grady had Stockholm Syndrome.

Tonight, Max didn't text him. That was weird. Grady didn't think Max was constitutionally capable of ignoring a dick trick—scoring four goals in a game.

Had Max played tonight? Was he injured? Grady pulled up the NHL app and found the Monsters' news and schedule. Max's game had ended half an hour before his. He'd played until the end of the third period, and there was no mention of him going down the tunnel to treat an injury. Grady watched the highlights to check, but no—Max had had an assist and a hooking penalty in his team's victory over Carolina and drew a penalty on Gorges for roughing, but it didn't look like he'd been hurt.

Probably he was out celebrating. The Monsters were at home, and they had a day off tomorrow.

But just in case he'd gotten hurt and checking up on Grady had slipped his mind, Grady sent, *Nice assist. What did you say to Gorges?* Whatever it was, the guy took a hell of a swing at Max.

Grady only watched that clip once. Thinking about what could've happened if that hit connected differently did unpleasant things to his stomach. But Max could handle himself. He was a big boy. He knew the risks of playing a contact sport. He didn't need Grady coddling him.

Grady didn't even want to coddle him, and just because he didn't want Max to get hurt didn't mean he *liked* him. Hockey was just better when everyone was at their best. That was it.

When the bus pulled into the hotel parking lot and Max hadn't texted him back, Grady huffed and turned his phone off. Whatever. He didn't want to talk to anyone anyway.

The next day was a travel day with nothing else scheduled. Grady turned his phone on in the morning and found a text from Max from the early hours of the morning. *Asked him what perfume he was wearing cuz i wanted to get some 4 my sister. Guys a douche.*

Gorges was the hypermasculine type, so Grady could see that.

A few minutes after the first message, Max had sent, *nice dick trick [eggplant eggplant eggplant eggplant]. Too bad the rest of ur team sux. Also wtf was that temper tantrum????*

In the light of day, Grady felt childish for breaking his stick. It had seemed like a better idea than lashing out at his teammates, but it made him look like a sore loser with an anger management problem. And sure, he didn't *like* losing, but dealing with losses maturely was part of the game.

Breaking his stick was not mature. Sulking alone in his hotel room and not speaking to anyone probably wasn't a great look either.

He sighed.

*It really sucks to score 4 goals for nothing. But I should've handled it better.*

He didn't expect a response right away, but a moment later, his phone buzzed. *Fuck it id have done the same. Cant even celebrate a dick trick. Fuckin travesty.*

The Grady from a few months ago would have recoiled in horror that today's Grady found comfort in that.

Today's Grady opted not to think too much about it and went down to breakfast.

After they checked into their hotel in Quebec City, he called his sister.

Jess didn't bother answering with *hello.* "You want to talk about the four goals or the suspension?"

"Neither. Fuck." Grady slumped against the headboard. "Talk about something else, please."

"Oh God, you *must* be feeling pretty dumb. You know the rules, Grades."

He groaned. "You're not even going to take pity on me after I got suspended?"

"Your own dumb temper got you suspended. Pay the piper and prove you're holding up your end of the deal."

Grady could've made up dating horror stories, but he wasn't that creative, and it had been a while since he filled her in. He'd been doing all his venting to Max instead.

He had just finished regaling her with the story of Byron—his actual wallet name; Grady made him prove it—whose most fervent ambition was to be a sugar baby, when Jess asked an apparently burning question.

"So, okay, wait, did you sleep with *any* of these guys? Have you been shelling out money to hang with losers without even getting laid for your trouble? You didn't meet even one guy worth testing the mattress springs with?"

That made him sound pathetic. "There was *one* guy," he said before he could think better of it.

"Uh-huh, all right, I'll bite. And what did you do on your date?"

Fuck. Grady closed his eyes. "*American Ninja Warrior* gym."

"*What*?" She sounded aghast. "Grady Armstrong! How could you keep this from me? That sounds amazing!"

"It wasn't *that* great."

"Why?" Jess asked astutely. "Did he beat you?"

*Fuck.* Technically, he kind of had. "Uh—"

"*Oh my God*!"

"He cheated."

Jess laughed so hard Grady thought she might choke. Finally her chuckles tapered off and she gasped, "This is incredible. Oh man. Okay. What did you say this guy's name was?"

"Shithead."

She howled. "All right, we're coming back to that. But this is the guy you slept with?" She paused. "I guess that makes sense."

Grady was pretty sure he was going to regret asking, but he did anyway. "How do you figure?"

"I know you. He outperformed you in an athletic setting? You wanted to put him in his place. Uh." Now she sounded like she wanted to eat her words. "Not in, like, an abusive creepy way, just in a maladaptive competitive man way."

He pinched the bridge of his nose. "Thanks."

"So anyway, you slept with Shithead. It was hot, right?"

Well, it wasn't like he was going to tell her Shithead's real name. "Jess. It was *insane*."

"Knew it!" She laughed. "So what's the problem?"

Grady blinked. "Excuse me?"

"Why'd you bother with those other guys? Is he ugly or something?"

"No." Actually, with the nice shampoo Grady had so selflessly provided, Max was alarmingly… presentable. He always looked kind of smug, but Grady had been conditioned into finding that attractive. "He's just an asshole."

"Sounds perfect for you."

"Oh, fuck off. Come on, I told you mine. Distract me, for the love of God and hockey."

With a long-suffering sigh, Jess relented. "Fine. First things first, though—you're so lucky gay guys don't bring up IVF on the first date."

Grady whistled. "Wow. And I thought the U-Haul joke was an exaggeration."

"It is—sometimes. Okay, let's see. I've had three dates since I gave you the rundown. The first one lied about her age and it was so obvious. Like, child. There's no universe in which I believe you're a day older than twenty-three."

"Jess, you dog."

"That's too young. I am literally old enough to be her mother. Gross."

He smiled and let her voice wash over him. At least for a few minutes, the shitshow with his team took a back seat to someone else's dating drama.

And then she got to the part where she said, "But, like, I don't know. Maybe I should cancel the whole trip."

"No!" Grady blurted. He hadn't realized she'd been getting so down about it. "Jess, come on. You've needed this closure for actual years." He'd always felt partially responsible for her breakup with Amanda, which had happened a few months after their parents died. Twenty-five-year-old Jess should have been living her own life, not driving Grady to practice, making sure he went to therapy, and helping him with his homework.

She groaned. "I know. I know. But, like, part of me doesn't want it."

And here he thought she'd been making progress—she'd at least agreed to date, to make an effort, to try. She wanted something to insulate her from her past with Amanda. "Hey, come on. You're not going to go back on your promise, are you? I suffered fake ice cream for this."

"No, you're right," she relented. "Personal growth is supposed to suck. I'm just venting."

It didn't sound that way to Grady. A suspicion formed in his mind. "Don't tell me you're still…?"

Jess blew out a breath. "I don't know, Grades. I feel pathetic about the whole thing. Like, it was fifteen years ago."

"Did you ever think about telling her you still, you know…?"

"Of course I thought about it. But every time I started to get up the nerve to say something, she'd have another girlfriend. I'm not gonna be that girl, you know?"

He knew. "The heart wants what it wants, I guess."

Jess sighed feelingly. "Ugh."

There wasn't much left to say after that.


GRADY HAD spent his share of games watching from the press box. Usually he was injured, though.

This time he felt the weight of every set of eyes on him as he took his seat next to the glass to watch the game. He couldn't decide what would hurt worse—watching his team lose and knowing they might've had a shot with him on the ice, or watching them win without him despite their piss-poor performance the other night.

Okay, that wasn't true. He still wanted them to win without him, but he felt dramatic about it.

He didn't think much about the other occupants of the Nordiques' press box until someone sat down next to him and he recognized Baller— the Nordiques' captain.

Grady blinked. "Did you get suspended too?"

"No." Baller grimaced and looked over his shoulder. Right—they were literally sitting with people who got paid to write stories about them. Grady should remember that too. "Think they wanted to give a couple of the rookies another look before they send one of them back down."

And Baller was the guy they chose to sit out instead? Grady didn't buy it. It was only fall, but no team was going to sacrifice points like that by sidelining such an important player. They could've picked one of their bottom-six guys.

But if he was actually nursing an injury, he wasn't going to tell Grady, and if something else had landed him here, it was none of Grady's business. So he accepted the explanation at face value. "Makes sense." It didn't. "Whoever's team gets scored on first buys the first round?"

Smiling, Baller held out his hand to shake. "Deal."

Baller lost, but he was cheerful about it. "C'mon, let's go for a walk. Better drinks in the exec lounge."

"Oh, we're fancy?"

"Tonight we are."

Someone would probably comment that they weren't at their post watching the game, but Grady decided to care about that later. He'd given his agent the go-ahead to request a trade. People were talking about him anyway.

Grady should've remembered Baller's drink of choice was fancy tequila, though.

"This is the good stuff," he promised as he handed Grady a rocks glass with a slice of orange. "Cheers."

What the hell, right? "Cheers."

They didn't head back to the press box right away. Grady figured Baller didn't want an audience, and he couldn't blame him. They sat across from each other at a high-top in an otherwise deserted lounge. Grady raised the glass to his lips. At some point Baller had acquired good taste in tequila, at least.

Grady rolled the bottom of his glass against the tabletop, considering. "Can I ask you something?"

Baller spread his hands. "I'm an open book."

Grady snorted. "I've heard that." He sipped his tequila. "You ever sleep with someone from another team? Before you and Gabe, I mean."

Baller gave him a wry look. "Bro, I didn't even realize I was bi before Gabe." Then he raised an eyebrow. "Why do you ask?"

No point being cagey about it. There was only one reason Grady would need to know. "I was hoping you had advice on how to keep it from getting weird."

"Not unless you're looking to put a ring on it."

Grady imagined it for a second and then immediately washed the thought down with tequila. "Uh, no."

Baller grinned at him. "Hey, don't knock it 'til you try it." He leaned forward in his seat. "So, another team, you say? Is it *actually* weird, or is it just super competitive and hot? Anyone I know?"

"I plead the Fifth." There weren't that many out guys in the league. Baller didn't need any more information, even if Grady trusted him not to blab.

"I'll take that as a 'yes to all.'" He finished his drink and set the empty glass on the table. "How's it getting weird?"

Now that, Grady actually wanted to answer, but he struggled to put his thoughts into words. He could barely put his finger on it, even in his head. "I don't know. It's…. We're not dating, and we're not friends. But we're sleeping together, and sometimes we talk." He paused. "We went out for dinner once." *I slept over at his house. I've met his dog.*

Baller's brow creased. For a moment he didn't say anything. That was strange—when they first met at the US men's team development camp, holding his tongue had not been his strong point.

Finally he shook his head and said, "Hate to tell you, bud, but you're friends." He looked like he was going to laugh.

"Shit."

Grady was right—he did laugh. The sound echoed in the strangely empty lounge. "You didn't answer my question, though. Why's it weird? Like… I don't know, you start sleeping with somebody and your relationship changes. That's normal. By definition, the opposite of weird." Then he paused again and considered. "Well. Unless the relationship changes *before* you start sleeping together, but we can't all do things backwards."

Grady grimaced. "I don't *want* things to change."

"I think you picked the wrong Dekes captain for this conversation." Dante shook his head. "Look, you don't need my advice. I'm not older or wiser or more experienced or whatever. Any tips I could give you on maintaining a casual, uh, acquaintances-with-benefits situation would be outdated. But everything changes. I mean, you asked for a trade. Change is coming."

Grady's shoulders slumped under the weight of that truth. In a few weeks or months he might not have to worry about this. The Firebirds wouldn't trade him within their division. They'd ship him halfway across the country into the Midwest or Florida or something—or even to Canada—and he could stop wondering whether he had the energy to make the hour-long drive to Newark for sex, because it wouldn't be an hour-long drive. It'd be two, or four, or twelve.

Why didn't that make him feel better?

Before he could worry about it, the goal horn echoed from the ice. Baller glanced up at the TV screen above the bar and grinned. "Aw, look at that—it's your turn to buy a round."

MAX'S TEAM was not having a good game. In the middle of the second, they were down 3–1 to the Orcas. From a puck-possession standpoint, it felt more like 30–1, thanks to Max's teammates, who seemed determined to spend the period in the penalty box.

They finally got a breather at a commercial stoppage, and Max skated over to the bench for the ritual scolding.

Instead he got a call to arms.

"We need to break their momentum," Coach said. "Three penalties back-to-back killed us. We need a chance to get back on top, put some shots on goal, get the crowd going for us." He looked at Max. "Think you can draw a penalty?"

Max considered the options. Kirschbaum had an even keel, but Max might be able to goad White into doing something if he laid a big enough hit on his boyfriend.

A month ago he wouldn't have thought twice about it. Now he had a voice in his head—one that sounded annoyingly like Grady—pointing out that Max could get what he needed without hitting below the belt. So to speak.

"Put me on against Nordstrom." The guy had a habit of escalating. If Max could sneak in a couple digs, he'd eventually retaliate with something the refs would have to call.

Coach smiled. "Attaboy." Then he turned to the group and said, "Listen up, we're going to change the matchups here for a minute and give Mad Max some room to make a mess...."

In the end it took Max three shifts to get under Nordstrom's skin. The last straw was a little love tap with the butt end of Max's stick right under the edge of his chest protector.

Nordstrom whirled on him against the boards, stick in both hands as he shoved Max's chest. Max's head snapped back and something in his neck spasmed. Another shove and Max went down, jarring his shoulder against the ice.

Somewhere the whistle blew. One of Max's teammates was pulling Nordstrom away. Max stared up at the rafters and winced.

Hedgie leaned down next to him, brow creased. "You hurt?"

*Yes.* Nothing broken, Max didn't think. Muscle tear, probably. But his neck screamed at him not to turn his head to the right, and his left arm had pins and needles from his elbow to his shoulder. "Roll me onto my right side," he said through gritted teeth.

Hedgie's eyes went wide. "Are you kidding me? If you can't move—"

"I didn't hurt my spine. I can't turn my head and my left arm is fucked. Feels like I pulled everything from my neck to my delts. Help me roll over so I can get up."

Hedgie did, and Max hobbled off the ice, half bent to keep his strained muscles as happy as possible. There was no way he could play the rest of the game. He limped off to see a trainer.

As he left the ice, he could hear the penalty announcement— number 39, Nordstrom, two minutes for cross-checking.

All this for a lousy two-minute man advantage. The Monsters better fucking score. Next time Coach could get someone else to draw a penalty.


THE NEXT two hours were misery. The trainers gave him something for the pain, but he had to have diagnostic testing just in case. In the end the doctors ruled it a partial tear and told him to take at least a week off from doing anything more strenuous than walking.

They hooked him up with muscle relaxants and painkillers and put him in a cab home. At least he wouldn't be stranded without a car, since Hedgie had his spare key and could drive it home.

Not that Max could safely check his blind spot at the moment. Or drive under the influence of this drug cocktail. Or even bend down to give Gru some love when his precious baby came to meet him at the door.

Instead he let the dog out, waited for him to come back in, and then made his painstaking way to bed. Getting comfortable could be a challenge.

Gru climbed in with him, but he didn't snuggle much at bedtime. He simply curled up and collapsed like all was right in the world.

Max was still low-key in pain and needed a few minutes' distraction to let the drugs work their magic before he could sleep. He propped himself up against the headboard and put his phone on a pillow on his lap, since holding it at the wrong angle made everything hurt.

He had half a dozen unread texts from the team, everyone wanting an update on how he was and when he'd be back, and another notification from the NHL app that the Monsters had lost in overtime. At least they'd recovered some momentum.

Max didn't want to get his hopes up, but he did anyway when he saw the unread message from Grady.

*That hit looked bad. Are you okay?*

It was a dumb text. Seven tiny words. It didn't mean Grady gave a shit. Grady didn't even like him. This was only the second time he'd texted Max first if he didn't want something—like advice, or to bitch about one of his stupid dates. Which he was still going on—yet another reason Max didn't need to let himself get any more invested. Grady wasn't, and that was fine. He didn't owe Max anything just because Max was an idiot who'd caught feelings.

But Max *was* an idiot who'd caught feelings, so instead of turning off his phone and going to bed—or deleting Grady's contact and forgetting this whole thing ever happened—he typed out a reply. *Rumors of my death r greatly exaggerated. Sorry 2 disappoint.*

*Fucking Nordstrom is a menace. He should be suspended.*

Max shoved down the warm fuzzy feeling that wanted to well within him. Grady wasn't pissed on Max's behalf. This wasn't some fairy-tale white-knight bullshit, and Max would hate it if it was. Grady was only stating a fact. Nordstrom's conduct was suspension-worthy.

*Ya but u know the department of player safety.* What a joke.

*Department of Pretending to Give a Shit.* Max could almost see Grady's bitchy face, hear his voice saying the words. *I'll let you get some rest.*

Except Max didn't think he could sleep. Eventually he plugged his phone in and tried to get comfortable. He managed to find a position that didn't hurt, but his eyelids felt like sandbags. The rest of his body throbbed distantly.

But his brain was stuck on Grady.

The cat was officially out of the bag that he'd requested a trade. Max didn't know how, and it didn't really matter. It could've been someone in Philly's front office or it could've been Grady's agent intentionally letting other teams know he wanted to be on the market. The Firebirds didn't have to deal him, but Max had snooped into his contract situation, and he figured they probably would. Rumor had it that they'd send him to the Anaheim Piranhas, who were looking for some offensive star power to kick their game up a notch. Grady would fit in there—not a traditional hockey hotbed, so less pressure, and with talented young teammates.

But Anaheim was on the other side of the country. The Monsters only played them twice a year. That would spell the end of their casual hookups.

Maybe that was for the best, though. Then Max would have to get over it.

That was what Hedgie thought he should do. El was on the fence, possibly because her pregnancy hormones had made her extra invested in his sex life. "*Grady Armstrong* is the guy who edged you for half an hour in his hotel room in Toronto?"

Hedgie made a horrified face and put his hands over his ears. "El!"

Max sighed gloomily. "Yeah."

She wrinkled her nose. "I can't see it. Good for you, though."

Apparently Hedgie heard her through his earmuffs. "El!"

"What! I'm the sex confessor friend. You're the relationship advice friend. This is not my territory. Shouldn't you be asking if there's a chance Grady likes him back or something?"

"That guy doesn't like anything."

None of this was helping Max sleep.

He needed a plan. Once he figured out what to do, he could stop thinking about it.

So, okay. He could wait until Grady got traded and deal with that when it came. But Max didn't have that much patience. He could go back on his word about keeping their sex life strictly off-the-ice next time they played each other, and Grady would get pissed off at him and break it off. Except Grady kind of had a point about it being shitty, and Max had been the used party in relationship-adjacent scenarios before, and it had left a bad taste in his mouth. Plus that seemed like a coward's solution.

Straight-up asking Grady about it was a hard no. With any other guy, Max could put himself out there. But Grady? No. Max couldn't imagine doing that and then having to play hockey against him, knowing Grady knew about Max's feelings and didn't reciprocate them and was too good a person to chirp him about it.

Which left one option.

All he needed now was for his body to cooperate.

Decision made, Max finally succumbed to the painkillers and fell asleep.

GRADY GOT home from the road trip on Wednesday. On Friday he had a date.

David was a handsome guy in his twenties, maybe slightly younger than Grady preferred but with a mature personality. He was artsy but not pretentious, and the graphic tee and skinny jeans he wore fit him well.

On the app, he'd asked Grady, *Do you trust me to plan this? Just go with it, you'll have fun.*

If Grady never had to plan another date, he'd die a happy man. Someone else wanted to take the initiative? Sign him up. *All right. I guess I'll see you Friday.*

David had gotten them tickets to see the immersive Van Gogh exhibit. It wasn't something Grady would've chosen on his own, but he enjoyed it anyway, and David's lively, casual-but-not-dumbed-down talk of postimpressionism and the use of color and imagery was actually interesting. Besides, he was funny and engaging and didn't seem to mind that it took several prompts to get Grady to express an opinion on art beyond "I like it."

David laughed. "Yeah, I'm getting that. But how does it make you *feel*? What does it make you think of?"

"Sunflowers?" Grady said. But he owed it to himself and David to dig a little deeper than that. He was supposed to be trying to connect with the guy, after all, and he'd put thought and effort into this date. "Uh, August, maybe? Like, sitting at my mom's kitchen table the week before school went back in, with the sun streaming in the window. She always had flowers on the table in the summer, but she wasn't great about pulling out the wilted ones, and they'd sort of flop over after a few days."

He thought maybe David would laugh again, or point out some way in which Grady's answer was flawed, but instead he smiled quietly. "There, see? We'll make an art critic out of you yet."

But Grady kept his thoughts on *Starry Night Over the Rhone* to himself, even if it was silly. The two people walking together in the foreground with all of the beauty of the universe behind them—paying no attention—and somehow all he could think of was that little splash of red on the woman's dress, and how it reminded him of Max's lobster tattoo.

The second half of their date was eating Philly cheesesteak sandwiches from a food truck, walking down the street toward the parking lot.

"The duality of man," David said, wiping a smear of sauce from the corner of his mouth. "Fine art and food trucks."

Grady felt uncharacteristically philosophical. "Man cannot live on cheesesteak alone."

David laughed. "Don't let anyone else in this city hear you say that."

Grady offered to drive David home—he didn't drive, he said, and used a bike rental program to meet Grady earlier. They made small talk in the car. It felt nice, natural. David was objectively attractive, clever, engaging. He was a little more femme than Grady usually went for, but Grady liked it. It suited him. All Grady's friends were jock types, but he was pretty sure David would charm them too.

But he didn't feel the slightest spark. He didn't want to hold his hand or kiss him or have sex with him, though he wouldn't mind another guided tour of some art.

That sucked. He felt like a jerk. This was the best actual date he'd gone on maybe ever, and... nothing.

To make matters worse, he had no idea how he was going to explain this to Max. Usually Grady texted to vent about everything that had gone wrong, and Max made fun of him and his date in turn and then sent him dick pics to take his mind off it.

Grady didn't have anything to complain about tonight. David was great. He'd chosen an interesting activity. Grady enjoyed himself. What was he going to say to Max? "Everything went great, but I don't want to fuck him"?

Then what? Would Max still sext him after?

When had going on these dates become more about Max than the people he was with? He had no intention of pursuing a relationship with Max. But apparently he didn't want to have sex with anyone else.

Finally he put the car in Park in the driveway of David's townhouse, took a deep breath, and turned to David.

Who was smiling at him, unperturbed. "No second date, huh?"

David was too good for Grady anyway. He could hardly believe he was having this conversation. It felt like his mouth was working on autopilot while his brain went around in circles with unproductive thoughts. "Believe me when I say it's not you. I haven't had this much fun doing something out of my comfort zone in a long time."

"I'll take that as a compliment."

"If something like this ever crops up again and you want someone to explain art to, call me up." Then Grady's brain kicked in for a brief moment and he snorted. "Or if you're ever trying to impress someone with really mediocre taste in hockey teams, let me know. I'll get you the best seats in the house."

"Well, I do like jocks." He dimpled in the glow of the streetlight that filtered through the car window. He reached for the doorhandle. "I hope it works out for the two of you."

Grady's mouth dropped open. "For who?"

David lifted a shoulder, easy nonchalance. "You and whoever you were thinking of when you looked at *Starry Night Over the Rhone*."

Then he opened the door and got out. "Drive safely, okay?"

Grady watched him until he made it into the house. Then he brought his right hand to his forehead and tried to rub away the tension starting there.

It was just that particular shade of red that caught him. That was all.

And if he told Max later that night that the date had been a bust, no one ever had to know.


AT THE beginning of November, the Monsters had a road trip. Max didn't go.

It didn't make sense to travel with them—they'd only be gone a little over a week, and he probably wouldn't get cleared to skate until they returned, even though all his issues were upper-body.

He could deal with the separation from his team, but the boredom ate at him. He was only supposed to work out his legs.

The lack of structure made him feel like time had no meaning. At least when he trained in the summers, he had a schedule—swimming this day, weights that day, resistance training another. Eat this many calories. Start at this time. Finish at that time. Check in with your trainer. This? Max ate, took his pills, worked out on the stationary bike or leg press for as long as he was allowed, and then… nothing. The whole day stretched in front of him with nothing to fill it. He didn't even need to finally put in that research to find a replacement dishwasher, since Grady had taken care of that.

Max made it a total of thirty-seven hours. At that point his neck and shoulder *hurt*, but he could move them enough that he wouldn't be a danger on the road. He would, however, be a danger to himself if he didn't get something to do.

He could go to El and Hedgie's. He knew he was always welcome there. But El had reached a fun new stage of pregnancy where she was either throwing up or sleeping. He'd already arranged for a dog-sitter for Gru because Max didn't want to impose while she felt like crap. He could cancel that.

Or.

*Or*, he could take advantage of the fact that the Firebirds were in the middle of a home stand. He could drive to Philly and surprise Grady at home. If he couldn't work out, he could *get* worked out. And maybe while he was getting fucked, he could figure out *how* utterly fucked he was. If Grady sent him home, well, Max would know how he felt and he could get over it.

And if he didn't, Max could fool himself a little longer.

"This is a terrible idea," he said out loud to himself.

Then he went next door to ask if he could trade cars with El for a week. Maybe Grady's neighbors were less nosy than Max's, but he didn't want to leave it to chance and end up not getting laid because he accidentally outed their arrangement and Grady was pissed about it.

He had Grady's address from their failed attempt to meet up in the preseason, so all he had to do was slide behind the wheel of El's car—"I'd say make good decisions, but too late for that," she said as she handed him the keys—and follow the directions on his phone.

An hour and ten minutes later, he pulled into Grady's driveway.

He'd expected a bland modern cookie cutter of a house, with white siding or stucco and grass trimmed within an inch of its life, maybe a boxwood hedge with perfect ninety-degree corners.

He was half right. The house *was* a modern monstrosity, bland and flat, though the stucco was gray.

But he'd been wrong about the yard. It didn't have a lawn at all, but row upon row of planter boxes—mostly empty—with neat brick paths in between. The few remaining plants looked like some kind of squash.

For a few seconds Max stared. This had to be the wrong house. The sensible part of his brain refused to accept the possibility that Grady Armstrong grew his own vegetables.

*He does get his eggs from a farm*, the horrible, inconvenient part of Max's brain chimed in. *It's not impossible that he gardens.*

The rational part responded with an image of Grady as a grumpy old man, chasing rabbits out of his lettuce with a rake.

Fuck it. Every second he spent sitting there, his judgment of himself grew. He needed to act before his common sense reminded him what an idiot he was.

Max took out his phone. *R u home?*

Only a few seconds passed before the response came. *Yeah. Why?*

*Open the door*

This time the reply came quicker. *What? No.* Then, *How did you even get my address?*

Max bit his lip. *Uh u gave it to me before that preseason game bud. Remember?*

*Don't call me bud.*

But the front door was opening, so obviously Grady wasn't as bothered as he pretended.

That restored Max's confidence, or enough of it that he could fake the rest. He sauntered up the front steps, smirking. "You really want me to use a pet name, eh? Babycakes? Honey bear?"

Grady rolled his eyes as he let Max into the house. His hair was damp at the ends, and he smelled like the stupidly fancy shampoo he'd bought for Max. "I want you to shut up."

Max closed the door behind himself and grinned. "Well, you know how to make that happen."

From the look in Grady's eyes, he had every intention of cashing all the checks Max's mouth was writing.

Then he frowned like a grumpy thunderstorm and said, "You're injured."

Max blinked at him. "Yeah, but I didn't break my mouth, so…."

Grady huffed and stomped farther into the house. Max toed off his shoes and followed. The décor was inoffensive and functional, and that was the nicest thing he could say about it. At least the place had good natural light. "I'm not having sex with you when I don't know what your injuries are."

Translation—he didn't know which ways to be careful to keep from aggravating something.

They were in his kitchen now—industrial white, twelve-foot tray ceilings. An herb-pot wall provided the only splash of color.

Max pursed his lips. He didn't come here to be treated with kid gloves. He also didn't want to examine his feelings about the possibility that Grady cared enough not to hurt him. "I'm not telling you my diagnosis." Teams kept that shit to generic "upper-body injury" for a reason—so other teams couldn't target their weaknesses.

"Then we're not having sex."

Oh, come on. "Seriously? Because I won't tell you where I'm hurt?"

Grady's nostrils flared. "If you don't trust me not to hurt you, why the *fuck* are you sleeping with me?"

Max flinched. He could afford to be reckless with his heart, but not his body. Only, what was more reckless? Trusting that Grady wouldn't use his injuries against him, or fucking him without talking about them?

Finally he relented. "I strained my neck so it's hard to turn my head to the right. And I have a partial muscle tear in my left shoulder."

Grady's eyebrows doubled in size and volume. "And you were going to let me fuck your face in the foyer?"

Let, nothing; Max was angling for it. "No pain, no gain. I'm open to alternatives."

Grady appraised him, gaze lingering on Max's mouth, his shoulders, his crotch. Max's skin went hot.

Then Grady said, "Bedroom's to the left."

Max didn't need to be told twice. He reached for the zipper for his hoodie and pulled it down as he went.

Grady's bedroom looked like he'd purchased everything directly from the display at an expensive furniture store. It all matched too well. But Max only cared about the king-size four-poster bed and how quickly they could ruin the sheets.

By the time he got his hoodie off his left arm, Grady had folded the comforter and put it on the chair in the corner. "How much can you move it before it hurts?"

"Don't worry about it. I can take it."

Grady rolled his eyes. "I didn't say you couldn't. But if I hurt you, it's going to be because I did it on purpose, not because you didn't tell me something. So how far can you move it?"

Max's mouth went dry and a shiver went down his spine, which actually hurt a little when his neck spasmed. Still, he demonstrated his arm's range of movement, feeling naked under the weight of Grady's gaze.

"Now this."

Suddenly Grady's hands were on his face, tilting Max's head up and to the side.

Max's breath caught in his throat as Grady met his eyes.

Somehow he didn't expect Grady to kiss him. It was slow and thorough and hot, and the hair on the back of Max's neck stood up. He curled his hands into the fabric of Grady's T-shirt and held on as Grady scraped his teeth over Max's lower lip, but when he bit down, Max jerked instinctively and then cursed into Grady's mouth as his neck protested.

"Guy did a number on you," Grady commented. He hadn't let go of Max's face. "Guess you'll have to be a pillow princess today."

Max squawked in indignation as Grady pushed him back onto the bed—except it was less of a fall and more of a controlled descent, nothing that jarred his strained muscles. "Excuse you," he protested into the cotton of his own T-shirt as Grady eased it over his head, careful of his left arm. "I'm perfectly capable of participating—"

Grady made a hot, surprised noise and thumbed the right side of Max's chest. Max hissed and squirmed back into the pillows as Grady toyed with the barbell. "What's this?"

"It's a nipple piercing, genius."

Grady flicked it. Max writhed as pleasure shot through him. "I've never seen it before."

"I don't—" Grady found the piercing on the other side and put his mouth around it. Max's central nervous system went on strike. "—ah, fuck—I don't wear them during games for obvious reasons." Catching one of them on the inside of his pads during a nasty hit could result in some gnarly nipple trauma.

Grady pulled his mouth away and rolled the wet nub through his fingers. "But you like this."

"Yeah? That's why I got them pierced—"

Grady pinched. Max was gonna die of sex. "They're sensitive."

They were basically hardwired to Max's dick. "What tipped you off?"

Now he was twisting. Max groaned and arched into it, then hissed when his neck muscles pulled.

"The piercings aren't exactly subtle." Grady's voice sounded gravel-rough. "Stop moving. You'll hurt yourself."

Max opened his eyes and glared at him. "How the fuck—"

Grady skimmed his palms over Max's chest, brushing the tips of Max's nipples. God, he was barely touching him and Max's dick was leaking in his underwear.

"I could just stop touching you if you move."

Max could just die of a heart attack right now. "Fuck you."

"Next time," Grady promised lightly.

Max wasn't owning up to the skip his heart gave at the words—or the fact that it was the promise of next time, and not sex, that caused it. "Take off your pants, you smug asshole."

It must be Max's lucky day, because Grady actually did what he asked. Max squirmed out of his too. By the time he was naked, Grady was kneeling between his legs, looking hungrily at Max's cock and the mess it had already left on his thighs and stomach.

Max couldn't muster the focus to feel embarrassed when Grady was reaching for the lube, obviously as eager to get his dick in Max's ass as Max was to have it.

The problem came when Grady pushed inside and Max arched his back again and sent his neck into agony.

"Fuck!" Max liked a good slap on his ass in the heat of the moment, but this was the bad kind of pain. He gritted his teeth and tried to breathe through it.

Grady put a palm in the center of Max's chest and pushed down until his shoulders went flat to the bed. Max grunted. "I'd joke about tying you up, but I don't think your arm could handle it."

Max exhaled through his nose and consciously relaxed his neck and shoulders. Then he canted his hips; Grady should remember he had a job to do here. "Put a pin in that thought."

Grady took his cue without further prompting. He snapped forward and nailed Max's prostate just right. Biting his lip, Max closed his eyes and let himself get lost in it. He braced his right arm against the mattress and wrapped his legs around Grady's waist.

But Max wasn't designed to lie there and take it, and he only lasted a handful of deep, perfect thrusts before he dug his left elbow into the mattress and tried to use it for leverage.

Huffing, Grady pulled out.

Max opened his eyes. "Hey!"

"You're a danger to yourself," Grady said. "Turn over."

All the wires in Max's brain crossed in his haste to obey *that* particular annoyed, turned-on tone. Grady tugged his hips as Max wrestled to get his right arm beneath him. He had to rest his head on the pillow because the angle would've been murder on his neck, but otherwise Grady had the right idea—there was little Max could do to aggravate his injuries in this position.

"Stop squirming," Grady complained again when he was back inside Max.

"Get the angle right, then," Max bitched. "What is this, amateur hour?"

Grady fucked in hard enough to rattle Max's teeth, adjusted the angle of Max's right thigh, and fried most of Max's remaining brain cells. "Anyone ever tell you you're high-maintenance?"

Max swallowed a laugh with a gasp and curled the fingers of his left hand into the bedsheets. That was a new one, but Grady *would* think so. "Not—*ah*, do that again—not really." He thrust his ass backward to meet Grady's hips.

"For fuck's sake, stop *moving*."

Easy for him to say; *he* didn't have to try to hold still while his central nervous system liquified. "Fucking make me. Jesus. You think *I'm* high-maintenance."

Grady dug his fingers into Max's hips. Max would've sworn he could feel the slap coming—Larry was ready for it—but it didn't land. "That's what you want, isn't it? But I'm not going to."

Max opened his mouth to protest. It figured—of course Grady wouldn't give him what he wanted; Grady was a contrary asshole—but then he continued,

"If you want me to spank your ass so bad, you can behave yourself. It's only a punishment if you don't like it."

At that point Max's spine stopped working, and he couldn't have moved if his life depended on it, because his brain went offline. An embarrassing moan escaped his mouth because Max didn't have any control over that either.

"Knew you could do it," Grady said, like the smug asshole he was.

The flat of his palm landed against the meat of Max's ass, sending fire along his nerve endings. Max bit his lip, but the gasp came out anyway, and his body spasmed around Grady's dick.

But he didn't move—not voluntarily—until his cock was dripping between his legs, his right arm was shaking with the effort of holding him up, and his ass stung so good from being slapped he couldn't take it anymore. "Fuck," he groaned into the pillow. "Grady, I gotta—"

"Yeah," Grady said, sounding every bit as wrecked as Max felt, and Max wasn't gonna ask twice.

He didn't have a perfect range of motion on his left arm, but he could get his hand around his dick. One more stinging slap on the back of his thigh and he hurtled into orgasm, shuddering and shaking and making a mess of Grady's sheets.

Grady followed like he always did. His grip on Max's hips tightened and he bit off a curse Max only vaguely heard through the roaring in his own ears, and his balls twitched against Max's ass as he came.

With the endorphins leaching out of his brain, Max gave himself a moment to recover. He kept doing this. Realistically, he was going to *keep* doing it until he couldn't anymore, which was stupid. Eventually he'd break and his feelings would come flooding out, and Grady would be horrified.

But right now Grady was too come-dumb to notice if Max waved a sign advertising his feelings in front of his face, so it was fine.

Grady collapsed on the bed next to him, breathing hard. "Not that I don't appreciate the booty call," he mumbled into the pillow, "but what are you doing here?"

Max could've taken offense, but Grady clearly didn't mean anything by it. "Getting laid?" He patted Grady's hip. "Good job, by the way."

"You're the worst." Grady peered at him with his face half smashed into a pillow. "And that's not what I meant."

Max rolled onto his back so he could pretend Grady couldn't see him. "Don't be so hard on yourself. Sex is a pretty good motivator."

Grady muffled a sigh.

Fuck it. He wouldn't believe the truth anyway, if Max told it right. "Couldn't stomach the idea of spending a whole week in my own company, so I figured I'd impose on you instead. Knew you were on a home stand. So here I am."

Blessed silence for all of three seconds. Then, "A *week*?"

Max braced himself. "My bag's still in the car."

"The car?" Grady squawked. Max looked at him. His eyes were as big as pucks. "You parked that monstrosity in my driveway? The lime-green one with the vanity plates? Are you nuts? *Do you know how nosy my neighbors are?*"

Max rolled his eyes. "Relax. I took Hedgie's wife's car. You saw it when I came in, remember?"

"Fantastic," he said wryly. "They can think I'm screwing her instead."

Yeah, it was probably best if that rumor didn't circulate. "What was I supposed to do, *rent* a car?"

"Or park it in the garage like any normal person having a clandestine hookup."

Max laughed. "That's a bit rich coming from you, since Hedgie and El already saw *your* car in *my* driveway overnight."

That stopped Grady cold. "Oh shit, seriously?"

"I had to answer so many awkward questions, Mr. Pennsylvania Plates. But I'd be happy to park in your garage to save you from the same fate." He waggled his eyebrows. "I'm sure your teammates will appreciate the good mood all the extra vitamin D will put you in."

"Gosh. Awfully gracious of you." Grady gave a theatrical sigh. "Fine, you can stay. But you're not sleeping in my bed."

From the way he said it—no trace of annoyance, an amused twist to his lips—it was clear he neither believed that nor was he particularly bothered. Max grinned sunnily. "That's cool. Can I still fuck you in it?"

Grady hit him with the pillow.

Then he said, "I need lunch first. You want an omelet?"


GRADY WAS a call-first kind of guy. When Max presented himself on his doorstep, it threw him.

But he was also having a tough week—news had broken that he'd requested a trade, so now he got to deal with fans dragging him for disloyalty on the internet and a combination of accusatory questions and sympathetic understanding from the Firebirds' beleaguered beat reporters. Having Max around provided a distraction, not to mention an outlet for some of Grady's pent-up energy. Feeding him seemed like the least Grady could do.

Grady made the omelets while Max watched from the breakfast bar, brow furrowed. "Why're the yolks so orange?"

"Farm-fresh eggs are always richer in color." And flavor. But he'd figure that out soon enough.

Grady plated up and Max dug in, then made an orgasmic, outraged sound through his closed mouth. Once he'd swallowed, he looked at his plate in disbelief. "Oh my God, this is amazing. How is it so much *eggier* than a regular egg?" He looked up at Grady and his expression became accusatory. "How am I supposed to go back to grocery store eggs after this?"

Grady finished his own lunch around a self-satisfied smirk. "That sounds like a you problem."

Laughing, Max tossed his balled-up napkin at his head.

And then Grady made good on his promise and spread himself out on his bed with Max between his thighs.

Max hadn't missed the mark when he accused Grady of being a control freak, but he didn't miss it in bed either. He kept his thrusts slow and steady and perfectly aimed, which left Grady without anything to complain about.

Well—he could have complained Max didn't have a hand free to wrap around his dick, but that seemed in poor taste since Max was injured and Grady's arms worked fine.

He did drop the condom on the sheet afterward, so Grady bitched about that instead, even though the linens were already destroyed from earlier.

Max snorted into Grady's shoulder and wiped his lube-sticky hand on Grady's stomach. "I don't know why I thought this would make you mellow."

Objectively, they were disgusting, but Grady was comfortable and Max wasn't *that* heavy. They could shower later. "Me neither. You really misread that situation."

Max's laugh tickled the hairs on the back of Grady's neck. Neither of them got up for several minutes.

Grady didn't have a game that night, but if he thought spending the entire day with Max would be awkward and strange, Max surprised him again. Grady did an off-day workout in his home gym while Max helped himself to Netflix, and then they argued about dinner for twenty minutes before settling on gnocchi with kale, Italian sausage, and a browned-butter sauce.

"If you turn the heat up in the pan, you can get the kale to crisp up on the edges," Max commented as he drained the pasta.

Grady didn't remember telling him where to find the colander. "Maybe I like it wilted."

But he turned the heat up when Max wasn't looking.

Everything went surprisingly well until bedtime rolled around and they realized they'd forgotten about the state of the sheets.

Max pursed his lips in consideration. "So when you said I wouldn't be sleeping in your bed… you meant that you wouldn't either?"

Asshole. Grady pointed. "Guest bedroom's upstairs."

Last time they'd shared a bed, Max slept ass naked, passed out facedown. This time Grady woke up to find him curled into a ball on his side like a kid, wearing Grady's stolen boxers since he'd been too lazy to get his bag out of the car.

Maybe he thought it was rude to sleep naked in someone else's bed.

Probably he was just a weirdo.

Grady had practice in the morning, so they made a quick breakfast before he left. He had no idea what Max planned to do while he was gone, but as long as he didn't burn the house down, Grady didn't care.

His agent called when he was halfway home. "Keep this quiet for now, but things are in motion. Don't be surprised if you get scratched this week."

For years, Grady's shoulders had been gradually tightening with stress about the team. Half a dozen seasons now he'd spent training up a new linemate, working to generate chemistry, only for management to turn around and trade him for a defenseman or picks because Grady'd played with him enough to inflate his numbers. They seemed to expect Grady to play just as well with anyone.

Now the tension finally started to relax. It felt… strange.

Of course part of him was sad too. He liked Coop and Zipper. He liked his home here.

But he could like it somewhere else too. "Any idea where they're sending me?"

"Looks like Anaheim."

Anaheim had a stable full of young talent. When they clicked, they steamrollered their opponents. When they didn't, they could blow a 5–0 lead in a single period. It made sense that they'd be looking for a few veterans to keep the hotheads in line and keep them on an even keel. Grady could see himself fitting in there.

It was on the other side of the country, though—kind of a long way to go for a booty call. He should enjoy this time with Max while he could.

"Thanks, Erika."

When he entered the house, Max was sitting in the living room in his boxers, eating a bowl of cereal. He paused the TV and looked up when Grady entered.

Grady looked over Max's shoulder at the TV screen. Apparently he was fifty-seven minutes into *Pride & Prejudice*.

"Don't judge me."

Grady raised his hands. "No judgment." Max could watch whatever he wanted.

"So." Max craned his neck to meet Grady's eyes. "Where are they dealing you?"

He must've been paying attention after all. "Erika thinks Anaheim."

Suddenly saying it out loud exhausted him. He sat down on the opposite end of the couch from Max, and they finished watching the movie together.

Grady expected to get scratched for the next game as a preventive measure, since an injury could kill a trade. But Coach put him in the lineup at the last minute. "Don't look at me," he said. "I do what they tell me. Suit up."

So he did. He got a few shifty looks in the locker room, but at least soon it wouldn't be Grady's problem.

He went out and put up three points against Pittsburgh, which was good enough to earn him first star of the game but not good enough to get the Firebirds a win against their second-most-hated rival team.

Grady did his standard postgame media bullshit, spent long enough on the bike to keep from cramping, hit the shower, then hit the road.

He hoped Max wasn't expecting much from him tonight. Between the exhaustion and the frustration, he didn't feel particularly social.

As had become routine, Max had the TV on when Grady got home. TSN was playing highlights from the Nordiques game—no, not just one game. The video flashed to a shot of Dante Baltierra in an away jersey. He'd been playing at home in the first one.

Had Baller hit a milestone tonight?

Grady looked away from the screen and met Max's eyes.

Max said, "I'm really sorry."

With a sinking sensation, Grady turned back to the television. This time he read the ticker along the bottom. *Nordiques trade Dante Baltierra to Anaheim in three-way deal.*

If they'd taken Baller, they weren't taking Grady. Not without significant other moves, or an injury, or a roster overhaul that made no sense at this point in the season.

Which meant Grady wasn't going anywhere for now.

"Fuck."

"Yeah." Max regarded him for another moment and then turned off the TV. "You want to get high about it?"

MAX DIDN'T make a habit of smoking. He needed his lungs in top condition. But sometimes he needed to unwind more.

He'd been pretty sure Grady would turn him down—Grady was uptight by default, and weed wasn't legal in Pennsylvania.

So when Grady blinked at him and then laughed and said, "Fuck it, YOLO," Max kind of thought he was hallucinating.

It turned out weed made Grady tactile. They sat shoulder to shoulder on his back porch, passing the joint between them.

Grady was warm and solid against him, leaning with a good amount of weight, and he smelled good. Max suspected he'd made a terrible mistake, so he reached for the conversational equivalent of a bucket of cold water. "So. How's the dating going?"

"Fucking terrible." Grady turned his face until his forehead was pressed to Max's shoulder. He snickered. "I quit."

Well, that backfired. "What?"

"It was a dumb idea." He slumped and rotated again as he held out his hand for the cigarette. Automatically, Max handed it to him. "I could've been traded anyway. And, like, it's already November. I don't wanna spend the holidays with some guy after dating him for a month. That would be weird and clingy."

"True."

Without dislodging himself from Max's shoulder, Grady held the joint up to Max's lips. Max took a drag. The paper was slightly damp in his mouth.

Grady sighed theatrically and flopped backward onto the deck. "I don't know what I'm gonna tell Jess, though."

The high was hitting now—it always took a little longer than Max expected—and his head got that detached floating feeling. "Hmm?" What did Jess have to do with it? Max didn't remember.

"'Cause, like, she's gotta go. If she doesn't see Amanda again and get closure, she's gonna pine forever, you know?"

Max nodded. He might not remember what Grady was referencing, but he understood the *pine forever* bit and why it was bad.

"And she's all I've got, but she's also my big sister, who raised me since I was fifteen." He exhaled a cloud of smoke toward the sky. "They broke up because of me, 'cause Amanda wasn't ready to be a parent."

"Oh fuck." That was a lot to hang on a fifteen-year-old.

Now Grady let out a frustrated groan and rolled his head against the deck boards. "But if Jess finds out I have nobody to spend Christmas with, she won't go."

And this was the moment Max *knew* smoking was a bad idea, because his brain didn't even *try* to stop his mouth from saying, "So spend it with me."

Why was he such a dumbass?

Grady turned toward him with dazed eyes and smiled a high, uncomplicated smile. "Yeah?"

Max was completely fucked. "Yeah. I mean, it'll be chaos. It's me, my parents, and my brother and sister and their families. Last year my sister's best friend was getting a divorce, so she tagged along. We rent a place."

"What, you don't have room for them all at your house?" Grady laughed. In the dim porch light, Max could make out the crinkles around his eyes.

Sometimes Max forgot how handsome Grady was when he smiled, since he didn't do it often. This laughing, relaxed Grady was like kryptonite.

Max's chest hurt. He blamed the pot.

"I could buy a bigger house," he said, aiming for levity. "But then I couldn't leave it when my mom starts getting on me about my love life."

Grady flat-out giggled. It was adorable. "Okay, but, like, that brings up a good point. What do we tell your family? Like, 'Mom, I brought home a stray hockey player for the holidays'?"

"Fuck no. I'm not going to New Brunswick. There's, like, six feet of snow." It'd take him the entire break to dig his car out. "We're going to Florida. But it's fine. We'll just tell them the truth—you're hanging out with me so your sister can get a second shot with the one that got away. They're big suckers for True Love."

Squinting, Grady said, "That's not the truth, though."

Max snorted. "Isn't it?"

"Amanda's girlfriend is coming." He sounded unsure. "What am I supposed to tell Jess?"

If he didn't want to come, he could say no instead of prolonging Max's agony. "Look, if you don't want to—"

"I do!" he said. He looked surprised at himself, but he didn't take it back. Instead he said, "I'll figure out what to tell Jess tomorrow." Then, "Thanks."

Christ. Max took the last of the joint from Grady's unresisting hand and finished it off in one deep pull. When he exhaled, he pretended it had eased the anxious knot in his chest. "Don't mention it."

MAX LEFT before noon the following day, apparently needed back in Newark for evaluation. Afterward the house felt too quiet, which rankled because Grady had lived alone for eight years. A few days with a houseguest shouldn't have been enough to shift his baseline.

God only knew how he'd feel after Christmas, after spending three days in a house with Max's family. He'd probably have to start sleeping with the TV on.

Truth told, he felt a little weird about agreeing to spend the holidays with Max, but he couldn't deny it solved his problem. Jess would be able to go on her trip with Amanda and company guilt-free. Grady would probably get laid. If Max's family members were anything like him, they wouldn't care that Grady played for a rival team, and if for some reason things went south, they'd be in Florida, so at least Grady could escape someplace warm and sandy.

Which left only the logistics of telling Jess.

Fortunately, Grady had accidentally come up with the perfect strategy when he gave her the names-redacted account of his "date" with Max. Grady picked up his phone and sent her a text.

*Bad news/good news. Bad news: I quit internet dating. Good news: Going to Florida with Shithead for Christmas.*

The house stopped feeling so quiet after that, because Jess called him within five minutes. "I cannot wait to hear this."

"Hi to you too," Grady said.

"Don't even, little brother. First you're having hot dates at the *American Ninja Warrior* gym, then you're having super competitive sex with the guy, all the while complaining that he's as much of an asshole as you are, and now you're spending the holidays with him. I'm going to need details. Not sex ones!" she added quickly.

He tried not to smile at how easily she'd taken the bait. "He invited me to spend Christmas with his family in Florida."

"What? *When*?"

"Yesterday."

"Wait, have you been fucking this guy the whole time? In between all your other dates?"

Now he needed to choose his words carefully. He didn't like lying to Jess, even if it was for her own good. "It was casual." It was still casual, but Jess didn't need to know that.

"Except what, now you've decided you have feelings so you're giving up on dating anyone else?"

*No*, Grady wanted to say. But that was exactly what he needed her to think. And….

And he *was* giving up on dating, and in part it *was* because he didn't want to be with anyone but Max. He'd gone on a very nice date with someone else and had a good time and thought about Max the whole while. Max had left his house and Grady immediately felt the loss of him—off-kilter in his own home.

But it was still casual… wasn't it?

He cleared his throat and pushed aside a wave of impending panic. It was casual. Everything was fine. "Something like that."

"Oh my God. Grady. Only you." She was laughing, though. "God, I told you so. Are you going to tell me his real name now?"

Ah, fuck, he hadn't thought of a good way to evade that question. "If we're still together at the trade deadline I'll tell you everything."

There was a suspicious pause. "At?" Jess asked.

Shit. "*By*," Grady corrected. *At* maybe made it too obvious Shithead was another hockey player.

"Uh-huh," Jess said. "All right. Fine. You held up your end of the deal, so I guess I have to go skiing."

"Please. How many black leggings and soft sweaters with too-long sleeves have you bought for this trip?" Grady knew how Jess dressed when she wanted to appear touchable. She had it down to an art form.

Now she mock gasped. "How dare you." But he heard the grin in her voice. "You should see this cable-knit scoop neck I bought. It is softer than a newborn puppy and I look like I belong in a Nespresso commercial."

Grady snorted. That was Jess, all right. "You're a terror, sis."

"You're damn right."


MAX SLOTTED back into the Monsters' lineup two days after he left Grady's, but he was only back for one game before their star defenseman took an awkward fall into the boards and went out with a hip injury.

On the one hand, that sucked. The Monsters had a lot of firepower, but they'd built their defensive core around Jimmy, and the whole team felt his absence. Their first game without him should've been a blowout—they were playing Winnipeg, who were currently in last place in the Central Division—but they barely eked out a win, 4–3 in overtime.

Max liked a lot of things about his job. He loved the game, loved his teammates, loved the fans. Truth told he loved being the center of attention. He'd miss all of that when he inevitably got too old for pro hockey.

But he'd never miss the spicy takes from Twitter, the fan sites, and even the beat reporters who covered the team. A rumor that the Monsters were days away from trading Hedgie for a replacement defenseman kept him from dwelling on his holiday plans. He could've done without the stress for El, though.

Between games, practices, and travel, Max had barely enough time to confirm the last details of the vacation rental with his mom. He didn't have to worry about Christmas shopping—he rented the house and paid for groceries and travel for his family as their gift. Max might only be able to stay for a few days, but he rented the house for two weeks so everyone else could enjoy some time away from the snow. Both Logan and Nora had seasonal affective disorder, and the injection of sunshine helped them get through the long winter.

Of course, Max liked spoiling Logan's kids, so he'd gotten the family Disney passes and, to make it up to their parents, virtual reality headsets that would keep the little ones busy in the event of poor weather or a day spent recovering from sunburn.

But apparently his mother wasn't on board with Max's plan of "not worrying about the holidays." He rubbed his eyes and glanced at the bedside clock in the hotel room as her voice came through the phone. "…and I set up the grocery delivery for the day we arrive, so we'll be all set when we get there."

It had gotten to the part of the hockey season where Max's body didn't know what time zone it was in, just that it was tired all the time. But those words woke him up. "Oh shit."

"What do you mean, 'oh shit'? Don't you mean 'thanks, Mom'?"

He put the phone on speaker so he could turn onto his side and curl up. "I do mean 'thanks, Mom.' The 'oh shit' was for me. I forgot to tell you we're going to have one more."

"One more what?"

He bit his lip. "Guest."

"Oh! Do we have enough bedrooms? Do we need to look into getting another place? I think all the beds are spoken for, but there might be a pull-out—"

This was her subtle way of asking whether Max and his guest were sleeping together. "It's fine. He can share with me."

"So it's that kind of friend! Why didn't you tell me earlier? I didn't know you were seeing anyone!"

*It's complicated* didn't cover this situation. Fortunately his mother was used to her children bringing strays home for the holidays, including Max's occasional casual sex partners. "I'm not. I mean, he really is just a friend." Maybe Grady wouldn't put it that way, but Max couldn't afford to spend a lot of time having feelings about that. "Sometimes we have sex, but seriously. Just friends."

"Okay, sweetheart. As long as you're being careful."

She said the same thing to his sister when she dated, so Max didn't take it personally. "Promise, Mom."

"Well, I'll add another adult's worth of food to the grocery order."

Yeah, that wouldn't be enough. "Better make it another me worth of food." A hockey player's midseason calorie intake was more than twice the average adult's.

"Oh?" Max knew that voice. That was her *I'm about to go fishing* voice. "Who *is* this friend? Someone from work? Do I know him?"

Unbidden, Max got a mental image of his parents' faces when Max showed up at Christmas with his media-designated archrival in tow. "You'll meet him soon enough."

"Max! So mysterious!"

"Sorry, Mom. A guy's got to have a few secrets in his life, eh?"

"I can't believe you're going to keep me in suspense." She tutted teasingly. "See if you get anything but coal in your stocking this year."

However enthusiastic his mother was, Max didn't expect the two thousand questions Grady fired at him in the weeks leading up to the break. Things like *Is Gru coming along?* and *Does your mom have any hobbies?* He wanted to know the names and ages of Max's brother's kids, and what his sister was like, and did his dad drink scotch.

It took Max longer than it should've to realize Grady was trying to figure out what to get people for Christmas.

Max almost sent him a message to say he didn't have to do that. Nobody would expect Grady to get them anything. Their relationship was casual. Hell, Max wasn't planning on getting Grady anything either. He'd made it clear where they stood—they had a weird friendship and great sexual chemistry.

And then he remembered Grady's parents were dead and the only family the guy had left was abandoning him for the holidays to get closure with the woman who'd left her when she became Grady's legal guardian, and he physically could not do it. He couldn't tell Grady not to pretend he was having a normal family Christmas for the first time in fifteen years.

But he also couldn't let Grady come to Christmas and not *receive* any presents.

Fucking *shit*, he was going to have to buy a gift for someone who legitimately had a subscription to Consumer Reports—a man who Max was in love with and who *could not find that out*. Max's life was officially the worst.

Due to the game schedule, Grady couldn't fly out with Max and Gru. Instead, he flew right from his last game in Nashville, and Max met him at the airport in Miami, hoping to every deity that no one recognized either of them and took a picture for the internet.

"Nice goal last night," Grady commented when he met Max in baggage claim. "You really committed."

Max had basically followed the puck into the net because Kipriyanov tripped him, which was the only reason the goal hadn't been called off for goaltender interference. "Commitment is my middle name," he said, and then immediately wanted to punch himself in the face.

Fortunately Grady wasn't paying him any attention—he was down by Max's feet, ruffling Gru's ears. "Hey, buddy. Were you a good boy on the flight? Ready to get out of here?"

Gru licked his chin.

Max refused to be jealous of his dog, even if it had been weeks since he'd gotten his mouth on any part of Grady's body. Time to get going. The sooner they got to the house, the sooner he could rectify that problem. "You get everything?"

"Shockingly, the airline did not lose my luggage." He stood up and gestured to the full-size suitcase behind him.

"Holy shit. You know we're only here for three days, right?"

Grady's cheeks went slightly pink as he tugged up the handle of the rolling bag. "The presents wouldn't fit in a carry-on. But I could take yours back if you want—"

Max mentally upgraded his punishment from punching himself in the face to kicking his own ass. If Grady was this adorably awkward for the next three days, Max would give himself away in seconds, and wouldn't *that* be uncomfortable for Grady, having to share a bedroom with him while being aware Max had somehow caught feelings.

Yikes.

"Let's not be hasty." He grabbed his own bag—a much more reasonably sized one, because Max had only had to pack real presents for Grady and Gru—and led the way toward the arrivals area. Gru trotted along beside him, nails clacking on the floor.

"Hey, hold up a second." Grady had taken a slight right and had to correct himself to catch up. "Don't we need to go to the rental car counter?"

Max slowed down enough to be able to glance over without running into someone. "Nah. My parents drove down. They're picking us up."

Grady's eyes went wide and he caught his foot on the edge of a stray carpet. He righted himself before he could fall. "They drove down from *New Brunswick*?"

"They like having a car when they're down here. Plus my dad hates air travel."

Grady puffed his cheeks out on an exhale. "I guess that makes sense. But you couldn't have given me a heads-up I'm meeting your parents first thing? What's our story?"

Max snorted. "Bit late to ask now, bud."

Grady bumped his shoulder.

"It's fine. I told them the truth—we're friends who sleep together."

If Grady disputed the term *friends*, Max was going back to the departures desk to book himself a ticket to Antarctica. But he simply said, "And they're cool with that? Even though your niece and nephew are going to be there?"

"What, you think my brother raised his kids to be homophobic?" Max asked, amused.

"I just don't want to explain 'friends with benefits' to an eight-year-old."

Okay, that was fair. Max wheeled his bag through the exterior door and grinned as the humid Miami air swamped him. "We can leave it at 'friends' for the ankle-biters. Tell them we're having a sleepover."

Grady laughed. "Are we going to stay up late and talk about our crushes?"

Max's heart squeezed. "I was thinking more lingerie-clad pillow fights, but if gossip's your thing—"

"Max! Over here!"

Showtime.

"Game face on," Max said. "Here's your last warning—my mom's a lot."

"What a surprise."

That was the last thing he heard before his mom launched herself into his arms. "Merry Christmas, nerd!" She smacked a kiss on his cheek and then pulled away. "Your father's waiting in the car. He sent me to find you."

Before Max could react, she'd reached for his bag, leaving him holding Gru's leash, and turned to Grady. "And this must be—"

The words cut off, and Max turned to watch the look of realization dawn on her face.

Grady let go of his suitcase and held out his hand to shake. "Hi. Um, I'm—"

"Grady Armstrong." Max's mom sounded like she was meeting Elvis or something. She took his hand in both of hers. "Hello. I'm Linda."

"Nice to meet you, Linda." Grady smiled—the real one that made Max's breath catch. "Thanks for letting me join you."

"Oh, any friend of Max's," she said with a pointed look in Max's direction. "Come on, car's this way."

Grady followed after her with a bemused smile.

Max sighed and glanced down at Gru. "Buddy, are we gonna hear it later."

Then he hurried to catch up. He didn't want to miss his dad's reaction.

GRADY MET Linda first, and the expression she leveled at Max let him know that Max had been a little vague about who was coming for the holidays. Grady couldn't exactly blame him, since it wasn't like he'd been forthcoming with Jess.

They put their bags in the trunk of a white SUV with New Brunswick plates, and then Linda got in the front and Max opened the rear driver's side door. "Hey, Dad," he said cheerfully as Grady got in on the other side. "Merry Christmas. This is Grady."

"Oh you little shit," said Max's dad.

Grady was *pretty sure* he was talking to Max.

Then he continued, "I owe your mother twenty bucks."

Max cackled.

His dad turned around in his seat and offered Grady his hand. "Big Max."

Of course he was. "Grady."

"Oh, I know." He shook his head. "Max played this one close to the chest."

Grady looked at Max, who was still grinning. "Something tells me he enjoyed it."

Max had been right about his family—they were nuts. Grady didn't mind, though. It was kind of like spending the holidays with a multigenerational coed hockey team, but not like the Firebirds or his juniors team—one that actually liked each other.

Nora had graduated dentistry school in April, but she wasn't allowed to do Max's teeth because, in her words, "After the way we

went at each other as kids, he's not letting me near his face with a drill."
She had the same manic gleam to her eyes Max got when he was about
to start shit, so Grady figured that was probably the right call.

Stay-at-home-dad Logan was built more like Big Max, who stood
close to six foot four, than his brother. Maybe that explained why his
kids, Carly and Milo, seemed to view him as a human jungle gym. Tanya,
his wife, worked as a software developer; she took one look at Grady and
said, "Oh thank God, a sane person."

Behind her, Logan covered a laugh. "Babe, that's Grady Armstrong.
Max's, like, archnemesis from the Firebirds."

"Nemesis is such a strong word," Max said, at which point Carly
and Milo swarmed him demanding he throw them in the pool.

He let them carry him off, leaving Grady alone with Tanya and
Logan.

"You want a drink?" Tanya offered into the sudden awkward
silence.

Perfect icebreaker. "I knew I liked you."

The house they'd rented was on the beach, with a beautiful pool
area and an airy open-concept design. Grady and Max had the ground-
floor bedroom, while the other four were upstairs, so Grady had a
small amount of insulation from the Lockhart family circus. The bright
sunshine and warm weather meant it didn't quite feel like Christmas,
but someone had strung fairy lights over a potted palm tree on the patio.
Grady approved of swapping out eggnog for margaritas and sangria and
didn't care who knew it.

If it weren't for his phone buzzing like crazy in his pocket, he might
have forgotten to miss Jess at all.

Grady let himself out of the kitchen and took the call in the
bedroom. "Hey, Jess."

"I can't do it," she hissed.

Alarmed, Grady closed the door. "Do what? Is everything okay?"

"No!" She was still speaking in a shouted whisper. "Half the girls
canceled at the last minute, so they put us in a smaller chalet!"

Uh-oh. "Who's 'us'?"

"Me, Amanda, and Polly."

Grady winced. Her, her ex, and her ex's new girlfriend. "Yeah.
That could be awkward."

"That's the problem."

"That it's awkward?"

"No. Polly keeps being *nice* to me."

Oh, the horror. Before Grady could be a smartass, Jess went on. "Like, okay, she was the one who organized the whole trip because Amanda was having this crisis about turning forty, I guess. So we've been emailing back and forth a lot. And she's been nice the whole time. And funny."

"Well," said Grady, at a loss. "How dare she."

"I'm being serious."

If Grady was the only one who could end up in a friends-with-benefits arrangement with a guy he regularly referred to as Shithead, Jess was the only one who could complain about a woman being nice to her. "Is she, like, Canadian nice, or Minnesota nice?"

Jess groaned. "I don't know, Grades. She made me a hot chocolate and put my hair in a crown braid. It looks awesome."

Grady didn't see the problem. "Is that weird?"

"It is when it's your ex's girlfriend!"

"She probably wants you to like her. You and Amanda were always close."

Jess blew out a long breath. "I guess. I just wish she'd be annoying and unlikable. And ugly."

Under the circumstances, Grady decided not to point out she'd barely even mentioned Amanda, the love of her life. Let Jess realize she could finally get over it in her own time. "Gosh. Stuck in a ski chalet with two people who are nice and easy to get along with. How will you ever survive?"

She blew a raspberry. "You're the worst." And then, predictably, changed the subject. "How's Florida?"

"Hot. Loud. Chaotic." Like Max, really. "It's like being on vacation with a hockey team."

"Hopefully it smells better."

There was a shout and a loud splash from outside, and Grady glanced out the bedroom window into the yard. "I gotta go. Shithead's niece and nephew just pushed him into the pool."

"You weren't kidding about the hockey team thing. All right, I'll talk to you later, Grades. Have fun."

"Don't let anyone be too nice."

He was tucking his phone back into his pocket when Max came in. He must have left his T-shirt and jeans outside to avoid tracking water through the house, because he was wearing only boxers and a towel slung around his neck, and he was still dripping wet.

"So the kids are definitely Lockharts," Grady said, slightly later than he should've because he was having trouble keeping his eyes on Max's face.

Max threw the towel at him. "Careful or you're next." He gave Grady a once-over, his gaze lingering on Grady's crotch. "Want to help me shower off the chlorine?"

CHRISTMAS EVE unfolded in a flurry of activity. Grady couldn't remember the last time he'd spent a holiday with so much to do.

He and Max exchanged hot, sloppy hand jobs in the shower. Max came when Grady bit the side of his neck, spurting hot and slick over Grady's fingers. Grady followed right after him, head spinning.

They spent the next few minutes drying off and unpacking, and then Logan asked Max to watch the kids in the pool while the others prepared dinner. That lasted a few minutes until Nora let Gru outside and he tried to launch himself into the water.

In a flash, Max stood up, cursing, and intercepted the dog with an arm around his middle. Gru yelped and struggled, frantic to get into the pool. "Nora!"

"Fuck! Sorry!" Nora slid the door open again and Max deposited Gru back on the other side of the glass.

Grady glanced at the kids—both in the shallow end, both gaping at their aunt, wide-eyed. "Aunt Nora!"

"I mean fudge!" Nora said. "Sorry."

Max closed the door again, but Gru just sat on the floor, barking his head off.

Grady kept his eyes on the kids as he asked, "What's his problem?"

Max sighed. "We're not sure. Either he has severe FOMO, or he's convinced that any human in a body of water is drowning and he has to rescue them. Either way, Gru plus swimming equals claw marks."

Poor Gru did seem distressed, from the sounds he was making. "That's… sweet but inconvenient. You want me to take him for a walk around the block? Maybe he'll forget about it."

"That would be great. Thank you."

It took a handful of treats to get Gru to leave the house, but once they did, he was happy enough to sniff along the sidewalk and pee on every third bush.

"Seriously, again?" Grady asked.

Gru gave him a look like he was actually being quite restrained.

When they got back to the house, the kids were still in the pool, but Grady lured Gru to the bedroom with another treat and then figured, *Fuck it*. Gru didn't know if Christmas was today or tomorrow, and besides, it wasn't like Grady had only bought him one present. He pulled the brand-new Minions bed out of his suitcase and presented it to the dog. "What do you think, buddy?"

There was a loud laugh and a splash from outside, and Grady thought the jig might be up, but then Gru put tentative paws on the bed and curled up.

Success!

Grady gave him another treat and went back to the kitchen to investigate the dinner situation. "What smells so good in here?"

Linda clacked a pair of stainless steel tongs at him. "Fresh New Brunswick lobster."

As if on cue, Grady's stomach rumbled and his mouth watered. Suddenly he remembered that he'd skipped lunch. However—"Wait, you brought a *live lobster* across the border?"

Linda chuckled. "Oh, Grady, honey, don't be silly." She patted his shoulder and turned back to the stove. "We brought seven."

Grady might weep with joy.

"Christmas Eve tradition," Max told him. He and the kids had just come in from the pool. His nose was starting to turn red. "Grandpa was a lobster fisherman."

What a great tradition, Grady thought. It had only been him and Jess for the past ten years, plus the occasional partner if one of them happened to be in a relationship. The first year after their parents died, Jess tried to make a full turkey dinner, but the bird was half burned and half raw and they ended up ordering Chinese. Grady thought it was kind of funny at the time, but that night he heard Jess crying in her room. For the next year, he spent his limited free time learning to cook so he could take care of Christmas dinner.

They still ordered Chinese every Christmas Eve, though.

Maybe he could convince her to switch to lobster.

"Grades? Hello?" Max waved a hand in front of his face. "Stop looking at my mom like you're going to propose. You want a beer?"

"I just really like lobster," Grady said, though he could feel himself flushing. He didn't want to explain the direction his thoughts had gone. It would bring down the mood. "And yes, please."

Miraculously, that was Grady's only lapse of the evening. For the rest of the night, Max's family kept him busy eating, laughing, and following their absurd sibling rituals. Before dinner, for example, Max and Logan had to arm wrestle for the kids' benefit, because "My dad's older, so he's stronger." Milo said this so matter-of-factly Grady had to tamp down on a laugh.

"But if they already know that, why do they arm wrestle?"

Carly rolled her eyes. "Because boys are stupid."

"Carly," Logan scolded.

"What? Aunt Nora said 'fuck'—"

"And Aunt Nora's in big trouble," Tanya said. Nora nodded along, her expression a passable impression of remorse. "We don't use that word. Try again."

With a long-suffering sigh, Carly corrected, "Because boys are ridiculous."

As Max fairly obviously threw the arm-wrestling match to make his brother look good in front of his kids, Grady couldn't disagree.

At that point Big Max directed them to set the table, and everyone was too excited about food to dwell on the outcome.

Grady had never tasted a lobster so perfect—tender, juicy, flavorful. Thank God it came in a shell that made it impossible to shove the whole thing in his mouth, or he would have embarrassed himself. "Why is this so good?" he hissed to Max while he was cracking open a stubborn claw.

Max glanced up from his plate. A smile lurked at the corners of his eyes. "Same reason your omelet was."

Oh, that asshole. "You *ruined lobster for me*," Grady accused under his breath.

Max patted him on the thigh under the table. "Payback's a b—a you-know-what."

The two of them pulled dish duty after dinner, since everyone else had helped cook. Grady didn't mind—there was a dishwasher for the plates and cutlery, and washing a few pots seemed like the least he could do. It might have felt strange if not for the time Max had spent at his place in November. Grady had gotten used to working with and around him in a kitchen.

He'd switched to drinking wine with dinner, which had the effect of making everything feel soft-edged and pleasant. The kids' laughter drifting in from the dining room added to the ambience. Whatever they were doing involved a lot of teasing. It reminded him of him and Jess.

"Hey." Max bumped his shoulder. "You okay?"

Without meaning to, Grady smiled. He must've been lost in thought again. "I'm good." Then he frowned at the pot he was drying. "This still has potato on it."

Max flicked dish suds at him. "I just make 'em wet. You make 'em clean."

Grady wiped his damp face on his sleeve. "Really."

Max grinned. "What are you gonna do about it?"

For a second, Grady considered the hose attachment to the sink. But when Max caught him looking at it, Grady upended the last of the water in the pot on his head instead.

Max squawked and reached for the dish sponge.

"Are you boys behaving in there?" Linda called from the dining room. "No!"

A moment later she appeared in the doorway. "Oh, for goodness' sake. Children."

Grady hid the damp dish towel he'd been scrubbing in Max's face behind his back.

Linda rolled her eyes. "Oh, leave the dishes for now and come play a game with the *other* children. Carly refuses to start without you, Max."

"You gotta come and be first lobster!"

Grady raised his eyebrows.

"I'm always first lobster," Max said loftily. He tossed the sponge back in the sink. "Come on. I'll introduce you to the next tradition."

In the dining room, Carly had already set up a board game on the table. Milo, Nora, and Logan sat around it, and Max gestured for Grady to sit next to him. "So, back when Logan and Nora and I were kids, Grandpa was in charge of keeping us entertained while everyone else cooked. And if you recall, Grandpa was a lobster fisherman...."

Apparently, the object of the game depended on your token. The lobster was trying to get to the sea. Everyone else—a butter pat, a lemon wedge, a trap-looking thing Max kept calling a "pot"—was trying to get to the lobster before it escaped. There were multiple paths, but you had to move your full roll in a single direction. The lobster only had to get as far as the sea, but everyone else needed an exact roll to catch the lobster. If they did, the lobster player was out and the one who'd caught him became the next lobster.

"I get to be the butter," Carly announced. She narrowed her eyes at Grady and then selected a token and handed it to him. "Uncle Grady, you can be the lobster cracker."

Nora stifled a laugh, and Logan cleared his throat and looked away. But Grady was torn between a sudden fascination with the redness in the apples of Max's cheeks and his own complicated reaction.

*Uncle* Grady. Obviously he wasn't, but what was he going to tell her? And it would be weird for a kid to start calling an adult by their first name, right?

He wasn't touching the significance of the lobster-cracker thing.

Fortunately, Linda chose that moment to swoop in with the wine bottle. "Who needs a refill?"

All the adults raised their glasses.

The game was raucous. Despite a few close calls—Grady had been sure it was over for Max when Logan and Milo cornered him down a dead-end path—eventually the lobster prevailed. By that time they'd finished another two bottles of wine between the seven adults, and the kids were begging Uncle Max to tuck them into bed.

"I should take Gru for his nighttime pee," Max said regretfully.

Under the table, Gru perked up his ears and wagged his tail.

"I'll take him," Grady offered. Max should enjoy as much time with the kids as he could. Clearly they had a mutual admiration society going on. Besides, Grady wanted some time alone with his thoughts.

He couldn't count the number of invitations he'd declined to his teammates' family holidays over the years. Even before he grew fed up with the Firebirds' management, he'd held a part of himself back from the team. Now he was starting to understand how that had impacted his life.

He barely had a relationship with most of his teammates. Plenty of the other players' kids called other guys on the team "uncle," but none of them had ever called Grady that. Carly was the first—the niece of the guy Grady had cheerfully remembered punching in the face not that long ago.

What had happened to him?

Grady thought he knew. When his parents died, he buried himself in hockey and used that as his armor against his feelings. There was no time to grieve when there were games to win. The only person he let in was Jess, because she was already family. That way he only had one person to lose—like there was a cap on potential suffering. And Jess was enough.

Until she wasn't. Until Max slid past his defenses like some kind of Trojan horse, and now here Grady was, being treated like family by his rival's parents, siblings, and niece and nephew, and thinking about how much Jess would love it. About whether it would be okay if he invited her along next year.

And now Grady was casually assuming he'd be welcomed back, when there was nothing at all casual about that assumption.

Gru butted against his leg, and Grady realized they'd reached the end of the sidewalk. He bent down to ruffle Gru's ears. "You're a good boy."

Gru nudged Grady's hand with his wet nose in acknowledgment.

When he returned, the house was mostly dark but not yet quiet—everyone must be upstairs. Max wasn't in the bedroom, so Grady picked up his wineglass and took it out to the pool, where he sat with his feet in the water.

The holidays were hard. He always found himself missing his parents more than usual. Only now he found himself missing them in a different way. He wished they could've met Max. He wanted to know what his mom would have thought about him, if she'd be scandalized to know about Max's tattoo or if she'd think it was hilarious. Would his dad be upset Grady was sleeping with one of his rival team's star players?

Jess might know. She'd gotten to interact with their parents as an adult. Grady wondered if it had felt like a more familiar, comfortable version of this—warm and safe and inviting and joyous. Full of love, even if it wasn't for him.

Except—wasn't it? Max treated Grady with the same teasing affection he had for his family. He'd invited Grady here to join them. He listened to Grady's stupid problems with his team, to his recaps of dates Grady had no business going on, and to Grady's guilt over Jess's disastrous love life.

He invited himself to Grady's house when he was lonely. He let Grady walk his dog. Everything Grady had wanted but never let himself reach for, not just sex but companionship, family, Max had put within his grasp. And he hadn't asked for anything in return. And the way he looked at Grady sometimes, when they were high, when Baller went to Anaheim instead of Grady, when Max fucked him the first time—

Four months ago, Grady could never have been comfortable on a night like tonight. Too many strangers, and he didn't have much experience with kids. He knew he came across as standoffish.

But it was easy to be around Max. To loosen up and let himself have fun.

Grady would've said it didn't make any sense, except he had the sneaking suspicion it *did*. Max had offered to help him navigate dating like a person instead of a prickly, perpetually annoyed asshole. The thing was, Grady was still a prickly, perpetually annoyed asshole. But Max treated him like a person anyway, and Grady didn't want to give that up.

Before the horror of the realization could fully dawn on him, the patio door slid open. "Hey. Mind if I join you?"

Grady wished he did mind. He shook his head. "Water's nice."

"How can you tell?" Max teased as he sat beside him. "You're barely touching it."

Without meaning to, Grady leaned over until their shoulders touched. His heart was still pounding too fast, but the panic receded. Max was loud and sometimes crass, but never cruel, and his arm against Grady's was warm and solid, just like the rest of him. "Didn't want Gru to freak out."

Max ran his fingers across the surface of the water. "No worries there. He's passed out cold on the bed you got him."

Grady leaned back on the cement pad and smiled at the sky. "That's from Santa."

"Oh, my mistake," Max laughed.

Grady reached for his wineglass only to discover it was empty. Tragic. But judging by the lethargy in his arms and legs, he didn't need any more alcohol.

"You all right?" Max asked after a minute. "I know we're not the most chill family. Not what you're used to."

"You're great," Grady said without thinking. But he wasn't ready to say the rest of it—didn't know how—so he added, "Your family, I mean."

Max let it slide. "So how come you're sitting out here in the dark by yourself?"

*Everyone else was upstairs.* But that wasn't the real reason. "Just thinking. Holidays are still hard. Not like they used to be, but...."

"I understand. This is only the third year we've played the game without my grandfather."

"Super Max?" Grady guessed.

Max's laughter blended softly into the night. "He was a Henry. He'd have loved that, though."

With Max's warmth beside him, the alcohol in Grady's blood seemed that much more potent. He succumbed to gravity and lay back against the cement. "How come you're always the lobster?"

Max laughed again. "What?"

"You're not a lobster. Lobsters have tough shells, and they snap." He made a little pincer motion with his hand. "You're, like, a fake lobster. Maybe you're only a lobster on the ice. Off the ice, you're soft." To demonstrate, he used his pincer to nip the flesh at Max's waist.

"How much did you have to drink?" Max sounded amused.

Grady ignored him. "I'm the lobster. I'm prickly."

"Oh yeah," Max said. "Look at you. You've got half a palm tree in your hair." He carefully carded his fingers over Grady's scalp. "Terrifying."

But now he was leaning over Grady, too close to ignore that softness any longer. It called to Grady's, a reassuring whisper that he could take off his armor. "I should be the lobster," Grady repeated quietly when Max's fingers traced down the side of his face. "You crack me open."

For a long moment Max held his gaze. Then he kissed him softly, slowly, his body braced over Grady's like a shield. Grady anchored himself with a hand on Max's shoulder and let the earth spin around them.

Eventually Max pulled away and stood. He held a hand down to Grady. "Come on. We should go inside. Santa can't come if you're not sleeping."

Grady let Max pull him up and lead him inside. He left the weight of his shell by the pool with his wineglass.


MAX WOKE up to his pillow rumbling quietly.

The room was still dark except for a faint glow that had to be Grady's cell phone. Max stretched slightly and got Grady's fingers threaded through his hair for his trouble.

He never wanted to get out of bed.

*You crack me open.* Max couldn't know exactly what Grady meant by that, and he wasn't going to ask tonight. But he couldn't ignore the way Grady'd looked at him when he said it.

And he definitely couldn't ignore the pounding in his own heart when he pulled slick fingers out of Grady's body and reached for a condom and Grady put his hand on his wrist and said, "Do we need…?"

They didn't. Max let the condom fall from nerveless fingers and slid in bare, hopelessly overwhelmed.

Max had spent his whole life around hockey players. He *was* one. It had never surprised him that Grady played things close to the chest.

But tonight a dam had broken, and now Grady was talking quietly on the phone in the middle of the night, still wet with Max's come, basically petting Max's head while Max used him as a body pillow.

"You could ask them about it," Grady said lowly.

If Max strained his ears, he could make out the female voice on the other end of the call—almost certainly Grady's sister Jess. Something about two women named Amanda and Polly and a ski chalet bedroom? He tilted his chin up to let Grady know he was awake, in case he wanted privacy.

Apparently he didn't. "Jess. I have no idea. It's weird, I'll give you that, but…."

Max inhaled and rested his head against Grady's chest again. He was glad his parents kept the air conditioner cranked, or this could be uncomfortable.

"What am I going to do? I can't send them back to their room to freeze—"

Max's brain did a record scratch, and he blinked a few times and started listening more closely. But the longer he listened, the funnier it got. There was no way it was a coincidence that Jess's ex-girlfriend and her new girlfriend had planned a vacation where everyone else had canceled, insisted Jess take the room with the bigger bed, and then *coincidentally* discovered that the heat in their bedroom didn't work.

He lifted his head again and reached up for the phone. "Gimme." Grady obviously had no clue what was happening here.

"What?" Grady said. "No, don't. Max—"

But Max already had the phone in his hand. "Jess. Hi. Did I hear you right?" He listed off the details he'd overheard.

He half expected her to ask who he was or why he'd been eavesdropping, but instead she said, "How is this my life?"

"No, I have a better question. Why are you asking *Grady* what to do?"

"Hey," Grady grumbled without pausing in his scalp massage.

Jess groaned. "Oh God, you're right. The man has the emotional intelligence of a garden snail."

"I'm very fond of him," Max said, because it seemed rude to agree out loud when Grady could hear him. "But listen. You're on vacation with your ex and her new girlfriend. It was supposed to be a group trip, but everyone else *supposedly* backed out at the last minute. Somehow, despite the fact that you're a single person on vacation with a couple, you got the bigger bedroom. And now your friends' heat is out and they're trying to bunk in with you. Kind of a coincidence, don't you think?"

It took a moment for it to sink in. Then Jess said, "Oh my God."

"You're either in a porno or the first-ever lesbian triad Hallmark Christmas Special."

"Oh my God," Jess repeated.

"Oh my God," whispered Grady.

"Bad news is you probably have to actually talk to them to figure out which one it is." Max considered. "Or you put on your sexiest pajamas and let the cards fall where they may."

"Holy shit."

"Merry Christmas!" he said cheerfully. "You want to talk to your brother again?"

She did, so Max passed the phone back and closed his eyes.

This time Grady didn't talk for long—he and Jess exchanged holiday greetings, and then she apologized for forgetting about time zones and promised she'd grill him about "Shithead—I mean *Max*" later.

Finally Grady set the phone on the nightstand, and the room fell back into darkness. "Sorry. Didn't mean to wake you at… three in the morning. Jesus Christ, Jess."

*Didn't mean to drool all over your chest in my sleep, but here we are.* "'S fine. Siblings, right?"

"Right." He settled deeper into the pillows and adjusted the sheets around them. "I thought women were supposed to be better at talking about their feelings."

"Eh," Max said. "Two of them are still hockey players." Best not set the bar *too* high.

Grady snorted. "Good point." He settled the hand that had been in Max's hair on the small of his back instead. "Are you seriously comfortable like that?"

"Mmm-hmm." He forced himself to raise his eyelids. "Why? Too heavy?" Only Max's head and part of his chest were resting on Grady—the rest was on the mattress or supported by pillows—but he wasn't exactly a featherweight.

"No. I have a weighted blanket at home, remember?"

"'Kay." Max closed his eyes again. "Night."

Christmas was a huge success. The house didn't have a fireplace, so they hung stockings off the breakfast bar, and Max's mom was all too happy to include one for Grady.

Grady took the stocking with his name on it with big, bright eyes and a smile that was a little brittle, and Max desperately wanted to watch him open it, but he felt too protective to let anyone else do the same, so he chased Milo and Carly around the living room and threatened to eat their candy while Grady pulled out the usual stocking staples—toothbrush and toothpaste, socks, lip balm, an organic chocolate bar (Max might've helped with that one).

He wasn't sure if the hugs that resulted surprised Grady or his parents more.

Max's heart did a little somersault just from watching it.

Then Nora sat down next to him at the breakfast bar and lowered her voice to a conspiratorial whisper. "So you sent him to a dentist, eh?"

Max shook himself and turned toward her. "What?"

She gestured with her head toward Grady. "For a night guard. The shape of his jaw's changed. No buildup of muscle means no more teeth grinding."

"I didn't. I've never seen him wear one either." Not that he spent every night with Grady, but he seemed like the kind of guy who'd wear the night guard in company anyway, even if it was deeply unsexy, because it was for his health, and would glower menacingly if Max ever dared mention it. Now that Max thought about it, he'd never heard Grady grind his teeth at night.

Nora was right, though. Grady's jaw did look narrower.

Max could feel her gaze on the side of his face when she said, "Huh. He must've figured out a really good way to manage his stress, I guess."

She went to the fridge to grab more orange juice, but Max sat there for he didn't know how long, wondering if he could get up and press a kiss there, feel the difference under his lips.

"Uncle *Max*," Carly said, like she'd been trying to get his attention for several minutes. "Can we open your gifts now?"

Max shook himself into the present. "Hmmm." He glanced at Tanya and Logan over Carly's shoulder and got a slight head shake. "After breakfast. Why don't you and Milo help me set the table?"

By early afternoon they'd cleaned up the wrapping paper massacre and decamped to the beach, which was too cold for swimming but ideal for lounging. Milo and Carly took turns burying each other up to their waists, impervious to the slightly chilly—for Florida—weather, as any New Brunswicker would be.

Grady went back to the house to catch up with Jess, which left Max free to take Gru for a stroll down the beach and organize his thoughts.

*You crack me open.*

The words echoed in his head. He felt them in his chest.

He'd never expected Grady to let him in. He was pretty sure *Grady* never expected to let Max in. But something had given. Something had changed. And now....

A lot could happen. They were still professional hockey players, and Grady was looking for a trade. But they'd still see each other a few times a year, and they would still have summers off. They could train together.

Without intending to, he ended up back at the house. Gru beelined to his water bowl for a long drink, and Max hung his leash by the door and went looking for Grady. He found him in their bedroom, sitting on the bed and doing something on his phone.

"Hey."

Grady put the phone down and smiled. "Hey."

Max closed the door behind him and sat on the end of the bed. "How's Jess?"

"Giddy," he said wryly. "Guess they worked everything out."

Grinning, Max crawled up the mattress to lie next to Grady. "Awesome. Merry Christmas to her."

"Please don't make a joke about Christmas coming more than once a year."

"Of course not," Max said. "That would be derivative."

Grady turned onto his side and bit his lip, and Max took a deep breath. Time to lay the cards on the table.

"We should talk—"

"Do you think we can—"

Their eyes met. Max felt his cheeks go warm even as Grady flushed too.

Then the back door slid open and someone said, "Gru, *no!*" and Max groaned and pulled a pillow over his head.

Grady rescued him from suffocating himself. "Maybe when we have a little more privacy?" he suggested. "We play in Newark this week. Meet you after the game?"

"Yeah." Max could feel his face smiling a little too widely, but he couldn't do anything about it. "Sounds good."

"Are you in town for New Year's? Jess is bringing her girlfriends."

"I'll have to double-check we're not flying out a day early, but I think I can make it."

"Cool," Grady said. He was such a dork. "It's a date."

Max's heart did a stupid little flip, like it thought it was a figure skater instead of a hockey player.

"Max! Come get your dog!"

Groaning, he pulled the pillow back over his head. "Next year I'm going to Cancun without them."

For a moment Grady said nothing. Then he lifted the corner of the pillow. "Does that mean I can have your share of the lobster?"


GRADY EXPECTED to leave Miami more than ready to go home. After three full days of not only Max but Max's family, who were all variations on the theme of Max, Grady thought he'd be—well, Maxed out.

But he was only half right. He didn't mind leaving behind Linda, Big Max, Logan, Tanya, Nora, and the kids. But he couldn't seem to keep his hands off *his* Max. The morning of the twenty-sixth, they spent half an hour in their bedroom with the door closed and made out until their airport shuttle arrived.

Never in a million years could Grady have seen this coming.

He felt kind of stupid about that. It seemed obvious in retrospect that he'd spent the past few months falling for Max. Max was the one he wanted to talk to about his terrible dates, and the standard he hadn't been willing to admit he was holding them to. Max was funny and offbeat and kind in an irritating way, like a dog who could tell when you were sad and kept putting its drooly head in your lap for pets.

And he was—though Grady could never admit this either—*silly*. In Max's eyes, the world and all the people in it were there to poke fun at. The only person who'd seen that side of Grady in the past fifteen years was Jess, who couldn't reject him because he was the only family she had. Being with Max gave Grady permission to be silly too. He hadn't realized how much he'd missed that freedom.

It turned out there was such a thing as *pleasantly surprised*. Max still got on his nerves, only now Grady felt all sappy about it.

Finally the alarm on Max's phone went off and they couldn't put it off any longer. They gathered their bags and opened the bedroom door.

Nora looked up from reading on the couch, raised her eyebrows, and cleared her throat.

"Subtle," Max said.

Grady thought maybe she had a point. Max's chin and neck were blotchy red with beard burn.

"Not the word I'd use," Nora said cheerfully. Then she started singing "Leaving on a Jet Plane."

There was a pileup in the driveway as everyone lined up to say goodbye while the driver handled the luggage. Even Grady got hugged within an inch of his life, though the embraces took less time than Max's did. Max was still talking to his parents when Grady made it to Milo and Carly at the end of the line.

Milo was shier than his sister, and Grady didn't think the kid had spoken more than two sentences to him outside the board game on Christmas Eve and a thank-you for his gift. So it knocked Grady for a loop when the kid squinted up at him in the sunshine and asked, very seriously, "Uncle Grady, are you and Uncle Max going to get married?"

Grady's first impulse was to say no very loudly. He'd spent the past fifteen years determined to keep everyone he could at arm's length because he couldn't lose what he didn't have.

His second thought was, *I should be so lucky*, which made him want to run screaming into the Atlantic. It was a wild swing from his gut reaction and a huge leap from where they stood now—they hadn't even used the word *relationship*, never mind defined it—to that potential future.

Somehow his feet stayed planted and his mouth stayed shut, for which he was grateful. No one else seemed to have heard the question.

Grady took a deep breath and held it for a moment. Then he pitched his voice low enough not to be overheard and hoped he wasn't jinxing anything. "Tell you what. If I'm around for Christmas next year, ask me again."

And then that was it. Grady went home and slept like a log. The Miami house Max had rented was nice enough, but the mattress in their bedroom left something to be desired.

Practice on the twenty-seventh felt like a new beginning. Grady didn't know if it was because he was in a good mood or everyone else was, but the guys were flying. Even Fletch, the dour-faced defenseman Grady usually resented for not pulling his weight, brought his A-game energy.

"You have a good break, Ace?"

Grady smiled at him, and it felt natural for the first time in a long time. "Yeah, actually. You?"

"Really good. Nice to catch up with the whole family."

Not long ago, the words would've made Grady bristle, like it was a reminder that everyone else *had* a whole family, and he only had Jess. Looking at it from the other side of a mental breakthrough, Grady couldn't detect any intentional malice.

"How's your sister doing?"

"Jess?" For a minute the question didn't register as being related. "She's great. I'm picking her up at the airport after this." Fletch didn't need to know about her relationship situation, so he left out the bit about her girlfriends.

Frowning, Fletch said, "Oh. I assumed she was with you for Christmas. What did you do?"

*Went to Florida and accidentally got a boyfriend.* "Vacation in Miami."

"Oh, good call. We'll get enough of the snow."

It was the friendliest conversation Grady'd had with the guy in years.

He was still in a good mood when he picked up Jess, Polly, and Amanda from the airport. Jess flung herself into his arms like a kid. Her grin stretched from ear to ear. Grady didn't need to ask what had put her in such a good mood.

He remembered Amanda from the first time Jess dated her; she was a tall, pretty blond with broad features and an easy smile. "Merry Christmas, Baby Armstrong."

Grady hugged her too. "Good to see you, Amanda. Merry Christmas."

"And this is Polly."

"Nice to meet you." Polly was probably a normal height when she wasn't standing between Jess and Amanda, who were both close to six feet. She wore a nose stud and a bright red undercut.

Grady might need to put a king bed in his guest room. "Same," he said. "Car's this way."

Mercifully, Jess held off on interrogating him until Polly and Amanda excused themselves to go to bed. Grady needed to go to sleep soon too—the Firebirds would play Pittsburgh tomorrow and the Monsters the next night—but he wanted to talk to Jess more.

As soon as Polly and Amanda were upstairs, Jess turned to him in the armchair and curled her legs up in her seat. "So. Tell me about *Max*."

He'd thought for sure she would realize Max meant Max Lockhart, the hockey player Grady had been bitching about for years. But nothing in her expression or tone suggested any suspicion. Then again, she probably hadn't thought much about Grady's love life for the past few days. "What do you want to know?"

"Well, for starters, when did he get upgraded from Shithead?"

That one was easy. "Officially? The night my trade to Anaheim fell through."

She put her chin on her folded arms and leaned closer. "Why then?"

"He found out before I did." Grady thought back to that night. "The game was a shitshow, but I kept thinking to myself, 'At least it'll be over soon,' because Erika had told me a trade was in the works. Then I got home and Max had TSN on and they were running the story about Baller getting traded." He huffed. "He could've been an asshole about it. I can't say I wouldn't have been, if I were him—"

"If you were him?" Jess interrupted. She narrowed her eyes. "Wait a second, are you saying Max is also a hockey player?"

*There* it was. "Yeah."

"And he was hanging out at your house instead of playing? Does he play in the AHL or something?"

"No." Grady braced himself. "He was injured."

It still took her a moment. "Grady," Jess said slowly, "are you sleeping with *Max Lockhart*?"

He couldn't read her expression. "Surprise?"

"What the fuck! Grady!" She ran a hand down her face. Okay, that didn't fill him with confidence. He'd thought she'd be happy for him. "Since when?"

"World Cup."

"What!"

"It's your fault," he accused. "You're the one who downloaded Grindr instead of an actual dating app—"

"Oh my God."

"And then Max and I matched, and he didn't believe I was really me because I used my headshot from NHL.com. Apparently that's a no-no—"

"Oh my *God*!"

"So he said if you're really Grady Armstrong then prove it, and one thing led to another...."

"*Oh my God*!"

This was getting rude. Grady was only dating one guy he used to hate. Jess had started dating her ex-girlfriend *and* her ex-girlfriend's girlfriend, and he was being way more chill about that. "Anyway, the sex was"—great, amazing, transcendent—"good. So we kept hooking up. And I explained why I had Grindr in the first place, and Max helped me download an *actual* dating app. But it turns out I suck at dating, so Max was giving me pointers—"

Jess made an incredulous noise.

Finally Grady stopped trying to explain. "What? You asked." Besides, she was the one who'd ended up in a porny Lifetime movie.

"Yeah, but you just... trusted him?"

"Believe me," he said, "nothing Max suggested could've made the situation any worse."

That, at least, Jess seemed to accept. "Okay, but dating a rival player who once *broke your arm*?"

"That was an accident." Of that, Grady had no doubt. "Look, it just happened. Like I said, I found out Baller got traded instead of me, and Max could've been a dick about it, but he said he was sorry and the situation sucked and then he asked if I wanted to get high."

"Grady!"

If she was reacting like that over a little recreational marijuana, he definitely wasn't telling her he'd let Max fuck him bare. "Don't even, Jess. You live in Colorado. It was pot. We ended up talking and he invited me to Christmas with his family." Jess didn't need to know she was the whole reason Grady had gone in the first place.

"Just like that?"

"I don't know what you mean 'just.' We'd been sleeping together for months by then." Grady squared his shoulders. "I get that you're surprised—I was too—but Max is great. I mean, he's the one who figured out what was going on with you and Amanda and Polly, right?"

From her expression, this hadn't occurred to her. She looked like she'd bitten into a lemon. "I guess."

Grady didn't know what else to tell her, or how. *He feels safe? He's kind and generous and makes me laugh? He helps me remember what it's like to be able to rely on someone other than you?* Everything seemed too emotional, or too private, or too… damning. He didn't know how to say those things to Jess without her taking it personally. She'd done the best she could raising him. He'd always be grateful for that.

So he settled for, "I like him a lot, okay? He's a different person off the ice. I mean, he's the same, but he doesn't take any of it seriously, if that makes sense. I could learn a few things."

Finally Jess cracked a smile. "Who are you and what have you done with my baby brother?"

"Hey," he protested. "A guy can't grow as a person?"

"*A guy* can, sure. But you?" Her smile softened. "I'm sorry I'm being so… whatever. It's not like I don't have teammates who ended up with someone from a rival team. But I thought the two of you hated each other."

Grady shrugged sheepishly. "So did I. But Max never did."

Jess reached out and squeezed his hand. "I worry about you, is all. Big-sister thing. I don't want to see you get hurt."

"I know." Grady had worried about that in the beginning too. "He's not going to fuck me over on purpose, okay? We had that talk way early in the…." *Relationship.* God, he'd been dumb.

Judging by Jess's raised eyebrow, she thought so too. "Oh? What did he do?"

It didn't seem fair to hedge now. "He brought up our, uh, off-ice activities on the ice. I said we could fuck around off the ice or on it but we weren't going to do both."

She snorted. "Nice phrasing." Then she shook her head. "Okay, tell you what. I'll reserve judgment until I meet him in person."

"Great," he said immediately, "because I invited him for New Year's."

"Grady!"

She was going to wear out his name at this rate. "Come on. It's not fair if you get two dates and I don't even get one."

"Fine." She shot him a small smile. "But I better not hear you having sex."

"No promises."

The next day Grady and the Firebirds played their best game of the season—maybe the best game they'd played in years. He was thrilled to get to do it while his sister and her girlfriends watched from glass seats. Barny stopped all twenty-seven shots for his first-ever career shutout, and the whole team mobbed him afterward.

There was no way Grady could skip out on the celebration, so he texted Jess that he'd be late and not to wait up.

Then he texted Max. *Barny pitched his first no-hitter. Go easy on us tomorrow, we're gonna be hungover.*

*send me a drunk naked selfie and ill think about it*

No, he wouldn't, but Grady smiled anyway.

The twenty-eighth dragged. Grady wanted to prove to himself— okay, and Jess—that he and Max were on the same page. Ever since she'd voiced her concerns, he'd been a little on edge. It was normal to be nervous before a define-the-relationship talk, right? And Jess had him second-guessing himself.

But he knew what he wanted. He thought he knew what Max wanted. He was pretty sure it was the same thing. The last step was admitting it out loud to each other.

And he'd have his chance after the game.

"All right, boys, just like last night, eh?" Coop said as they headed onto the ice in Newark. Grady bumped his fist the same as everyone else.

Monsters fans hated Grady the way Firebirds fans hated Max— they booed every time he set foot on the ice, every time he touched the puck. They cheered when someone knocked him on his ass. But the noise never bothered him. It always felt right.

Tonight it sent a frisson of energy down his spine. Grady caught Max's eye during warm-ups and Max winked at him. Grady skated away laughing.

If anyone on the team thought his good mood suspicious, no one said anything to Grady. Maybe they attributed it to last night's win, to momentum. Either way, it felt good to give the Monsters a fight for once. Puck possession and scoring chances were about even going into the second, with the score tied at zero. Coop spent two minutes in the box for tripping Max, the Monsters' goaltender got slapped with a slashing penalty for trying to break Grady's ankle—just another rivalry grudge match. Grady's bruises had bruises and his blood sang in his veins.

Early in the second, he and Max got into a puck battle against the boards. Grady was fighting for possession with everything he had, and if Max's cursing was any indication, he was too. After fifteen seconds Max let out a giggle at the absurdity—they were wedged into the corner with their sticks on the puck, neither of them giving ground. It *was* kind of ridiculous, enough that Grady found himself fighting back a laugh too.

But that was all the window Max needed to leverage Grady's stick off the puck and flick it back to his team. Grady cursed and took off for the defensive zone with Max on his heels.

He shouldn't have let his guard down, but he couldn't blame Max for it. Besides, he might've lost that battle anyway. He'd win the next one.

With a few minutes left in the period, Grady chased the puck into the corner and got the business end of one of the Monsters' sticks across the cheek. The crowd roared as the ref blew the whistle, and Grady pulled off his glove to touch tentative fingers to the sting on his face. They came away bloody, which meant a power play for the Firebirds.

Grady went to the bench to have the cut glued shut and then skated back to the dot to take the faceoff.

Hedgie lined up across from him, smirking. "Hey, Ace. You have a good Christmas?"

Max probably told him they spent it together. That was a normal thing to tell a friend, and it wasn't like he was being mean. He was making small talk, hoping it'd throw Grady off. That wasn't Max's fault. He couldn't control what his teammates did.

Grady exhaled sharply, rapped his stick on the ice, and bent over to signal he was ready for the linesman to drop the puck. "Better than yours."

But uneasiness ate at him, even after the Firebirds scored. Could Jess have been right? Had Grady made a mistake trusting Max?

Doubt crept in. He did his best to focus on the game, but two minutes after the Firebirds scored, Grady turned the puck over to a rookie defenseman who had no business picking his pocket, and the Monsters tied the game.

He took another deep breath. Things happened. He couldn't control everything.

Coop patted him on the shoulder as he went back to the bench, a show of wordless support.

Grady let himself lean into it and refocused on the game.

The clock ticked away to the end of the period, and Grady went over the boards for the last shift. All of Newark jeered when he got the puck on his stick and crossed the blue line into the offensive zone.

He was ready for the hard check to his shoulder—he'd already dropped the puck back for Coop.

But he couldn't account for his skate blade catching in a crack in the ice, and he went down hard. He lost his stick, and the player who'd hit him tripped and fell too. He landed half on top of Grady and knocked the breath out of him.

"Fuck. Jesus," Hedgie said. Somewhere in the distance, Grady registered the horn signaling the end of the period. "Think I just cracked you like that lobster you like so much."

Grady's mind went blank.

Oh God.

*You crack me open.*

Max had told him.

Shaken, he got to his feet and collected his stick, ignoring Hedgie. Coop met him at the tunnel, concern etched on his features. "Hey, you okay?"

"Fine," Grady said, numb. Nothing hurt—not his chest or his arm where Hedgie had landed on it or the cut on his face. "I'm fine," he repeated when Coop tried to catch his elbow, and jerked his arm away.

Coop raised his hands. "Okay! All right, I just—"

"Armstrong!"

At his coach's voice, Grady glanced over.

"Trainer!" Coach barked. "Get yourself checked out."

Fair enough—they'd want to make sure he hadn't injured himself, disinfect his face again, and reglue the liquid stitches. As a bonus, Coop would have to stop looking at him like Grady might break at any second. "Yes, Coach."

But even after the trainer and the team doctor had checked him out, they kept Grady in the trainer's room. Did they know he was having a personal crisis? Had he somehow let on that he'd developed feelings for Max? Was he going to get chewed out for that? That might almost be better, if someone else yelled at him. Then at least he could stop being so hard on himself.

He felt sick, but he knew he hadn't hit his head. This was a different kind of sickness, even if it was as disorienting as a concussion.

He'd trusted Max. He'd let Max in—he'd let down his guard and he'd…. Should he get tested? Had Grady put himself in physical danger, as well as emotional?

The third period had to have started by now. Why hadn't the trainers released him? Grady clenched his hands into fists. He needed to get back on the ice. He needed to prove this mistake wouldn't affect him. He—

The door opened to reveal not one of the trainers but Dan, their most junior coach. "Armstrong. Hey."

Fucking finally. Grady pushed himself off the table. "Am I good to go?"

"Kind of." Dan smiled softly. "Looks like you're getting what you wanted."

Grady blinked. So far nothing tonight had gone the way he wanted it to.

Then Dan said, "Hit the showers. You're on the next flight to LA. You've been traded."

# Third Period

AFTER THE game, Max sat in the locker room, waiting for his phone to buzz. There was no word from anyone on Grady or why he hadn't returned to the ice after the second, and he was worried. Surely Grady hadn't been hurt too badly after Hedgie basically fell on him. He'd gotten up and skated away under his own power.

Anything could happen in hockey. Max had heard enough horror stories—someone he knew in juniors had taken a fall like Grady's while in the early stages of appendicitis. The pressure caused the organ to burst, and he'd spent a month in the hospital with sepsis. If Hedgie had landed wrong, he might've cracked one of Grady's ribs, punctured a lung.

And no one on Grady's team knew they were together—or *would* be together, hopefully, if they ever managed to talk—so Max was in the dark with no one to give him an update.

He was in the middle of sending Grady a third text—the first had been *r u ok?* followed by *ill kiss it better later*—when a notification popped up.

Max was halfway through dismissing it when he realized it was a trade notification. *Firebirds trade Armstrong to LA Condors.*

His heart hit his knees. No wonder Grady hadn't written back. He was probably on a plane by now, heading to the opposite coast. About as far from Max as he possibly could be and still play in the NHL.

Max's stomach turned over. His palms felt clammy, and he wiped them on his suit pants.

Grady wasn't going to come tonight, obviously. They wouldn't get to have that talk. But would he still want to be with Max?

And why hadn't Grady texted him to let him know he wasn't going to make it?

A quiet voice in his head whispered that Grady had wanted this trade all along. Maybe Max had only been a distraction from his unhappiness with the Firebirds. Now that he'd been traded, he didn't need Max anymore.

Max pushed those thoughts away. Grady wouldn't do that to him. His nighttime confession by the pool had rung with truth. Even if it hadn't, he'd asked—he'd trusted—Max to fuck him, skin to skin. Max knew Grady's type. If Max had never done that before, Grady hadn't either. So Grady had feelings for Max. He was surprised by the trade, which Max couldn't blame him for. Midgame trades for players of Grady's caliber didn't happen every day or even every season. It was all very dramatic and only reinforced Max's low opinion of the Firebirds' management. They clearly didn't give a fuck about their players.

Anyway, Grady was probably working through some conflicting feelings. Max could give him space for now.

But once he was on the opposite side of the country, how much more space could he need?

GRADY DID not have a restful flight.

He called Jess on his way to the airport. She'd already heard the news and cursed up a storm over how the Firebirds' front office had handled it. But on the plus side, at least Grady had someone on hand to pack up some of his things and ship them to California, and to arrange for his houseplants to get watered.

Erika called as he checked in for his flight. "I'm sorry to do this to you." She sounded like she meant it. "Talks only started an hour or so before the game. They were going to wait until it was over to make it official, but then Hedgewood fell on you and they worried that you'd get injured and it would fall through. I knew you wouldn't want that."

Grady wouldn't have wanted that a month ago. Did he want it now?

He couldn't say. He didn't hate the idea of leaving the Firebirds. In hindsight he realized he was part of the problem, that he'd let the chip on his shoulder about management's bad decisions color his interactions with his teammates. He could've tried to make the best of the situation. Now he'd never have the chance. But at least he knew better than to make the same mistake in LA.

If it weren't for Max....

Grady pursed his lips, but he couldn't help thinking about it. If Hedgie hadn't hinted that he knew things Grady told Max in private—deeply personal things Grady hadn't even fully voiced to Max—*during a game,* when Grady had asked Max to make sure that never happened…. If Grady weren't so angry and hurt, and sick over his own recklessness—

The flight attendant came by Grady's row. Grady eyed the tiny bottles of whiskey but asked for water. Flying made him dehydrated, and he wouldn't sleep much tonight as it was.

He downed the water and let himself finish the thought.

If Grady didn't care so much about Max, this trade would make him happy. The Condors were a strong Cup contender. They had a solid core, with lots of guys in their prime and enough talented younger players to give them staying power for years. They'd lost the Cup Final just the year before. The team was primed to win and win now—no more endless rebuilds.

So the trade didn't bother him, even though being sequestered in a trainer's room, told nothing, and then traded midgame made him grind his teeth.

Which meant his turmoil was because of Max, who'd betrayed his trust on a fundamental level. It was like he'd flayed Grady open and put his guts on display.

Grady had spent so long avoiding attachment because he was afraid of getting hurt. Well, now he hurt, all right. He should've stuck to his guns. He should've told Max to go fuck himself back in September.

Jess was right.

At least she wasn't the kind to say *I told you so*.

The flight attendant came by again and refilled his water glass. This time Grady sipped it more slowly and tried to concentrate on releasing the ball of tension that had coiled in his stomach. His jaw ached, and he rubbed it distractedly.

In a few hours, he'd land in LA. Someone from the Condors would meet him at the airport and drive him to his temporary accommodations for a few hours of sleep. Then he'd meet his new team, learn a new coach's system, and look for somewhere more permanent to live. He didn't have time to dwell on Max.

So he took out his phone and pulled up Max's contact.

A handful of texts had come through before Grady put his phone in airplane mode. *R u ok?* and *ill kiss it better*. And then, ten minutes later, *Fuck just saw the news. Call me when you can? XOX.*

As if nothing had happened.

Grady slid his thumb over to the three dots in the top right corner. He only hesitated for a moment.

Then he hit Block Contact.


MAX GAVE it an entire day before he freaked out about the radio silence from Grady. Sure, a trade to another conference put a crimp in their relationship, but if that was going to be a deal-breaker, Max deserved to hear that from Grady instead of having to guess.

With his stomach knotted, he took out his phone and opened a text.

*hope cali is treating you well*

Was that too spineless? Too passive-aggressive? Max deleted it and tried again.

*guess I have to take a rain check on that talk*

God, no, that reeked of desperation and self-pity. Max couldn't make Grady's trade about him.

This was so stupid. What did he *want* to say?

*I wish you hadn't been traded.*

*I miss you.*

*I was looking forward to spending the rest of my life getting you to pretend you're annoyed with me.*

*I know all this started with a stupid bet, but I think I'm in love with you.*

*I think you're in love with me too.*

Max couldn't say any of that—not when Grady was ghosting him, and even if he wasn't. Max had made all the moves—the bet, the follow-up, the offer to help Grady learn how to date. He'd shown up at Grady's house. He'd invited Grady to Christmas.

Never had Grady reached out to him first. Max should scrounge up a modicum of self-respect and wait for Grady to text him this time.

But Max wasn't very good at doing what he should, so he tried one more time.

*i guess were not rivals anymore.*

He couldn't decide if that sounded sappy or pathetic, but he couldn't spend another minute thinking about it or he'd lose his mind. He sent the text, put his phone on Do Not Disturb, and did his best to go to sleep.

In the morning he crawled out of bed to make breakfast. He didn't have much of an appetite, but he still had to eat to keep his energy up. He got out the eggs and put some bread in the toaster.

He took out his phone, thinking maybe a new recipe from the internet would make breakfast more appetizing. He was opening the pantry to get the dried chives when the text message icon lit up.

Fucking finally. Weak with relief, Max opened it.

But it wasn't from Grady at all. *Your message could not be delivered.*

Could not be delivered.

Grady had blocked him.

Max stood in the kitchen, numb.

The UV garden Grady gave him for Christmas had a bright light that was often still on when Max went to bed, so he'd put it in the pantry, where he could close the door. That meant he didn't look at it every day. Today, when he put his phone down with a shaky hand, for the first time, he saw tender little shoots coming up.

He grabbed the chives and firmly closed the pantry door.

But no matter how much he tried to ignore it, suddenly the house felt like it was full of ghosts, all of them Grady's. When he put the bowl he'd cracked the eggs in into the dishwasher, he gritted his teeth, remembering Grady sitting at his kitchen table, researching which model to get. Max loved that dishwasher.

Now he wanted to rip it out.

The frying pan he was using to make breakfast was the same one he'd scrambled eggs in that morning. It matched exactly the one in Grady's kitchen in Philadelphia.

Gru's bed in the corner of the living room, just visible from the stove, had been a gift from Grady. Gru was lying on it right now.

Even later tonight, when Max went upstairs to go to bed, he couldn't escape, because Grady's memory was all over his bedroom. He was even in the shower.

Max should throw all that stuff out. But Gru loved that bed. And it wasn't easy to throw away a dishwasher. And that was his *favorite frying pan*, goddammit.

But the UV garden could go. Those tiny sprouts didn't mean anything to Max. In fact, he wanted them out of his house right the fuck now.

He threw open the kitchen pantry and yanked the cord out of the outlet. Then he grabbed the garden in both hands and carried it into the garage, where he threw it against the floor to smash it into pieces.

But he couldn't leave it like that. Gru could cut himself. So Max snatched the broom off the wall and furiously swept the broken plastic into a dustbin. Then he dumped everything in the garbage.

By the time he finished, the kitchen had filled with smoke. The moment Max opened the door, the smoke alarm went off.

The eggs he'd left on the stove had melded with the frying pan. There was no saving either of them.

Max's eyes stung. He told himself it was from the smoke. "Fuck." He swiped his hand over his face and squeezed his eyes shut.

Then he threw the frying pan in the garage trash too and went to get Gru's leash. He could try breakfast again after a walk.


GRADY SPENT New Year's jet-lagged.

His new captain was a defenseman named Howard Barclay. He was all of nineteen and still had acne and went by the imaginative nickname of Dawg.

Dawg did not invite Grady to a New Year's party at his place after Grady's first home game as a Condor. Grady figured that was because Dawg lived in a white-walled apartment with enough furniture to seat one and couldn't legally buy alcohol. Instead, Grady's new goalie, Mitch, invited him to the team gathering at his place. Grady went and enjoyed himself, even if he did spend half an hour petting Mitch's idiotic cocker spaniel, but he caught a cab back to his hotel at twelve thirty, already gritty-eyed.

Being around people was better than dwelling on the party he'd have had back in Philly, with Jess and the girls and Max and maybe Gru.

But when he got back to the hotel, he found himself dwelling on it anyway. He couldn't fall asleep.

He hated himself for it, but after twenty minutes of tossing and turning, he took out his phone and opened Instagram. Max might be an asshole, but Gru hadn't done anything wrong, and Grady missed him too.

Except he didn't see any posts from Gru on his feed, and when he searched for the profile, only a little gray box appeared. *No posts yet.*

Gru's Instagram was public.

Max had blocked him.

Grady put his phone back down and scrubbed his hands over his face.

Now he was back to thinking about Max. He'd made an appointment for a blood draw on the third, even though it was probably too soon to know anything. How could Max have touched him the way he did, and been there for him like he was, and turned Grady into this version of himself who could make people like him, and then betray him like that? *Why* would he do it?

It didn't make any sense.

He curled up on his side and forced himself to go to sleep.

He woke up January 1 groggy and disoriented, with his temples and face throbbing, and reached for his phone to check the time. He had a handful of New Year's wishes from teammates—not just Firebirds and Condors, but Team USA guys too. Hedgie had sent a middle finger, but that wasn't uncommon. Grady deleted it without thinking about it, because if he did, he'd get sucked down into a festering swell of heartbreak and resentment.

Baller had sent *HEY HAPPY NEW YEAR. We should get sushi sometime, you in????*

That, at least, Grady could seize on as a distraction. *Aren't we supposed to be rivals now?*

He expected it to be a while before Baller texted back—it was pretty early—but maybe he had practice or maybe you didn't get to sleep in very much when you had a kid, because he got a reply almost right away. *Bro we could go on a date to Disneyland and no one would even notice. Ask me how I know.*

Then, a moment later, *Ok my husband would notice but you get the point.*

Grady's schedule for the day included looking at houses with his Realtor, because when you were staring down that kind of commission you didn't worry about holidays, but he was free for dinner. Baller volunteered to make a reservation.

He spent a conscientious five minutes in the shower—the water conservation would take getting used to—then grabbed a bite in the hotel restaurant and met his Realtor out front.

Every one of his teammates had an opinion on the listings he looked through online, but Mitch was the judgiest and most helpful. *Who has that much lawn in LA???* he texted after Grady sent him the third one. *Fucking irresponsible smh.* He shut down another as "soulless." Grady agreed. He'd rather live somewhere with character. The others were too far from the arena.

So the list of properties to look at wasn't long—just three Grady had picked out based on meticulous research of the neighborhoods, amenities, and location. He'd made up his mind to put in an offer on the third, but then his agent asked if he wanted to come with her to a fourth property she was just taking the pictures for prior to listing.

It was only two blocks from the third property, and Grady wasn't ready to be alone with his thoughts, so he agreed and they pulled into the driveway of an older two-story white stucco home with a red tile roof, half of which was covered in solar panels. The front yard was landscaped with drought-resistant plants. Grady squinted up at the roofline and made out what might be a rooftop patio.

It was a beautiful house. Open and airy, with plenty of natural light for Grady's house plants. It boasted several environmentally friendly features he'd specifically looked for in the other places, and the setup— with a master suite on the south side of the house, common areas in the middle, and a guest suite on the north—made perfect sense for Jess's visits.

He held his tongue while his Realtor took pictures, but he couldn't stop staring at the backyard, which had a lap pool and lounge chairs and threw him forcibly back to Christmas in Florida with Max.

The house was perfect. The patio had built-in planters where he could grow his vegetables year-round. The owners had planted clover in the backyard, which meant no watering or mowing—"And it's not affected by dog urine," the Realtor added when she finished explaining why it was a good choice. "Do you have a dog?"

Grady didn't have a dog, but maybe he should finally get one. His life had been too empty for too long.

It took him two tries to manage, "I'd like to make an offer."

The ensuing paperwork made him late for his reservation with Baller, but this was a common enough occurrence in LA that he didn't mention it.

"Took the liberty," he said when Grady arrived, and nodded at a tall sweating beer glass.

Grady collapsed into the booth across from him. "You're a saint."

Baller hooted. "I'm telling Gabe you said that." In a polo shirt and shorts, he looked relaxed and at home. The restaurant he'd chosen was some kind of Mexican-sushi-fusion thing, and when the server came around, he spoke to her in rapid, familiar Spanish for a few minutes before asking if Grady knew what he wanted to order.

Grady raised an eyebrow. "You eat here often?"

"Yeah, I mean, I kind of hate our kitchen here, so probably once a week." He grinned.

"It's more like twice a week," the server corrected fondly. "But usually he brings the baby for me to coo at."

"You'll have to make do with Grady this time."

"Why don't you order for me," Grady told him. "I'm not picky."

Baller made puppy eyes at the server, who rolled hers. "I'll bring the usual."

"Thanks, Carla!" Then he turned back to Grady. "So, California. How's it feel? Was the trade everything you wanted?"

*Not really.* But it would be embarrassing to admit that Grady had been part of the problem all along—or at least he hadn't been part of the solution. "I like the team so far," he said instead. "Everyone's been nice. Dawg's a bit... young."

"He's so earnest, though," Baller said, propping his chin on his hand. "He *believes*. It's adorable. And the name is the icing on the cake. I mean, Howard Barclay. It's like his parents were expecting a golden retriever."

Grady smiled. "So you've met him."

"Just to play against. Gabe used to put on his press conferences whenever I whined about being captain, so I could hear what an old man I sounded like." His mouth twisted in obvious affection. "Asshole."

"How do you like not being the man anymore?"

"Oh, it's weird for sure, but the Fish are fun. Everyone knows I'm here as a rental, but they don't treat me like it." He eyed Grady cautiously. "I kind of thought you might be mad I ended up here instead of you."

"No," Grady said immediately. "Come on, it's not like you orchestrated it."

"True."

The conversation stopped for a moment as Carla delivered two plates of appetizers—some kind of gyoza thing and veggie tempura. Curious, Grady pulled one of the dumplings onto an appetizer plate and bit into it, surprised to find it filled with Mexican spiced pork. Delicious. He made an appreciative noise.

"Right?" Baller said around a mouthful of tempura. "Anyway. What else is new with you? Did you figure out your enemy-with-benefits situation?"

Swallowing the gyoza—and his emotions—gave him an extra few seconds to figure out how to respond. But while the gyoza stayed down, the feelings refused. He thumbed the condensation on his beer glass. "Not really."

"What do you mean, not really?" Baller pushed the plate to the side and leaned across the table, as though he could sustain himself on hockey player gossip. If anyone could do it, it would be him.

What had Baller said when Grady had asked, back in November? *Unless you want to put a ring on it*.... Except Max didn't want that. Grady had thought he did, but he'd been wrong. If Grady had taken Baller's advice on the subject, he could've figured that out in November and been over this by now. "I mean maybe I should've asked for your advice after all."

Maybe.

"Oh shit. So what happened?" He backtracked. "I mean, if you want to talk about it."

Sadly it turned out Grady did want to talk about it, with somebody who wasn't his sister.

So, hunched over increasingly enormous plates of delicious food, Grady spilled the whole story. He kept Max's name out of it, but Baller wasn't stupid. He'd guess, and they'd both let plausible deniability protect them.

"Well, fuck," Baller said when Grady told him about Hedgie's on-ice comment. He had to pick his way around it, because the words had been private when he'd said them to Max and now that they'd been thrown in his face, he didn't know if he could repeat them. "You're sure it was on purpose to fuck with you?"

Grady poked at the last of his sushi. He'd eaten way too much already and his appetite had fled. "It wouldn't be the first time. I warned him."

"That's weird. Sucky, but weird." He shook his head.

Now Grady was frowning at Baller instead of his spicy tuna. "Weird how?"

"I mean, Hedgie's not really the type to get personal, you know?"

Grady felt the blood drain from his face. *Hedgie*. Fuck. He'd managed to keep Max's name out of it, but he'd forgotten about Hedgie. "I don't know what to tell you," he said. "That's what happened. And then I got traded in the middle of the game before I could even yell at him."

"Jesus." Baller was not having the same issue with fullness Grady was, because he popped in another piece of sushi. When he'd swallowed, he said, "Tell me you at least left him a nasty voicemail."

No, he hadn't. Because he was a coward. Grady shook his head. "Blocked his number."

Baller had been leaning on his elbow, but now he slipped and his hand slapped against the table. "Seriously?"

Grady flinched, but the other diners didn't seem to notice.

"Seriously?" Baller asked again, quieter this time. "You had feelings that intense and you didn't even break up with him in person to get closure? That's fucked, dude."

"How was I gonna break up with him in person from a plane over the Midwest?" Grady said, bitchy.

"On the phone, then, dipshit. You know what I mean."

Grady crossed his arms. Suddenly that sushi wasn't sitting well. "I didn't want to talk to him after that, okay?"

For a few seconds, Baller quietly sipped his beer. Then he said, "Can I give you some free advice?"

"Are you going to tell me anyway even if I say no?"

"Yeah." He leaned forward again. "Look, I can't blame you for not wanting to talk to the guy if he really ran his mouth to his team."

Grady waited for the *but*.

Because Baller was a contrary asshole, he went with another word. "*However*. What if he didn't? What if he didn't say anything and you ghosted him and he has no idea why? How are you going to know if you don't confront him about it?"

Grady flexed his hands under the table as his gut twisted.

What if? That would explain the texts he'd gotten before he blocked Max's number. None of them struck him as something Max would've said if he felt smug about siccing Hedgie on Grady. Or even if he'd done it accidentally and regretted it.

But that could've been part of the game, right?

"I'm just saying." Sometime during the past few minutes, Baller had signaled for and paid the check without Grady noticing. Damn. Now he slid the folder toward the end of the table. "I once broke up with Gabe because he canceled a dinner reservation for my birthday when I had a dislocated elbow. I figured he was still too afraid people would find out and I'd be his dirty secret forever, so I bounced. Turned out my birthday present was my dream couple's vacation. What if I never found out?"

Grady was used to Baller as a joker, a smiling, easygoing guy who loved hockey and being the center of attention. He could be serious— Grady had experienced it firsthand—but he preferred not to be. Now, he was solemn and even sad. "No husband. No Reyna. Maybe no Cup either. I might've been traded earlier if we couldn't play well together."

Grady let out a slow breath, but the nausea didn't subside. Had he made a mistake? The only way to know was to talk to Max. But he didn't know if he was ready to know the truth. "What if he doesn't…?"

Baller didn't make him finish the question, just gave a minute shake of his head. "At least you'll know."

Would it be better, though? If Max had loved him and Grady had fucked it up, would knowing be better?

Grady didn't know.


THE YEAR turned over and Max hit a funk.

He was sure it would be temporary, but in the meantime, he was suffering. He grinded his way through games, but his production went down. He spent a lot of time on his couch with Gru, rubbing the soft places behind his ears.

But today he was on El's couch with her while Hedgie was filming a promo spot for Gatorade or something. Two days ago the team got test results back for their injured defenseman. He'd separated his shoulder and would be out indefinitely.

Which meant the Monsters were in danger of losing their season, and the internet was abuzz with rumors that management would trade Hedgie for a replacement defenseman.

"I swear to God," El said, "if they send us to Winnipeg—"

"Why Winnipeg?" Max broke in.

El popped a handful of peanut M&Ms into her mouth, threw the last one at Max's head, and then drummed her fingertips on the curve of her belly. "This is a worst-case scenario, Maximus. Pay attention."

Max caught the candy left-handed and crunched down on it. "Sorry. Why's Winnipeg the worst, though?"

She shot him a flat look. The effect was ruined by the way she was lying, which made her look like her chin came directly out of her boobs. "Imagine being stuck in the house with a baby for six months because there's ten feet of snow on the ground."

"You could get a little snowmobile," he said. "Maybe a dogsled. And at least the baby won't be a newborn in the winter." Another M&M hit his forehead dead center. "Ow. Hey."

El huffed. "You're not helping."

*You're not usually this dramatic*, Max wanted to say, but he didn't want to get pegged with another chocolate, so he kept it to himself. El was growing a whole new human. She could be as dramatic as she liked. "Sorry. You know there's nothing to those rumors, right? Hedgie's agent confirmed it."

She sighed and rubbed her stomach again. "I know. But I'll be on edge until the trade deadline passes anyway. Hormones are seriously the worst."

"I believe you."

El turned onto her side and regarded him seriously. "What about you? How are your hormones doing?"

Oh Jesus. "Did I relapse into a teenager when I wasn't looking?"

"I'm just saying. Pretty sure I heard you blasting early Taylor Swift the other day. If the shoe fits…."

"Harsh, but fair."

"You still haven't heard from Armstrong, huh?"

Max reached for the party-size bag of M&Ms and grabbed a fistful. "My last text came back as undeliverable. Pretty sure he blocked my number." Chocolate might not fill the void inside him, but he'd never know until he tried.

"What the fuck."

"That's what I said," Max mumbled around a mouthful of candy. Depending on the day, thinking about it made him either angry or depressed as fuck. In any case, he needed chocolate.

"Save some of those for me," El said.

He passed her the bag.

On the television, Hugh Grant and Julia Roberts kissed.

El sniffed. "This is so dumb. I miss action movies. I hate that I'm loving this. I hate that I'm crying about it. I hate that I want to watch *Ever After* next."

*A bird may love a fish,* Max thought, *but where would they live?* A secret romance story with a happy ending would hurt to watch, but maybe it would be cathartic. "Done."

But Hedgie came back in before they could put it on. "Hey, turn on TSN." He sat on the ottoman.

*Oh fuck.* Max automatically reached for the remote and obeyed before his brain could process.

*... replacing Monsters head coach Jason Saunders. New Jersey's front office released a statement of support for Saunders, who has taken a leave of absence in order to seek treatment for addiction—*

"Jesus *fuck,*" Max said. He snapped the TV off. "Addiction to what?"

"Isn't it obvious?" Hedgie raised a hand to his face and touched the side of his nose.

"Christ." Max groaned. "Who's in charge now?"

"Well, if you'd left the stupid thing on—"

Max turned the TV back on, but the program had switched over to something involving a doping scandal. "Damn."

Hedgie rolled his eyes. "They're promoting Wells."

Their assistant coach thought Max's best use was drawing penalties because his goals didn't make the highlight reels. Max assessed the M&Ms along with the mounting pile of bad news and made a prediction. "We're gonna need more snacks."

"Yeah. About that." Suddenly Hedgie's shoulders tensed, and his head drooped between them. He looked miserable. "I got a text from Baltierra while I was out."

Try as he might, Max couldn't connect the dots. He glanced at El, who shrugged, then looked back at Hedgie. "Is this you coming out as bisexual and telling us you think he's a snack? Because I agree, but dude's taken."

Hedgie rubbed a hand over his forehead. "No, that's not.... Look. He said I needed to tell you what I said to Armstrong on the ice."

Max went cold all over. "What? Why would he say that?"

"Because apparently I'm the reason he's ghosting you." He raised his head. "I swear to you, Max, I didn't do it on purpose. I have no idea why he'd get so...." He spread his hands.

Fuck. Max swallowed. "What did you say?"

"That's the thing. I barely remember. Like, it wasn't super memorable to me, but I must've set him off somehow. I probably said something about Christmas? Because I knew the two of you spent it together."

No, that couldn't be it. "He knew you knew about us. He might not have appreciated it, but he wouldn't have ghosted me over it."

On the other side of the couch, El had called up the game on ESPN+ and was fast-forwarding through it. "What about here?"

The TV showed the end of the second period, when Grady went down with Hedgie on top of him.

"I was mostly apologizing," Hedgie said. "I basically tripped over him. I probably made a joke."

Max needed to understand what had happened to make Grady react the way he did. "Please try to remember."

El turned the volume up. Neither Hedgie nor Grady had been wearing a mic, but the rattle they made as they hit the boards got picked up anyway. Finally Hedgie's expression brightened. "Okay, so I was thinking about the sound it made when we collided, and you and Grady, which, sorry bud, but I see your tattoo way too often and know way too much about your sex life. So I said something like 'didn't mean to smash you like a lobster.'"

Max's bile rose. "Oh fuck. No wonder he hates me."

El sat up and put her hand on his leg. "Hey, come on. He doesn't hate you—"

"No, he would." He pressed his balled fist into his thigh to distract from the churning in his stomach. "I know it was a coincidence, but he thinks I told Hedgie something really personal and then he used it against him on the ice."

Hedgie flattened his lips. "Okay, but he didn't have to assume the worst and then ghost you."

No, he didn't. The least he owed Max was to tell him to fuck off in person, even if he didn't believe Max's explanation. "I didn't say I wasn't pissed, I said I know why he thinks I'm an asshole."

His stomach turned over again. He felt like he'd been gut-punched.

Why was Grady so fucking determined to believe the worst of Max? Hadn't Max treated him well enough to deserve the benefit of the doubt? The least Grady could do was have the spine to tell Max why he ditched him.

Max rubbed his face. "Well. That's that mystery solved, I guess." He wished knowing made him feel better.

El picked up the M&Ms bag and handed it over. "You need these more than I do."

Max already regretted eating so much chocolate. "I think I better eat something more substantial." With a sigh, he stood up and considered the contents of his kitchen. "Forget the snacks. I'm going to go find myself some dinner."

El and Hedgie exchanged glances. "We could order takeout," she offered.

"Thanks." Max shook his head. He needed to fume in private. "Maybe next time."

GRADY WASN'T sure how road trips were going to go with his new team—a lot of people had travel superstitions and designated seat partners—but right after he sat down, Mitch took the seat next to him, so he didn't have to worry about being left out.

Then Farouk took the seat in front of him and turned around, hugging the top of his seat as he put his head on his arms.

"So listen," Farouk said, "we've got a weird tradition."

Grady glanced from him to Mitch, who said, "It's not *weird*."

From this, Grady gleaned that it definitely was. "Okay."

"And you're the new guy, so it's your turn for initiation into tattoo roulette."

Grady's first reaction was *no way*. He didn't need another permanent mark on his body.

But he wanted to try to fit in with this team. He didn't want to spend the rest of his career bouncing from city to city because he didn't have strong ties anywhere. He'd bought a house in anticipation of signing a contract extension. He could at least hear them out. "Tattoo what?"

"Roulette."

Mitch took over the explanation. "See, Farouk here is the second-most-junior member of the team."

If Grady remembered right, Farouk had signed with the Condors in the off season.

"And every time we have a new guy on a road trip, we make a bet."

Naturally. "'We' meaning?"

"The new guy and the second-newest guy."

At least Grady would only be subjected to this twice. "And what are the terms of the bet?"

Farouk grinned. "Okay, so, if I get more points than you on this road trip, you get a bad tattoo. If you get more points, I do."

That was so stupid. No wonder the team loved it. Everybody loved a good story, and ugly tattoos made great ones. "Bad meaning crappy or bad meaning, like, ridiculous?"

Farouk rolled up his shirtsleeve to show off a well-crafted image of Baby Yoda drinking a bubble tea.

Grady snorted. "Okay. Before I agree to this… saying I lose—and I don't intend to—do I get to choose my own dumb tattoo and where it's going?"

Farouk and Mitch had a silent conversation. Mitch eventually answered, "Subject to approval as sufficiently stupid, yes."

Fuck it. "Why not." He and Farouk shook on it. "You're going down, though."

Farouk laughed at him. "We'll see."

Three minutes later, a WhatsApp message came through from Hedgie.

Grady almost didn't open it. He couldn't imagine it said anything he wanted to hear. But curiosity got the better of him, and eventually he opened it.

*Max had no idea why you were mad at him. Whatever I said to you that pissed you off, it was a coincidence. He didn't tell me shit.*

Then: *PS you're a dick.*

For a few heartbeats, Grady stared blankly at the messages. Then questions started to creep in. How did Hedgie know why Grady was mad, if Max hadn't told him?

Baller, of course. He loved to meddle.

But did Grady trust the three of them?

And did it matter? At the end of the day, if he gave them the benefit of the doubt, then he and Max might still have a chance. That was worth the leap of faith. Grady might like his new team, might even like his new life, but he missed Max. He missed the person Max made him want to be.

Max had given him permission to be the kind of man who could make a bet about a stupid tattoo. But he also accepted Grady as a petty asshole who judged people for serving palm oil dessert and calling it ice cream.

Maybe Max was innocent and Grady had fucked up. If that was the case, he had to figure out how to fix it, if he could. How could he apologize?

But that wasn't even the first question. The first question was how he could get Max to hear him out when they both knew he didn't deserve it.

The Condors didn't play Newark until the end of the regular season, three months from now. Grady would never forgive himself if he didn't attempt to clear this up before then.

With nerveless fingers, he navigated to his contacts list and scrolled down to Shithead.

God, he'd been such an asshole. He made himself sick.

Grady unblocked Max's number. Then he hit Edit Contact and erased the name. Max didn't deserve that, and Grady was past caring what other people thought.

He entered Max's full first and last name and touched Save.

Now for the hard part.

*I fucked up.*

No shit. But what else?

He took the rest of the flight to figure it out.

MAX CONSIDERED himself an easygoing guy. He got up, he worked out, he ate, he played hockey, he went to bed. The circle of life. He left work at work. He had, like, Zen chill or whatever.

But Coach Wells was an energy-sucking vampire who consumed all Max's chill and fed it back to him as distilled rage. Considering Max was already having a certified Bad Time, he didn't need Coach Wells in his life.

They were halfway through the third period, trailing 3–2 in a game they had no business losing, but Wells had his idea of what each player's strengths were and didn't care about reality.

When he finished telling Hedgie to make a play that was way more in Max's wheelhouse—Hedgie had good hands but Max had him beat for speed, which this plan called for—he turned to Max. "Lockhart—"

"Yeah, yeah," Max said. "Tie up the third man and piss him off so he takes a penalty." He bit down on his mouthguard hard enough that he heard an ominous crack.

That was the second one this week. Max was going to have to see a dentist if this kept up.

Nora would gloat. Horrible.

Wells gave him a look that said Max would pay for his insubordination after the game, but Max didn't care. If Wells scratched him, at least he'd have a game off to rest. Max had taken more retaliatory hits in the past two games than in the two weeks before that. Bruises marked his skin from elbows to shoulder and down his flanks. He'd even taken a spear under his ribs, and the skin there had turned a mottled purple.

But he did his job. He got up in that third man's space and took it away. He got in the way. He didn't worry about making plays, but he made sure this guy couldn't even look at the puck. Finally, in frustration, the guy slashed Max's legs—at least he'd chosen a place Max wasn't already black-and-blue—and Max exaggerated enough to get called for embellishing.

Oh well, he thought as he skated to the box, maybe Wells would stop asking him to do this.

Needless to say, the Monsters did not pull off a surprise win. Max did his media duties as blandly as he could, even when a reporter tried to bait him into criticizing Wells. Max had been in the league ten years. He knew a trap when he heard one.

By the time he got back to his hotel room, he was so exhausted he considered turning his phone off when the screen lit up with a notification. But he unlocked it instead and found a message from Grady.

*I fucked up.* Then another, *I want to apologize.*

Max went over the edge. He stabbed Call before he could think about what he wanted to say.

Grady picked up on the second ring, but Max didn't let him get a word out.

"You have a lot of fucking nerve."

"I know—"

"No, you don't. Shut up." The words poured out, filled with acid. "You ghosted me for weeks and now you think you're going to get a word in?"

"Max—"

"Fuck you," Max said. "You spent months convincing yourself I'd fuck you over, but guess what, Grady? You not only fucked yourself, you fucked me too. I thought we were going to—but you disappeared without a trace. You didn't even have the stones to say something to my face. You're a coward."

"You're right."

God damn him. Max clenched his jaw and closed his eyes. He had a whole list of shit to read Grady the riot act over, but he couldn't get the words out past the lump in his throat.

Grady took advantage of his silence. His voice was rough and quiet and left no doubt as to his sincerity. "Max, I'm sorry. I jumped to a stupid conclusion and I hurt you. I ruined something good that could have been—"

*Could have been.* But now it wasn't.

"Could have been great," Grady finished.

"You're an asshole," Max said. "Who just stops talking to someone they—?"

"Someone they love?" Grady's voice cracked.

Fuck. *Fuck.* "*Now* you say that to me?" Max's hands shook and his eyes burned. "Now?"

"I should have told you in Miami, but I've never—it's been fifteen years since I said that to someone who wasn't my sister."

Max's grip on his anger was slipping. With anyone else, he might have questioned the truth of that statement, considering the timing. But he knew to his bones that Grady had never said those words to a lover. It shouldn't have been enough to sway him, but he didn't want to stay mad. He wanted Grady to apologize so they could be together for real.

And it looked like he might get his wish. "I was stupid. Hedgie said—you know what he said, I guess. And I panicked. I assumed the worst. Then they stuck me in a trainer's room to make sure I didn't have a concussion and let me stew for an hour, and I kept going around in circles. By the time they told me they were trading me, I'd convinced myself…."

Max bit his lip until he tasted copper.

"And then I was going to California, and I thought, well, it's not like we could even…."

Max exhaled shakily.

"But I was wrong about you telling Hedgie, and I think I was wrong about that too."

Maybe he was. Max curled onto his side on the bed.

Was he still mad? Yes. Could he get over it?

Yes. He could get over it and let Grady back into his life and have that great thing that they would have had if Grady hadn't fucked everything up.

And he could set himself up to get hurt all over again.

All of a sudden Max wasn't angry. He didn't have any more anger in him. He'd never been good at holding grudges, and right now he needed something to feel positive about.

As long as Grady was willing to put in the work, Max was too. And there was one good test to find out. "Say it for real."

"Max." Max swallowed hard and held his breath while Grady paused. "I'm in love with you."

There—*that* was the feeling Max had been waiting for. He went warm all over and his mouth smiled without his input.

Long distance be damned. This might really work. Actually, right now the distance felt like a welcome buffer. It would give Max some time to work through his residual hurt. By the time he saw Grady face-to-face again, he'd be ready.

"Okay," he said.

"Okay?" Grady didn't quite squawk, but it was close. "I tell you I'm in love with you and that's what I get back?"

"Oh yeah." Max rolled onto his back. He might've forgiven Grady, but he wasn't ready to pick up where they'd left off in Miami. Grady would have to prove he deserved to be there. "Just because we're dating now doesn't mean I'm going to go easy on you."

Grady laughed. It was the second-best thing Max had ever heard. "No, of course not." Then, "Dating, huh?"

"Yup." Max popped the *p* and stretched out to get comfortable. This phone call could go on for a while. "Don't worry, though. I know how much you hate going on dates. But look on the bright side—you have until we play each other in April to plan one."

MAX COULD have restrained himself, but restraint had never been his strong suit. He could only go so long without pushing Grady's buttons. So the next time he was out with the team after a win—and one too many shots—he found himself replying to one of Grady's bland but somehow endearing texts with *how good r ur dick pics?*

Then Hedgie distracted him, and he forgot to look at his phone again until he was back at yet another hotel room, brushing his teeth.

He had three new messages from Grady.

When the first picture loaded, Max snickered. That was Dick van Dyke. A white whale followed—Moby Dick, presumably. Then a comic-book character in red and green with a yellow mask. Robin? *Funny*, Max said. *whos the last one?*

*Dick Grayson.*

Of course. *At least u didn't send dick cheney*

*I'm not actually TRYING to piss you off.* Then, a moment later, *Saw the game tonight. What's Wells smoking?*

They'd won, but Wells had been up to his usual bullshit, making Max his designated pain in the ass. Max's fledgling good mood waned. *Dont joke abt drugs :(*

*Shit, sorry. I hope Saunders is back soon.*

Max did too, but he didn't want to talk about hockey. *tell me something good.* He flopped on the bed with his phone.

Grady's next message said, *I made another bet.*

How mysterious. *Oh?????*

*I lost.*

Max smiled at his phone screen. *Whats the forfeit?*

*I'll tell you when it's done.*

They texted back and forth a few more times, but Max's eyelids were heavy. With Grady to distract him from his frustration with Wells, he fell asleep.


TWO WEEKS after the Condors returned from their road trip, Grady woke up with regrets.

Not about the tattoo. Farouk won the bet fair and square, and somehow it did help Grady bond with the team. Their schedule had kept him from holding up his end of the agreement until last night, but that gave him plenty of time to come up with his idea. Mitch cried tears of laughter when Grady showed him the design he'd chosen, and he and Farouk stayed for the whole appointment, cracking jokes and telling stories about the team.

But if Grady had to do it again, he'd pick another location. The bowl of his hip had been a poor choice. It was going to be a bitch to play with.

He should probably get some analgesic cream or something, because he might have the whole day off from hockey… but not from moving.

Today Grady got possession of his house.

Groaning, he got up and made himself coffee. Not touching the ink on his hip took a surprising amount of focus. He definitely needed caffeine to manage it.

He had forty minutes before he had to meet the movers at his new house when someone knocked on the hotel-room door.

Blearily, Grady opened it and was surprised to find Farouk and Mitch, as well as Dawg and a handful of other guys, standing on his doorstep. Or whatever you had when you still lived in a hotel room.

"Rise and shine," Mitch said. "It's moving day."

Grady blinked at him. "I know. What are you doing here?"

"Helping," Dawg said like it was obvious. "Are you going to get dressed?"

Was Grady being bossed around by a nineteen-year-old off the ice? "I hired professional movers," he protested.

"They're not gonna unpack your kitchenware, dude." That was Farouk. "Hurry up. If we get going early, we can be done in time for beach volleyball."

"Hey," said Dawg before Grady could find a shirt, "is that a new tattoo?"

Grady hadn't explained it to Mitch and Farouk, and he sure as fuck wasn't going to explain it to Dawg, a kid Grady'd taken aside and told to stop washing his face with Irish Spring. "Eyes up here, Captain."

Dawg flushed so brightly Grady felt bad for calling him out.

"Help yourself to some coffee while I get dressed." Hopefully that would distract everyone from teasing Dawg.

By two o'clock, Grady had to admit that moving went smoothly when you had professional hockey players as well as professional movers. Granted, he'd sold a lot of furniture with the Philadelphia house and had only kept his master bedroom set, personal touches like art and framed jerseys, and his kitchenware, wardrobe, and linens. He had his old TV and media console and one ugly armchair the new homeowners didn't want, and the nice patio set that came with the new house because, he suspected, it was too heavy for anyone to want to move it.

His decorator had ordered all his other furniture to be delivered over the next few weeks. But for today, they were making do with the pool, the patio furniture, and the towels Grady pulled out of his box of bath linens. He made a beer run and had an embarrassing number of pizzas delivered, and they ate outside in the winter sunshine. The thermometer read seventy-five degrees.

It was almost perfect.

As if on cue, a notification popped up on his phone. Max, of course—though he'd missed one a few hours ago, from Jess.

Hers said, *How's the move coming?*

*All done*, he sent back. He texted her a picture of the pileup of pizza boxes and beer cans. *Hanging out with the boys.*

*Nice!!!!!*

He decided not to think too hard about what it meant that Jess used that many exclamation points to mark her approval that Grady was making friends.

Max's text provided a handy distraction. He'd sent a selfie taken on the team bus. He had his noise-canceling over-ear headphones on, with the waves of his hair fluffed out to the side like he was in a Disney movie that took place on a boat, and his expression as he stared into the phone camera suggested he was having his toenails pulled out with rusty pliers while being forced to watch paint dry. Behind him, just in frame, Grady made out the profile of the Monsters' interim coach's face as he addressed the team.

He winced in sympathy. Wells used Max like a blunt object when he was more of a Swiss Army knife, and then acted like it was Max's fault he wasn't a hammer.

He sent back a selfie of his own, sunglasses and all, pool in the background.

"Hey, are we taking pics for Insta?" Grady snapped his head over to see Dawg pulling himself out of the pool. He reached for his towel. "What's your handle?"

"Dude." That was Farouk. "Not everybody wants you in their thirst trap pics. Or to share their thirst trap pics with you."

*Oh God.* Grady sent the picture, locked his phone screen, and hoped his sunburn covered any physical reaction.

Dawg wasn't so lucky. He'd gone blotchy red down to his shoulders.

Did Farouk not realize Dawg had a crush, or was he giving him shit for it? Grady didn't even know if Dawg was out.

Fuck. "It's a private account. I pretty much only follow my sister and a dog." It was Max's dog—blessedly, Max had unblocked him after they made up—but Grady wasn't going to give that away unless he had to. "I don't post anything."

Unfortunately, this invited a follow-up question from Mitch, who was lounging with his arms out of the pool, looking at Grady over the tops of his sunglasses. "So the selfie was for someone in particular?"

On the other hand, maybe he could be vague enough to discourage Dawg without spilling the whole story. "Yeah."

Mitch grinned. "Nice. Get it, Grades."

Probably not for another few months, but Grady grinned back anyway. "I will."

Meanwhile, on the patio chair next to him, Dawg was vigorously rubbing a towel over his face. When he pulled it away, he seemed to have regained some chill. "Hey," he said, "the Fish have a game tonight. We could watch, keep an eye on our competition."

Farouk booed—a day off should include not being forced to watch other teams' games, he said—but Mitch wanted to watch for a little early scouting on Baller before the Condors played the Fish in two weeks.

"Besides," Dawg said, "we need to get Grades here hating on the Fish."

"I hate them plenty." Otherwise they'd have to kick him off the team. The Fish were the Condors' main rivals. Grady knew how sports rivalries worked. He'd been part of one of the more volatile ones in the NHL for his entire career.

If, lately, hating another team seemed like a waste of energy, his new team didn't have to know that.

"We could move the TV out here," Mitch suggested. "Then Farouk doesn't have to get out of the pool and Dawg can do his homework."

So Grady and Dawg moved the TV, and Grady streamed from his phone. Ten minutes into the game, Farouk climbed out of the pool, shivering, and pulled over a patio chair.

Grady went inside to grab some extra sweatshirts. Even he felt a bit of a chill now that the sun had gone down and the breeze picked up. But when he slid open the patio door to go back outside, he found his teammates hunched forward facing the screen.

"Jesus," Mitch said with a grimace.

Dawg blanched.

Farouk pulled his towel tighter around his shoulders. "Son of a bitch."

Apparently Grady had missed something big. He tossed a shirt at Farouk. "What happened?"

Without speaking, Dawg gestured at the television.

Well…. Grady could've figured that much. The replay showed one of the Ottawa Tartans hooking Piranhas number 68. When he went down, his other foot twisted under him. He landed on it with his full weight, skating too fast.

Fuck, that was a bad fall. Grady could tell the guy wouldn't be getting up again under his own power. "Who was that?"

"Baltierra." Mitch put his head in his hands. "Fuck, if he goes on IR, that gives them so much cap relief."

That meant the Piranhas would be able to trade for another good player during the regular season. For playoffs, Baller would be eligible to come back—assuming he'd healed from what was almost certainly a broken foot—giving the Piranhas a ton of firepower.

Which was presumably why Mitch was upset. "Show a little sympathy, dude." Grady already had his phone out to text Baller a message of support.

"Right. Sorry. I forgot you're friends."

"Injuries like that suck," Farouk said. "That could fuck him up for a long time."

Grady hoped not. He didn't want the Piranhas to get an influx of cap space and become that much more challenging to beat—especially since it looked like the Condors might come up against them early in the playoffs—but he didn't want Baller to be badly hurt either.

Dawg had already moved on to, "Who do you think they're going to go for?"

"Kirschbaum?"

"No chance, the whole city of Vancouver is married to that guy."

"People get divorced all the time."

"Could be Yorkshire. I mean, if they're going for a Dekes reunion, it would make sense. And the Fuel are rebuilding again"—that was generous, Grady thought; they'd never managed to build anything in the first place—"so they'd probably go for picks and prospects on a trade."

Grady tuned them out. He didn't know enough about the Piranhas' roster to know who they might be able to trade for another good forward, and it seemed in poor taste to speculate about it when there wasn't even a report on Baller's injury.

Instead, he pulled out his phone and found a video from Max—a ten-second clip of Gru chasing snowflakes. Apparently it was cold on the East Coast. Gru was wearing a little green sweatshirt with a hood that made him look like Creature, the Monsters' mascot. The eye stalks bobbled hilariously as he jumped to try to catch a particularly fat snowflake.

Grady couldn't believe he'd been so stupid that he'd almost walked away from this. He wouldn't make that mistake again.

MAX WOKE up the day before the trade deadline and checked his phone obsessively, the way he had for the past two weeks. No news about Hedgie being dealt, just the same unsubstantiated rumors. Realistically, if it were going to happen, Hedgie's agent would've given him a heads-up.

But sometimes things moved fast. She might not have time.

In any case, today was still a good day. He pressed a kiss to Gru's fuzzy nose and received a lazy blink in return, but by the time Max had finished putting on enough layers to go outside, the dog was waiting by the door, tail wagging.

Max slipped the harness over Gru's head, tugged a toque onto his own, and stepped outside into the biting wind.

Some dogs didn't like weather, but Gru approached walks with the same cheerful disposition no matter what the sky was doing. Max worried he was going to end up with frostbite. Every time he got ice stuck between the pads of his feet, he stopped, favoring the affected leg, and gave Max the most pathetic puppy-dog eyes until Max bent down and unstuck it.

But he hated his snow boots. Naturally.

Today Max kept the walk short, since he had to be at the arena early and it looked like the roads were going to be a mess. Gru didn't mind; while he loved the morning walk, it was mostly important as a ritual that had to be observed in order to get to breakfast.

A snowplow went by, the sound muffled by the toque pulled low over Max's ears to protect them from the howling wind. Driving snow stung his face and stuck in his eyelashes.

"Had enough?" he asked after Gru had dumped a load next to an ornamental cedar half bent under the weight of six inches of snow.

Gru kicked up a spray of snow behind him and pricked his ears.

Max bagged the turd. "Okay. Let's go have breakfast."

They had to walk into the wind on the way back. Max's eyes watered and his ears burned, even under the wool of his hat. The hairs in his nostrils froze, which was always disgusting, but not as disgusting as it would be when the snot melted.

He could never complain about any of this to his family, of course. They'd think he'd gotten soft.

He had a shelf of snowflakes on his eyebrows when he let himself back in the house. Gru shook himself vigorously, flinging snow and hair around the mudroom. Then he pranced to his bowl in anticipation of the next best part of his day.

"Yeah, yeah," Max grumbled as he tried to toe off his boots without falling over. "Give me a minute. I'm coming."

He was dumping the last scoop of food into Gru's dish when he heard a faint ringing from the mudroom. He'd left his phone in his coat pocket. "Shit."

It took so long to dig out past the crumpled Kleenex and roll of dog poop bags that he thought for sure the call would go to voicemail. Then his fingers were too wet to swipe Accept and he had to wipe them on his shirt three times.

Finally he picked up. "Hello?"

"Max. Thank God I caught you. I've been trying to reach you all morning."

Fuck. He recognized that voice. "Hey. Sorry, I was walking Gru and it's practically a blizzard out there. Probably couldn't hear my phone over the wind."

He already knew, when his agent didn't acknowledge what he'd said, that he wouldn't like what came next. "Listen, Max… there's no easy way to say this."

He closed his eyes and swallowed. "Where are they sending me?"

She released a long breath. "Miami."

His throat grew thick with emotion. "Okay. I'm guessing they don't want me to go in to practice this morning." He wasn't part of the Monsters organization anymore. No last chance to say goodbye, not when it meant he might see some new set play the team had drawn up—information he could pass on to his new team.

"The equipment manager's going to ship your gear down."

Well. That was that.

Gru must've sensed something was wrong, because he snuffled into the mudroom and pushed his nose under Max's chin. Automatically, Max wound his fingers into the thick fur at his neck. "Have you heard from Florida? When's my flight?"

"Still waiting to hear back from their front office. I got the feeling they're making multiple last-minute deals and haven't gotten all the details sorted out yet. I'll call you as soon as I know more."

Numbly, Max thanked her and hung up.

Gru whined and licked his chin.

"Okay," Max said after a fortifying breath. "First things first, right?" And Gru had to be first, because Gru was a dog and couldn't look after himself. "Let's get your harness back on, buddy."

He didn't want to ask for this favor, but he'd probably be living in a hotel for the foreseeable future. The hotel might not be pet-friendly, and it wouldn't be fair to Gru. He'd be better off with Hedgie and El.

"Florida, eh?" he muttered, half to himself and half to Gru, as he pushed open the door into the snow. "Figures."

Getting sent away from the snow, fine. But couldn't he have ended up at a team closer to Grady? They'd have the same weather and still be a six-hour flight apart, plus the same time difference.

Grady was probably still in bed right now, with no idea Max's life had gotten turned upside-down. He kept his phone on Do Not Disturb at night, so Max couldn't even call him and vent.

He didn't realize he'd made it all the way to Hedgie and El's front door until Gru barked, expecting to be let in. Belatedly, Max rang the doorbell.

Several minutes later, Hedgie answered it, bleary-eyed, dressed in pajama pants and with his hair sticking straight up on one side. He must have been asleep. "'M I late?" he asked, blinking through a yawn.

Then he noticed Gru, and suddenly his eyes opened all the way.

Max held out the leash and tried to keep it together. "I need a big favor...."

GRADY WENT to practice in a terrible mood.

He felt awful for Max. A trade was hard enough when you were expecting it. But a trade that blindsided you when—at least apart from the temporary coaching situation—you were happy with your team? When you were one of the team's core players? When you'd expected to wear the same jersey your whole life?

He called on his way to the rink for morning skate, in the hopes that maybe talking to Grady would help. Grady didn't know how, but Max had a way of making him feel better despite his own determination to be a grumpy asshole. Grady could at least try to return the favor.

But Max didn't answer, and now Grady wondered if they were going to have a repeat of his own dumb posttrade radio silence. If so, he deserved it, but it still sucked.

So he was surly through practice—enough that Dawg made sad puppy eyes at him when Grady snapped and then felt like a monster. After that, he kept a better lid on it, but he could tell Mitch and Farouk were giving him more space than usual.

Grady made a conscious effort to dial back "hate-the-world mode," as Jess called it, and get his head on straight. At this point in the season, every game counted—the more points they got, the better chance they had at an easier matchup in the first round of the playoffs. Grady could hardly remember the last time making the playoffs felt like a given rather than a struggle, and he wasn't going to waste it. Especially not since their game tonight was against San Jose—a divisional matchup. Winning tonight could mean the difference of a home-team advantage in the first round.

And all Grady could think about was Max in Miami, away from his friends and away from Grady, and the fact that the Condors had already played Miami twice this season. If Grady got to see Max before the playoffs were over, it would be because they were playing against each other in the Stanley Cup Final.

Grady gritted his teeth and did his best to focus, but he struggled. Finally he knocked a goal past Mitch in practice—right out of the air off a flukey bounce—and Farouk patted his shoulder. "Attaboy. You show that puck."

Grady checked him halfheartedly, but his shoulders unknotted and he relaxed. Settling into the groove got easier after that.

After practice, the team filed into the locker room. Jeremy, their PR guy, gave Grady a heads-up in the hallway. "You're on tap for media today."

Grady wanted to protest. Everybody else was in a good mood. Grady wanted to brood in peace.

But it was a team sport, and he had promised himself he'd make more of an effort to be a team player, so he nodded. "Got it."

It wasn't like media interviews were hard. Grady could've answered questions about their power play strategy in his sleep. The most difficult part was keeping his attention on the questions while the rest of the team dressed and chatted around him.

Grady talked a little about Farouk's landmark year—he was on track to hit forty goals by the end of the regular season—and how much the team supported him.

Then Sonia Goldstein, who covered the team for the *Athletic*, got her turn. "Grady, when you played for the Firebirds, you had a notable rivalry with Max Lockhart."

Grady schooled his features into neutrality as he waited for her to finish.

"How do you feel about rekindling that rivalry now that Max has been traded to the Piranhas?"

Blinking, Grady tried to untangle the question while his heart tried to escape his rib cage. "I thought he was going to Miami."

Sonia shook her head. "You must've missed the news. They flipped him to Anaheim an hour ago."

Grady could not have controlled his expression if his life depended on it. Without meaning to, he raised his hand to his face and rubbed his cheek. Oh—that was the edge of a smile under his fingers.

Oops.

"They did, huh?" He shook his head. "Guess he missed my pretty face."

Sonia laughed. "So that's a yes?"

*Yes* was such a small word. "Max is always fun to play against." Even if that wasn't what Grady looked forward to most. "But maybe I'll try a little harder to stay out of the box this time around."

Somehow he got through the rest of the questions, and then Jeremy ushered the media out again.

Grady could've used a few minutes to pull himself together, but he didn't even get ten seconds. As soon as the door closed, Mitch was on him.

"Grady. Bro. Buddy. Friend." He put his hand on Grady's knee. "What is that on your face?"

*Fuck.* Grady put his head in his hands. He was still smiling. "Shut up."

"Okay, wait, wait, wait." Farouk sat down on his other side. "Am I jumping to the right conclusions here? Your special friend you sent a shirtless selfie to the other day is your *archrival*?"

"Oh my God." Grady lifted his head. "I'm not a supervillain."

"This is amazing," Farouk said. "This is better than television. I don't believe this."

At least they weren't upset. On the other hand, this might be worse.

"When did this start? *How* did this start?" Mitch wanted to know. "How have you kept this quiet for so long when your face does *that* when you talk about him?"

"You have to tell us," Farouk said. "I will never be able to have my pregame nap with all these questions. Do it for the *team*, Grades."

He squared his shoulders. "I'm not going to do that without talking to Max."

Farouk shrugged, unbothered. "Oh well. Worth a shot. Seriously, though. I have so many questions."

"Leave them off the ice," Grady told him.

"Hey, hey, I can be discreet. Unlike that face—"

Finally Grady stood and mustered the remnants of his dignity. "I'm going to shower."

Farouk and Mitch heckled him as he walked away.

That didn't stop Grady's smile either.


By the time Max landed in LA, he was emotionally exhausted. His eyes were gritty. He'd barely eaten all day, and he knew he needed food, but the idea turned his stomach. Traded twice in the same day—who'd want to eat after that? Shaken, hurt, and stuck in an airplane for seven hours didn't make for a strong appetite.

His agent had told him the team would send someone to collect him at the airport, so at least he didn't have to worry about that. He spotted the person in the Piranhas polo with LOCKHART on a sign and followed them to their car.

The team had set him up in a hotel near their practice arena. The mini fridge was stocked with snacks, and they'd ordered dinner to be delivered half an hour after he arrived. Max took a shower, the heat cranked up as high as he could stand it.

He'd forgotten to refill his travel shampoo—the one Grady picked out for him.

That might've made him sad in Miami, but he was in Los Angeles, where Grady also lived. Grady was probably arriving at the arena right now for tonight's game. Max could, in fact, get out of the shower, get dressed, and get a ticket. He could be in the same building as Grady in a few hours.

But he was still too raw. He needed time to mourn his old life before he started his new one.

He ate dinner by rote, not really tasting it, brushed his teeth, and then looked at the bed. He shouldn't get in. It was too early. He'd screw up his internal clock.

But fuck it. He was tired.

Before he crawled into bed, he unlocked his phone and opened a new message to Grady. Realistically, the time he had to work through his hurt had passed. Now it was time to see if they could really make this work in person, instead of long-distance.

No pressure.

*Looks like im gonna miss that date in april. reschedule?*

Then he put it down and closed his eyes. He had a big day tomorrow.

MAX EXPECTED to wake up at an ungodly hour, given the time he'd gone to bed and his body clock.

Instead he opened his eyes to bright sunlight and a buzzing from the hotel phone. Max reached for it blearily and brought it to his ear. "Hello."

"Good morning, Mr. Lockhart!" chirped the voice on the other end. "This is the front desk. You have a visitor. Should I send him up? He says he's supposed to take you to the arena."

That sounded vaguely correct. Max sat up and wiped his eyes. "No. Tell him I'll be down in a few minutes. Thank you."

At least he'd showered last night.

Max quickly brushed his teeth and threw on a set of athletic gear. After a moment of frantic searching, he found his key card in last night's pants pocket. Then he picked up his wallet and phone and went down to the lobby to face whatever indignity getting collected from your hotel was.

Was this how Hedgie felt all the years Max had to herd him places?

Shit, who was going to do that now?

But Max didn't have time to be sad about it because, when he entered the lobby, he found not his chauffeur from last night, but Dante Baltierra in a T-shirt, board shorts, and sandals.

Well, one sandal. The other foot was in a walking boot.

Max blinked at him. "It's sixty degrees outside."

"In February!" Baltierra agreed. Max had never formally met the man, but apparently neither one of them was into introductions. "I love it. Too bad I'm just a short-term rental. You good to go?"

Yes, but…. "How are you driving us anywhere with that?" Max gestured to his right foot. He'd heard enough nightmares about LA traffic. It definitely didn't seem like the kind of time to fuck around driving with a broken brake foot.

Or gas foot, for that matter.

"Oh, I'm not. Gabe's out front. I call shotgun. You get to ride in the back with Reyna."

Max had more questions but sensed they would not lead to satisfactory answers. "Lead the way."

"Hi, honey," Baltierra said when he opened the door of the SUV idling out front. "Look what I found."

Max slid in the back and offered a wave to Gabe Martin, Baltierra's husband and Max's former Team Canada teammate. "Hey, Gabe. Thanks for the ride." Then he turned his attention to his neighbor, a chubby toddler with bright brown eyes and curly hair. "You must be Reyna. I'm Max." He held out his finger to shake.

Reyna ignored it, but she did yell, "Max! Max! Max!" so he couldn't be too offended.

He hoped his teammates were as excited to meet him as she was.

"Oh, yeah, that reminds me," said Baltierra from the front seat. "You can use my nickname around the team, but try not to around the kid. It gets awkward when strangers think she's talking about my testicles."

"Tetticles!" Reyna agreed loudly.

They stopped at a light. Gabe covered his eyes with one hand, and his shoulders shook with silent laughter.

"See what I mean?"

Gabe took his hand away from his face. "Day care *loves* us."

Gabe dropped them off at the rink, and Baller limp-swaggered down the hallway to lead Max to the GM's office for his introductory visit—security details and administrative stuff.

The GM took one look at Baller and developed an eye twitch. "Baltierra, what the fuck are you doing here? Go home and sit down. I said you could play chauffeur, not walk all over LA."

"I'm going," Baller said. "Going to go elevate it right now. Promise." He left with a wink at Max, who didn't believe him for a second.

The GM sighed, but he also shook his head fondly. "That kid, I swear. He's lucky he's so likable. Come in and sit down and we'll get this over with so I can get you on the ice with the team as fast as possible."

True to his word, the meeting took only a couple minutes. Max's new coach came in at the tail end and introduced himself as Barry, shook Max's hand, and said, "All right, time to meet the guys. You ready?"

Max wasn't. He'd been a Monster his entire career. Management had made him believe he'd be there forever. Usually he knew at least one or two players on a team—guys he trained with, guys who'd played for the Monsters before, friends of friends, players from the national team. But here, the closest thing he had to a friend was Baller, who he'd met this morning. It made him wonder why the Piranhas wanted him in the first place.

But he pasted on a smile and said, "Let's do it."

Of course, all his apprehension was for nothing. The team was the same as any other team, except maybe a touch younger. Max fit in well enough. His new captain, a six-foot-eight center who went by Bishop, welcomed him to the team with a back slap that rattled his teeth. "Fresh Fish!" he bellowed to the locker room.

"Beware the Fish!" the rest of the team yelled back, stomping their feet.

Oh God, Max had joined a cult.

Bishop patted his shoulder, gentler this time. "Let's see what you got."

Practice went well enough. The Piranhas played a fast, offensive game that focused on puck movement to generate even-strength chances. It was a change for Max, who was used to a defensive game at even strength and a scoring strategy that focused on the power play.

"We'll put you on third or fourth line a couple games until you get used to it," Barry told him after his third set of line rushes. He side-eyed Max. "You look like you could use the rest."

*Gee, thanks*, Max thought. But he couldn't disagree, so he didn't bother trying. "Okay, Coach."

It wouldn't be the worst if he didn't get fifty new bruises every game.

They'd had a closed practice, so there were no reporters present to ask Max how he felt about the trade. For that he was grateful to the Piranhas organization, because he didn't think he could do it without getting choked up. He'd feel more sure of himself after his first game in an unfamiliar jersey.

He expected to get passed on to another teammate for a ride back to the hotel—maybe Bishop, as part of his captain duties—or else to have to call an Uber.

But when he got out of the shower, Baller was waiting for him, his booted foot propped up on the locker room bench next to him. He had a battered romance novel in one hand and appeared deeply engrossed.

Everyone else had left. Was this some kind of setup? Max was suspicious.

"Oh good," Baller said when he noticed Max standing there. "I thought the shower might have defeated you."

Max tossed his towel in the laundry bin. "I'm a Fish now, remember? Water can't hurt me."

Baller beamed. "That's the spirit."

When Max had pulled on a pair of boxers and a T-shirt, Baller discarded his book and patted the wood next to him. "Sit down for a minute so I can be nosy."

*Figures.* "Is that why I rate special attention?"

"Yes. My foot's broken and I'm super bored. I need something to occupy me."

At least he was honest about Max being his pet project. Max sat. "I'm going to assume this isn't about hockey."

"It *could* be," Baller said with feigned offense. Then, "Okay, but it isn't. I'm definitely here to get the dirty on your thing with my boy Grades."

Max knew Grady must've told him something, or he would've had no reason to text Hedgie about it.

But Grady wouldn't appreciate him telling Baller anything he didn't know, so he wasn't about to spill his guts. *Well, I was in love with him, but he broke my heart, and then he apologized and we got back together, and now I'm low-key freaking out that it'll fall apart again now that we're in the same place* was not something you laid on a guy you'd met that morning. Especially when he'd called the man in question "my boy."

"No comment," Max said.

"Hmm," said Baller. He took out his phone, thumbed around on it for a moment, cranked up the volume, and said, "Do me a favor and watch this."

Before Max could object, Baller thrust his phone into Max's hands.

The video must have been taken in the Condors' locker room. Grady was wearing a sweaty team-branded T-shirt, looking intently at the reporter asking the questions. Max missed the first one, but the second came through the speakers clearly.

"How do you feel about rekindling that rivalry now that Max has been traded to the Piranhas?"

Rekindling. What a word choice.

Grady blinked at the reporter in obvious confusion. "I thought he was going to Miami."

Then Max got to watch realization dawn on Grady's face when the reporter said, "They flipped him to Anaheim an hour ago."

Grady rubbed his fingers over his stubble, but it didn't hide the smile, which crept all the way up to his eyes and made the skin at the corners crinkle. It was such an obviously besotted expression that Max couldn't help smiling in return.

Then Grady shook his head and said, "Guess he missed my pretty face," like he hoped it was true.

Max was going to melt onto the floor.

The video ended, but Max didn't move until Baller cleared his throat.

"So," he said cheerfully, "still no comment?"

Max put the phone down on the bench. He brought one hand to his mouth.

Baller patted his thigh. "Wanna find out if he's home?"

*Yes.* Wait. "You know where he lives?"

"I went to his housewarming party."

Grady Armstrong had invited a rival team player to his house? *Max's* Grady? Okay, so Max had also been to Grady's house, but he hadn't been *invited.*

He desperately wanted to be invited. No—he wanted to know he didn't need an invitation.

The shortest way to get there from here was to see Grady now, in person, before he lost his nerve.

Preferably while the memory of Grady's smiling, helplessly in love face was fresh in his mind.

"Yeah," Max said. "Yeah, yes, I do."

Baller grinned. "Cool. I'll call our driver."


*HEY ARE you home?*

Grady finished his wipe-down of the kitchen counters and tossed the paper towel in the trash. Over the past three hours, he'd obsessively cleaned every surface in the house. Not because they were dirty—he'd had the place professionally cleaned before he took possession—but because he needed something to do. Max hadn't answered his text from last night.

Max suggested they reschedule their date. It had taken everything Grady had not to share his Google Calendar and tell Max to pick the earliest time that worked for him.

Instead he'd said, *I'm free tomorrow and the next day. Flying out the day after, back on Sunday night. When works for you?*

He hadn't gotten a reply, hence the cleaning binge.

And now Baller wanted his attention for something. He wished the message had come from Max.

Grady sighed. The house was as clean as it could get. Maybe Baller could provide a new distraction. *Yes. Why?*

The reply came through two minutes later. *Special delivery.*

The doorbell rang.

Grady's phone clattered to the ground. He left it where it landed and went to the door.

Max stood on his front step, hands in his pockets, shoulders hunched. Out of the corner of his eye, Grady barely registered an SUV in the driveway. The person in the passenger seat waved jauntily as it backed out.

Grady ignored it. His heart thudded in his chest. "Hi," he said stupidly.

Max said, "I love you too."

Grady's brain shut off like his phone when he left it in the sun. He'd been desperate to hear Max say that for weeks and now he couldn't speak in return. He didn't even know what to do with his hands.

At least Max was smiling. Actually he looked kind of... giddy. Tired too, punchy maybe. He'd forgotten sunglasses, so he was squinting against the sun, his blue eyes sparkling.

He looked so fucking good Grady could hardly stand it.

"Are you gonna invite me in?" Max asked finally. The twitch of his mouth said he might be about to laugh.

Fuck it, he could laugh at Grady all he liked, especially if he was going to do it in Grady's house.

Grady laughed too, and then he had Max in his arms, kissing him. It felt like a pass connecting right before a goal. Grady let the electricity of it buzz through him, spark over his skin. Max felt warm and right and alive under his hands, and he clung to Grady's shoulders.

Of course that was when Grady's words came back. "I love you." He spoke the words between kisses, against Max's mouth.

Max curled his fingers into the back of Grady's shirt. Somehow they got the door closed.

Only now Grady's stupid mouth didn't want to stop talking. "I should've given you the benefit of the doubt. I overreacted and I hurt you and I'm *sorry*—"

Max took pity on him and put a finger to Grady's lips. His eyes were bright and his cheeks were flushed, and he was wearing just the hint of his old shit-eating smirk. "I forgive you. Now take me to bed."

Grady's body obeyed and started to walk Max into the bedroom even as he teased, "Are you sure, because I had a little more groveling planned—"

Max's laugh whispered against Grady's mouth, and then their lips met again. Grady got his hands on Max's hips and pulled him close.

They'd wasted so much time. Grady wouldn't waste another second.

All the times they slept together, Grady couldn't remember Max being so sweet or so quiet. His rib cage hitched under Grady's hands. When Grady pulled back to look at him, kneeling between his thighs, he took in the bruises on Max's body and the desperation in his eyes and thought, *Okay*.

It had been a fraught couple of months. Yesterday Max had been traded twice in a handful of hours. Maybe he needed someone to be gentle with him.

It didn't look like anyone had been gentle with him in a long time.

So Grady kissed him, and touched him, and held him, softly, in a way he'd never dared. He peeled away all their layers until they were bare.

They laced their fingers together. Max's calf hooked around his ass. The fingers of his opposite hand burned against Grady's hip as he aligned their bodies so they could slide their erections together.

But the tenderness remained. The steadily quickening beat of Max's heart stuttered in the space between their chests. Grady let go of Max's hand and slid his fingers into his hair, like that could tether him, like he could ground Max here in California, in his new home.

Finally Grady's arm slipped on the sheet. Max made a sudden sharp sound into Grady's mouth as his hair pulled, and then they were tumbling over the edge, messy and intimate and clinging to each other.

Grady kept kissing him, but the ache in his shoulders from supporting his weight forced him to move onto his side.

After a few more minutes, Max exhaled heavily through his nose and opened his eyes. "Can't believe I've been in California for, like, twelve hours and I need a second shower already. There's a drought on, you know."

Grady gave him a small smile. "Would it make you feel any better if I told you I have a gray-water reclamation system?"

Max laughed and sat up, pulling Grady with him. "Of course you do. Come on, we can conserve water together."

Their shower amounted to a quick warm rinse and some more kissing, which Grady wouldn't complain about.

Max's fingers tickled against Grady's stomach as he smoothed them through the slick mess they'd left there, until the glob of come washed down the drain. His eyes were dark and calculating as he did the same to his own abs. He must've known what Grady was thinking, because he smirked. "You should do me raw next time."

Grady's breath whooshed out like Max had boarded him. "Your pillow talk is something else."

It was all very lighthearted and silly until Max snatched away Grady's towel and his eyes went to Grady's tattoo.

He ran his thumb over the ink in the bowl of Grady's hip. Goose bumps prickled up Grady's spine. "What's this?"

The giddiness settled into a bone-deep happiness, edged with embarrassment. "That was my forfeit."

Max sat on the edge of the bathtub and pulled Grady closer to get a better look at the design. He traced his fingertips over the linework, the two handles, the jagged teeth of the jaw of the lobster cracker. Grady's skin jumped under his touch. It tickled. "This is what you got when you lost the bet?"

"I don't know if I *lost*," Grady said, echoing Max's words from months ago. "Doesn't feel like I lost. Feels like I got exactly what I wanted."

"Hmm." Max raised his eyes to Grady's. "Kinda risky. Might not have worked out between us. Then what?"

*It still might not*, Grady thought. But they both wanted it to. That was good enough for now. "Then I would have learned a very painful lesson. Physically and emotionally."

"One you were going to carry around on your skin forever."

What did that matter? It was under the skin that counted, and Max had already left his mark there. Grady shrugged.

"I love you, you know," Max said finally. He brushed a kiss over Grady's tattoo. "In case it wasn't obvious."

Grady did know. Hearing it again still made him feel like his heart was made of feathers. "I know." Unlike Grady, Max had always been pretty good about showing it. It had just taken Grady ages to believe what he'd seen.

He was starting to think they should forget the whole staying clean thing and go back to bed, when Max's stomach growled so loudly it echoed in the bathroom.

Max's face scrunched into a laugh that he hid against Grady's hip. Grady pulled him to his feet. "Subtle hint?"

Max smiled ruefully. He still looked tired, but the sadness around his eyes had faded. "I slept through breakfast."

"How?" He shook his head. "And then you went and did a full practice. I'd better feed you before you keel over. Baller will kill me."

They decamped to the kitchen, where Max took a seat at the island while Grady threw together some omelets. "What's his deal, anyway?"

An excellent question. "Baller?" Grady shook his head. It wasn't just that Baller was an incurable romantic and the league's biggest busybody. He wanted his friends to live happily ever after, and if that meant meddling in their love lives, that was what he'd do. "He thinks he's everyone's fairy godfather."

Max snickered. "Aren't you older than he is?"

"Four months," Grady confirmed. "He says it's because he became an Old Married at a young age."

"I'd buy it."

Grady plated the omelets and sat down next to Max with their knees touching, and Max ate like he'd never seen food before. Grady let him go at it for several minutes. "How the fuck did you sleep past breakfast if you're this hungry?"

Max looked up from his plate, sheepish. "Software glitch. Apparently putting my phone on Do Not Disturb also killed my alarm."

That explained why Max never texted him back. "Why did you put your phone on Do Not Disturb?"

He pushed a bite of omelet to the side of his plate. "I got overwhelmed reading all the goodbye texts."

Poor Max.

Grady nudged his ankle in support. He left it there until the meal was finished.

"WE SHOULD probably talk more," Max said in bed later. He was eye level with Grady's tattoo, dancing his fingertips over the ink. Despite the fact that it was obviously a joke, it was beautiful. Max was going to leave a hickey on it next time. "But first—did you deliberately get this on this hip so it would line up with Larry when we fuck doggy style?"

"I can neither confirm nor deny," Grady rumbled, which meant he absolutely had.

Max smiled and raised his head. "You romantic asshole."

Grady snorted and wrapped his hand around Max's upper arm. He tugged until Max crawled up the bed to lie down face-to-face. "You wanted to talk," he said.

Not so much that he wanted to, but playoffs were coming. This wouldn't have mattered so much when Grady played for the Firebirds, who had as much chance of making the playoffs as they did of winning the Nobel Peace Prize. But the Piranhas and the Condors were neck and neck for first place in the Pacific Division. They might play each other in the first or second round. Only one team could advance.

"Playoffs," Max said.

Grady lifted Max's hand and laced their fingers together. Apparently months of frustrated romantic tendencies had pushed to the surface now that the dam had broken. "Yeah. That's going to be interesting."

"One word for it." Max pillowed his head on his other hand. He had a good understanding of his own strengths and failures. He could handle a playoff series loss to the Condors without torpedoing his relationship with Grady, but if he did something stupid or played badly and fell into a funk because of that, it would complicate matters.

On the other hand, Grady had never compartmentalized well. If the Condors lost to the Piranhas, Max anticipated a lot of sulking and bitterness.

But he wasn't going to come out and say, *Hey, babe, are you going to break up with me if my team eliminates yours?* That would be a terrible way to restart their relationship. It wasn't like Grady didn't know what he was like.

So Max said diplomatically, "How are we going to handle that?"

"Badly?" Grady guessed.

Max smothered a laugh. Grady knew what he was like, all right. "I'm serious."

"Oh, a role reversal," Grady teased. "Really, I don't know. It'll be one day at a time. We'll just have to…." He made a face as he trailed off.

"Communicate?" Max suggested wryly. "Not your strong suit."

"God, this is going to be awful."

"Hi, honey. I really love you a lot, but if you score on my team tonight, you're not getting laid for a week."

"I was thinking more along the lines of, you know, 'I need space for a few days.'"

Max could handle that. And it seemed like Grady was willing to give it a try too. "A whole week does seem like kind of a stretch."

"We'll figure it out," Grady promised.

Max wasn't so sure, but he decided to believe anyway. There was no point borrowing trouble before he'd even played his first game in a Piranhas jersey. "It's a plan."

"Then there's one more thing we should talk about."

At Grady's tone, Max narrowed his eyes. He sounded sheepish but also nervous, like this was the beginning of a different kind of confession.

Grady cleared his throat. "Uh, so yesterday in practice our beat reporter asked me about our rivalry...."

Max found himself grinning all over again as he remembered Grady's smile. "Yeah, Baller showed me the video."

With a groan, Grady turned his face into the pillow. "Of course he did." He huffed out a breath. "Anyway, it's kind of making the rounds online, so...."

"So?" What was he driving at?

When he spoke next, his words were muffled. "So it's fueling a lot of wild speculation that I'm secretly madly in love with you."

Oh. Max pursed his lips on a smile. "I mean, if it's all over the internet, I think the secret's out."

Grady sighed and lifted his head again. "Just... this was supposed to be private. We agreed. And I fucked that up. So... I'm sorry again."

What a doofus. "Oh yeah," Max said. "I'm super upset that you're so into me you can't hide it in front of the media. How dare you."

"You're not mad?"

Max shrugged. It wasn't Grady's fault, and that video had made Max so stupidly happy that it seemed absurd to get upset. But it could make their professional lives interesting. "Not at you. If a reporter asks me what you're like in bed, I'll give them so much detail they'll never be able to print any of it."

Grady made a pained face. "Please don't."

"I'll tell them about that bite mark you left on my—"

Grady clapped a hand over his mouth.

Max licked it.

"I should've seen that coming." Grady wiped his hand on Max's chest. "I figure PR'll make the media check those questions, but my actual point was that my team knows now, so that's weird."

Well… yeah, Max could see how that might pose an issue. "Is it going to cause problems with the team if one of them lays a hit on me, you mean?"

"Or vice versa."

As long as no one got injured, Max figured things would be fine, but players got injured all the time, accidentally or not. "There's nothing we can do about that other than play and hope for the best. Like, I'm not going to intentionally hold a grudge, you know?"

"Me neither, but I'm grumpier than you."

And more suspicious, Max didn't add. "And then if, I don't know"—*we broke up*—"we had a fight—"

"It could paint a target on our backs." Grady half shrugged. "But that's hockey. I'm used to that."

"What did your team think?"

Grady rolled onto his back and admitted, "Mitch and Farouk think it's hilarious and they've been blowing up my phone asking if I've seen you yet. Dawg hasn't said anything, but that's because he has a crush on me and it's awkward now." He turned to face Max with a horrified grimace. "You *cannot* tease him about that."

"Not on the ice," Max promised, gleefully filing away the tidbit. He was more likely to torment Grady with it, but hey. "Anyway. What I'm hearing is there's actually no problem with your team and everything's fine so you're borrowing trouble."

"I need to prepare for the worst."

Max opened his mouth to snark—*what happened to you that you're always convinced things will go wrong?*—but he bit his tongue. He knew what happened. If Max's parents had died young in a horrifying accident and his grieving siblings had put their own dreams on hold to raise him, he'd be a little different about it too. "Tell you what," he said instead as he slid his leg between Grady's. "You prepare for the worst. I'll plan for the best."

"Deal." Grady craned his neck and glanced at the clock he had on the bedside table like an eighty-year-old who didn't have a cell phone. "And now I have to prepare with a pregame nap. You're welcome to stick around, but I need to sleep."

"Maybe I'll go skinny-dipping in your pool." But he made no move to get up. A few minutes later Grady's breathing evened out into sleep.

Max followed.

THE NEXT day Max was on a plane to Vancouver for the start of a four-game Western Canada road trip.

It would've been stupid to miss him. They'd spent more of their relationship—however loosely you defined it—apart than together. Besides, he was too busy to think about Max. He had his own games to focus on. They beat San Jose, and then he had to pack.

He did it with the game on in the background, which turned out not to be very efficient because he kept stopping to watch.

Max wasn't having a great game. He made three bad zone entries, and Grady was pretty sure the last one was going to cost the Piranhas a goal for being offsides.

He double-checked his toiletries as the officials reviewed the goal. Max looked frustrated, and Grady didn't blame him. The Orcas were a tough team. Max specialized in finding room where other players couldn't, working in close quarters to score dirty goals. The Orcas' defense excelled at keeping opponents out of those areas.

On top of that, he was playing on the Piranhas' shutdown line, which meant he was playing *against* the Orcas' top line, centered by Nico Kirschbaum, who was on a nine-game scoring streak. But the Piranhas' shutdown line didn't work anything like the Monsters', and Max kept falling out of position. Grady found it painful to watch, so he couldn't imagine Max was enjoying it.

In the third he got so frustrated he broke the Piranhas' strategy entirely and started looking for someone to take a swing at him or trip him or grab his stick because he was an annoying little shithead.

Grady winced and turned the game off, but he set a reminder to text when it had ended.

He'd finished packing and was watering his houseplants when his phone buzzed to signal the end of the game. The Orcas had won 5–2.

That would be a tough loss for Max to swallow, held to no points and at a minus two for the night. For his first game with a new team too.

Would he want to talk? Grady didn't know for sure. But he texted in case. *I'm still up if you want to call when you get back to the hotel.*

Twenty minutes later he got a text notification. *Plz tell me u didn't watch that shitshow.*

*I mean… I was mostly packing*, Grady sent back. *But I can lie if it'll make you feel better.*

Fifteen minutes after that, his phone rang.

"I haven't played a game that bad since my rookie year," Max moaned.

Sugarcoating wasn't in Grady's nature. "I've seen you play better."

"I've played better games hungover." Max sighed. "They're probably regretting that trade right about now."

Defeat sounded wrong on him. Max *never* took games personally— it was his superpower.

His other superpower was knowing what to say or do to snap Grady out of a funk. He'd been doing it, Grady realized now, ever since they started sleeping together. And Grady had no idea how to return the favor. That bothered him. He couldn't just *suck* at… boyfriend things. He couldn't be a *worse boyfriend* than Max.

So making Max feel better was something he'd have to practice, like any other skill.

It would've been easier if Grady could've given him a blow job. But he couldn't, and he also sucked at phone sex, so he'd have to make do with regular words. "I'm pretty sure you're the only one who expects you to master a whole new hockey system in one game."

"Ugh," Max said. "You sound so reasonable. It's disgusting."

Grady smiled. There. Maybe Max didn't feel *better*, but at least Grady had distracted him. "You're welcome."

His next game was better. Grady only caught the tail end of it, from a bar in Raleigh. He couldn't watch as closely as he wanted because Farouk kept chirping him, but he caught Max's assist on a goal to seal the Piranhas' win against Calgary, so hopefully that would cheer him up.

*Nice apple*, Grady texted.

"No sexting at the table," Farouk said. "Save it for your hotel room."

By the time Grady got there, he'd have just enough energy to take his clothes off and fall into bed. Their game had gone to a twelve-round shootout. He was whooped. And Max would just be finishing his game.

"Yes sexting at the table," Mitch said, "but you have to read them out loud."

Grady pretended to consider it. "Just mine, or Max's too?" Not that he'd do either, but Mitch didn't have to know that.

"Fuck," Farouk said. "I take it back. Sext all you want, but keep that shit to yourself. I don't want to know about any Fish's weird sex kinks. Instant buzzkill."

Victorious, Grady reached for his beer. "Agree to disagree."

He fell asleep in his hotel room before Max texted him back. In the morning he had a new text message—*That shootout goal was [fire emoji]*.

They kept up a steady correspondence while Max was gone. Grady loved playing for the Condors. Winning wouldn't get old anytime soon. Having friends on the team—beyond Coop, who still texted him a couple times a week—made for a completely different experience even when they lost.

And he didn't feel like the success of the team rested on his shoulders alone. He wasn't sure if it was the team or the media or the fans or his own ego that made him feel that way in Philly, but he didn't miss the pressure. And with Farouk on his line, he was scoring more points than he had in years.

Watching Max struggle while Grady flourished was weird. Max was one of the most consistent players in the league. It used to drive Grady crazy. It was strange to hate seeing him play poorly when not so long ago he would've reveled in it.

"I feel like I'm on another planet," Max confided one night from Winnipeg. Grady assumed this wasn't a comment on the weather, which was approximately the same in Winnipeg in February as it was on the surface of Pluto. "Why would they even trade for someone whose game is so different from their system?"

None of the usual reasons—cap relief, tanking for draft picks, incompetent management—applied, so Grady said, "They obviously think you can adapt. It's been like a week. Give yourself a break."

"Eleven days," Max corrected.

"Oh, I'm sorry, eleven days, including a transcontinental move, some pretty severe jet lag, and your boyfriend fucking your brains out—"

Max made a tiny sound that might have been a laugh.

"—twice—"

"That's pretty generous."

"You're right, there wasn't much there to begin with."

"Wow, you suck at this pep talk thing."

Snickering, Grady thought, *What would Max do?* "You're right. Let me try again. Suck it up, figure out what your coaches want from you, and when you get home, I'll be mean to you in bed about it."

There was a pause. Then Max said, "Hey, what are you wearing right now?"

So maybe Grady was better at this than he thought. Or at least he had a pretty good learning curve.

Unfortunately, he needed an entirely different skill set to deal with the other most important person in his life.

The day before Max returned from his road trip, Grady had just finished his morning swim when Jess, Polly, and Amanda showed up from Philadelphia with the rest of his plants.

"Hey, loser." Jess pushed a cardboard box laden with herbs into his arms. "Nice place. Got room for a few more?"

"Come in," Grady said belatedly. "And uh… I guess that depends how long you're staying and how you feel about roommates?"

He set the box on the kitchen counter. Jess, Polly, and Amanda followed him in, each hauling a box of plants and with a duffel over their shoulder.

"Roommates?" Jess dropped her bag, gave him a hug—a quick one because he was still damp—then stepped back and narrowed her eyes.

Grady probably should've put on a shirt so he didn't show off the bite mark Max left on his pec. "Uh, I mean, maybe more like occasional overnight guests?"

"Oh my God," Jess said. "I admit that I wondered after that video went up, but you really *took him back?*"

"Oh look, a pool," Polly said brightly. "Amanda, let's go check that out. Okay bye!"

The sliding door closed audibly behind them.

Grady huffed. "I begged for forgiveness for being an asshole."

Jess's eyes went flinty. "He broke your arm, Grady."

"During a hockey game *six years ago*, and it was an accident."

"You didn't think so at the time."

"I didn't know Max at the time." Max didn't hurt people on purpose. "Besides, Amanda broke your heart and you gave her a second chance."

"That's different."

"Why? She broke up with you because our parents died and you'll take her back ten years later just fine, but I broke up with Max because of a dumb misunderstanding and we made up after a couple weeks and that's not okay?"

Jess crossed her arms, radiating displeasure. "You were really upset."

"So were you ten years ago, and you don't see me getting in the way of your happiness now. You think only older siblings get to feel overprotective?"

She broke his gaze. "I'm… sorry. I pushed you to start dating and you slept with Max instead, and you were so happy and then you weren't, and it just… felt like my fault."

Grady stared at her. "What the fuck. How was it your fault I thought Max was blabbing secrets about our sex life to his teammates?"

"I didn't say it was *rational*." She dropped into a seat at the breakfast bar.

Grady joined her. "If it helps any, I've definitely, like, been there. For example, when you and Amanda broke up."

Jess looked at him in surprise. "Grades. That wasn't your fault."

He resisted the urge to cross his arms in the same defensive gesture Jess had used earlier. "If I'd been older, or if I hadn't existed, Amanda wouldn't have had a freakout about becoming a stepparent. She wouldn't have dumped you."

"Jesus." She leaned closer over the counter. "I never blamed you for that, okay? We were both doing the best we could."

Grady put his hand over hers. "Yeah. And we still are."

For a second, Jess only blinked at him. Then she said, "Motherfucker, did Max make you this sappy?"

Grady grinned. "Yeah, he did."

"Ugh." She rolled her eyes, but she was smiling. "Fine. I guess I'm happy for you. Loser."

"Thank you." He smiled. "I think we should hug now?"

"Oh my God, Max really *did* change you." But she laughed and stood up to hug him, and she clung tighter than he could remember in years. Grady sank into it. They should hug more often.

Then she pulled away and looked him up and down, her gaze lingering on the waistband of his swimsuit, which had slipped down under the weight of the damp material until the top of the lobster cracker was just visible. "Is that a tattoo?"

MAX GOT off the plane from Edmonton blinking sandpapery eyes and dragging his feet.

The bruises from his time as a Monster had mostly healed and been replaced by new ones, though not as many. He'd finally scored his first goal in a Piranhas jersey, slick and dirty from the paint, the way he liked it.

The Piranhas had taken him out to celebrate, and Max's liver would never be the same.

But at least he had the proverbial monkey off his back. Now he could… go back to his hotel and be alone.

He unlocked his rental car and dropped into the driver's seat, where he texted Grady. *This is going to sound dumb but I really miss my dog. Facetime isnt the same.*

Gru didn't react to the sound of his voice, and Max couldn't pet him through the screen. It only made him feel lonelier.

Grady's response lit up his phone before he could start the ignition. *So come over and you can rub my belly.*

Horrified, Max dropped his phone and started the car. His hands-free lit up with a second message before he even put it in Drive. With many misgivings, Max pushed the button to have the car read the text.

*Ok, that was really bad. Sorry. I've spent too much time listening to Jess flirt with her girlfriends. I promise I did not just casually suggest pet play by text. That's an in-person conversation.*

"Jesus," Max muttered.

"Do you want to respond?" the cheerful Android Auto lady asked.

Fuck it. He really didn't want to be alone, and he had to meet the in-laws sometime. At least he wouldn't be stuck in the house with them for three days. "Yeah, tell him 'Be there in half an hour, freak.'"

Max assumed Grady was the only one home when he got to Grady's, because Grady dragged him into his bedroom by his tie and—after half tearing the rest of Max's clothes off—used it to bind Max's wrists behind his back.

Then he shoved his own pants down and pulled Max over his lap.

Before Max could do more than catch his balance, Grady pressed two slick fingers inside him. Max was still groaning in ecstasy at the stretch when Grady replaced them with his cock.

Max exhaled sharply and arched his back.

A steady stream of filth fell from Grady's lips as Max rode his dick, and he twisted Max's nipple piercings almost as mean as Max could ever want.

Max came when Grady slapped the inside of his thigh, blindsided by an orgasm that ripped out of him and left him boneless.

Before he could gather the strength to move so Grady could jerk himself off, Grady's eyes went wide and his mouth opened and he made a hurt sound and thrust up into Max's body one more time.

A few seconds later, when he pulled out, Max felt the slick of his come dribbling out of him. He shuddered in pleasure when Grady wiped his thumb up the wetness on the back of his thigh.

They were both shaky when Grady untied him. He made a wry face as he tossed the silk into the trash. "I think I owe you a new tie."

Max collapsed face-first onto the mattress. "Call it even." He never wanted to move. "Feel free to defile all of my ties. I'll start buying them at Costco."

"Absolutely not." Grady lay down beside him, still breathing heavily. Max turned onto his side to look at him. "No boyfriend of mine will be seen with a bulk-purchased tie. What would people say. I'm putting my foot down."

Max still felt gooey inside when Grady said *boyfriend*. Or maybe that was something else. "What are you gonna do about it?" he teased.

"I told you. You like Tom Ford?" He danced his fingers over the hollow of Max's neck. "I'll buy you a new tie. I'll buy you fifty ties."

For a moment Max had to bury his face in the pillow to hide his grin. Either sex completely fried Grady's brain, or he was one of those guys who was prone to spoiling his boyfriend outrageously. Max knew where he'd put his money. "You just want to show me off."

Grady tapped his nose. "Maybe I do."

The kicker of it was, Max believed him. And it sounded kind of nice.

He took a deep, happy breath and let himself nap.


HE AWOKE to muffled voices.

At some point Grady'd gotten out of bed, because Max was alone with the sheet pushed down to his waist. He sat up and scrubbed a hand over his face as he tried to gauge the time. He'd probably been asleep for an hour and a half.

If Grady was up and talking to someone—and the voices coming from the direction of the kitchen suggested actual humans and not the TV—then chances were Jess and her girlfriends were home, which meant Max needed to put on pants.

Scratch that. Max needed a shower, *then* pants.

He scrubbed down quickly in Grady's en suite, then decided it was better to ask for forgiveness than permission and raided Grady's dresser. He wasn't wearing wrinkled suit pants to lounge around Grady's house.

Besides, how thirsty would that look to Grady's sister—that Max had been so desperate for it that he hadn't even bothered bringing his travel bag in from the car.

Max *was* that thirsty, but he didn't have to advertise it to anyone but Grady. He slipped on a pair of loose exercise shorts—looser on him than on Grady, because Max's metabolism made keeping an ass like that impossible—and a T-shirt, and went to go find his boyfriend.

Maybe he should've borrowed a swimsuit instead, since everyone was gathered around the pool, with the sliding doors open to let in a breeze.

Picking out Jess was easy, since he'd seen her at the NHL Awards, but given enough time Max would have recognized her anyway. She looked a lot like Grady, with the same serious face, dark hair, and blue-green eyes. She had a starfish-patterned towel wrapped around her hips over a red two-piece swimsuit, and her hair was wet.

The other two women were still in the pool, batting a beach ball back and forth. Max assumed the taller, blond one with the broad shoulders was Amanda—she had a hockey player's musculature—which made the redhead standing in the shallow end Polly.

Grady was sitting in the shade near the door with his phone in his lap. He glanced up and smiled when Max walked out. "Hey. You're up."

"Looks like I'm late to the party. And overdressed." He perched on the end of Grady's lounge chair.

"You could always take your shirt off," Grady said sweetly, like he didn't know Max's nipples were currently not safe for public consumption. He rearranged his feet on either side of the lounger to give Max room.

"Oh no. My delicate East Coast princess skin needs time to adjust to the climate." He turned toward Grady's visitors. Now or never. "I'm Max, by the way. Hi."

"Oh my God," Amanda said quietly. "Seriously, Jess?"

Across the pool, Jess threw up her hands. "It wasn't my place to tell you."

Amanda must have recognized Max as Grady's archnemesis. "Surprise?"

Polly and Amanda waved and introduced themselves. Then Grady cleared his throat and Jess stood up from the other side of the pool and walked over.

She held out her hand. "Hi. I'm Jess."

Max stood to shake it. She was a tall woman, not quite eye level with him, and she had a firm grip that said she'd dealt with a lot of men having handshake pissing contests in her life. "Nice to meet you in person. I don't think that phone call counts."

Polly and Amanda had climbed out of the pool, and now Polly glanced over. "Phone call?"

Jess cleared her throat as her demeanor went from aloof older sister to chagrined girlfriend who really didn't want him to elaborate. "Ah, yeah. Thanks... for that, by the way."

Max grinned. "Any time."

When the breeze picked up, they went inside. Grady and Polly headed toward the open-concept kitchen to discuss a late lunch, and Jess and Amanda cornered Max in the living area.

"So." Amanda propped her chin on her hand on the edge of the sofa. "How long has this been going on?"

"What's 'this' exactly? The official relationship? When we started banging?" Maybe they wanted to know how long since Grady picked out Max's dishwasher?

"That's the wrong question anyway." Jess tucked her legs up on the couch. "The real question is, are you ready to play against him again the day after tomorrow?"

Max snorted. "I don't know if you know this, but I've played against your brother a few times this season. He got traded in the middle of the last game, though, so that sucked." Not to mention the whole breakup thing.

"At least we're past the trade deadline?"

True. "Anyway, believe it or not, I'm actually good at leaving the game on the ice."

With a glance toward the kitchen, Jess said, "That's not what I was worried about." At first Max thought she meant Grady—which, fair enough; Grady wasn't the most graceful loser Max had played against. But then she said, "I meant the media circus that's going to happen because the internet isn't sure if Grady's in love with you or in love with the idea of punching you in the face."

Grady carried over a tray of sandwiches. "I mean, it's both." Behind him, Polly had a stack of cups and a pitcher of iced tea.

Max blinked. He'd forgotten all about that. His phone had been a social-media-free zone since the trade.

Grady set down the tray and put his hand on Max's shoulder.

"Right." Jess cleared her throat like she was somehow trying to draw attention from Max's vulnerable moment. "So anyway, yeah, have your agents not been in touch about how you want to handle that? Because Grades, no offense, but subtlety isn't your strong suit and the media is definitely going to ask for Max's take on your comments."

Unfortunately, she was right. Max had mostly escaped having to talk to the media as the newest Piranha so far because he hadn't been scoring much. The questions had focused on how he was adapting and then, last night, how it felt to finally get that first goal in his new uniform. But hockey reporters loved rivalries. Instead of the same bland answers and feigned respect—you could never say anything that would get you characterized as arrogant when the entire hockey fanbase expected players to act humble, even if the other team objectively sucked—rivalries brought out sound bites like *they hate us as much as we hate them* and *if my sister dated a Monster? I'd probably disown her*.

Grady had said he wanted to show Max off, and Max had slept soundly wrapped in the warm fuzzies from that declaration, but how was that going to play with their jobs? He tried to think what he'd say about Grady now, if a question caught him off guard. He'd probably make the same dumb besotted face Grady had and whatever words came out of his mouth would sound exactly like *However the game ends, I'll end the night with Grady's cock in my throat.* "Shit."

Polly grabbed a sandwich and a plate and perched on the arm of the sofa, her knee against Jess's shoulder. "Eat your lunch first," she said. "Strategize after."

AS EVERYONE who knew him could tell you, talking was not Grady's strongest point. He sat on the end of his bed and ran his hands through his hair as he tried to order his thoughts.

Annoyingly, he had no one to blame but himself. He was the one who'd lost control of his face when he'd learned Max would soon be back within arm's reach.

Even more annoyingly, he hadn't given a second's thought to what the almighty Narrative would be, this time around. In the fall, he'd used the inevitable public fallout as an excuse to keep his thing with Max in a vault labeled CASUAL.

Or, well, to try to keep it there, at least. Sometime when Grady wasn't looking, Max snuck in and picked the lock and got feelings all over everything.

"Are you freaking out?" Max asked finally from where he'd sprawled out next to him.

Grady thought about it. "Weirdly, no." They needed to figure out how to handle this, but it was a minor nuisance, not something he dreaded. Actually, it was kind of funny.

"Okay. Cool." Max nudged his hip, and Grady flopped backward and turned his head to face him. "So what do you want to do?"

"I don't know. This is going to sound so stupid, but I actually never thought about it."

Max snorted. "Bull shit." He made it two words to emphasize his disbelief. "You were so paranoid, Grady, don't even front. We went to get milkshakes in the middle of the night and you were looking over your shoulder like the hockey rivalry police were going to come for you."

Yeah, Grady would give him that one.

"And yet you were still dumb enough to park your car in my driveway and then you tried to give *me* shit—"

"I meant the second time," Grady blurted. "Once I fucked up, all that mattered was fixing things with you."

God. He would've been embarrassed, except Max made a sound like he'd been punched and smushed his face into the mattress. "You think my pillow talk is rough. Have you listened to yourself talk about your feelings?"

"I try not to," Grady said honestly, and smiled when Max shook with laughter.

"Okay. So what's our objective here?" he said when he'd recovered. "Full-on star-crossed lovers treatment? Are we leaving them guessing? What do you want?"

"Art Ross? Stanley Cup? Hall of Fame induction?" Grady was spitballing. He had what he wanted. He did kind of want to show Max off, but Max had fallen asleep before he could agree to that, and anyway that was gravy.

Besides, Grady didn't know if he could say that out loud a second time.

Max snorted and slid his knee between Grady's thighs. "Settle for a hot boyfriend and a blow job?"

It seemed like he wouldn't have to. Grady threaded his fingers through Max's hair. "For now."

But he kept thinking about it afterward. It was easier to think about what he *didn't* want, and harder to imagine saying it. He didn't want to be expected to say cruel things about Max. He didn't want people to think Grady hated him. He wasn't going to pull his checks on the ice—he'd play as hard as he always had. But he wanted the rivalry to stay on the ice—and okay, maybe in the bedroom sometimes, but only if it was in fun.

He wanted to play hockey, *good* hockey, and learn how to bully Max out of his rare bad moods, and come home from road trips to a bed that Max had slept in, was still sleeping in, would sleep in again. He didn't want to care what anybody thought about it.

That would be enough.

He hadn't napped earlier, and Max was warm and heavy on his chest, the perfect living weighted blanket, and Grady was doped up on orgasms and content for the first time in years. He should finish his conversation with Max.

Maybe he would close his eyes for a moment. He and Max could talk afterward.

MAX HATED to leave Grady while he was sleeping, but he could only nap so much before it interfered with his ability to fight jet lag. After ten minutes he got up and crept out of the room, then closed the door quietly behind him.

Polly looked up from her seat on the couch, where she was curled up with a book. "Come to any conclusions?"

Max grinned. "Probably not in the way you're thinking."

Laughing, she closed her book and turned her full attention to him. "Are you heading out?"

"I probably should. We play against each other the day after tomorrow. I need to be able to lay a clean hit without thinking about my feelings." Honestly, Max didn't think he'd have a problem, but... well. They'd just gotten back together. He didn't want to push too hard, too fast. Grady wasn't the only one who'd cracked. Max needed a little space or he'd break himself open for Grady all over again. "I promise I'll text him something naughty from my hotel, though, give him something nice to wake up to."

"True love." Polly feigned a swoon.

Max slipped his feet into his dress shoes. Grady's stupid feet were too small. This was what he'd been reduced to—dress shoes in bare feet, borrowed shorts, and a T-shirt. If Grady could see him right now, he'd probably have a nightmare. "It was nice meeting you. I hope I'll see you again before you leave."

She smiled and pushed a lock of red hair behind her ear. "I think we'll have lots of time to get to know each other."

That sounded nice. He gave her a quick wave of acknowledgment, then turned around and opened the door.


## RIVALS' REMATCH
### By Sonia Goldstein

With a few weeks left in the regular season and the Condors and Piranhas neck and neck for the top seed in the Pacific Division, the stage is set for an epic rivalry showdown.

But this West Coast matchup has a little East Coast flavor in the form of former Philadelphia Firebird Grady Armstrong and onetime New Jersey Monster Max Lockhart. The question is, is that flavor as bitter as expected?

You might recall a time several seasons ago when Armstrong came out of an on-ice encounter with Lockhart with a fractured ulna, or a fight the year after that when Lockhart got the business end of Armstrong's fist to his nose.

But if you've spent any time on hockey Twitter in the past two weeks, you've also seen Armstrong's now-infamous reaction to learning Lockhart would be joining him in California. Anyone could be forgiven for interpreting his expression as sweet rather than salty.

So did Lockhart truly miss Armstrong's pretty face? Tomorrow night's game should shed some light—or blood—on the subject.

**Comments:**

I'm here for the blood! Let's go Condors!

Get you a man who smiles like that when he thinks about you.

I have watched this video 27 times and I cannot come up with another explanation. They are in love. I will be retiring to my bedroom to scream into my pillow. Thank you for your understanding in this trying time.

Who cares if they're sleeping together as long as they give us a good show. And I mean *on* the ice.

MAX AND Grady still hadn't made a decision about how to handle the situation by the Condors' practice the next day, so Grady was unprepared when Jeremy tapped him on the shoulder. "Hey, I need you in Natalie's office for a couple minutes after practice."

Natalie was the Condors' GM. "Okay."

But when he arrived, the atmosphere was very California. Natalie sat in a velour beanbag chair, drinking a green smoothie. Jeremy perched on one of those sit/stand chairs next to a wall-mounted desk space, fidgeting with something on a tablet.

"Hey, Grades," Jeremy said cheerfully. "Come on in and make yourself at home. You want a kombucha or something?"

Grady wanted a real chair and a drink that had only been fermented if it was alcoholic, so he said, "No, thanks," and sat awkwardly on the chaise longue.

"Cool." Jeremy moved to the beanbag opposite Natalie. "So, you're probably wondering why you're here."

*Not really.*

Before he could go on, Natalie gave an amused smile. "Jeremy's not giving you enough credit. Obviously you're here so we can ask if you're involved with Max Lockhart. Which you're well within your rights to be and we are not upset about, and if you'd like to call your agent for this conversation, we've made sure she's available."

Gee, they'd really thought of everything. Grady should absolutely call Erika and she'd be pissed if he didn't, so he nodded while they got her on the phone.

"Right," Jeremy said once Erika had picked up and introductions had been made. "So, tomorrow we've got our last regular season game against the Piranhas. Very big rivalry game. It's on their home turf, but the crowd should be split about fifty-fifty."

As if Grady hadn't watched an hour of video on the Piranhas in the past week. "Yeah, I know."

"What you might *not* know," Jeremy said, "is that we track engagement on our games on social media by geographic region. Generally speaking, nobody east of Colorado cares what happens in California hockey until the Cup Final. But whether it's because it's you and Lockhart and you're drawing from the Philly-New Jersey market, or if people are invested in you personally because of your interview, or both, we don't know, but we're seeing a 30 percent increase in engagement in the Eastern Conference states."

Either way, Grady guessed, they wanted to capitalize on that.

"It sounds like you're looking at this as an opportunity," Erika said neutrally through the speaker.

"Absolutely." Natalie set aside her smoothie cup. "I want to make clear up front that we don't expect Grady's on-ice behavior to change. However, if you're comfortable playing up the angles—speaking about the personal relationship between yourself and Lockhart, positive or negative…."

Grady blinked. Positive or negative? That sort of sounded like they didn't care what was going on with the two of them either way.

Erika cleared her throat. "I need a moment with my client, please. Grady, pick up the phone and take it off speaker."

He did.

"Okay," Erika said. "On the one hand, this is good. This lays the groundwork for you being able to do and say what you want about Max and having management's tacit approval. On the other hand, we want to make sure they're not going to feed you lines to say to generate clicks when those may work against your personal interests. Do you understand?"

Thank God he had an agent to navigate this shit for him. "Yeah, that makes sense."

"So I don't want you to agree to anything yet. I'm going to have them put what they want in writing and send it to me, and we'll have our lawyers look at it, and then you and I will talk. It's possible they're going to talk merchandise, and if they do, you and Max should each get a cut of it. The deal may not be done by the game tomorrow. Don't agree verbally or sign anything until you and I have talked."

"I won't."

"Great. And Grady?"

"Yes?"

"Next time you decide to fall in love with another hockey player, don't let me find out from the internet."

Grady's cheeks heated. "Kind of hoping this is the last time."

"Mazel tov. Okay, you can put me on speaker again."

The rest of the team had cleared out by the time the meeting ended. Grady drove himself home wondering if Max had had a similar experience of his own—but he didn't have to wonder for long.

His phone rang.

Grady stabbed the button to take the call on the car speakers.

"So," Max said, "did you have the same talk I just did?"

Grady signaled a lane change and slowed way down. The delay in leaving practice meant he'd hit traffic. Well, worse traffic than usual. "The one where our respective front offices think our relationship means dollar signs?"

"Yeah, I mean, I know we're commodities, but this is a whole new level. On the other hand, it seems like they're going to let us do whatever and not interfere."

"That was the impression I got too." Considering that only a few years ago the whole league would've flipped its shit over a player coming out, never mind two of them dating each other, Grady couldn't complain much. Maybe he should write Baller a thank-you note. "Like their own personal soap opera or something."

"Hey, if it works for pro wrestling," Max said wryly. "So… I'll see you tomorrow?"

Grady puffed out his cheeks. He wanted to say *No, come over tonight.* But he shouldn't. He didn't want to wonder if he'd have had a better night's sleep with Max out of the house, or if Max had sabotaged him somehow. He knew Max wouldn't, but he didn't trust himself not to have a weak moment and blame Max anyway, and ruin everything.

"Tomorrow," Grady said. "Bring your A game."

# Overtime

WHEN MAX walked into the Fishtank for his first home game, he could feel the electricity in the air crackling along his skin.

The locker room buzzed with anticipation. Max was buzzing too, not only with anticipation but with nerves. The last time he'd played against Grady, things had gone to shit. He needed tonight to go well to prove to himself—and Grady—that playing on rival teams wasn't a deal-breaking obstacle for their relationship.

No pressure.

Bishop bumped his fist as he headed into the workout room for the first part of his warmup routine. "Ready for this?"

*Guess we'll find out.* "Always."

Bishop climbed onto the exercise bike next to him. "You want to give me a real answer?"

Max gave him a sideways glance. "I'm saving that for media."

Snorting, Bishop slipped his AirPods in and let Max stew in peace.

After a few minutes on the bike and another ten of two-touch, Max felt more like himself. It helped that the Fish were a young, energetic group and only took themselves as seriously as they needed to and that Baller had shown up with his walking boot and was offering advice from the sidelines.

"Don't forget to make a lot of stick jokes. Oh—you could mention how you're going to try to keep his stick tied up."

Max feigned a long-suffering expression and turned to Bishop. "What's he even doing here?"

"Hey! I'm moral support."

"Lockhart." Their PR person poked their head out into the hallway. "You're up."

Bishop crossed himself. "Go with God, my son."

Max replied with a much ruder gesture.

It was easier sitting in the hot seat only having to think about Grady's reaction and not the team's.

The first question came from Piranhas beat reporter, Craig MacLeod. "Are you looking to start something tonight to get the team fired up?"

"I think the team's plenty fired up already, and it turns out I play better when I'm on the ice instead of in the box, so… no, I'm not going looking for trouble. But it usually finds me anyway."

He laughed.

"This is your first home game as a Piranha. What do you want to accomplish tonight?"

Max scratched at his chin where he'd nicked himself shaving. "That's a good question. I think last game I finally started to find my groove on the team, started scoring goals again, sort of fit what I can do into the system the Piranhas play, which is different from what I'm used to. So I'm looking to continue that and hopefully give the fans a good show."

"Max, how do you respond to Armstrong's comment that you must have missed his face?"

Oh, an easy one. Max put on his most innocent expression. "Guess I'll aim higher next time."

That was the last question for the session. Their beleaguered PR person gave him a look once they'd ushered everyone else out. "We might have to revisit that 'say what you want' rule."

In fairness to Max, he could've been talking about not spearing Grady in the dick instead of giving him a facial. He wasn't, but the internet didn't have to know that.

Half the arena booed when the Condors hit the ice for warm-ups, but they made enough noise to fill the space. Max laughed, invigorated all over again, and raised his stick in a salute when he took his own first lap on home ice. Half the arena booed him too, but the other half drowned them out.

Someone near the Condors' bench had a poster of a bird with a fish in its talons. A few seats down, a fan had rendered a Piranha chowing down on a chicken leg. Max grinned at them and tossed them a puck.

Around center ice, someone was holding a sign that depicted a muscular arm wrapped in chains and secured with a heart-shaped lock. Clever. The legend read LOCK IT DOWN, MAX.

Kind of early, but Max would take the suggestion under advisement. He winked at the fan holding the sign and skated back to start the shootout drill.

"How'd you get popular so fast?" one of his new teammates asked, mouth twisted with barely contained humor.

*I sucked Grady Armstrong's dick.* "Must be my sparkling personality," Max told him, and snagged a puck for his shot on net. It went bar-down. Perfect.

Max wouldn't shoot again for a minute, so he looped up to center ice to peek at the Condors.

Grady was stretching near the center line, and he glanced up as Max snowed to a stop next to him. "Really?"

"Gotta give the fans something new to talk about," Max told him cheerfully.

With a dead-eyed expression, Grady wiped ice shavings off his eyebrow and flicked them at Max. "Aim higher, huh?"

"You can get me back later."

When Grady made a vaguely threatening motion with his stick, Max laughed and skated away.

For obvious publicity reasons, Max and Grady took the opening faceoff. The ref eyed them both with the expression of a man facing the gallows. "I don't suppose I can talk the two of you into a nice clean game."

"You could try," Max offered.

Grady chomped his mouthguard and rolled his eyes.

The ref sighed. "That's what I thought."

Then the puck dropped.

Max won the faceoff by the skin of his teeth. The crowd roared as he regrouped around Bishop to follow the puck into the offensive zone.

Bishop dropped the pass back to Max, in perfect position to screen his shot. But Grady collided with him before he could pull the trigger.

The impact knocked Max's breath out of him, but it also made him laugh. Of course. He should've expected nothing less. Grady only played to win, even if that meant Max got steamrolled.

It was on.

Max's shot went wide. A Condors defenseman collected the puck from behind the net, and now Max and his team were chasing.

As Max burned toward the defensive zone with Bishop, something finally clicked. Max had spent almost two weeks on third line waiting for this feeling. Tonight he was getting his first shot at first line, and he *belonged* here.

And by the end of the night, everyone in this arena would know it.

The game got physical fast, not with fights, but with questionable checks and raised elbows. Max kept his head up and his elbows in and didn't run anyone into the boards, mindful of Barry's admonition in Winnipeg—*Your job here isn't to draw penalties, it's to score goals. Don't get injured. And stay out of the box.*

Max stayed out of the box. Damned if he was going to stay out of the box score.

The Condors drew first blood with a goal five minutes in, Grady from Barclay—the one he called Dawg. Instead of letting it ruin his night, Max let it fuel him.

Three shifts later he roofed the puck on a one-timer, and the Fishtank erupted in cheers. Bishop slammed into his side with a whoop and bellowed, "Fresh Fish!"

"BEWARE THE FISH!" the fans chanted. "BEWARE THE FISH!"

Laughter bubbled out of Max's throat as the sound of it washed over him. Beware the Fish. And he was one of them.

"Nice goal," Bishop said. "Let's get another one."

In the meantime, they had their hands full keeping the Condors from scoring again. Max might be keeping his elbows in and the butt end of his stick to himself, but that didn't stop him from laying legal hits.

"Hey babe, miss me?" he chirped his usual line as he slammed his body into Grady's, sweeping his stick out in front to try to get to the puck.

Grady responded with a variation on his own theme. "Maybe if you went away and gave me a chance—" He passed the puck, and Max didn't have a reason to hang on him anymore.

Not until *after* the game, anyway.

Grady's linemate scored again in the middle of the second. Both teams were rolling, and Max could already tell he had half a dozen shiny new bruises. Grady wasn't the only one who'd laid a hit on him, though Grady's had probably been the most legal.

Every time Max returned the favor, Barclay gave him the evil eye. Max blew him a kiss.

The Fish tied the game again, and Max added another goal eighty-three seconds later. So he knew, going into the third, that there'd be a target on his back.

Max's line didn't play against Grady's every shift. Nothing in hockey lined up that perfectly. But they played each other often enough for Max to lay another good hit early in the period, two shifts after Grady got away with holding Max's stick to keep him from taking a pass.

Max couldn't be mad about it, since it was Grady's job to get away with it, but he *could* retaliate.

He just didn't expect to turn half a second later and find Barclay's fist zooming toward his face.

Max dodged the first wild punch. Barclay was clearly an inexperienced fighter, because he'd left his gloves on and his footing sucked. But now his gloves came off and he grabbed the sleeve of Max's jersey with his left hand and swung again.

A solid part of Max's career had been built on his ability to take punches. Normally, though, he got more warning, and his opponents were players his own size and not teenagers who were 97 percent hormones by volume, and too hotheaded to give their opponents time to drop their gloves.

Max might not have the same soft hands as Grady, but they worked a hell of a lot better when his fingers weren't broken. He preferred not to test them on other people's faces—especially not guys like Howard Barclay, who'd grown out of his baby fat without growing into the ability to build muscle. If Max hit him, he'd go down like a sack of potatoes.

The second punch caught the side of Max's jaw and knocked off his helmet.

Somewhere a whistle blew. Max knew the linesmen were making a beeline for them, ready to break up the fight.

But he recognized the fury in Barclay's eyes, and he'd need a couple teammates to pull him back. Meanwhile, Max didn't want a concussion.

So he shucked his own gloves and twisted his arm out of Barclay's grasp. For the first time, reality intruded on whatever was going on in the kid's mind. Max saw the *oh shit* flash in his eyes.

Then he grabbed the front of Max's jersey instead, and fine, he asked for it. At least he still had his helmet on. Max hooked an ankle behind the kid's leg, knocked him to the ice on his back, and then followed him down in an undignified heap.

"You fucking asshole!" Barclay shouted. "You piece of shit!"

What the fuck. "Simmer down, kid." What did Max do?

Barclay was still trying to hit him, though with Max essentially sitting on him, the blows landed against his pads. It probably hurt Barclay more than Max.

It felt like an eternity passed before they separated, with the bewildered linesmen helping Max up while a couple of Barclay's teammates held his arms and tried to talk him down. One of them was Grady, who was bleeding from the nose.

"Did I do that?" Max asked under his breath as the ref sent Barclay down the tunnel. That would explain part of why Barclay went apeshit.

With a grimace, Grady swiped away some of the blood. "No, which is why you're not in the box."

Max blinked at him. Why was he so pissed off? "So then how…."

Grady pressed his lips together in a thin line. "Watch the replay."

So he was definitely pissed. Fantastic.

At least the game was almost over.

The refs called three more penalties in the last eight minutes, but the outcome didn't change—the Piranhas pulled out a 3–2 victory. Max hardly took any satisfaction in it. What had just happened didn't make any sense.

Somehow he managed to answer a handful of media questions after the game. By the time he'd showered and dressed, the rest of the team was making plans to go out to celebrate.

Max took advantage of their planning to send a message to Grady. *R u ok? wtf was that with ur captain?*

Grady hadn't replied by the time Bishop ruffled Max's hair and said, "You're coming. Hero of the hour and all that."

He should. A little hometown team bonding would be good for him, and it might stop him from obsessing over his phone all night.

"Obviously."

"Nice. Baller found this new place—"

It figured that Baller had become the de facto social coordinator.

Max made the most of his night out. A little alcohol, a few ridiculous stories, rookies being rookies, good music, and good atmosphere should have had him feeling fine. He didn't have to put on a show for these guys; they were young and fun and had Baller for that. Max only had to sip his beer and follow along and laugh when the occasion called for it, which was often because Baller was kind of a drama queen.

But he couldn't entirely keep the situation with Grady out of his mind, and he kept checking his phone. Finally, a little over an hour after Max had texted, Grady sent, *I'm fine. It's a long story. Talk to you tomorrow?*

Max released a breath, but the knot in his shoulders didn't go with it. He wished Grady had used a different word than *fine*. He wished Grady would just talk to him now so he could stop worrying about it. Not that Max was in a very good place to talk, between the alcohol and the volume in the bar.

He hunched his shoulders and reached for his drink. If it was this hard to talk to each other after a regular season game, how the fuck were they going to manage if they had to play against each other in the playoffs?

GRADY CAME out of his meeting with the coach in a black mood that he knew showed all over his face.

Showering didn't help, but at least he'd missed any postgame interviews.

He texted Max, feeling guilty the message had sat there so long while Grady endured a mortifying conversation, but the last thing Grady wanted to do now was talk about it some more.

In Philly, the guys on the team would've taken one look at Grady and studiously ignored him.

Farouk assessed him head to toe and said, "You need a drink. I'm buying."

Grady didn't want a drink. He wanted to go home and get into bed and pull the blankets over his face. But Jess was still there, and she'd never let him get away with it.

Fuck, they'd come to the game tonight. He was definitely going to hear about it if he went home.

So he sighed and said, "Fine."

"Sweet." Farouk patted his shoulder. "Let's go."

But alcohol did not solve Grady's problem. He stopped trying—and drinking—after the second beer and debated getting up and going home to face the music. Sooner or later he was going to have to read his texts from Jess anyway. But he was supposed to be entertaining the friend of the woman Farouk was trying to chat up, and he was aware that as an openly gay guy he was already not the ideal candidate for wingman. He didn't want to leave Farouk hanging, or this girl bored out of her mind while Farouk flirted. He didn't want to make the same mistakes he'd made in Philly and end up essentially friendless.

Across the table from him, Emily eyed Farouk and her friend, then leaned toward Grady. "Do you think they know they're adults and they can leave the bar and fuck whenever they want?"

At least he had good company. That made him laugh, which caused Farouk and Janelle to look over.

They didn't have to look that surprised about it, Grady thought. He hadn't actually tried to bite anyone's head off tonight unless you counted Dawg, but that had been in private and Dawg deserved it.

Except it turned out they weren't looking at Grady at all but past him, and Farouk's demeanor went from "charming pro athlete looking to get laid" to "alarmed pro athlete about to drag his teammate out of a fight."

Grady turned around half expecting an angry fan—

And got an eyeful of angry Max instead.

"Hey," Max said, way too belligerent for a guy whose team had won tonight's game. "You can't be here." He frowned. "We were here first."

Grady looked at him and then back at Emily, who wasn't even pretending she didn't find this conversation fascinating. The phrase *it's a free country* came to mind, but just because Max was drunk didn't mean Grady had to get down on his level.

The second thing that occurred to him was *yeah, well, we were here second*, which was not any better. Instead he said, "Hi, Max."

What he said didn't matter anyway, because Max continued talking over him. "You don't get to just, just, just be mad at me and not talk to me and then show up at my bar!"

Mad at him? Grady had texted and said they'd talk later! "I know this is going to come as a shock, but not everything is about you."

"Fuck you," Max said. "You're mad at me! I could see it in the game! You had the face, with the eyes, and the thing your jaw does when I'm annoying—"

Grady clenched his teeth.

"See!"

Farouk cleared his throat. "Maybe you should take this elsewhere," he suggested. "Before you get more of an audience."

Fuck. Angelenos were great about not giving a fuck who you were, but even if the participants weren't famous, a public argument would draw attention. Who could resist the chance to eavesdrop? Especially when Max was making it so easy.

With a huff, Grady stood from the table. "Come on. Let's talk."

The almost cold night air felt good. Maybe it would sober Max up into a semi reasonable person. Grady could hope, at least.

"You said you were fine, but you're not fine! You're pissed!" Max accused. "How are we supposed to, like, have a relationship if you're pissed off at me when I do my job?"

"I'm not pissed off at you!" Grady said.

"Then why are you yelling!"

Grady made a grand sweeping gesture with both arms. "Gee, Max, I don't know. Maybe I'm a little testy because my teenage captain lost his fucking mind on the ice tonight and started a fight with my boyfriend because he doesn't like it when you throw legal checks! Maybe it's really fucking embarrassing when a *nineteen-year-old* tries to defend your honor in a stupid macho sport!"

Max gaped at him.

But Grady had built up a head of steam, so he might as well vent the rest of it. "Some of us got to end the game the normal way, and *some* of us got dragged into a meeting with our captain and our coach where we had to explain what the fuck just happened and why it wouldn't happen again, and try to pass it off as Dawg retaliating because he thought you hit me in the face! And then we had to be thankful he decided to bench Dawg for two games anyway! When the truth is Dawg is a dumbfuck with a crush and zero personal judgment!"

Finally Max found his voice. "How *did* you start bleeding, anyway?"

Grady sighed and the tension in his jaw finally relaxed. The muscle throbbed. He wished Max had watched the stupid video. It was probably all over the internet by now anyway. "I butt-ended myself in the face."

His mouth dropped open. "*How?*"

"It doesn't matter! It's just been a really shitty night and I'm *allowed to be cranky about it.*"

The rest of the wind went out of Max's sails—he visibly deflated. "You're right. Sorry, I just... you said you were fine, but fine doesn't always mean *fine*, you know?"

Grady hoped the blankness of his face conveyed that he did not.

Apparently it did, because Max groaned and rubbed his forehead. "Sorry," he said again. "I think I was, like, primed for drama, and 'let's talk later' is, just FYI, something people in relationships take as a bad sign. I was having flashbacks to the last time we played each other."

When Grady had ghosted him and moved across the country. He winced. "I'm sorry too. I only wanted some space to wallow, I swear."

"You could've *said* that." He crossed his arms over his chest. He looked small and cold. Grady wanted to hug him.

"Next time I will." Grady paused. "Unless it's, like, the Conference Final or something, in which case can it be understood that the loser needs some space?"

"Okay," Max said. He uncrossed his arms, then crossed them again.

"Okay," Grady repeated. "Now come here and hug me. You look like you're freezing. I thought Canadians were supposed to be tougher than this."

Blessedly, Max obeyed. Grady felt better as soon as he had Max's body against his. It was both annoying and very nice.

However, there was one more issue he wanted to settle. "Since we're talking about next times… next time can you tear me a new one in private while you're sober?"

Max muffled a noise of regret in Grady's shoulder. "That would probably be a better idea."

At least they agreed on the important things.

Conscious of the fact that they were in public, Grady pressed a quick kiss to Max's cheek and then pulled back. "I think I've had enough excitement for tonight. Do you want to come home with me?" He was leaving for a road trip tomorrow, the final one before the playoffs—New York, Philadelphia, and New Jersey. Waking up with Max beside him tomorrow would go a long way toward putting his best foot forward.

Max tilted his head and gave him a crooked smile. "Actually, yeah. Let me just go say my goodbyes."

Grady should do that too. They were going to get chirped forever, but his teammates actually liked him, so he found he didn't care. "I'll come with you."

MAX SENT Grady off with a kiss and instructions to bring home six points, which came out of his mouth without his brain's input. They both stared at each other for a few seconds after, and then Grady kissed him again. They almost ended up back in bed, but Grady pulled away to leave for his flight.

Still, he was going to be gone for a week. Under normal circumstances, Max might have worried that their fight—could he call it a fight?—after the game was only a taste of what was to come, but Grady seemed determined not to let him.

The first text came in after Grady's flight landed in New York. *Do you need anything from your house in Jersey?*

Max didn't have *room* for anything from his house in Jersey. *Id say gru but my hotel does not allow pets. Or joy.*

Grady responded with a sad-face emoji.

So it seemed like everything would be fine after all.

The last week of the regular season flew by. Baller's cast had come off and he was pushing himself hard in rehab, but Max didn't know if he'd be ready in time for the first series. Whenever Max wasn't practicing, playing, sleeping, or talking to Grady, he was watching video, analyzing his opponents, or making notes of his own missed opportunities. He did manage one phone call with El and Hedgie and two just with him and El. During the first call, El fell asleep while Max was complaining about living in a hotel. On the second one, Max kept nodding off, and he didn't even have an excuse. It was only five o'clock in California.

He watched a lot of hockey and didn't get nearly enough sleep. Every night he checked the standings, and a ball of anxiety grew in his stomach as he tried to gauge the likelihood the Condors would play the Piranhas in the first round. The Pacific Division was a tight race, with only five points separating first place from third. Both the Condors and the Piranhas could end up in any of those spots, and the second- and third-place teams would play each other.

Grady's team kicked ass on their road trip and won all three games. Max didn't have a game the night the Condors played the Monsters, so he sat on the bed in his hotel room to watch it while he ate room service. Grady scored two goals and two assists and got first star of the game, which Max took as a mark of his affections.

*Aw babe u didn't have to*, he sent, followed by a number of heart emojis.

*That was for me, not you*, Grady replied.

*Well I enjoyed it anyway.*

This time the reply was a kissy-face emoji, which was adorable because Grady had never sent one of those before. *We're getting right on the plane home after media. Come over tomorrow?*

When Grady was jet-lagged and bleary-eyed, and Max had a game to nap for?

On the other hand, he hadn't exactly been sleeping well since Grady left. Maybe he could get his nap in at Grady's place. *Ok.*

At skate the morning of the last game of the season, the trainers decided Baller was ready to participate fully. "Let's try the two of you on a line together," Barry said. "Do some rushes. See how it feels."

Baller held out his fist for a bump. "We got this, right?"

"Hell yeah."

The first set of rushes wasn't quite right. Baller was a little slower than Max anticipated, probably because of his injury.

When they regrouped to wait their turn for another go, Baller said, "Let me carry it in this time and I'll drop it back for you and screen, and Bishop can pick up the rebound."

Bishop glanced at Max. "Kinda bossy for a guy who had his leg in a boot last week."

Max patted him on the back. "C'mon, Captain, like you wouldn't be going out of your mind if you'd had to sit out for this long. Let's give him this one."

"Yeah, Captain. Give me this one."

Bishop groaned theatrically. "The two of you are going to be like this all postseason, aren't you?"

This time Max exchanged glances with Baller before they both turned back to Bishop and chorused, "Like what?"

"Christ," Bishop laughed. "Have it your way."

They did have it Baller's way, and then Max's, and then Bishop got a chance to put in the rebound. When they'd scored on four out of six rush attempts, with their goalie cursing them vehemently, Bishop put his arms around them and said, "Okay. You win."

"*We* win," Baller corrected. "Or we will once I don't need a nap after ten minutes of ice time."

"Heal faster," Max told him.

The spring air was already hot by the time he got into his car in the parking lot. He yawned as he stretched a kink out of his neck and wondered if he should cancel on Grady and go sleep in his hotel room for a few hours.

But he wanted to see his boyfriend, and Grady's bed was more comfortable, so he texted *omw* and put the car in gear.

One godawful LA traffic experience later, he parked in Grady's driveway. One of the neighbors' dogs must've been out in the yard, because he could hear it going apeshit as he walked up Grady's front step. To his overtaxed, underslept brain, the dog sounded like Gru. What he wouldn't give right now for a good snuggle from his best boy. Maybe then he'd finally get a solid night's rest.

He was still thinking about it when the door opened and Gru shrieked and launched into his arms.

"Shit!" Grady lunged forward and caught Max by the elbow so he didn't go backward off the step. "Gru! Sorry, sorry, I didn't know he was going to do that."

Max looked down at his armful of barking, wriggling, tail-wagging dog, who was licking his face like Max had come home from the wars, and then up into Grady's apologetic eyes, and felt his lip wobble.

"Hi, buddy," he said softly, adjusting his grip to support Gru's butt. "Hey. Hey, I missed you too. What're you doing here, eh? Did you stow away? What a good boy."

Gru licked Max's nose.

"Oh, thank you. I needed that." Max kissed his snout.

Then, finally, he looked at Grady again. "And here I thought this was a booty call." If his voice rasped a little, Grady didn't mention it.

"Come in and pet your dog."

Max didn't need to be told twice. He parked himself on the area rug in front of Grady's sofa and rolled around with Gru for fifteen minutes, stroking his ears, rubbing his belly. The faint smell of the shampoo his Newark groomer used settled him in a way he hadn't felt since he landed in California the first time.

But eventually he had to address a few real-life problems. "How'd you get him here, anyway?" he asked, reclining against Grady with Gru in his lap.

Grady cleared his throat. "Uh, team plane."

Max tilted his head back to look at him. "Seriously?"

With a sheepish expression, Grady said, "I mean, I asked everyone first. No one was allergic."

Grady asked his Condors teammates, who'd recently lost a game to their divisional rival, in which Max had embarrassed their captain in a very stupid fight, if he could please bring Max's dog on the flight home. Max smiled and leaned back far enough to press an upside-down kiss on Grady's jaw. The muscle there was starting to shrink again. "That's sweet. But you know I can't have him in my hotel room, right?" And he didn't exactly need to add looking for a short-term rental that allowed pets to his to-do list.

"He can stay here." Grady ran his thumb over the curve of Max's hip. Max shivered at the touch. "I'll give you a key so you can visit whenever. If we're both out of town, we can find a dog walker."

*A key?* "We?" Grady's thumb took a southern detour. Max cleared his throat. "Kinda seems like you're looking for excuses to get me to come over more often."

"Don't know what you're talking about."

Yeah, right. There was a Minions-themed dog bed in the corner next to a suspiciously sized Amazon box.

Max kissed Gru's head. "Okay, down, please."

Gru sighed, but he eeled off Max and onto the floor.

Then Max turned around so he could look Grady in the eyes. "What's your end game here? In words." He caught Grady's hand before he could distract Max further. "Operating on unspoken understandings is not one of our strengths."

"I want...." Grady bit his lips. "I *do* want to see you more often. I brought Gru here because you said you missed him, and I want you to be happy. And he's a good dog."

"He's the best," Max agreed. "Keep going."

With a deep breath, Grady did. "I don't want to fuck things up with you because I'm acting like a sore loser. But sometimes I don't know how not to be alone. I'm trying to do better," he added before Max could recover from that emotional gut punch. "I felt better once I talked to you after our last game. I just don't know how to start the conversation."

Well, they were essentially both raised by wolves. But Max's wolves were the kind who'd sent the other two of their three kids to therapy. Max went to hockey instead. "And you think"—*giving me a key*—"me being here more often is going to help solve this problem?"

"When you struggle with a skill, you practice." Grady swallowed visibly. "I know I need to learn to let go of a game when it's over. But maybe *you* need practice letting me react to things without making it about you?"

Suddenly Max's heart was beating so furiously he was sure Grady could see it just as easily as if Max's skin were made of tissue. It terrified him—but the good kind of terror, like the moment before puck drop of a big game or that last click of the track at the top of a roller coaster. "Maybe." He licked his lips. "But chances are one or both of us will still need space at some point."

"It's a big house," Grady said. "I was thinking we could have separate chill zones? We could even sleep in different rooms on game days if it gets too much in the same bed. I can be kind of intense."

Max hadn't been able to get his brain to shut up at bedtime for the past week, so he said, "Yeah, I can see how we might keep each other awake, and not in the fun way." He pushed his tongue against the inside of his cheek as he thought, because he wanted to be clear about what was happening but didn't want to be the first one to say it out loud. "Kinda sounds like I'd be moving in with you."

"How often are we both going to be home at the same time, really? A couple days a week on average?"

Max's heart needed to cool its jets. "Okay, well, you've forgotten one small detail."

Grady hummed. "You mean tonight's game?"

The Pacific Division race was so close, if Max's team won tonight, they'd take first place. If they lost, they'd get third and have to play the Condors in the first round. "Could be awkward if we're playing against each other. It wouldn't be the greatest foot to start off on."

"You'll just have to win tonight, then."

Max smiled in spite of himself. "Oh really. That simple, is it?"

Grady cupped his face. His expression said *I'm being a shithead*, but his voice rang with sincerity. "I believe in you."

No one would ever believe Max if he told them what a sap Grady was. That only made it sweeter. "You can do one better. You can help me with it." Max got off the couch and tugged Grady to his feet. "First step to a good game is nap time."

## PIRANHAS TAKE BITE OUT OF ORCAS, SET PACIFIC DIVISION PLAYOFF SCHEDULE
**By Craig MacLeod**

With tonight's 1–0 win over the Vancouver Orcas, the Anaheim Piranhas claimed the top seed in the Pacific

Division. Max Lockhart scored the lone goal in the game. The victory means the Piranhas will face the Las Vegas Heatwave in the first round of the playoffs.

The Stanley Cup Playoffs kick off Tuesday night at 8:00 p.m. PST, when the puck drops in LA for the first game of the Condors-Orcas series.

"I DON'T know," Grady said for what had to be the fifth time. "Should I—"

"If you ask me if you should ditch the tie again, I'm going to rip it off you and stuff it in your mouth. Not even for sexy times." Max tossed his tablet onto the bed beside him. "You're a built guy wearing a custom suit. You look fuckable. It's extremely rude of you not to be following through on that right now."

Okay, so maybe Grady was being a little extra about this whole first-game-of-the-playoffs aesthetic. Sue him. It had been years since he'd gotten to play in the postseason.

But he definitely wasn't letting Max get the last word, even if fucking was technically off the table because they both got too into it and were too likely to pull something. He turned around and tugged the tie loose for the final time. "Everything I learn about Canadian notions of politeness is against my will." He balled up the tie and threw it at Max's chest.

"Ooh, now undo the top two buttons. Yeah, baby. Work it."

"I hate you," Grady said without heat.

Max batted his eyelashes. "Does that mean we can have nasty, disrespectful sex later? I miss it."

"I literally came all over your face this morning." In the shower, so it barely counted, but still.

"Maybe I want to disrespect you for a change."

Grady snorted. For all Max talked a big game, he also talked a lot *period*. It was hard to feel disrespected when Max kept telling him how hot he looked and how good he felt, but whatever Max had to tell himself to sleep at night. "As long as you leave me in game condition… also probably only if we win tonight."

"I accept your terms," Max said solemnly. "Now get out of here. You're going to hit rush hour traffic."

Grady stole a kiss, rubbed Gru's ears for luck, and left the house.

The rest of the day passed in a blur. Media, warm-ups, puck drop. Farouk put the puck in the net ten minutes into the game. Grady roofed one twenty-seven seconds later.

The Orcas pushed back. They were a good team and they wanted this victory. In the back half of the third, Nico Kirschbaum slipped through the Condors' defense like a hot knife through butter.

But Mitch shut the door on everything the Orcas threw at the net.

When the clock ran out, the Condors mobbed their goalie. Every fan in the building shot to their feet. Grady slapped the back of Farouk's helmet in appreciation and whooped into Mitch's face.

In the locker room, the guys were debating where to go to celebrate. Grady didn't care; the game mattered, but drinks were just gravy. Before he could say he'd probably go, but only for one beer, his phone buzzed with a new notification.

*This is what ur goal did 2 me*, Max's text said. The attached picture showed his hard dick straining the fabric of a threadbare pair of tiny sweat shorts. Max was framing the bulge with one hand.

The back of Grady's neck went red hot. "I'm out," he said.

Mitch took one look at his face and burst into laughter. Farouk whistled. "Get it, Grades."

Dawg hunched his shoulders, but he perked up again when Farouk brought up his beautiful center-ice empty-netter, and right now that was the best Grady could hope for.

Max—still naked except for the shorts—met him the second he set foot in the door. "Hi," he said. Then his mouth was on Grady's in a filthy kiss that made Grady's lips tingle and his hands itch to feel Max's skin.

He was light-headed already when Max grabbed his hand and moved it to his crotch. He broke the kiss with a last wet lick over Grady's tongue and put his other hand on Grady's shoulder. "You gonna let me disrespect you in the hallway?"

Right now Grady would let him do whatever the fuck he wanted. He went to his knees when Max pushed, and moved his hands to cup the backs of Max's thick thighs.

Max made a wordless noise of approval and pushed the waistband of his sweats down far enough to get his dick out.

Then he guided it into Grady's mouth and Grady's mind went static. He'd never seen Max like *this*. Normally he preferred to goad Grady into doing what he wanted, but tonight he was apparently not only too turned on to wait for Grady to come home but desperate enough to take charge physically. Grady's mouth watered as Max fucked it, and Grady took him down the best he could, deliciously aware of his own cock leaking in his pants.

But Max hardly let Grady get into it. He'd barely had time to work his throat open when Max swore and backed away. "Fuck, you're too fucking good at that. Come on, get up."

Before Grady could process, Max was pulling at his shoulders, urging him to stand. Then he shoved Grady around to face the wall and unbuckled his suit pants from behind.

Grady opened his mouth to remind Max about their agreement and snapped it closed again a second later when Max knelt behind him and spread his asscheeks. A pathetic gurgle slipped past his lips when Max flicked his tongue over his hole, but Max probably couldn't hear him over his own moans, so his dignity was intact.

Or not, as it turned out when Max pushed his tongue past the ring of muscle and Grady's knees tried to buckle. He braced his hands against the wall, bit his lip, and tried not to fall over while Max ate him out.

He was working up to asking Max what his plan was when that wet hot tongue pulled away and something harder slid into its place. Then Max slapped his asscheek, bit the side of his hip, and said, "Pull your pants up."

*What?*

But Grady's hands were already obeying even though his brain had no idea what was happening. Had Max put a plug in his ass and then told him to put his pants back on? *Why?*

His tongue felt slow, too thick for his mouth. The hard silicone in his ass hit the right spot to make him brainless. His erection tented the front of his pants, and the inside of his underwear was wet with precome.

The next thing Grady knew, Max was pushing him down on the couch and climbing into his lap. Somewhere overhead, music started playing. Grady couldn't identify it. Now the plug was grinding against his prostate and Max was grinding against his dick.

Grady raised his hands to Max's hips, but Max slapped them away. "You know the rules," he chided. "No touching during a lap dance."

How was Grady supposed to keep his hands to himself when Max's pierced nipples were right in front of his face?

"Hands on the back of the couch," Max instructed.

When he rolled his hips, Grady had no choice but to obey. He needed to hold on to something or he'd fly apart.

Max put his hands on Grady's shoulders. With his thighs trapping Grady's hips, he had Grady pinned exactly where they both wanted him. He looked incredible, with his eyes dark and his hair wild and his mouth swollen and shiny with spit. The pleasure mounted as Max rubbed his ass over Grady's erection, back arched like he knew how bad Grady wanted to bite his nipples, and wanted to drive him crazy.

Then Max fumbled in the couch cushions and said, "*Fuck*—where's the—there it is—" and the plug started to vibrate.

Grady's head fell back and his mouth dropped open. Max's full, round ass rubbed just right against his erection, and Grady's body wanted to turn inside-out to get closer to him.

"God," Max groaned. "Fuck, Grades, you see what you do to me? You see what you—" He cut himself off and shoved his shorts down far enough to get one hand on his cock.

Grady watched slack-jawed, too wrecked to do more than breathe and try to buck up, to fuck into the perfect grip of Max's asscheeks.

Max shoved the fingers of his left hand into Grady's mouth and Grady hurtled into orgasm, chest heaving as he clamped down around the plug. His underwear flooded with come. Max swore again and fisted the head of his dick until he shot all down the front of Grady's shirt and jacket.

For a few long seconds Grady thought he was shuddering with the aftershocks of an intense orgasm. Then he realized the plug was still vibrating and flailed vaguely on the couch, looking for the remote.

"Shit, sorry," Max said. He found it first, but he must've hit the button to turn it up, because Grady jolted with the sudden increase in frequency. "Sorry!" Finally it stopped.

Then Max collapsed against his chest, sweaty and panting.

Jesus.

Grady curled his fingers in Max's hair and tugged his face up for a kiss.

"Do you feel disrespected?" Max mumbled into his neck a moment later.

Grady found his voice. "Well my *suit* definitely does."

Max shook with silent laughter.

"You're doing the dry-cleaning run this week," Grady told him.
"Worth it."

WHEN THE phone rang in the middle of the night, Max woke up out of a dead sleep.

Blinking in the darkness, he tried to remember where he was. His house in Newark? No. Grady's house in California? He blinked and tried to remember.

Then he caught the orange glow of the Las Vegas strip creeping in around the blackout curtains. Right. He was in Vegas, because they had a playoff game against the Heatwave tomorrow.

Why hadn't he put his phone on Do Not Disturb?

Grumbling, he reached for the nightstand in the dark. The call display read *HEDGIE*.

Oh shit. Max scrambled to answer and belatedly realized it was a video call. "Hello? Is it happening?"

A few seconds later the video came through and he saw Hedgie in a brightly lit hospital room. Was it already morning on the East Coast? Max's eyes hadn't woken up enough to focus on the time in the corner of his phone screen.

"She's here!" Hedgie looked like he'd gone three rounds with the baddest defenseman in the league. His eyes were bloodshot and had bags under them, which made sense because Max already felt like that and he only had to play hockey, not stay up with a partner who was delivering their child. He was grinning like a maniac. "Why's it so dark where you are?"

"Because it's, like, six in the morning," El said from somewhere behind him.

Oh good, at least one of them could do math. "Looks like the baby takes after El, if she was actually on time." El's due date was today. Or yesterday. Max's brain wasn't awake enough to determine which.

Hedgie made a face. "You're the third one who's said that. Be nice to me or I won't let you see her."

"Yeah, right," Max said immediately. "You can't wait to brag about this kid. Show me the baby, Hedgie."

The phone jiggled for a moment, and then the camera flipped around and Max was looking at El sitting in a hospital bed, hair up in a knot, with a little pink-wrapped bundle in her arms.

"Looking good, Mama," Max said. Truthfully she looked better than Hedgie. "And who's this with you?"

Hedgie brought the phone closer and Max got his first glimpse of a squish-faced infant with Hedgie's nose. He immediately fell in love. "This is Amelia Kate."

"It's nice to meet you, Amelia," Max said. His throat suddenly felt tight. "Good job, guys. She's perfect."

"We're pretty pleased with her," El agreed. "We'll let you—and me, to be honest—get back to sleep now, but we wanted to say hi and everyone's doing fine."

"Congratulations, all of you."

When the call ended, Max blinked a few times in the darkness of the room. He'd wanted to be there for El and Hedgie's milestone, but the pang of missing out stayed brief. He'd meet Amelia this summer. Maybe he wouldn't get to watch her grow up the same way he would have if he'd been in Newark, but he had other people here. He had a good team who let him play a role he liked much better.

He had Grady, whose team had won their third straight game of the series that night.

And he had a playoff game to win today. So he should really put his phone down and go back to sleep.

THE MOMENT Grady's blades touched the ice for warm-ups in Vancouver, he could feel the energy of the building reverberating through his feet. The Orcas were on the brink of elimination, and half the city had turned up to support their efforts to turn the series around.

Grady was going to give everything he had to ensure those fans went home disappointed. It wasn't personal, but he wanted this victory more than those six hundred thousand Canadians combined.

The team stayed loose during warm-ups, and Mitch heckled them all during the shootout drill. He was easily the most laid-back goalie Grady'd ever met.

He expected the other end of the ice to be tense. If Vancouver lost tonight, their season was over. But at least to Grady, they seemed to be fine. Focused, but not grim. As Grady rounded the back of his own net, laughter rang out—Kirschbaum, it looked like. Weird. Grady had always thought he was kind of dour.

Warm-ups ended, and they filed back to the locker room for one of Dawg's pep talks—one they didn't need but responded to with cheers anyway. With the Condors, Grady had cut his Instagram meditation down to just a minute or two, and he didn't feel the need to leave the locker room. This team had a totally different energy for him, one he didn't find toxic.

Maybe he'd been part of that toxicity before, but he had a blank slate here. He was making the most of it.

In any case, he smiled when he checked Instagram and saw Max had uploaded a badly photoshopped picture of Gru peeing on the Orcas' mascot.

*Totally impartial*, read the caption.

Grady hit the Heart button.

The game started off with tight defense on both sides. Grady made a few forays into the offensive zone, but the Orcas had learned from their mistakes and quickly shut down any plays the Condors made.

Things opened up a little bit in the second. Kirschbaum put the puck between Mitch's legs five minutes in, and then a bad turnover from Dawg resulted in the Orcas getting a really good look at a 2–0 lead. Fortunately Mitch had that one covered.

Grady couldn't let momentum start swinging the Orcas' way. He chewed his mouthguard in annoyance. Next to him on the bench, Farouk nudged his knee into Grady's. "We got this."

Right. They did.

Three shifts later, one of the Condors dished Grady the puck at the center line, and it was like time slowed down. He could see where the Orcas were going to be and exactly how to get around them. He carried the puck all the way to the crease, then passed to Farouk at the last second.

The goalie never had a chance. Tie game.

"Holy shit!" Farouk screamed at him behind the net. "That was insane!"

Laughing, Grady crashed their helmets together. "Fucking nice finish!"

Ten minutes into the third, Grady was sure the game would go to overtime.

He had done everything he could to tip the balance in their favor. He won 70 percent of his faceoffs. He made nine shots on goal. The Condors needed a game-breaker.

And Grady thought he saw the opening for it, just like he had in the second period. Except this time, he didn't get two strides into the offensive zone before the breath got crushed from his lungs.

The first time he managed to inhale again he was on his back on the ice, the ringing of the whistle loud in his ears. He registered the sounds of a fight, then several more whistles as the linesmen tried to break it up.

The thing was, it didn't hurt. He hadn't hit his head. He just had to get up and he'd be fine.

He rolled to his left side and tried to push himself up with his arm, and it gave out under him. *That* he felt. That *hurt*. There was no strength in his arm.

He'd just have to play one-handed.

Farouk helped him up, but when Grady skated toward the bench, their coach shook his head. "Get it checked out. You can afford to miss a few minutes of one game."

Grady glanced back toward the ice. He needed to be here for his team.

But Dawg said, "C'mon, Grades. You got so little faith in us? Go."

The idea of going down the tunnel with the trainers made Grady's stomach hurt, but he could barely hold on to his stick. "I'll be back," he said finally. "Feel free to win without me."

Strength or not, he could still move his arm. Maybe not a full range of motion, and maybe not without gritting his teeth in pain, but it still moved. His hand opened and closed, even if his grip was limp. How bad could it be? He'd played injured before. He wouldn't leave his team in the lurch during playoffs.

He couldn't let this team down.


**PIRANHAS OUTLAST HEATWAVE, WIN SERIES 4–1**
**By Craig MacLeod**

The first series of the NHL Stanley Cup Playoffs has been decided as the Anaheim Piranhas defeated the Las Vegas Heatwave 3–1 last night to take the series four games to one. The home team had the possession advantage most of the game and held Vegas to 23 shots on goal, compared to the Piranhas' 37.

Emory St. Clair and Deniz Kaplan each scored their fourth goal of the series, and Max Lockhart added his first of the playoffs in the victory.

With the return of power forward Dante Baltierra anticipated for the second round, the Fish will prove a difficult opponent. They will play the winner of the Condors-Orcas series. Vancouver hosts game 6 tonight. The Condors lead the series 3–2.

IF HE played for any other team, Max would have attended game 7 to cheer on his man.

But Max played for the Condors' biggest rival, and he'd have to play the winner of this series. He didn't want to come across as a sore winner, or whatever; the Condors had let a 3–0 series lead slip away, and anything Max said about it would be salt in the wound. To make matters worse, he knew Grady was injured. Hell, *everyone* knew Grady was injured. *Shooters shoot* was a cliché for a reason, and right now, Grady wasn't.

He wasn't doing much around the house either. He kept his left arm close to his side and didn't take off his shirt, which probably sucked almost as much for him as it did for Max. He ate with his right hand only. It didn't take a genius to connect the dots.

So Max watched game 7 from the couch, Gru curled up next to him, and tried to keep breathing. He wanted Grady to be happy, but he *didn't* want to have to play against his boyfriend in the second round.

The game had him on the edge of his seat. Every breakaway made his stomach clench. Every glove save was a sigh of relief. The third period ended with the game tied 1–1.

Grady had only played eleven minutes. He should've played seventeen.

Max got up to get a drink and use the bathroom while the players got a short break before overtime, but even after doing the dishes, he still had fifteen minutes to kill.

And he couldn't sit around and wait. Restless energy filled him. He'd never had a problem watching high-stakes hockey before. But right now he wasn't a hockey player. He was an overly invested boyfriend.

He looked at Gru. "Walk around the neighborhood?"

Gru blinked at him, then flopped off the couch and padded to the door.

Max clipped the leash to his collar, jammed on his slides, and stepped out into the California night.

The neighborhood was mostly quiet, everyone tucked into their houses, many of the lights off. The breeze carried a hint of salt and diesel fumes. Max walked Gru aimlessly in the hopes that he could forget about the game, but no dice. So he kept walking until his phone vibrated.

Max released a long breath and unlocked the screen.

*FINAL: Vancouver Orcas 2, Los Angeles Condors 1.*

Shit. "Come on," Max told Gru. "Let's go home, buddy." He opened a new message to Grady and debated what to write. After another block, he decided on *want me to clear out tonight?*

It was almost an hour later when he got a response. *No.* That was it.

Max didn't know what he expected, but some of his anxiety eased. There was still time for everything to go to shit, but at least Grady wasn't in such a bad mood he didn't want to see Max at all.

Max waited another half hour before he heard the garage door, and suddenly he was second-guessing himself. Should he have watched the end of the game? Should he have gone to bed? Just because Grady didn't want him gone didn't mean he wanted to face him.

Gru, however, had no doubt of his welcome. The door jolted him out of a deep sleep, and he barked joyously and ran to the entryway with his tail stump wagging, ready to welcome Grady home.

Gru was an excellent buffer. Even Grady couldn't take his disappointment out on the dog.

"Hi, buddy. I'm back. Okay, calm down, you're gonna wake the neighbors."

When he hadn't made a move to come farther inside and the nails clicking on tile told Max Gru was changing petting positions, he heaved himself off the couch and went to face the music.

Bent down in the entryway to fluff Gru's ears, Grady looked exhausted. He had dark circles under bloodshot eyes, and he'd come home in athletic gear instead of his suit, which hung on the outside of the entryway closet. His face was lined with pain as he stroked Gru one-handed, because his left arm was in a sling.

"Hey," Max said quietly. "Good game tonight." It *had* been a good game—some of the best hockey he'd seen all season. He wasn't looking forward to playing the Orcas.

"Not for me," Grady said.

And—well, that was true too.

Grady didn't look up.

Max cleared his throat. "What's the verdict?"

Now that there was no chance they'd face each other in the postseason, Grady could tell Max what was wrong with him. He hadn't earlier in the week. Max would've thrown his words from months ago back in his face, but regular season was one thing. Playoffs was another animal. Part of Max hadn't wanted to know, because if he didn't know, there was no chance he could use the knowledge, even subconsciously.

"Not broken," Grady said. He sounded bitter instead of relieved. A break would've been a better excuse. He'd have been mad at whoever did it instead of at his own body. "Clavicle contusion. No strength in my arm. Feels like spaghetti, even when they shot it full of the good stuff."

Max winced. Taken out by a glorified bruise. No wonder he was bitter. "That sucks. You need ice? Heat?"

Grady shook his head. "Sleep."

He looked like he needed it. "All right. I'll join you in a minute."

Max's heart sank when Grady shook his head again. "I'll sleep in the guest room. Too many painkillers. I'm going to snore like a chainsaw."

Max bit his lip. "Okay."

He watched as Grady shuffled down the hall. Gru looked forlornly after him, tail still wagging slowly.

Sighing, Max scratched behind Gru's ears. "C'mon, buddy. Let's go to bed."

Gru curled up on Grady's side of the mattress, nose tucked under his tail. Max stroked him absently and tried to shut off his brain.

Grady was just trying to be considerate by sleeping in the other room, where he wouldn't disturb Max, who still needed to get a good night's rest, since he'd be starting round two of the playoffs in a couple days. Which sucked, because Max *also* needed a snuggle and someone to tell him that a goal and three assists in five games was a reasonable number of points and hockey was a team sport.

But that was okay. Grady would still be there to tell him those things in the morning.

Gru sighed in irritation, his cue for Max to stop petting him and let him sleep. Max tucked his hand under his head and took his cue from Gru.

GRADY WOKE up sore the day after the Condors' playoff exit.

But weirdly, it was mostly a physical soreness. His arm hurt, and he was disappointed, sure. Just not disappointed enough to let it affect the good things in his life.

He'd thought this was his year. He liked his new team. He got along with his teammates, who shared his work ethic. He wasn't ready for locker cleanout and everybody leaving town.

But that was what he'd gotten, and he still had Max. He could make the best of it.

Max was still in bed when he got up, so Grady took Gru for a quick walk—even mostly one-handed, he could do that much—and then braved the task of making breakfast.

It almost ended in disaster when he caught the egg carton with the edge of the sling and sent it teetering toward the edge of the counter, but Max came into the kitchen just in time and made the save.

"Thanks," Grady said as Max set the carton down. "I was going to make you breakfast, but maybe I'd better not." At least not until he was more aware of where his elbow was. "Want me to order something?"

Max stared at him for a moment, wearing kind of a funny smile, and then kissed his cheek. "Nah, go sit down. I got this one."

THAT NIGHT, Max came home from the first Piranhas-Orcas game with his shoulders slumped. Grady hadn't watched, but he'd turned on notifications on his phone, so he knew the Orcas had won 8–5. Losing the series opener at home like that would sting.

But what could Grady say? Anything he attempted would come across as patronizing or smug.

In the end, he said, "Hey."

"Hey." Even Max's hair looked kind of limp, though his playoff beard was starting to bush out to make up for it. "So that sucked."

Grady winced in sympathy. "Sorry." He gave himself a mental point for not adding *at least you're still playing*.

Max shrugged. "It is what it is. How's your collarbone?"

"Bruised." The sudden subject change disoriented him. "Getting better, though." He should have his strength and full range of motion back in another week.

"That's good." Max shifted from foot to foot. Gru nosed his kneecap for more pets, but Max ignored him. "Come to bed?"

Grady had been sleeping in the guest room, conscious that his tossing and turning could keep Max awake. But maybe having him sleep in a different bedroom was just as bad. Besides, he missed being close to Max, and he could see from the strain around Max's eyes that Max missed it too.

"Yeah. Let me take Gru out for a pee and I'll join you."

By the time Gru had finished showing the clover who was boss, most of the lights in the house were out. Grady locked the back door and left his slides on the mat, then used the screen of his phone to make sure he didn't stub his toe on the hall table as he made his way through the dark house.

The lamp on the nightstand on Max's side of the bed was lit to the dimmest setting when Grady entered. Max lay on his side facing the center of the mattress, one hand tucked under his head.

Grady turned on his own lamp and took a quick detour to the bathroom. When he came back out, Max's light was off, but he still had his body turned toward Grady's side.

Grady slid under the covers. "Do you want to talk about it?"

Max opened suddenly sharp blue eyes and narrowed them, but his mouth gave him away, the corner of his lip tugging up into a sort of smushed smirk under the beard. "Did it physically hurt you to ask that?"

"I'm not sure. It might've been my collarbone."

That earned a smile complete with eye crinkles, and Grady's heart skipped a beat. "Get over here and cuddle me."

Grady scooted closer, a little awkwardly since doing anything on his left side was still hit-or-miss, and wrapped his arm around Max's waist.

He thought Max had forgotten about the original question, so it surprised him when he said quietly into Grady's chest, "I lost my lucky cuff links."

Grady blinked. "The ones with the weird tentacle monster thing?"

Max's snort tickled his chest hair. "It's Cthulhu. Well, on one side. The other one's a big hairy foot, for Bigfoot. My parents got them for me when I got drafted. Monsters, you know?"

Grady rubbed his thumb in an absentminded circle over Max's hip. "Where's the last place you saw them?"

"I wore them the last night of the first series. We went out after, and I rolled my sleeves up. I usually put them in my jacket pocket when I do that, but I looked there. There's a hole in the pocket lining."

Probably gone for good, then. "Did you call the bar?"

"I even offered a reward," Max said moodily. "Maybe they fell out in the Lyft on the way home."

"Maybe." Grady kissed the top of his head. He wanted to say something about how Max didn't need lucky cuff links to win, but he thought that might be missing the point. But maybe there wasn't a point. Maybe Max needed to talk.

After a moment of silence, Max sighed and some of the tension melted out of him. "Thanks for listening."

Grady mentally awarded himself another point for guessing right. He could absolutely do this supportive-partner thing. "Of course." Then he paused. "Hey, Max?"

"Mmm."

"Can you be the big spoon? My collarbone is killing me."


MAX WAS already gone to practice when Grady woke up the next morning, infused with determination to do something to cheer Max up. He took Gru for a quick walk before it got too hot, fired off a text to Mitch and Farouk to see if they wanted to get lunch, and hopped in the shower.

When he got out, he had two messages waiting, along with a meeting invitation to a trendy but casual place with a great patio. Mitch had a Google Calendar obsession, but Grady appreciated people who made reservations too much to tease him. He accepted the invite and shoved his toothbrush in his mouth while he went to investigate his laundry situation.

An hour later he was sitting under an umbrella with Mitch and Farouk, nursing a beer and studiously not talking about the season.

Until Mitch said, "So has he reached out to you yet?" and suddenly Farouk started acting cagey. He grimaced and set his phone, which he'd been fidgeting with, facedown on the table.

Mitch had been asking Grady, who didn't follow. "Has who reached out?"

Mitch rolled his eyes. "The captain, obviously. I mean it's only his second season, but he does take being the captain pretty seriously. He's usually on the ball making sure nobody is blaming themselves, they know nobody else blames them, we'll get 'em next year, blah blah."

*Yeah, well, he didn't punch most guys' boyfriends in the face.* "I haven't heard from him." And he didn't need a pep talk from a guy more than a decade younger than him. Hard pass. "Are you sure he doesn't just do that with you?" Goalies were notorious for taking losses personally.

First Mitch looked offended, then like he was considering the possibility. But before he could answer, someone cleared their throat.

Grady looked up, and God damn it, there was Dawg, hunched awkwardly with his hands in his pockets, hiding behind a pair of mirrored sunglasses that had gone out of style before he was born. "Hey."

Grady tried to catch Farouk's eye, but Farouk was studiously looking anywhere but at him, so he had a feeling he knew who'd shared their location.

Dawg cleared his throat again. "Uh, Grades, can I talk to you?"

This was definitely a setup.

"Um, privately?"

Grady shot a warning look at Farouk, but he took one last sip of his beer and gestured toward the back of the patio, away from anyone who might overhear.

"Okay," he said mildly when they'd gotten as far away from other people as you could get on a patio in LA. "Talk."

And then Dawg squared his shoulders and lifted his head, his face set in determination, and shocked the hell out of him. "I owe you an apology. I shouldn't have made my feelings your problem, and I'm sorry. It won't happen again."

Grady blinked. Honestly he hadn't been sure Dawg could say *anything* to improve the situation, but though the apology was short, it hit on exactly why Grady had felt so upset. "Okay."

"Okay?" Dawg repeated. The maturity that had settled into his expression a moment before evaporated. "So, like… are we good?"

Were they good? Grady didn't know if he'd go that far. But they were going to be teammates for the foreseeable future, and he didn't want any drama. "Try not to punch my boyfriend in the face again. At least not without provocation."

Dawg smiled and held out his hand to shake on it. "Deal."

"Deal." Grady glanced back at the table. Mitch and Farouk both quickly turned away and pretended they hadn't been watching. Idiots. Grady sighed inwardly. In for a penny. "Do you want to join us for lunch? Fair warning, I invited them here to get relationship advice."

Dawg's shoulders straightened again. Grady was starting to think of it as his Captain Posture. "I can handle it."

They might as well test that somewhere he couldn't punch Max in the face, so Grady gestured him toward the table.

Their server ambled by when she noticed Dawg had joined them, and they all ordered another round and some burgers.

Then Grady figured it was time to get down to business. "So. You may be wondering why I asked you here."

Mitch and Farouk exchanged looks.

"It's Max."

"Told you," Farouk said, holding out his hand. Mitch pulled out his wallet and slapped a twenty into his palm. "But bro, it's too soon to be talking marriage."

*Not according to Max's nephew.* Grady shook his head. "It's not about that. More like… it's been a long time since I had a season as good as this one, and it got fucked up at the end, and that sucks. But I need to get over myself—"

"This is way above our pay grade."

Maybe Grady should get a *new* new set of friends. He glowered at them. "—and *do something nice for my boyfriend.* He lost his lucky cuff links. And it turns out I actually might want him to, you know…." *Win the Cup.*

It was too embarrassing—and unlucky—to say out loud.

Mitch and Farouk stared at him in horror.

But Dawg, though he wrinkled his nose in distaste, nodded. "That makes sense. I mean, you're not going to do it, so you might as well be happy for him."

Now Mitch and Farouk turned their stares on him. Dawg turned red. "What? Look, last year we went all the way to the Cup Final and lost and then my sister had a baby while everyone else was out of town."

Grady couldn't figure out how this story was relevant. A glance at Mitch and Farouk showed that they were similarly at sea. "And?"

"And babies are fragile and they cry a lot, and I don't know if you've ever had to take care of someone who just gave birth, but, like, I've seen some gross hockey injuries. This was not like that." His tone made it clear which one was worse. "But it was also kind of nice. I couldn't help my team win the Cup, but I could make dinner and run the dishwasher and change a diaper, you know? And meeting my niece for the first time was awesome. I couldn't spoil that for my sister by sulking about the playoffs."

Damn it. That was actually insightful.

Then Dawg ruined it by patting Grady on the shoulder and intoning, "I'm just saying. I'm proud of you for being so mature."

Mitch and Farouk fell over each other laughing.

Grady groaned but accepted his lumps. "All right, let's try to leave my reputation as a sore loser in the past."

Fortunately, Mitch and Farouk were too invested in taking apart Dawg's analogy to make fun of Grady.

"So, wait," Farouk said, "is Max the baby in this scenario?"

"No, the Cup is the baby. Max is the sister."

Fortunately their lunch and drinks arrived, so Grady only had to listen with half an ear as Farouk and Mitch debated what it would be like to give birth to the Stanley Cup. Grady was replacing them both with Dawg.

"Okay, new subject," he interrupted when things got a little too graphic. They all turned to look at him. No point beating around the bush. He was going to get shit for this either way. "I need a shopping recommendation. Specifically jewelry."


"GRADES?" MAX looked into the closet and cursed his own lack of foresight. None of his nice shirts' sleeves had buttons. He'd always worn his lucky cuff links.

"Yeah?"

Max hated to ask, but unless he wanted to show up looking like a slob, he didn't have much of a choice. "Can I borrow a shirt?"

After a moment, Grady poked his head into the bedroom. "Do you actually not have any shirts with button cuffs?"

"Not ones that are nice enough to wear with a suit." At least not during playoffs. He had another set of cuff links, but they didn't feel *lucky*. Maybe one of Grady's shirts would.

Grady opened the other closet. "Yeah, I might have something."

"Oh, you might have something," Max joked. "In your designer closet full of designer dress shirts—"

When Grady turned around holding a small velvet jewelry box, Max's words died in his throat and morphed into a strangled, "You're not gonna tell me there's a shirt in there."

Grady must've caught Max's runaway train of thought, because he gave a wry smile. "Breathe, Max. I am not a good enough loser to be proposing to you right now."

The nervous tension in Max's belly broke into a laugh. At least Grady could own up to it. "Thank God. I thought maybe you were concussed."

"No concussion." Grady rolled his eyes, but he was still smiling faintly, his cheeks tinged with red, like he was nervous or embarrassed. Maybe both. "Stockholm Syndrome, maybe."

What an asshole. Max grinned and made grabby hands for the box. "So what did you bring me?"

Wordlessly, Grady opened it and held it out.

On the left side of the box sparkled a tiny lobster studded with red and blue gems. On the right, a rose-gold fish with shiny dark turquoise scales bared sharp white mother-of-pearl teeth. Max swallowed. "You romantic motherfucker."

"I know they can't replace the ones you lost." Grady took a deep breath. Was he nervous? Why? Max was on the brink of tears over here. "But I thought maybe these could be lucky too—"

Max cut him off with a kiss. The box dropped to the bed as Grady wrapped both arms around him.

*Finally.* Grady hadn't touched Max like this since before the Condors' last game. Max had been starting to despair. He fell into the kiss.

"I love them," he said when the kiss broke. He waggled his eyebrows. "And they're definitely lucky."

Grady snorted at the joke. "I'm glad you think so."

Max thumbed the side of his mouth. His own emotions were doing an impression of a microwaved marshmallow, warm and sticky-sweet and exploding all over everything. "Do you think piranhas eat lobsters in the wild?"

"I don't think they meet in the wild. Piranhas are freshwater fish."

Of course he knew that, thereby spoiling Max's innuendo. He went in another direction with it instead. "Well, this fish wants to get fresh with you. And after tonight's game, we've got two days off before the next one."

Grady's hands drifted down to Max's ass. "Is that so?"

"It is," Max chirped. "And personally I think that if these cuff links turn out to be lucky, we should get lucky too."

"I do owe you for what you did to my suit." Grady kissed him briefly and then pulled back. "Can I pick the shirt?"

A little shiver went down Max's spine. "Kinky." He gestured to the closet. "I'm all yours."

Grady picked a black shirt off the hanger and held it out. It took Max a moment to realize Grady intended to slip it on him, but he turned around and Grady pulled the silky fabric up his arms. He stayed behind Max and buttoned his shirt from behind, his chin hooked over Max's shoulder.

The hair on the back of Max's neck rose. He licked his lips. "Are you torturing me on purpose?"

When Grady smiled, Max felt the curve of it against his jaw. "I'm just giving you incentive to play your best." He unzipped Max's suit pants and tucked in his shirt.

Max's throat went dry as Grady's fingers tickled the skin on his stomach. "Well. It's effective."

Grady kissed the side of his neck and did up his pants. Then he turned Max around and picked up the cuff links.

Max was pretty sure this shouldn't be so sexy, but then Grady brushed his lips over the skin of his left wrist before fastening the lobster cuff link.

Grady repeated the treatment on the other wrist before helping Max into his jacket.

Max cleared his throat. "How do I look?"

Grady gave him a long, slow once-over. "Good enough to eat."

*Flirt.* "I'll hold you to that."

"Go win your hockey game."


## PIRANHAS BITE BACK
## By Craig MacLeod

It's not often you get a playoff series with multiple high-scoring games. Even rarer when the teams trade off scoring eight-plus goals.

But that's what happened last night in Anaheim, as the Piranhas bounded back from an 8–5 game 1 loss to win 9–6 last night.

After facing fan criticism for "underperforming" in the first round, Max Lockhart notched his first playoff hat trick, including the game-winning goal.

The series is now tied 1–1. The next game will take place Wednesday night in Vancouver.

# Postgame

**Rivals Take Relationship to the Next Round—Kind Of**
**By Sonia Goldstein**

It would have been easy to dismiss it as a rumor. When I asked LA Condor Grady Armstrong about rekindling his rivalry with former New Jersey Monster Max Lockhart, his reaction had people speculating if *rivalry* was the right word.

Turns out, not so much.

Hockey fans love a good narrative, and the sport gives us plenty to talk about. But Armstrong's surprise romance with Max Lockhart has all the hallmarks of a classic love story. With a history that reads like the first chapters of a romance novel and a smush name, Strongheart, that sounds like a Care Bear, it's no wonder people are paying attention.

After the Condors' disappointing playoff exit, Armstrong hasn't done much in the way of public interviews or appearances. But that didn't stop him from attending the first game of the Piranhas' series against the Colorado Altitude. Even in "civilian" clothes—black T-shirt, black ball cap—Armstrong stands out in a crowd, so it's no wonder fans spotted him right away.

It might be a *little* surprising he showed up to each game after that wearing a shirt with a different kind of sea life on it. My personal favorite was the electric eel.

When I caught up with him after the Piranhas clinched the Western Conference Championship, he was candid about his wardrobe choice—this time featuring a cartoon crustacean playing the drums with the legend

Rock Lobster. "It's my way of toeing the line, I guess," he said, pulling at the fabric of his shirt. "Trying to find that balance between being a supportive boyfriend and not, uh, betraying my own fan base."

He'll be in the stands for the Cup Final too, sitting with Lockhart's family as the Piranhas take on the New Jersey Monsters.

No matter the outcome of the series, it looks like love wins.

"I STILL can't believe you're doing this." Jess shook her head. "It's like I don't even know you."

"You don't have to sound so happy about it."

"I'm just saying. It's nice to see you loosen up. I take back all my objections over your love life."

"I'm still not getting you a VIP access pass."

Jess laughed. "Cold. Say hi to your man for me."

Grady flashed his pass at the security guard, who rolled her eyes. By now the Fishtank staff recognized him, even if they pretended to give him a hard time for playing for the opposition. "Tell him to finish it for us, would you?"

"I think he's pretty set on finishing it for himself." The New Jersey Monsters had taken the Eastern Conference Championship. Max didn't have to say anything for Grady to know he was taking the Cup Final matchup as an opportunity to make Monsters' front office regret the trade that had upended his life.

Even if it had worked out well for him so far.

The Piranhas were up 3–2 in the series, and tonight they had home ice. The Cup was in the building.

Grady wanted to see Max lift it. At this point he didn't even feel jealous.

But there was something he wanted to say before the dream became reality.

The locker room door was open when he walked up, and Baller saw him before he could knock. "Hey, Mad Max! Your man is here for your pregame ritual." Then he added, to Grady, "You didn't see my husband and adorable child by any chance?"

Grady was about to say he hadn't, but then he saw Gabe coming down the hall with Reyna in his arms, talking to a few of the other Piranhas' partners. "You might as well tell the room everyone is incoming."

Before Baller could respond, Max slipped out the door and pulled Grady away. "Hey."

"Hey." Grady tilted his head up for a kiss—in skates, Max was taller than Grady.

He was also currently a lot hairier. His playoff beard had gotten wild. *Mad Max* suited him well at the moment.

"You ready?"

"Ready." Max shifted from foot to foot, vibrating with anticipation. "Mostly. Oh." He reached for Grady's hand and deposited two body-warm pieces of metal into it. "For safekeeping."

Grady curled his fingers around the cuff links. Max's hands were on the outside of his own, and he brought Max's knuckles to his lips and kissed them, "for luck."

"Gross!" Max said happily. "You know being a good boyfriend isn't a contest, right?"

"Yes it is," Grady said, "and I'm going to win." Provided he could figure out how to say what was on his mind without jinxing anything.

Max laughed at him—Grady would never get tired of the sound—but then he shook his head. "Come on. Something's on your mind. Out with it."

Grady could not "out with it." He had to work up to it. "Keep your stick on the ice. Keep your head up. Stay out of the box."

Max nodded seriously. "Sage advice. Very original. Please go on."

"Full sixty-minute effort," Grady continued. He was getting there. "Stick to your game—"

"I'm kind of wondering how long you can keep this up for."

"Don't go easy on Hedgewood just because he's a dad now. He's not going to go easy on you—"

"I promise to take full advantage of his sleep deprivation." Max crossed his finger over his heart.

Finally Grady cracked. "I love you."

"Hmm," Max said. He tucked his hands into the back pockets of Grady's shorts. "I think I've heard that before too."

"Well, here's a new one." Grady met his gaze. "You tell anyone who asks that I will get my own ring, okay?" He'd achieve that dream through his own luck and hard work or he'd make the most of his happiness without it. He waved his hand toward the other partners, who'd convened farther down the hall. "I know everybody else is getting theirs to match—"

Max squeezed his butt, eyes dancing. "Do not buy Grady a Cup ring. Check. Anything else?"

"I thought some more about your mom's invitation." Max's parents were staying at their house after a multiday train journey from the East Coast.

The first time Linda had said, "You'll have to visit us in New Brunswick this summer," Grady thought she was just being polite. But she kept on him. Now he thought she was angling to make sure he was there for Max's Cup party but was too superstitious to say the words out loud.

Max hadn't pressed the issue, but maybe it had been bothering him more than he'd let on, because he straightened. "Oh yeah?" He cleared his throat. "What did you decide?"

"I think I'll take her up on it. I hear New Brunswick's nice this time of year." Then he slid his hand down and discreetly patted Max's leggings above the tattoo of Larry. "Besides, you know I can't resist fresh lobster."

Keep reading for an excerpt from
*The Inside Edge*
by Ashlyn Kane

# Prologue

"I, KELLY Marie Ng, take you, Caley...."

Nate Overton had been to plenty of weddings in his time. He'd even stood up in a lot of them—playing professional hockey led to the kind of intense friendship that lent itself to groomsman duties.

But this was the first time he'd held a bouquet as he stood up for a bride.

Just a few feet away, Kelly slid the ring onto Caley's finger and wiped away a tear, her smile so bright it almost hurt to look at.

The two of them were embracing even before the officiant finished pronouncing, "You may kiss your bride.

"Please rise for the newlyweds!"

Nate let out a quiet breath that he hoped went unnoticed, and applauded with everyone else when Caley retrieved her bouquet. Then it was just the private witnessing of the certificate to get through and he could have a drink and relax.

Kelly insisted she talked enough at work, so there weren't any speeches. Nate couldn't say he minded, since he was in the same boat. Besides, it was nice to enjoy the meal without an hour of other people failing to prove they could've had a career in stand-up.

Instead, he got to ride herd on his co-bridesman, who was currently peeking up at him from under the tablecloth.

Nate bent down to speak to him in a stage whisper. "You know, there's no green beans under the table. But there isn't any cake either."

Carter Ng stared back at him thoughtfully. At three and a half, he was painfully shy and just getting to that age where vegetables were the enemy.

Nate had been the favored team babysitter for the thirteen years he'd played in the NHL, and he wasn't above bribery to keep the kid on the correct side of the table, at least until the photographers had pictures of him dancing with his mom and stepmom. Then he could get as dusty as he liked. "If you come up here and eat two more bites of vegetables, I'll eat the rest and tell your mom you did. And then you can have cake."

Carter considered this wordlessly for a moment before climbing back into the chair between Nate and Kelly, who threw him an amused but grateful look and then returned her attention to Caley's great-aunt something-or-other, whose pontificating Nate had tuned out.

"So much for no speeches," he said sotto voce to Kelly when the woman finally—blessedly—left.

On Kelly's other side, Caley smothered a snort in her hand. He was pretty sure Kelly would've smacked him good-naturedly, but Carter was in the way.

"At least we're the only ones who had to hear it," she said, and then the emcee was calling them up for their first dance as a couple.

Nate surprised himself by making it through all of the ceremony, dinner, and the official dances—including a very short one where he swayed around the floor with a toddler giggling in his arms—without a single traumatic flashback or bittersweet memory. But when he put Carter back down, it was like he'd set down his shield against reality. He looked around quickly to ensure no one would miss him and then let himself outside for some fresh air.

Immediately he found it easier to breathe, which was stupid. He didn't have anxiety or asthma. He didn't have a reason to struggle with witnessing the beautiful wedding of two of his very dear friends.

Unless you counted what he had to do tomorrow.

The door behind him squeaked open, and he sighed. Caught.

"Hey," Caley said, coming to sit next to him on the bench outside the door, heedless of her pretty white dress. "I thought I might find you here. It's all too much, isn't it?"

Nate tried to frown at her. "You're missing your party. You should be celebrating."

"I will." She nudged closer until their shoulders bumped. "When I'm done checking on you."

There was nothing for it; she hadn't been the captain of multiple gold-medal-winning Olympic women's hockey teams for nothing. He sighed. "I'm fine. I promise."

"Forgive me if I'm concerned about the well-being of my friend, who's putting on a very good front of being happy for me despite the fact that he's about to fly to Texas tomorrow to sign divorce papers." She leaned her head against his. "The timing sucks, I know."

"We've been separated almost three years," Nate said. Part of him thought repeating that should make it suck less, but no dice. "It's past time. Not your fault there's a scheduling conflict. I could've asked to push it back."

"You should've," Caley said darkly. "Just been conveniently busy until the delay would've ruined *his* wedding plans. I'm just saying."

Nate smiled, tilting his head back. "I'm not going to say I didn't think about it."

"Pretty presumptuous planning a wedding before you've even got the ink dry on your divorce, if you ask me."

Nate had suspicions about what Marty had been up to before their separation, never mind before their divorce, but he didn't have any proof, and in the end it didn't matter. They wouldn't have lasted anyway. He'd only delayed filing for so long because it felt like giving up.

Nate's parents hadn't raised a quitter.

"I appreciate your support."

"There's an open bar, you know," she told him unnecessarily. Then her voice turned teasing. "And you know, Kelly has this cousin…."

Oh no. No, Nate was not ready for that. But before he could protest, the door opened and Carter ran toward them, followed a few seconds later by Kelly.

"Uncle Naaaaaaate," Carter said, patting Nate's knees. "They're doing cake!"

"Cake!" Nate said, standing and swooping Carter into his arms. He tossed him once, just a few inches, and caught him. "Cake sounds much better than this conversation. What a nice guy you are. Did you know I needed a rescue?"

Kelly indulgently watched the three of them. "I see you've successfully threatened him into a good mood."

Caley grinned. "What can I say, it's a gift."

Nate craned his head back so he could look Carter in the face. "God help you when you're a teenager in a sulk, kid. I'll make sure you have my number."

But he let Kelly and Caley flank him on the way back into the hall, and his maudlin thoughts didn't catch up to him for the rest of the night.


THE PHONE call came in just after Aubrey finished in Makeup, but long before he had to be on set. Had it been any other day or any other person, he probably would have ignored it. He hadn't met his co-star yet and he was supposed to be on the air in an hour. It was his first day on the job; he didn't need to be taking calls at work. He was having a hard enough time wrapping his head around the show, which was mostly news, analysis, and women's game coverage during the week, with a featured play-by-play on the weekend.

But it was his mother calling from home in Vancouver, and she called infrequently enough that he was inclined to take it.

And maybe a tiny part of him held some hope that she was calling to wish him well and let him know she'd be watching—though he didn't know how she would, since she didn't live in their broadcast range.

"I'm sorry, I've got to take this," he said to the makeup tech. "Thanks, though—I look great."

The man laughed and shooed him out of the room.

Aubrey took a deep breath and answered the call. "Hi, Mom."

"… no, I think the roses if you want traditional and the gerbera daisies if you want something a little more fun. Lilies are a bit morbid for a wedding— Oh! Aubrey?"

He could already feel his hackles rising. "Yeah, Mom. You called me, remember?"

"I'm sorry, I was distracted. I've been helping your cousin choose flowers for the ceremony."

Aubrey glanced at his watch, counting down the minutes. He hoped his mom didn't want to chat for long. He couldn't remember the last time he'd had a conversation with her that didn't end with one or both of them frustrated or angry. "It's all right," he said, trying to be patient. "So, why'd you call?"

*Can't a woman call to catch up with her only son?* he half expected her to say. Lord knew he'd been burned by those words enough times. They inevitably led to invasive questions about his love life, followed by *Mrs. Society So-and-So has a gay son about your age*, or *Your father and I miss you; when are you going to move back home?* As if they'd ever spent time with him when he lived there.

If he was really lucky, she'd find a new facet of his life to disapprove of, like his diet or—

"Well, like I said, I'm here with Rachel, and she tells me you haven't sent in your RSVP for the wedding yet."

Aubrey's stomach soured. "The wedding."

Right. His cousin was getting married. Well, Rachel wasn't actually his cousin. She was more like the kid his mom had always wanted, the daughter of his parents' friends. Aubrey had won multiple Grand Prix events, two World Championship figure-skating titles, and an Olympic silver, along with a handful of junior medals. None of it had been good enough. Why did he have to go clubbing so often? Wasn't he interested in a more rewarding long-term relationship? Didn't he want to take some business classes so he could take over his parents' hospitality business one day?

Why couldn't he be more like Rachel, basically.

He'd always been jealous of Rachel's relationship with his parents, but when her mom and dad were killed in a car accident four years ago, it added a healthy dose of self-loathing to the mix. Because how could he be jealous of an *orphan*?

"It's December 23," his mother reminded him. "RSVPs were due last week."

"Well, we both know I can't do anything right, so it can't surprise you that I forgot."

Aubrey winced. That was a little more combative than he'd meant to be, but he couldn't take it back now.

His mother sighed. "For God's sake, Aubrey. Just tell me if you're coming. Your father and I would like to see you."

"Sorry, I don't think so. The NHL plays until the twenty-third. I'll probably have a game to cover."

"Fine," she said, her tone frosty. "Was that so hard?"

Aubrey gritted his teeth. He'd even reminded her about his new job, which was starting today, and she couldn't take two seconds to wish him luck? "I've got to go, Mom. I'm needed on set. Unless there was something else?"

"No, that was all." She sounded resigned. At least he wasn't the only one. "Goodbye, Aubrey."

The call disconnected before he could say anything else. "Goodbye," he said to dead air, fighting the urge to bang his head against the wall. Next time she called, maybe he could do that instead. It would be less painful.

For now, though, he had a job to do. He summoned all the good cheer he could muster and headed toward the sound stage. His mother might consider him beneath her notice, but Aubrey could get the attention he thrived on elsewhere. All he had to do was show up and be charming. And charm was something that came very naturally to him—as long as his mother wasn't around to see it.

# Chapter 1

NATE TIPPED his driver extra; the guy had made it from O'Hare in record time. He sidestepped around the office workers in the plaza like they were opposing defenders and entered the enormous revolving door as the big lobby clock struck the hour. It almost felt like beating the buzzer—he was going to just barely make it in time for makeup and a brief rundown, but barely was good enough and far better than he'd hoped, after spending an hour waiting for a gate at the airport. The stress of being late—Nate hated tardiness in himself as much as in others—was only eclipsed by the situation at the network.

"Don't worry about it; it's handled," Jess had told him in their too-brief call before the flight took off. That didn't make him feel better. The few subsequent messages they exchanged during the flight hadn't helped, especially as it felt like he was also getting texts from everyone he'd ever met—all variations of the theme: *So what the hell is up with John Plum?* Not that he'd answered. Nate had already gotten a very firm, if unnecessary, voicemail form his agent that he should not, under penalty of torture, say anything but "no comment" about the situation.

What would he even say? *Sorry my cohost is a xenophobic misogynist douchebag with no control over his basest impulses?* Silence was the better part of valor.

"You're late," Gina the PA told him, falling into step next to him as he beelined for Makeup. "I sent a rundown of tonight's show to your phone. You have time to look at it?"

Nate shook his head. "It died halfway through the flight. Too much Candy Crush. Forgot the charging cord in my hotel room." He glanced around as they walked. "Is Jess around? She told me not to worry, but—"

"Yeah, on second thought, maybe I better let her tell you in person. I think she's with—uh." Gina pasted on a smile. Good thing her work was mostly behind the camera, because she didn't convince Nate. "You know what? I'll just go tell her to find you."

That didn't inspire confidence, but Nate didn't have a lot of time to argue. He had a call in... well, basically now. "All right," he agreed, but Gina was already scampering down the hallway, talking on her headset.

Jess didn't come in while he was in Makeup, and the usual chatter was suspiciously free of office gossip and sports talk, focusing exclusively on the relative merits of different varieties of Girl Scout cookies. Nate happily shared his opinion (Samoas best, the peanut butter ones disappointing, but he found it weird that no one was even referring to the elephant that was no longer in the room, and that made him feel wrong-footed. Someone had passed him a portable charger for his phone, so he was able to read through the rundown he was now expected to do by himself. It might be a little flat with just one body behind the desk, but they were going to cut away to the game in Brampton, and Kelly was always good. Maybe they'd use this as an excuse to give a little extra time to the women's game. John would hate that. Nate couldn't resist smiling at the image of him fuming about it.

"You're done." Samira batted him on the shoulder as she finished. "Now get out of my chair and y'all have a great show."

*Y'all.* Plural. Was that significant? Nate turned to ask, but Samira had already scooted out of the room.

Something strange was definitely going on.

"*Nate Overton to the set.*" The voice over the PA made it clear he didn't have any more time to wonder. In fact, he barely had time to change—he unbuttoned his shirt on the way to Wardrobe, where Tony was already waiting to help him into its replacement.

"Little behind today?" he asked, turning to grab the jacket and tie—helpfully already tied—while Nate buttoned up.

"O'Hare," Nate said grimly.

"Say no more." Tony held the jacket for him. "Not going to miss your old cohost's wardrobe peculiarities, you know?"

Nate figured Tony wouldn't miss him, period. "Maybe his replacement will be easier on the eyes."

Tony opened his mouth to say something, but Nate didn't have time. He took the tie to go, waving his thanks over his shoulder.

"Cutting it a little close," their primary camera operator commented as Nate stepped onto the soundstage.

Jeez. You get twitchy about people being late a few times and you'd never get any slack. "Yeah, yeah," Nate said. "Point taken." He took another three steps—

And stopped.

Someone was sitting in his chair.

A handsome—very handsome—dark-haired man had his elbows propped on the desk as he leaned forward, grinning at something Carl the camera operator was saying. Carl gestured with his hands, and the handsome brunet laughed, tossed his head back, and turned a million-watt smile on Carl. If Nate didn't know better, he'd think the guy was flirting with their straight, married, sixtysomething grandfather of three. Whatever. The guy was in Nate's chair, and Nate needed to politely inform him of the fact and give him the opportunity to move... and maybe to introduce himself, since no one else was going to tell Nate who he was. Where did they get him from? Nate squinted as he approached. The guy looked vaguely familiar. Local news? A weatherman maybe?

"Nate!" Carl intercepted him before he could make his case to the usurping newcomer. "Glad you made it! I thought I was going to have to join Aubrey up in front of the cameras tonight," he joked.

"Uh, yeah." Nate pasted on a smile, more confused than ever. He tamped down on a surge of change-induced panic. "You kn—"

"And Emmy would've loved that," Carl continued, still chuckling.

"Well, I'll make sure she gets that autographed picture," the guy—Aubrey—said. "Always happy to hear about a fan. Give her my love, Carl."

There was more batting of eyelashes until Carl ambled back to his station. "Hi."

And now the guy was making eyes at Nate. Nate, who'd just spent twelve hours in travel with a dead phone. Nate, who hadn't been able to wrangle a straight answer out of his producer all day. Nate, who had *no fucking idea* what was going on and needed to be on the air in *minutes.*

Right now Nate didn't care if Aubrey was the only other gay man on the planet. He wasn't going to flirt with him. Definitely not at work, and *especially* not while he was sitting in Nate's chair. "You're in my seat," Nate said.

The eyelashes stopped fluttering and instead narrowed around clear gray eyes. "My apologies," he said smoothly, and all the warmth of his initial greeting faded. "Ms. Chapel told me to sit here."

*Why would she do that?* Nate knew ratings had suffered with John. Had Jess decided to go in a totally different direction? Would she call him to set just to fire him?

The guy in Nate's chair leaned back, eyes still narrowed in assessment. The movement drew Nate's eye to his suit—cut very close, expensive too, and Nate knew expensive suits. This one had a silver line of stitching around the lapels. Flashy, but with class. John would've hated it.

"I'm Aubrey Chase, by the way," the guy said, holding out a hand, and oh. That was why Nate recognized him.

"The figure skater." It came out sounding a little more cringeworthy than Nate intended. He had nothing against figure skaters. He knew what kind of tremendous athleticism the sport demanded. But this was a hockey show. "Uh, nice to meet you," he offered belatedly and shook the guy's hand. "Nate Overton."

"My pleasure." Aubrey's smile was polite, if not warm, as if he could read Nate's thoughts. "You're the senior now, so I guess that's why you get

John's old spot. Kind of surprised it looks just like a normal chair, you know? It's not like it's velvet or ermine-lined or anything."

Nate adjusted his earpiece since he couldn't manage to adjust the nagging sensation of disorientation.

"Two minutes," Gina's voice said in his ear.

Nate glanced over the paper in front of him. To his right he noticed Aubrey smoothing his own sheet and shrugging and shaking out his shoulders a bit as if he were about to step into a spotlight on the ice. He was getting ready for his audience, obviously. Just Nate's luck that after all the times he'd dreamed of getting rid of an overbearing bigoted buffoon like John, the replacement would be a different sort of diva.

"I see we're hashing out Kazakov's new contract."

"That's what it says," Nate replied. He hated that he felt he'd gotten off on the wrong foot, but somehow blaming Aubrey for his own lack of grace made him feel better.

"Five and a half by five. That's going to be a squeeze with Dallas's cap issues," Aubrey offered.

"Well, it's not like top-four defenseman grow on trees, and Popov's not getting any younger." Nate probably sounded more definite than he felt about the issue, but it had been a long day.

"Dallas wouldn't know if they did grow on trees, unless they were trees in Russia. They can't seem to draft one from anywhere else." Aubrey clicked his pen for emphasis.

Nate swiveled on his chair to glare at the handsome but misinformed face. "They traded for Svensson at the last deadline!"

"Trading for a thirty-four-year-old isn't the same as developing or draft—" Aubrey insisted, but Gina's voice interrupted.

"Forty-five seconds."

Nate felt like his nose was going to hit the desk in forty-five seconds. He should have chugged an energy drink or three, and now a figure skater was trying to debate him on the finer points of building a blueline.

Worse, he wasn't entirely off base. At the very least he was competent, which was better than John, and unlikely to spout some of the more offensive bile that seemed to fall like flowers from John's mouth. Nate needed to focus on that and on staying awake and alert, and then he could apologize to his new cohost and try to start over.

"I really need a coffee," he grumbled, and Gina piped in over his earpiece.

"I'll get you one for commercial break."

"*Thank you*," Nate said fervently. He made a mental note to buy her something really nice for Christmas this year.

"Thirty seconds."

He took a deep breath. He'd be fine. He could talk about hockey in his sleep. He had, in fact, done so on enough occasions that he'd chased Marty out of bed to the guest room, which probably hadn't helped when everything went to hell. And wow, he needed to think about something else. Anything else.

"Are you okay?" Aubrey asked, one eyebrow raised. "You look a little… gray."

Despite himself, Nate prickled. Now Aubrey was calling him old. *Great.* As if he needed a reminder that he'd just stepped into the senior role. Nothing like feeling your age. "I'm fine," he snapped. "Let's just get this over with."

"Live in ten!"

"I love your enthusiasm," Aubrey deadpanned. But then Gina held her hand up for the countdown, and Nate could see the moment he switched into broadcast mode. He sat straighter, corrected his posture, and his features relaxed into something open and friendly instead of just openly hostile. He brushed a hand through his hair and somehow avoided messing it up. Instead it looked like he'd just paid a hairdresser a hundred dollars to do it. Nate would have sworn his *skin* even looked nicer, which was patently ridiculous.

Of course. On top of being a charming, shmoozing flirt, his new cohost was hot. Fuck Nate's life.

The red broadcast-indicator light came on and Gina gave them the signal—they were live.

"Good evening and welcome to *Off the Ice*. I'm Nate Overton and this is Aubrey Chase. Tonight, the Chicago Snap take on the Toronto Furies. We'll have that game for you live, as well as news updates, scores, and highlights from around the leagues. The puck drops in ten. For now we're going to our women's correspondent, Kelly Ng, live with Snap Captain Dominique Ryan. Kelly?"

ASHLYN KANE likes to think she can do it all, but her follow-through often proves her undoing. Her house is as full of half-finished projects as her writing folder. With the help of her ADHD meds, she gets by.

An early reader and talker, Ashlyn has always had a flair for language and storytelling. As an eight-year-old, she attended her first writers' workshop. As a teenager, she won an amateur poetry competition. As an adult, she received a starred review in *Publishers Weekly* for her novel *Fake Dating the Prince*. There were quite a few years in the middle there, but who's counting?

Her hobbies include DIY home decor, container gardening (no pulling weeds), music, and spending time with her enormous chocolate lapdog. She is the fortunate wife of a wonderful man, the daughter of two sets of great parents, and the proud older sister/sister-in-law of the world's biggest nerds.

Sign up for her newsletter at www.ashlynkane.ca/newsletter/
Website: www.ashlynkane.ca

MORGAN JAMES is a clueless (older) millennial who's still trying to figure out what they'll be when they grow up and enjoying the journey to get there. Now, with a couple of degrees, a few stints in Europe, and more than one false start to a career, they eagerly wait to see what's next. James started writing fiction before they could spell and wrote their first (unpublished) novel in middle school. They haven't stopped since. Geek, artist, archer, and fanatic, Morgan passes their free hours in imaginary worlds, with people on pages and screens—it's an addiction, as is their love of coffee and tea. They live in Canada with their massive collection of unread books and where they are the personal servant of too many four-legged creatures.

Twitter: @MorganJames71
Facebook: www.facebook.com/morganjames007

HOCKEY EVER AFTER    BOOK ONE

# WINGING IT

Falling for his
teammate wasn't in
the game plan....

# ASHLYN KANE
# MORGAN JAMES

Hockey Ever After: Book One

*Hockey is Gabe Martin's life. Dante Baltierra just wants to have some fun on his way to the Hockey Hall of Fame. Falling for a teammate isn't in either game plan.*

But plans change.

When Gabe gets outed, it turns his careful life upside-down. The chaos messes with his game and sends his team headlong into a losing streak. The last person he expects to pull him through it is Dante.

This season isn't going the way Dante thought it would. Gabe's sexuality doesn't faze him, but his own does. Dante's always been a "what you see is what you get" kind of guy, and having to hide his attraction to Gabe sucks. But so does losing, and his teammate needs him, so he puts in the effort to snap Gabe out of his funk.

He doesn't mean to fall in love with the guy.

Getting involved with a teammate is a bad idea, but Dante is shameless, funny, and brilliant at hockey. Gabe can't resist. Unfortunately, he struggles to share part of himself that he's hidden for years, and Dante chafes at hiding their relationship. Can they find their feet before the ice slips out from under them?

# www.dreamspinnerpress.com

HOCKEY EVER AFTER  BOOK 1.5

# THE WINGING IT HOLIDAY SPECIAL

ASHLYN KANE
MORGAN JAMES

Hockey Ever After: Book 1.5

Hockey's started, holidays are looming, and NHL player Dante Baltierra's husband is keeping secrets.

Of course, secrets aren't unusual this time of year, but Dante is pretty sure Gabe isn't being squirrelly about a new flat-screen or tickets for a second honeymoon. Whatever is eating Gabe is more serious than a surprise under the tree. But as much as Dante wants to help, asking about it would be fruitless. Besides, he has a theory about the problem—and the solution.

He's just not sure Santa has the power to deliver what Gabe really wants this Christmas.

# www.dreamspinnerpress.com

HOCKEY EVER AFTER  BOOK TWO

# SCORING POSITION

You miss
100 percent of
the shots you
don't take.

ASHLYN KANE
MORGAN JAMES

Hockey Ever After: Book Two

*Ryan Wright's new hockey team is a dumpster fire. He expects to lose games—not his heart.*

Ryan's laid-back attitude should be an advantage in Indianapolis. Even if he doesn't accomplish much on the ice, he can help his burned-out teammates off it. And no one needs a friend—or a hug—more than Nico Kirschbaum, the team's struggling would-be superstar.

Nico doesn't appreciate that management traded for another openly gay player and told them to make friends. Maybe he doesn't know what his problem is, but he'll solve it with hard work, not by bonding with the class clown.

It's obvious to Ryan that Nico's lonely, gifted, and cracking under pressure. No amount of physical practice will fix his mental game. But convincing Nico to let Ryan help means getting closer than is wise for Ryan's heart—especially once he unearths Nico's sense of humor.

Will Nico and Ryan risk making a pass, or will they keep missing 100 percent of the shots they don't take?

# www.dreamspinnerpress.com

For Jax Hall, all-but-dissertation in mathematics, slinging drinks and serenading patrons at a piano bar is the perfect remedy for months of pandemic anxiety. He doesn't expect to end up improvising on stage with pop violinist Aria Darvish, but the attraction that sparks between them? That's a mathematical certainty. If he can get Ari to act on it, even better.

Ari hasn't written a note, and his album deadline is looming. Then he meets Jax, and suddenly he can't stop the music. But Ari doesn't know how to interpret Jax's flirting—is making him a drink called Sex with the Bartender a serious overture?

Jax jumps in with both feet, the only way he knows how. Ari is wonderful, and Jax loves having a partner who's on the same page. But Ari's struggles with his parents' expectations, and Jax's with the wounds of his past, threaten to unbalance an otherwise perfect equation. Can they prove their double act has merit, or does it only work in theory?

# www.dreamspinnerpress.com

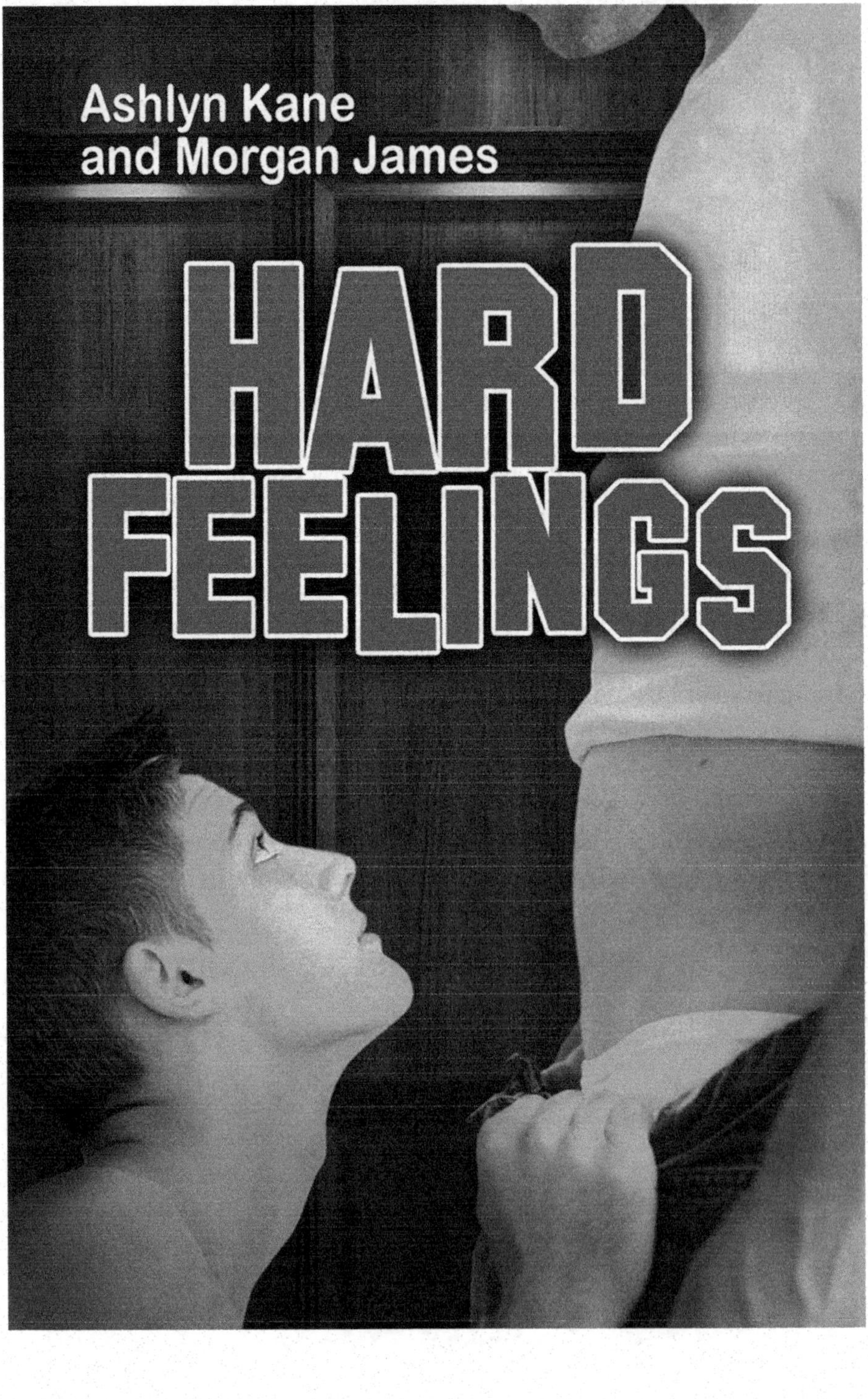

Ashlyn Kane
and Morgan James
HARD
FEELINGS

Rylan Williams hates conferences: too many people, not enough routine, and way too much interaction with strangers. When he gets stuck in a broken elevator with Miller Jones, the kid who fell asleep in his lecture, he figures things can't get worse. Then Rylan realizes he's the same guy he just spent an hour perving over from afar.

Rylan wants to await rescue in silence, but Miller insists on conversation, or at least banter. But just because they don't get along doesn't mean they don't have chemistry, and Rylan breaks all his rules about intimacy for a one-time-only conference hookup. He'll probably never see Miller again anyway. So of course, two months later Miller shows up at Rylan's office, having just been hired to work on a new computer program—with Rylan.

And Rylan thought being stuck in an elevator with him was bad.

Soon Rylan and Miller learn that they get along best when they take out their frustrations in the bedroom. Their arrangement goes against everything Rylan believes in, but the rules are simple: Don't stay overnight. Don't tell anyone. And don't fall in love.

# www.dreamspinnerpress.com